Secrets on Emma's Porch

Secrets on Emma's Porch

Rebekah Wyre

Library of Congress Control Number:		2008901553
ISBN:	Softcover	978-1-4363-2405-2

To order additional copies of this book, contact:
Xlibris Corporation
1-888-795-4274
www.Xlibris.com
Orders@Xlibris.com
44808

This book is dedicated in memory of my son, Jim (1980-2004) and to my daughter Katy, both of whom have been my life's inspirations. I would also like to thank my husband Rex, who encouraged me to pursue the emotional healing powers of putting my thoughts and heartaches in writing.

Chapter 1

Lilly met Emma on a miserably hot and humid August day. She was writing a magazine article on historic barns of the Midwest and earlier that week she had called to tell Emma her barn had been chosen. Lilly asked if she could come by and take pictures and talk to her.

Lilly watched the dust from the gravel road engulf her Jeep as she traveled down Emma's road that morning. Emma's directions were detailed and Lilly had no trouble finding her drive. Large willow trees lined both sides of the gravel drive, which was easily a quarter mile long.

There stood a two-story white farmhouse with red shutters on the windows and a white picket fence around the front yard. The front yard was full of wildflowers and the barn was made of native stone and stood a short distance from the house. It was of such stature that it dwarfed the farmhouse.

Lilly got out of her Jeep as the cloud of dust billowed around her and rested on her black bumper and rear window. Her skin immediately felt gritty from the dirt. She looked back and then approached the gate.

"Are you the young woman here to see my barn?" Emma asked. She was a petite woman with a round face and short, choppy hair, which was once a golden blond but had now been highlighted with white. It was a mixture many women would pay a pretty penny to achieve. She wore overall shorts with a bright yellow t-shirt underneath and white canvass shoes.

Lilly extended her hand and Emma returned with a firm handshake. "Yes, I am. You must be Emma."

"I am. Please come on in. This heat is a killer, isn't it?"

Before Lilly could answer Emma had opened the gate. A beagle and a very shaggy schnauzer greeted their guest. The schnauzer stepped back into the iris that lined the brick walkway and a kitten let out a terrible screech. "Gracie, how many times do I have to tell you to watch where you are stepping? You tell Hootie you are sorry for stepping on her tail." Lilly would quickly learn that

Emma spoke to all of her animals as if they were her children. The schnauzer and kitten scampered off, none the worse for wear.

"Would you like to sit on the porch a spell or do you want to see the barn right away?" Emma asked. Her face was tan and she bore a scar from the inside of her right eye across her cheekbone and up to her temple. When she squinted to protect her eyes from the sun, the lines of time blended in with the scar, making it barely noticeable.

"I would like to sit and ask you a few questions about the barn if that is alright with you."

"Heavens, I have all day. I am on your schedule. Been looking forward to this all week. Not many people want to come see my barn anymore." Two tabby kittens weaved in and out of her feet and as Lilly watched she wondered what kept them from tripping Emma as she walked up onto the porch.

Emma motioned towards two oversized wicker chairs on the porch. "Please, sit down. Would you like a glass of tea or water? I don't have any pop. Only buy the stuff if I know the grandkids are coming."

"Ice water would be wonderful, thank you." Lilly glanced at the barn. All native stone. It appeared to be in perfect condition and she was already planning her photos in her mind.

"You're welcome to go on out there and see her if you like. I can bring the water to you." She opened the screen door and pushed it against the hindquarter of a golden Labrador lying against it. "Sam, move so I can get in to fix Miss . . . I'm sorry; I can't remember your name. Wrote it down on the pad by the phone but that doesn't do me any good right now, does it?"

"My name is Lilly Ballard." I'll wait until you are ready to head to the barn too. We can go over some of its history first."

"Lilly. That was my great grandmother's name. I like it!" Let me get that water. Make yourself at home." Sam ignored her pushing the door against his hind end so she slid in with a sigh and a slight grumble of his name once again.

Lilly sat in one of the chairs. There was a slight breeze and the smell of honeysuckle drifted across the porch. The flowers were abundant everywhere she looked. The front yard was a mixture of iris, gladiolas, lavender, daylilies and more. As she thought about how much time Emma must spend tending to all these flowers, the screen door opened and Emma came out with a tray with two tall glasses of ice water and a pitcher filled with more ice than water. Sweat was already forming on the glasses and trickling down the sides.

"Thank you, Sam, for moving." The dog gave Emma a disgruntled look and rested his head on his outstretched paws. "Here you go. We can go in where it is air-conditioned if you want. This heat!" Emma wiped perspiration from her lip with the back of her hand and handed Lilly a glass of water. Lilly took a drink, shaking her head "no". "That tastes wonderful. No thank you. We can stay out here for awhile."

"Emma, what do you know about your barn?" Lilly asked.

"Well, I know that it was built in 1892 and it is still all of the original stone but it has had to have the roof replaced over the years. Isn't she just beautiful? When my husband Rylie and I first married and he moved into this place, it was our intention to turn that old barn into our home but life got in the way and we were content to stay here in this house."

"It is beautiful and it looks like you have loved it all of these years. Didn't you say you moved here over 25 years ago?"

"Yes. I fell in love at first sight with this place. Wanted the kids to have a quiet place to live, to bring their families to some day. I think we got the job done."

"I'm ready to head out there and see it if you are. Do you mind if I take my ice water with me?"

"Of course not. Come on Lilly, let's get started. Sam, you stay here on the porch."

Chapter 2

As they walked toward the barn, Emma told of the history and of the original owners who homesteaded the property. Her eyes were so blue and she seemed to fall in love with her home all over again as she talked about it.

As she slid the large door open and they stepped inside, Lilly noticed a vehicle with a tarp over it tucked safely in one section of the barn. There were three horse stalls that were neatly cleaned to perfection. "I have two horses out in the pasture, Sally and Pie" she said. Bought them for the grandkids and for my own mental therapy. They are so therapeutic!" Sam wandered alongside Emma as she talked. "Sam, didn't I tell you to stay on the porch?" She then patted his head and the tour continued, Sam alongside Emma as if he had never been ordered to stay behind.

They talked more about the history of Emma's barn and Lilly asked if she could begin taking pictures. "You take as many as you like," Emma said.

"Emma, I will take most of the pictures in different phases of daylight but I want a few of the inside also. Do you think it is possible to move the stored vehicle out for a few pictures?"

Emma's whole demeanor changed. "No, that isn't possible. You will have to work around it," she said. Lilly nodded and said she would honor Emma's wishes. Emma said she would give Lilly some time to take pictures and she would start some of her chores. As she and Sam left the barn, Lilly wondered what it could be about the vehicle that changed Emma so when asked about it.

Lilly stepped outside the barn and began checking the light and taking pictures. Emma began watering her garden and Lilly could hear her talking to Sam and some kittens as she worked. "Sam, you stay out of my garden or your feet will be muddy and you won't come in the house tonight," she scolded. At that moment Gracie, the schnauzer, came barreling through the freshly watered garden. "Gracie!" Emma then turned the hose on the unsuspecting schnauzer and Sam ran in the other direction. Gracie ran up to Emma as she knelt down to wipe mud off her own feet and Emma was met with doggie licks and lots of love. As Lilly watched, she wondered why a woman of her late sixties would choose to live alone in the country with the closest neighbor a mile away. Emma laughed and talked to each animal as if she were spending those moments with her child or grandchild.

Emma continued to water, feed animals and work in her flowerbeds, always keeping an eye on Lilly's whereabouts. Lilly spent nearly two hours taking pictures before Emma came back to check on her.

"Shall I plan on you having a bite to eat with me?" she asked. "I can throw a little something together for both of us. It won't take but a while and we can sit and talk if you would like."

"I think that would be nice. Do you mind if I continue to take pictures while you go inside? I am guessing another twenty minutes should do it."

"Another twenty minutes it is. I will see you inside". Emma carried a kitten like an infant in her arms as she walked away, caressing its round little tummy as she discussed the menu with it.

Lilly took several more photos and then stepped outside the barn to see the two horses chasing one another. The rooster chased some unsuspecting hens into the hen house. She leaned against the fence and took in the sweet smell of hay and felt a twinge of envy for Emma that she had such a wonderful, peaceful life here on the Kansas prairie.

Chapter 3

"Emma?" Lilly called as she stepped inside the front door.

"Come on in. I am just about finished with putting the meal together. I hope you like fresh garden vegetables." She was setting the table with what appeared to be a feast. Lilly walked into the dining room. The walls were painted a barn red and the border was chair rail height with chickens and roosters and a red striped pillow ticking wallpaper on the lower portion. French doors overlooked a brick patio bordered with wildflowers and gladiolas.

"Sit down, sit down". Emma motioned to a dining chair. "Do you like iced tea?" Before Lilly had a chance to answer she asked "Sweetened or unsweetened?"

"Unsweetened, please."

Emma chuckled and said, "Just like my Rylie liked it. A southern girl raised me so all I ever knew was sugared tea but Rylie was a Kansas boy and he hated sweet tea. Although I have known some Kansas folks that take theirs sweet so maybe Rylie just didn't know what was good. I'm sorry, that would be insulting your choice in tea, wouldn't it? I apologize for my rude comment, Lilly". She went back into the kitchen and Lilly could hear the sound of an ice dispenser.

Emma returned with a large glass of tea. She hurried back into the kitchen, returning momentarily with even more food. The table was set with sliced garden tomatoes, corn on the cob, a relish tray with radishes, cucumbers, pickles, carrots and celery. Next to that tray was a pan of cornbread still warm from the oven. There was a bowl of green beans and a platter with grilled pork chops.

"Emma, you've gone to way too much trouble."

"This is no trouble. The tomatoes and relish tray are always ready so that I can grab a quick bite when I am working outside. Didn't take any time to boil the corn and cornbread is no trouble. Green beans are heated up from yesterday and I threw the pork chops on the grill and had them done in no time. Do you want to say grace or shall I? Hope that is no offense but here we thank the Lord for what we have been given."

"I'll let you do the honors," Lilly said, a little surprised at the offer.

"Thank you, Lord for the food we are about to receive. Give Lilly a safe return home. Watch over those that have gone on to be with you and let them know I look forward to being with them some day soon. In your time, Lord, I will join them in your time. Keep us safe from all harm. In thy name, Amen."

Emma began to pass the food in Lilly's direction and, as they filled their plates, she told about the first time she saw the farm.

"I came here with a realtor, just the two of us. I was ready for a new beginning in life and had been looking at many different homes. This one was not in the same school district that the kids were in and I was hesitant to make an offer but that old barn kept calling my name. I came back to look at it three more times and then I brought the kids out to see it. My son said, 'This is a party house where I can bring my friends.' Which is funny because he didn't drink or party. Just wanted to be able to have his friends over. I asked if he minded moving away from the subdivision we lived in and he said he was fine with it. My daughter, Kate, was all about being able to have more animals so I made an offer."

"Rylie had no input on the decision?" Lilly asked.

"Rylie and I hadn't even met when I looked at this place. It was just me and the kids."

"How many children do you have, Emma?"

"Rylie has three and I have, or had, two. My son Jim passed away when he was only 24 years old. There is no greater loss than that of a child. My life was never the same. Kate lost her best friend and he was my best friend, my confidant, my wondrous blessing."

"I am so sorry, Emma. I should not have asked."

"No, no, it isn't anything to apologize for. I love talking about my family and he was my first-born. I want folks to know what a fine young man he was so don't ever feel bad that you asked."

"You say Rylie has three children. Where are they and where is your daughter Kate?"

Emma passed the green beans. "Seconds?"

"No, thank you". Lilly continued to finish her meal as Emma spoke of her family.

"Bill is Rylie's oldest and he and his wife live about fifteen miles from here. Their children are both grown and live in Topeka and Jason is Rylie's middle child and he, his wife and their son live in the country up north by the Indian Reservation. Their daughter, Kelsi, is grown and on her own. Danielle is Rylie's youngest and she lives with her daughter in Topeka. My Kate lives in Denver. She is an Interior Designer and she is married to a sports medicine physician. She established her career and now she is pregnant with a little boy. Needless to say, I can't wait to spoil him rotten. Rylie's grandkids have never known anything but having me as their grandma and that makes it work out just fine."

"Tell me about your son, Emma."

Emma's eyes began to well with tears as if the loss of her son were only hours before. She set her fork down, folding her hands on the table. "Jim. His legal name was James Edward but he went by Jim. Tall, standing at 6 foot 5 inches. All of the ladies loved Jim. He was such a handsome boy. We received a call in the night from one of his roommates saying he had collapsed and we needed to get to the hospital right away. Seemed like forever before we got there. That was the one time I hated living out here. He was gone when we got there. Poor Kate. Lost her big brother when she was only 18 years old. I sat by his lifeless body for hours. I cried, I prayed and I told him stories about how much he meant to me. Coroner said he died of an aneurysm of the ascending aorta of his heart. He was gone in seconds. That's his mustang in the barn. I drive it on his birthday, the anniversary of his death, Christmas Day and St. Patrick's Day. Sometimes if it is a sunny day, I just drive it up to the cemetery to see him. Come look."

Emma led Lilly to the front door. "There on the hill. See all of the pine and cedar trees? That is the cemetery. I can watch over him and when I go to his grave, I can see our house. And when I sit on my front porch, I can watch the breeze blow those trees on that cemetery hill and I know that Jim is waiting in Heaven for me."

"That must be such a comfort to have his final resting place so near to you."

"I wish I had given him a better life. I always tried and did the best I could. Come and I will show you pictures if you would like, of all of our family." They walked into the living room where family pictures covered the staircase wall and the sofa table. "This is Rylie. Look at his dark brown eyes. Here is Bill and Jason with their families. They look like their dad, don't you think?"

"They have a lot of the same features. Who is this, Emma?"

"That is Kate. Tall and beautiful. Not short like me. Both of my children grew tall. I hate to think how tall they might have been if I hadn't runted them out. This is Jim. Such a handsome young man. Here they are as babies." Emma held picture after picture up telling in detail about each child and grandchild. "Rylie and I married when I was 45 and he was 43. We always said it was a good thing we didn't meet when we were younger or we probably would have had even more kids. I am happy we had the ones we were blessed with."

"It is a wonderful family. Did Rylie's children have the opportunity of living here?"

"No, just my two, Rylie and myself. His boys were grown when we met and Danielle lived with her mother. It was good though, just the four of us. Jim was 19 when we married and he lived with us until he was 22. Kate left for college the year Jim passed on. Then this place was so quiet and empty. That is when I started adding to the menagerie of animals. Rylie brought Sam home. Found him on the highway. Told me we would take him to the pound if no one claimed him. We ran an advertisement in the paper. As you can see, that was ten years ago and Sam is still with me."

"And Rylie? When did he pass away?"

"That has been six years now. I laid him to rest next to Jim. Well, my plot is between Jim and Rylie. When Rylie passed on, I had a headstone made for both of us. I can sit and talk to both of them when I go up there. Mercy, you probably think I talk like a crazy woman! Talking about visiting with the dead."

"No, no. I lost my mother eleven years ago and I tell her things when I go to her grave. I think it is therapeutic."

"Come sit and visit while I clear the table."

"Oh, Emma, let me help you. You've been so kind and you've let me take up your day and eat your delicious food."

"No, you're company!"

"I insist."

They began to clear the table. Lilly loved the old house. The original woodwork and Emma's taste in décor made the home feel cozy and lived in. Her kitchen was so welcoming. The house was spotless and uncluttered. Emma insisted that Lilly sit at the kitchen table while she rinsed and loaded the dishwasher. They discussed family and Lilly's career. Emma seemed genuinely interested in every detail. Lilly felt like they were old friends reminiscing.

"Oh, Emma, look at the time. I need to get back and work on this article and these photos. May I call you when it is complete and bring the finished version out for you to see?"

"I would love that. Now, Lilly, do you know how to get back onto the main highway?"

"I do." Emma walked Lilly out onto the porch where they were greeted by Sam and Gracie. Lilly took another look at the barn with the door still open, revealing the black tarp over Jim's mustang. "I'll close her up after I do the evening chores" Emma said. "You need to head back before dark. These gravel roads can be so dusty this time of year and you can barely see where you are heading."

Emma walked Lilly to the gate, picking up a large, fat gray cat along the way. She opened the gate and smiled, "You make sure you come back to show me the finished product."

"I will. Thank you for everything. I have enjoyed meeting you and visiting with you."

Sam ran in circles barking as if he wanted Lilly to know he was also saying goodbye.

Lilly got into the car and as she drove away she could see Emma in the rearview mirror waving, kittens and Sam at her feet.

"Sam, get on in the house. This has been a full day, hasn't it?" Emma said as she closed the picket gate.

Lilly enjoyed the drive home and thought about the time she had spent with Emma. She smiled as she thought about Emma's animals, especially Sam.

Questions began to fill her mind. What caused that scar on Emma's face? An accident of some sort? Why had Emma chosen to stay on the farm all alone?

The thought of writing an article about Emma and taking photos of her in her own element intrigued Lilly.

Would Emma allow Lilly to delve into a past Emma seemed to have buried deep inside her?

Lilly chuckled to herself as she thought about Emma's conversations with animals and with the dead. How many times had Lilly gone to her own mother's gravesite and unburdened the problems of the day? She admired Emma's honesty about how intimate her times at the cemetery could be and how important those times were to her.

Obviously Emma loved her family. Lilly would be sure to find out more about them when she returned. Maybe she would be able to take pictures of the family.

In her mind she reviewed all of the family photos she had seen displayed throughout Emma's house.

Lilly had already fallen in love with Emma's home and her barn. And she thought about how relaxed she felt as she sat on Emma's porch and their time spent together. Obviously Emma loved to entertain and enjoyed guests. She was quite adept at making a person feel welcome and at home.

This woman held many mysteries, in Lilly's opinion. Lilly was so anxious to develop the pictures and write about the barn. More than that, she was anxious to learn more about Emma.

After Lilly's visit, Emma sat at the kitchen table, running her index finger over the time-worn wood. How much should she share with Lilly?

She picked up the phone and dialed. "Kate? What's the weather like there?"

She continued to run her index finger across the table in a circular motion as she chatted with her daughter.

She told of the day's events and of the new friend she had made. Mother and daughter laughed and shared stories of the week's events.

Each ended the conversation with "Love you" and Emma hung up the phone.

Chapter 4

It was nearly three weeks before Lilly would see Emma again. Emma sat on the porch-swing with her menagerie of pets around her feet.

"Afternoon, Lilly. Did you bring the pictures?" Emma smiled, the long scar disappearing into the lines on her face.

"I brought the pictures and the article too." Lilly was relieved this day was much nicer than the previous meeting. She walked up on the porch, patting Sam on the head as she sat in a chair. She opened her briefcase and handed the pictures to Emma.

Emma began to look at the pictures and said, "Isn't the barn beautiful? Look at the Kansas sky. Oh, Sally and Pie are in this one!"

She looked at each picture, sometimes running a finger over one and then looked up at Lilly, her clear blue eyes smiling. "You did a wonderful job, Lilly. How blessed you are to have the talent and the freedom to travel, take pictures and write articles about places and people. Folks are going to fall in love with my barn just like I did years ago."

"Emma, this is your copy of the article to read whenever you like. These are also your pictures to keep."

Before Lilly could say another word, a green SUV rolled down the drive and pulled up to the front gate. When the driver opened the vehicle door, Lilly knew from pictures Emma had shown her on her earlier visit that this was Kate, Emma's daughter.

"Kate! Good Lord! What brings you here with no notice? Did you drive from Denver? Is everything O.K.?"

Kate opened the gate, picked up a kitten and walked up on the front porch. It was obvious that she had been crying. Kate put her arms around her mother. Lilly noticed Kate was much taller than her mother, which seemed to make Emma seem even smaller.

"Momma", Kate whispered.

"Oh, Good Lord, Kate. Something is wrong. You're calling me Momma. Is it the baby? What is it?"

Kate took a deep breath and spoke, "Dad passed away in the night. Heart attack, they think. His neighbor found him when she went over to visit him. I drove back as soon as I got the call and I wanted to stop here before I went to Wichita to make arrangements. I didn't want to wake you in the night with a phone call. Joshua is flying in from Denver tonight to be with me."

"Oh, Sugar. This is the day I knew would come and I wish your brother was here to support you. But Joshua is a wonderful husband and he will be there. Kate, do you want me to be there because I will if you say the word?" Emma seemed hesitant in her offer and Lilly wondered why she didn't want to help her daughter at this time. Lilly felt like an intruder at a very personal moment so she excused herself and walked to the barn.

Emma and Kate sat on the front porch for quite some time before Emma called out to Lilly to come meet Kate.

Sam walked alongside Lilly, his tail wagging continuously, as she walked back to the house.

"Lilly, this is my baby girl Kate. Kate, this is Lilly Ballard and she is doing the article on the barn."

"It is so nice to meet you. I'm so sorry about the loss of your father."

"Nice to meet you, Lilly. And thank you for your condolences. Mom told me you were out here taking pictures of the barn and writing an article about it".

Kate's eyes were an emerald green, but her smile was her mother's. Lilly guessed she resembled her father more than her mother. Kate was tall with an athletic build and she was dressed in designer jeans and t-shirt. Kate appeared to probably be seven months along in her pregnancy. She did not appear to have been raised on a farm. She looked like a city girl instead of a country girl.

Before they could say more, Emma broke into the conversation. "Kate, do you want to eat something before you head to Wichita? Do you want me to pack something for you to take along? Some fruit?"

"No, I am not hungry. But if you have bottled water I will take one with me. I need to get going."

"Of course. Come on in and I will get you set up."

Kate followed Emma into the house. Lilly started to sit on the porch swing when Emma called out from inside the house for her to join them. When she entered the living room Kate was talking. "Mom, I see no reason for you to have to come to the funeral unless you think you need to. Joshua will be there and Aunt Patti. I will let you know when we make the arrangements but you don't need to put yourself through that. Give me a kiss and I need to hit the road." Kate kissed her mother on the cheek and Emma kissed Kate, both of them teary eyed. Kate gave her mom a big hug and walked toward the door. "I'll be fine, Momma. Jim is with me in spirit. He's my guardian angel. You know that!"

Emma's eyes brimmed with tears and she spoke quietly, "I know he is."

She tossed the kitchen towel she had in her hand over her shoulder and said, "Take care of my grandbaby. Don't get too tired. Eat right. Don't get too stressed. I am here, you know that."

"I know. I will keep you posted."

Emma walked with Kate outside. As Kate got into her SUV, she blew a kiss to Emma. "I love you!"

"I love you too, sugar!"

Kate drove down the drive, a cloud of dust following her vehicle.

Emma came back onto the porch. Lilly stood at the screen door not knowing whether to step out onto the porch or stay in the house. Emma picked up Gracie, the schnauzer. "We can sleep at night, Gracie. No more fears. He can't hurt us ever again." She kissed Gracie's little black nose and set her down. Lilly stepped away from the door with the uncomfortable feeling that she had just witnessed a very private moment. Lilly wondered what Emma meant by her comment to the dog.

Emma entered the house. "Well, Lilly. You got in on some excitement there, didn't you?"

"Emma, I am so sorry about the loss of your former husband. Poor Kate. I feel like I should not even be here. Shall I leave? I probably should have left when Kate first arrived."

"No, don't feel that way. Kate is very open. She would have told me if it made her uncomfortable with you here. She's a tough cookie. Life's lessons have made her strong. She'll be fine."

"Are you sure you don't want to be there? After all, he is the father of your children."

"No, no. Kate will not need me there. Lilly, there is a lot of history here. It is sad to say but Richard was never a father to my children. He doesn't deserve Kate's grief but I know she feels a loss. She has always tried to be a good daughter to him in spite of himself."

There was an awkward silence and then Emma said "You don't need to hear all of this," in a softened tone as she shuffled papers on the table.

"Would you like to read the article now or maybe you want time to read it alone?"

"Alone would be best if you don't mind. Can I get you anything to drink? Are you hungry?"

"No thank you. I am fine. I can't stay long. I really would like to someday write an article about you, Emma and how you came to Kansas from Missouri and how you came to this home."

"An article about me?" Emma laughed. "There isn't much to me."

"I think it would be fun for both of us. Would you consider it and give me a call when you are ready?" Lilly gathered up her things and glanced Emma's direction.

"An article about me. Will you put down things I tell you not to? Can I tell about my family?"

"Of course you can tell about your family! If you don't want something published, I won't put it in there. I promise." As Emma had pointed out earlier, Lilly enjoyed the freedom of being a freelance writer and the fact she could make her own decisions.

"I'll think about that and let you know. I might talk it over with the kids first. They might not want me talking about them to someone."

They walked onto the porch. Emma sat down on the porch swing and the fat gray cat jumped up beside her. "Can you sit for awhile?" Emma asked.

"I really should go. I truly want you to think about my offer, Emma."

"I will. Let me walk you to your car. Are you married Lilly? Guess I've never asked you about yourself. If you do that article, I will have to question you too."

"I would like that, Emma. Engaged. I'm engaged. No wedding date set."

"Hope he is a good one like my Rylie."

"He is. Maybe I will bring him out here some day so you two can meet. I really need to go. May I call you sometime?"

"Of course. If I don't call you first!"

Lilly placed her briefcase on the passenger seat and turned to wave goodbye to Emma. She, of course, had a cat in tow and waved back. "Drive careful!"

Thoughts of Emma and the happenings of the day raced through Lilly's mind as she headed back to Kansas City.

Emma sat on the sun porch as nightfall approached, thinking back to the frequent nights she would sit in the darkness, eyes trying to focus on the night shadows, wondering if Richard was out there hoping to catch a glimpse of Emma or do her harm.

She thought of all the times she had phoned for help when he would make himself known to her and her children and yet the authorities often arrived too late to catch him. Darkness had always held so many fears for her and this freedom had such a strange unfamiliar feeling. She cursed Richard under her breath for never giving her or the children peace. She longed for Jim and Rylie's presence so they could share memories and good times.

Emma felt robbed of so many things. She had been robbed of her youth and yet she held fond memories of being a mother those years. If she had nothing else with Richard, she had her children. That would never be taken from her. He had taken her dignity, her self-esteem and, in part, her health, but never could he take the joy of motherhood from her.

Something rustled in the underbrush along the hedgerow. Emma struggled to see what it was but her eyes weren't as keen as they once had been. Probably a possum or a coon, she thought to herself. Sam growled, only adding to Emma's fears.

"Silly old woman", she whispered aloud. "He's gone, don't you know?"

She sighed and whispered again, "Gone".

Thoughts of Rylie flooded her mind. He always told her she was safe and she could never accept it. Then there were the times when even Rylie was reminded Richard would never give Emma or anyone associated with her the peace that was deserved.

Emma thought of that day in court when she felt she was finally free from the abuse and how quickly Richard reminded her that there was no peace. He promised to haunt her always until one of them was taken by death.

Death had given Emma her peace. But would Kate be able to put it to rest or would she also have haunting memories of her father? Only time would tell, Emma told herself. Time . . . . something Emma hoped they all would have.

Bitterness swept over her in the darkness. She felt robbed that her children had also been victims and she blamed herself. Doubts and questions flooded her mind.

She stood up and glanced toward the shadows outside. Was it her own haunting memories that made her feel as if she were being watched?

"Crazy old woman", she whispered. "Get to bed."

Emma motioned for Sam and Gracie to follow her. Sam's hair stood up on his back as he continued to watch the lengthening shadows outside the sun porch window.

"Stop it, Sam. You're making me nervous. You heard Kate. He's gone. He's finally gone."

She made her way through the house, still with the uncomfortable feeling someone was watching her and that haunting feeling she always carried with her that she would never have peace.

She chuckled out loud. Sam looked up, wagging his tail.

"Wouldn't my kids get a kick out of me feeling like a ghost was watching us, Sam? Feels like the old days, doesn't it? We were always wondering if we had to deal with the boogie man. Boogie man, Sam? More like Richard, wouldn't you say?"

She turned off the last light and walked toward her room.

"Angels, watch over me. Let this lifetime of haunting and consequences end. Please let it end."

She longed for a restful sleep, something that seldom came to her in the past. Rest; finally she felt she could rest. She also tried to put the past to rest for the night. She had a feeling Lilly would not let it rest. She would deal with that when the time came.

Chapter 5

It was a warm September day when Lilly returned to Emma's house. Emma sat on the porch steps with a basket full of flower bulbs in her lap.

"Morning, Emma".

Emma smiled. "I'm glad you're here, Lilly. I've given this a lot of thought about talking about my life. Things I haven't told a soul except the Good Lord himself. Most things I am ashamed of. Some folks think I should just keep it light and casual with you and not tell you my story but Kate thinks it might be a good thing so that is why I had you come out. So you say we will be doing this on a regular basis?"

"I think so. I have no idea how long it will take. I brought my bags and I am staying in a hotel in Topeka this week. That is one reason I became a freelance writer, the luxury of being on my own schedule and able to travel some. I thought I would just schedule some times over the next however many months to come see you. Is that all right with you?"

"Heavens, yes. Come on up and sit and visit. Sam, move off the walk so Lilly can get through. You lazy bum! Oh, good Lord, Lilly, please excuse that old dog's manners."

Lilly ended up stepping over Sam, as he would not budge from his spot. Emma stood up and moved off of the steps. She sat down in a chair on the porch. "Need anything to drink?"

"No, I'm fine, thank you". Lilly removed a notebook from her briefcase and a recorder.

"You aren't wasting any time are you?" Emma crossed one leg under the other and a very pregnant calico cat jumped in her lap, rubbing against her chin.

"I just thought I might start keeping notes as we go if that is all right."

"Fine with me. You just make sure you tell it just like I tell it."

"Emma, where shall we start? Your child hood?

Emma looked off towards the barn and quietly spoke, "I was born the younger of two daughters. My dad was a banker and my mother was no doubt mother of the year. My sister was ten years older than me so I basically was an only child because she married when I was nine years old. My parents were strict Christian people."

Emma began to swing slowly and looked off into the distance.

Lilly tilted her head and asked, "Did you attend college? Anything else about your younger days? You're not giving me much here, Emma. How about you just start wherever and I will listen?"

"Start wherever, huh? I had a pretty uneventful childhood. We attended church every Wednesday night and Sunday morning and Sunday evening. I was active in the high school plays and choirs. I had a best friend, Beth. She was the daughter of a minister and my folks were very religious, so we had a lot in common. Beth introduced me to Richard."

"Richard. Tell me about how you met him."

"Lilly, for so many years I have kept a large portion of my past hidden not only from the ones I love but also from friends and neighbors. It has only been recently that I have decided folks should know more about me. Kate has always said I have kept it buried deep within my soul way too long and the memories will haunt me as long as I keep it in. So maybe this is an excellent time to share with you."

Emma tilted her head back, closed her eyes and slipped back in time as she spoke, "It was a blind date the summer I graduated from high school. I was preparing to attend Bible College in Springfield, Missouri. Beth was dating a boy that went to college with Richard so they set us up on a blind date. I worked at Woolco and he came in there to see what he was getting into. He always told me after that day how disappointed he was that it was me and not the other girl in the next checkout. Wish it had been her instead of me." Emma looked down at the floor and seemed to remove herself from the present. "Richard" she whispered.

"Tell me about Richard, Emma. Would you do that?" Lilly wanted to know more but felt somehow that she should not push Emma.

"Richard was so handsome. Charming. That is, until you lived with him. Well, even before that."

"How so, Emma?"

Emma shook her finger at Lilly and said, "Now, Lilly Ballard, keep in mind I've kept much of my life to myself and not many folks around here know the Emma of days gone by. I am not sure I want them to know what a fool I was."

Lilly smiled and reassured Emma nothing would ever be published without Emma's approval but that she would appreciate any and all honesty on Emma's part.

Emma sighed and said, "We met in June. Began to date regularly by mid July. One day I was at his apartment waiting for him to change out of his work clothes when the telephone rang. He yelled from the bathroom for me to get it. I answered and another woman asked if he was there. When I asked her name, she said Kathy. By then he was standing beside me. He was furious. Told her he would have to call her back. He hung up the phone and turned to me and slapped me in the face. Then he spit in my face. I should have left and never returned but he began to cry and say he was sorry. He would never do it again. I asked who Kathy was and he told me it was none of my business. I should have seen then that he was abusive and a womanizer who would never change his ways. Good old hindsight, huh?" She smiled, sipping her iced tea.

"So, what you are saying is that Richard had an abusive side?" Lilly asked, knowing the answer and yet not wanting to hear that inevitable answer.

Emma did not look at Lilly but answered, "Yes."

"Emma, why did you marry him if you knew he could possibly harm you?"

"I thought that I could change him because I loved him. I believed him when he said it would not happen again. But, you know, the night of our wedding rehearsal he became jealous of my high school friend that was going to sing in the wedding. His name was Loren and he was a wonderful young man. Richard became angry and pushed me against the wall in the church basement. I felt I had gone too far to turn back by then."

Emma picked up Gracie and held her in her lap. She leaned down and kissed the schnauzer's little black nose.

"How long was it after you married that he harmed you again, Emma?"

"Three days."

Lilly saw the shame on Emma's face.

"What happened then?"

"I had developed a urinary tract infection and there was blood in my urine. I was running a fever and only nineteen years old and scared as the Dickens. I called my mom long distance to ask her advice. He was listening from the kitchen. We lived in a little one-bedroom apartment and the walls were paper-thin. After I hung up he came into the room. 'Stupid Bitch!' he said. 'Do you have to call Momma to tell her how sick her little girl is? I'll give you something to cry about, cunt!' He pushed me to the floor and began to kick me. Now being a Texan, he always wore cowboy boots and let me tell you, those boots could do some serious hurt. I kept saying, "I love you. Please, I love you!" He kicked me until I blacked out. I woke up in our bed with him placing a cool, damp rag on my forehead and he was crying like a big old baby."

"Oh, Emma. You look exhausted. Do you want to stop for a while? We don't have to continue if you don't want to."

"I don't mind so much really. It is why I am the person I am today because of those choices I made when I was young. How about we take a little break and go inside? I have family pictures."

Emma put Gracie down and stepped over Sam. She opened the screen door and motioned for Lilly to enter the house.

Chapter 6

Emma went to the bookcase and began to take out photo albums.

"Where do you want to start on pictures?" she asked, crossing her legs in an Indian style as she gathered albums around her on the living room floor.

Lilly sat down next to Emma. "Let's just open one and start."

Emma opened an old wedding album. "I always thought Kate would someday want this but she keeps saying she will get it the next time she visits. I still have all of her high school things. That girl is in her thirties and still hasn't consolidated all of her belongings."

Emma smiled and pointed to the first picture. "That is my folks. They sure didn't want me to marry Richard but I did anyway. They did put on a nice wedding for us though." She turned the page and pointed to a handsome young man "Richard" she said, not looking up. She flipped through page after page telling who was in each one.

"Where did you live after you were married, Emma?' Lilly asked.

"We moved to Grandview, Missouri. We moved close to his family. He wanted nothing to do with my family."

"Did either of the families know of the abuse?"

Emma chuckled. "The first time his parents knew was one day when I came home from work and he wasn't there. I went downstairs to the lower level of the apartments where the mailboxes were and there was Richard coming out of this girl's apartment. They did not see me and they embraced and kissed in the doorway. I was just sick. Hurt, mad and just sick. I went back upstairs and when he came inside I confronted him with it. He immediately became angry, I think because he had been caught. He pushed me against the kitchen wall and began to choke me. I reached over on the cabinet and grabbed a paring knife and held it up, telling him that I would use it if he didn't let me go. He grabbed my arm and shoved his knee into my stomach. He knocked the wind out of me and I fell to the floor. Then he kicked me over and over and I ended up in the living room. I could feel the carpet burning my face as he kicked me. All of a sudden he stopped. I was afraid to look up. I just lay there not moving. I heard him walk into the kitchen. I thought for sure he was going to come back and kill me. I heard him dialing the phone. 'Mom, Emma just pulled a knife on me. You need to get over here now', he said. He had called his parents!"

"He walked back into the living room and said 'Get up and wash your face. Mom and Dad are on their way over.'

Emma paused. "He sat down and lit a cigarette and I went into the bathroom. It was about 10 minutes and I could hear their voices in the living room. I didn't want to see them but he came into the bathroom and told me to get out there."

"His mother motioned for me to sit down next to her. She began to tell me that I needed to accept the fact that he had needs and that I needed to accept the fact that there would be other women. I also needed to accept the fact that there would be physical punishment when I had upset him. 'That is the way it is and always will be,' she said. Richard's dad then jumped in on the conversation and told me the very same thing! I thought I was going crazy! They then got up, she gave me this fake little hug and out the door they went! It wasn't until years later that my folks knew what was going on. I felt so much shame."

"What happened next, Emma?"

"Richard told me to get into the bedroom. I began to cry and kept saying "No" so he grabbed me and drug me into the bedroom, throwing me on the bed. I knew what he was going to do. He unzipped his pants and crawled on top of me. He kept kissing me and saying, "You need to learn a lesson." I kept my eyes closed, turning my head away from his disgusting kisses. I felt him thrust his penis into me." Emma stopped. "Is this more than you want to hear Lilly? I think we may be getting into things that you really don't want to hear."

Lilly closed the wedding book and looked at Emma. "No Emma. I want to know what your life was like. If it is not too painful for you, then I think you should continue."

"He raped me. He then got off of me and spat in my face. I continued to stay still, afraid that any move would provoke him. He zipped his pants, walked out of the room and I heard him go out the door. I waited another ten minutes or so and then went and filled the bathtub and soaked in it. There was blood in the water and I could not figure out what had happened. I then took a closer look and realized he had thrust himself into me so hard that he had caused me to bleed. I just sat in there crying, wanting to go back home."

"Why didn't you go home, Emma?"

"I was raised that divorce was a sin and that those vows were sacred. I was ashamed to go home and admit that I was wrong and that they were right and I really didn't know how my folks would react."

"Did he stop the abuse after that or did it continue?"

"It continued. We bought our first house. The day we moved in was such a mess. His folks and some friends helped us and after they left I asked if he would hook up the washer and dryer. I saw the darkness come over his face. I tried to get up the stairs. The laundry area was in the basement. I kept saying "Never mind, it can wait. Never mind." He pulled me down the stairs and head butted me in the face. I had on my glasses and the force of his head on my face caused a terrible cut. Right here." Emma ran her fingers over the scar that went from the inside of her eye, across her cheekbone and to her temple."

"How many stitches?"

"Twenty nine stitches and some butterfly type of bandages. The doctor asked how I got it with Richard sitting right there. He glared at me. I told the doctor we had been moving things and I had tried to put some stuff up on a shelf in the basement and the shelf and the boxes fell on me. The doctor looked at Richard with his little cut from my glasses on his forehead. He asked where he got his little scratch and Richard said he got it as he was trying to help me. You know, back then they didn't do things for domestic violence like they do now."

Emma picked up another photo album and opened it. Lilly could not get over how petite and thin Emma was in the pictures and how tall and muscular Richard was. She wondered how such a small woman held up under such abuse.

"Where was this picture taken, Emma?" Lilly pointed to Emma and Richard standing in front of a large home.

"That was Richard's parent's house. His dad was an executive and they really didn't want for anything, except happiness. That old saying 'Money can't buy happiness' sure fit the mold when it came to this family."

"Did you get along with his parents? Did he have siblings?"

"No, I didn't get along with them. His dad was a sick, abusive man and his mother was just plain evil. He had one sister and a brother. You remember Kate speaking of her Aunt Patti? I have always loved Patti. She is the best of the bunch. She has always been good to me. I sometimes think her dad put her through a living hell. She ran away from home when she was only fifteen years old. Had a baby and gave it up. She never came back. I am guessing life under that roof was pure hell. She deserved better."

They continued to look through albums. Emma stopped and looked at the clock. "Good night! You are probably starving! Let me fix you something to eat."

"I owe you a lunch, Emma. Are there any restaurants near that we could go have a bite to eat?"

"Well, there is the Corner Café about 4 miles from here. It is just good old home cooked meals. I think I will take you up on that."

Lilly got up off of the floor and looked at Emma. Emma continued to sit there for a moment, holding her children's two baby albums. "We'll cover these two angels later," she said. She got up off of the floor and smiled at Lilly, the scar disappearing. Lilly's heart ached at the thought of what Emma had gone through.

"Do you want to take my car or yours?" Emma asked.

"Mine is already out so let's take it. I'll let you be the co-pilot." Lilly opened the screen door. Sam quickly got up and moved from his napping spot. Emma closed the door and locked it. "Sam, you take care of things."

Chapter 7

As Emma and Lilly ventured towards the Café, Lilly enjoyed the countryside. The rolling hills and the beautiful farmland mesmerized Lilly.

"Emma, how did you end up in Kansas when you and Richard started out in Missouri?"

"Richard worked for a company that transferred him here before the kids were born. We were first transferred from Kansas City to Poplar Bluff, Missouri. I was just a stone's throw from my mother's family but Richard would not hear of having any of my family around. We lived there only a year when he was transferred to Topeka. That was a lifetime ago and I never left."

Lilly saw a red brick two story building on the southwest corner of the street. The sign read 'Corner Café'.

"Just pull in anywhere." Emma said.

They walked into the café and Emma quickly went to a table in the corner. It was a small café with only a few tables, all covered in gingham tablecloths.

"Hey, Emma, haven't seen you in a few weeks. Where you been keeping yourself?" A man in his eighties in bib overalls smiled at Emma. He wore a K-State hat and his face was tanned to the point of leather. Lilly guessed that he had spent his years farming or working in the sun.

"Why, I've been around, Earl. Just haven't had a chance to come over and eat." The waitress and two other women greeted Emma.

"When is that article about the barn coming out?" Earl asked.

Emma turned to Lilly. "In March," Lilly said to Emma, not audible enough for Earl to hear.

"In March," Emma told Earl.

"You gonna autograph copies for all the locals?" he asked, winking and then smiling.

"Oh heck, Earl." It seemed to Lilly that Emma blushed. "That might depreciate its worth some day if it had my name on it." Emma smiled and Earl pulled his cap off and scratched his bald head.

The waitress asked what they were going to have. "What do you recommend?" Lilly asked Emma.

"I recommend any of it. Can't say that there is a single thing that isn't worth eating."

Lilly ordered chicken fried steak, mashed potatoes and gravy.

"Full order?" the waitress asked.

"Sure" Lilly answered.

"Are you sure?" asked the waitress.

Lilly hesitated and as she answered, her response sounded more like a question than an answer. "I think so."

Emma touched Lilly's arm and said, "It is pretty big. I usually get a half order with a salad. How hungry are you?"

"Change that to a half order with an iced tea and, do you have cole slaw?" Lilly looked over the menu.

"Sure do"

"I'll take cole slaw with it please." Lilly said.

"Emma?" the waitress asked as she looked at Emma.

"I think I will have the ham steak with a baked potato and salad."

"Iced tea as usual?" The waitress was already writing it down.

Emma nodded her head and said "Please".

As they waited on their meal, the local people would stop at the table and Emma would introduce Lilly to them, only as her friend. She did not mention the fact that Lilly had written the article. One woman asked Lilly where she was from and Lilly answered "Kansas City."

"Are you a friend of Kate's or Jim? Emma doesn't have many young visitors except her kids' friends or her grandkids."

"I am a friend of Emma's. I met Emma a few months ago." Lilly answered.

"Can't pick a better one to have for a friend. But, she will tell you like it is in a heart beat too," Barb said as she sat back down at her table with some other women.

"You have to remember that these folks all look out for one another and there are no secrets around here. I would rather they not know that you are writing something about me. You won't put it in a magazine or anything, will you? The things I have been telling you?" Emma frowned.

"Emma, I will only write what you approve and I will only publish it with your consent." Lilly looked into Emma's clear blue eyes and smiled.

"I trust you, young lady. You had better not let me down." Emma took a sip of her iced tea.

The two chatted like old friends as they ate their lunch. People came in and out of the café, each one speaking to Emma. Lilly wondered how much these people knew of Emma's life since she seemed to try to shelter them and herself from her past. The waitress brought the ticket and Lilly paid the bill. They walked out to the car and started back to Emma's home.

Chapter 8

Just as Lilly turned onto Emma's road, Emma's cell phone rang. Emma looked at the phone and said "It's Kate!"

"Hi, sugar!" Emma smiled and then said "Joshua? Where's Kate? Is she doing all right? How far apart are her contractions?"

Emma would nod her head once in a while and frown, then smile and then nod again.

"Tell her I love her more than meat loves salt and I am waiting for my grandson to arrive. You will call as soon as he is born, won't you?"

"Take care of my baby girl and that baby boy." Emma clicked the phone off and turned to Lilly with tears in her eyes. "Kate is in labor. She is doing fine. She has been in labor for four hours and they are at the hospital. I wish I could be there as it all takes place. You know, Lilly, I loved being pregnant with my babies and I would not trade a moment of the labor or the delivery. My children have been my greatest gift in life. And now the cycle continues with my grandson!"

"Emma, do you want to go to Denver to be with her? I will come back another time if you want to go."

"Heavens, no. I want to wait until they are settled as a family at home and then go when I can hold that boy and tell him all about what he has missed out on. I want him to hear all about his Grandpa Rylie and Uncle Jim. I want to pass on the history and the stories my own mother told me. I know Kate will tell him all of these things but a Grandmother has her own way of telling a story." Emma turned to look out the window as they drove up to the house. "Wish Rylie and Jim were here for this. That Rylie would take that grandson fishing and Jim would have him into some sort of fancy motorized toys before he could even walk. They would spoil him rotten."

Lilly stopped the car and Emma reached for the door handle and then turned to Lilly. "It is times like this that is so hard to be alone. It is when the emptiness almost overwhelms me."

"Oh, Emma. Thank goodness you have Kate and you have Rylie's kids. Why do you continue to stay out here in the country all alone?"

Emma opened the car door and stepped out. Lilly got out of the driver's side. Emma looked at Lilly over the top of the car, resting her elbows on the hood. "I stay here because this is where I belong. This is where I planted my roots and where I buried my son and my husband. This is where I came to start over in life and this is where my life will someday end. Then the children and grandchildren will bury me beside my soul mate and my son. And, there again, the cycle continues, Lilly. I just hope that Kate will somehow keep this place or the other kids will keep it. If they don't keep it, I hope that someone will buy it that loves it as much as our family has."

Emma opened the gate and motioned for Lilly to go ahead of her. Lilly bent down and picked up a cat and walked onto the porch. Emma was quiet for a few moments and then sat on the porch swing.

"I hope she isn't in labor long." Emma patted Sam on his head and motioned for Lilly to sit down. "Where were we, Lilly? I need to tell stories to keep my mind busy."

"We were in the early years of your marriage to Richard. You were telling me about your first home and his family." Lilly took out her notepad and recorder. She sat in the chair Emma had motioned to and looked up at Emma. Lilly could see the worry on Emma's face and wished she could keep her mind busy. "You just start talking, Emma and leave the rest to me.

Emma took a deep breath and leaned back as she spoke, "We had settled into our first home in Independence, Missouri. It was a cute little house in a nice little neighborhood. I was so proud of it. I wanted my family to see it but I had to wait until a time when Richard was away so that they could come and see it. It was right about that time that the company Richard worked for started him traveling during the week. It was a blessing for me in a way. But in another way it gave Richard every opportunity to have affairs. One Saturday he was working on the car and he asked me to find him his keys. I looked all over and then decided to look in his coat pocket. I felt a piece of paper so I took it out, opened it and began to read it. He had written the letter to a woman by the name of Karen and in the letter he professed his love and told her that whenever he was with me, he thought of her. He talked about how she felt, her kisses, her touch. He told her he loved her and that someday they would be together. I had just finished reading the note when he came into the house and yelled 'Did you find them?' He came into the room and there I stood, trying to hurry and fold that letter back up. He had caught me and, although he had been caught in his lies and affair, he became angry with me for finding the letter. Each time I would try to question him and ask for answers, he would tell me to shut up. I started to walk into the spare bedroom and all I remember after that was the terrible pain in the back of my head. I fell to the floor and he began to kick me over and over in the head. I blacked out. When I came to, he was gone and I could feel the blood running out of my ears and mouth. I tried to get up but I was so dizzy I couldn't focus long enough to sit up let alone stand. I crawled over to the wall and placed my back against it. I began to work my way along the wall until I reached the phone jack. I grabbed the cord and started to pull the phone to me. I called a friend that I worked with at the bank who knew he was abusive. I told her to come over but if she saw all of the vehicles in the drive, that meant he was still in the house or yard and she should under no circumstances come into the house. She wanted to call the police and I told her not to. I was afraid that, if they released him, he would kill me because he had told me so many times he would. I sat there waiting for her, listening to each sound, praying he would not come back into the house or into that room. It seemed like forever and then I heard someone say "Emma?" When I saw Melody's face, I began to cry. When she saw me, she also cried. "Oh, look at you, Emma. What did he do? Why are you bleeding so much from your ears?" She helped me up and then helped me into the bathroom. "We have to get out of here before he comes home, Mel." I told her. She washed me up as best she could and helped me into her car. "I am taking you to the hospital." She said. "No! Just take me to my doctor's office. He will know what to do." She drove me to the clinic and helped me inside. She told the receptionist I needed to see the doctor. When I got into the examining room and undressed, the nurse came in. She looked so surprised. "You need to file a report," she said. My doctor came in. He took a light and looked into my eyes, turned my head this way and that and then looked into my ears. 'You have an eardrum that is ruptured and I wouldn't be surprised if you have a concussion. I want to get some x-rays.' The nurse took me down the hall and through a corridor to the radiology section. She went in and talked to the girl that was working there. Soon they called me in to take the x-rays. Then the nurse took me back to the examination room to wait for the doctor. After about twenty minutes, he came in. 'You have a cracked skull. A hairline fracture. There really isn't anything we can do other than keep a close eye on you since you have the concussion and the fracture. I am sending you to a specialist who will check out the eardrum. Emma, this can't continue or the next doctor to see you will be the coroner.' He looked at me over the rim of his glasses. I looked him straight in the eye and said, 'I can't leave. He says he will kill me. He says if he can't have me, no one can.' My doctor frowned and said 'I am scheduling you an appointment with the ear doctor and a re-check with me in a week. You are not to work until I see you and release you. Do you understand, Emma?' I nodded my head and knew that I would not be able to miss that much work or be able to go to the ear doctor. Richard kept a close eye on all of the bills and he would punish me for even going to the clinic let alone anywhere else. Melody and I left the clinic and she drove me home. Richard's motorcycle was now in the driveway. He came out to the car. 'Hi girls, where have you two been?' He looked into the passenger side of the car and smiled at me. My heart raced. My mind raced. What lie could I tell him?"

"Melody smiled at Richard and didn't even flinch. 'Emma and I had planned this day quite some time ago to go garage sale shopping. I can't believe she forgot to tell you, Richard.' Melody looked at him with her huge blue eyes and smiled that sultry smile. Any time Richard thought a woman might be even remotely attracted to him, he would put on the charm so he focused on her and I got out of the car. 'What did you girls buy?' he asked. Melody again came to my rescue and pulled a bag of clothes out of the back seat. 'Emma didn't find much. You know Emma, always looking for something for the house and passing over stuff for her. I bought some clothes, though.'

Melody held up the bag. Richard smiled and patted her arm as it rested on the car door. 'Do you want to come in and model for us?' he asked. Melody smiled and made the excuse of having to go pick her dog up from the groomer and waved goodbye to me."

Emma looked at her watch. "We've been sitting here over an hour, Lilly. Do you want to go inside?" Lilly knew that Emma was worrying about Kate and the baby. "Emma, I want you to sit wherever you are most comfortable. If that is inside, then that is where we will go."

Emma picked up a cat and took a deep breath. "I love my porch. Let's stay out here"

"Emma, did Richard do anything to you when you went inside that day?"

"He went inside and went on and on about how beautiful Melody was and how he would like to get a piece of her. He did that a lot over women. It was no wonder I had no self-esteem. Not once did he mention what had happened earlier and I knew better than to bring it up."

"Did you return to the doctor and keep the ear appointment?" Lilly was fairly sure of Emma's answer.

"No and I went back to work that next week. It worked out well that Richard was out of town during the week. I confiscated the medical bills and insurance information and had it paid by money order before he ever saw it. To this day, I have a substantial hearing loss in my left ear. Let's go inside and look at some pictures." Emma set the cat down and got up off of the swing. Lilly followed.

Just as they entered the living room, Emma's phone began to ring. "This might be my grandson call, Lilly!"

Chapter 9

Emma hurried to the phone "Hello?" She covered her mouth and began what appeared to Lilly as a little dance. "He's here? How's my girl and her little guy?" Is he healthy? You're right, Joshua. I'll hush while you fill me in." Emma would nod and smile and then she turned to Lilly. "He's here! Nine pounds 11 ounces. Twenty-two inches long. He's a chunk!" Again she did a little dance. "Put her on the phone, Joshua." Emma waited a few seconds and then the tears began to roll down her suntanned cheeks. "Kate? Are you doing well? I know he's beautiful. There is no doubt in my mind. Lots of hair? I can't wait! Now, don't overdo it and if you need me, you call. What's that? I will schedule a flight out there within the next couple of weeks or sooner if I can't stand the wait. Give him love from his grandma. I love you. Bye."

Emma hung up the phone. "Conner James has arrived, Lilly. Come on, there is something I promised myself I would do when this day arrived." Emma opened the screen door, reached back onto the washstand in the foyer and grabbed some keys. Lilly followed. Emma hurried down the front steps and through the gate. She headed towards the barn. As she opened the barn door, she turned to Lilly and smiled. "I've waited a long time for this day, Lilly." She slid the barn door open and removed the tarp from Jim's car. It was a beautiful black mustang. "Get in, Lilly. I am taking you with me on this ride."

Lilly opened the door and slid into the passenger seat. She felt she was on sacred ground because she knew how much this car meant to Emma. Emma started the engine. The glass pipes made a loud repercussion in the barn. She eased the mustang out of the barn and headed down the drive. At the end of the drive, she turned towards the cemetery. Lilly was quiet. She knew what a special moment this must be for Emma. Emma had suffered so many losses in her lifetime and such heartache. This was a joyous moment in Emma's life and Lilly felt honored to be a part of it.

Emma shifted gears and drove into the cemetery. She went to the furthest section. Lilly knew instantly which graves were Jim's and Rylie's. Beautiful fresh flowers adorned the graves. On one headstone was the picture of a young, handsome man. Lilly knew that was Jim's final resting place. To the south of his grave stood another headstone. Jim's was black granite and stood about two and half feet tall. This other grave marker was deep green granite with no picture but also as tall. Between the two sites was a tall bald cypress tree. Flowers were planted around each headstone and also fresh flowers in each granite flower container.

"Come, Lilly. Today is a happy day and we need to share that with Rylie and Jim. Emma walked towards the gravesites and Lilly followed.

Emma stood before the gravesites. "Lilly, this is my Jim and Rylie. Don't think I am crazy. To this day Kate and our friends will ask "Have you been to see Jim and Rylie today?"

Emma knelt down in front of Jim's headstone, meeting the picture of her son eye to eye. "Jim, Kate had a little boy today. She named him after you. He is healthy and a beautiful little boy." Emma's tears flowed down her cheeks. She ran her fingers over Jim's picture as if she were actually touching her son's face.

"I need to tell Rylie." She got up from her kneeling position and stepped over to Rylie's grave. "Grandpa, you have a new one! He's a big one and he's healthy. I am counting on you and Jim to watch over him. I want him to be all boy and into everything. Kate needs a livewire, don't you know?"

Emma kissed her thumb and placed it on each headstone. Lilly read Jim's headstone and the realization of how young he was, only twenty-four, swept over her. How sad it must have made Emma, Rylie and Kate to lose him so young. Lilly read Rylie's headstone "Beloved Husband and Father". On the back of the headstone in small print Lilly read "Beans".

"Emma, what does this mean on Rylie's headstone?" Lilly pointed to the word.

Emma laughed and ran her finger across the word. "Kate's nickname for Rylie since she was a young teen was Beans. His name was Rylie Dean and at first she would call him Rylie Bean and then within a short period of time he was Beans. He became so used to it and even the grandkids started calling him Papa Beans. We had to put it on his headstone because it was a part of him."

Emma arranged all of the fresh flowers, making sure each one met her criteria of being suitable for the two men she most loved. Hanging in the bald cypress tree were several bells, some being rusted. "Emma, what are these bells?"

Emma reached out and made a bell ring. "Every time a bell rings, an angel gets its wings. Haven't you heard that, Lilly? These bells are from some of Jim's friends' weddings and when I get them, I bring them here to tie onto the tree. And this one is from our granddaughter's Christmas play so Rylie hung it on the tree. On a breezy day, you can hear the bells ring. It is such a sweet sound."

Emma leaned over to smell a rose and then began to walk away. "Are you ready, Lilly?" She ran her hand over each headstone, again kissed her thumb and turned to smile at Lilly. "This is a good day, Lilly. My grandson was born."

The two women walked back towards the mustang, not talking. Lilly looked out over the surrounding farmland and took in a deep breath. She turned to look towards Emma's house. Emma was right. From the gravesites Emma's house was clearly visible. The barn stood proudly over her plot of land.

"Told you, Lilly. They watch over me and I watch over them. I wouldn't have it any other way. Except that I would rather have them alive and here with me but I am not the one that decides that." Emma opened the car door and slid into the driver's seat. She started the engine and Lilly sat down beside her. Emma drove slowly out of the cemetery. As they turned towards the house, she looked back one last time. "This is a good day." She said.

Chapter 10

Emma and Lilly entered the house. Gracie greeted them. "Lilly, I need to call Rylie's kids and tell them about Kate and Conner. Do you mind going through pictures and I also have some journals that I have kept over the years."

"Go right ahead and make your calls. I know where the photo albums are but where are the journals?" Lilly headed toward the cabinet with the photos.

"I keep them in the pie safe. I knew having all of these antiques would come in handy. I keep photos and my journals in there also. I bet you thought those photo albums you have seen are the only ones I have." Emma walked to the pie safe and opened the doors. "Help yourself. Someday I will set you down and have you watch videos of the family."

Lilly began going through albums and Emma picked up the phone. "Denise? Kate had her baby! Both mother and son are doing fine. Yep." Lilly listened to Emma give all of the vitals and talk about the new arrival. Lilly opened up a journal. It read: July 11th

We moved to Poplar Bluff today. I don't know a soul here and Richard has told me there is no way my folks can come see us or I can go three. He says nine hours is too far for me to travel and he doesn't want to take a chance of me not coming back. Richard tied the dogs up in the back yard with no water and it is so hot here. I snuck some water out to them while he was talking to the movers. Richard let me bring the dogs in this afternoon. They are covered in fleas and Richard has beat both of them. I am going to get flea soap and spray. We think it came from the sand box that he tied them up to. Richard let me sleep in the bed tonight. He had told me that he didn't want me near him because I had brought the dogs with us. I don't think I am going to like it here so far away from friends and family. I wish I could go see mom's family in Kennett and Piggott. He says I can't but maybe there will be a time.

July 12th

I really love this house. I think partly because it is so much like mom's family's homes. Every place I have seen looks like "down home". Mom would love knowing I was in such a nice place. I can't believe I am so far away from everyone. I hope Richard does not feel an extra sense of security because I don't know anyone here and I have no one. I should research where the nearest hospital is and look into getting a doctor. I pray I don't need one.

July 17th

I met one of the neighbors today. She seems really nice. She has a husband, Max, and two children. Her son is a teenager and her daughter is eleven. She seems so happy. I guess I have forgotten that some couples love each other and are happy. I wonder how we appear to others?

August 1st

I found a job today with the local dentist. His assistant, Sheri, is so cute! She looks like a movie star. She said she would like for us to come and have dinner with them some time and meet some of the other couples in town.

August 7th

My first day of work. I can't believe we have been here this long and Richard has not raised a hand to me all of this time. Do you think it will last? Me either. Work went well. Richard questioned me a lot. He said I had better not make friends with any men.

September 27th

I am sorry I have not been able to write. Richard and I went to dinner a few weeks ago at Sherri and Ed's. There was another woman there with her husband. Her name is Becky. I found her and Richard on the patio kissing. He now sees her regularly. I hate the nights we have "couples" night because I have to see them making eyes or she plays "footsie" with him under the table while we play cards. I hate my life.

Chapter 11

"Lilly? What are you so engrossed in? I think I said your name four or five times. All of the kids are so excited. I have a feeling Kate will probably get a lot of calls in the next few days and Denise loves to shop for babies so Conner will probably be getting a package from Kansas. Do you want to continue to read or shall we talk?" Emma sat down on the sofa.

"Let's talk, Emma. Tell me more about your time in Poplar Bluff."

Lilly studied Emma's face as Emma replied, "I would have to say that Poplar Bluff was one of the easier years we were together. The Christmas we were there was hard. Richard made me meet my family in a motel room in Columbia, Missouri. I was so glad to see them. Somewhere in all of the pictures are several pictures of that day. I really wanted to tell them then that life with Richard was not what they thought but now that I look back, I know they knew some of it. They had to since he would not let them come around.

My uncle passed away. My uncle Bill. I had grown up spending part of my summers with him and my aunt Vesta. When he passed away Richard was away on business in Dallas. My folks flew into Poplar Bluff. They got to see my house and I got to go with them to the funeral. That was the first time I had seen my mother's family in all of the years we had been married. It wasn't long after that when Richard received the call that he was being transferred to Topeka.

The Poplar Bluff people had a big going away party for us. Richard sent me on home that night and he spent the night somewhere else. I am guessing it was with Becky or some other woman. He came home late that next morning. The movers arrived and started packing all of our belongings. By the end of that week we were on our way to Topeka. I was looking forward to being near my parents and by that time Richard's parents had been transferred to Saint Louis, Missouri so I knew I would be further away from them. I had hopes of a better life.

We bought a brand new house that had never been lived in. It was in a quiet neighborhood with lots of young couples with children. I loved setting up house and we worked at putting in trees and shrubs and flowers. After about a week, the neighbor kids, most of them in their early teens, started coming around. I think they liked that we were a little younger than their parents. We were in our mid twenties and Richard would throw the football with the boys and the girls would sit on our front porch and talk about all the things teenage girls talk about. After about three months, I began to notice that Richard would sit and hug the girls and touch them in inappropriate ways. It was also at this time that he became interested in having my teenage niece come visit or he would suggest we go there and see my family. He began to buy lots of porn magazines and movies and he started going with his friends to the bars where they had strippers. Still, he wasn't hitting me or anything, so I thought things were better.

One day one of the neighborhood mothers came to our house while Richard was gone. She accused him of making sexual advances towards her daughter and some of the other girls. I was hurt but I wasn't surprised because I had been noticing some of his strange behavior." Emma stopped and looked at the clock. "Lilly, I need a break. Let's take Jim's car for a little ride. I feel like I am ruining this special day by talking about Richard."

"I would like that Emma." Lilly got up out of the chair.

"Lilly, why don't you just plan on staying here and not even bother with a motel or hotel? Surely you still have time to cancel your room. I have plenty of room and I would love to have you stay here. How about it?" Emma smiled and the scar disappeared with the lines of time.

"I would be honored to stay with you, Emma. Let me make a phone call or two." Lilly took out her cell phone.

"Use the house phone, Lilly." Emma walked over and took the cordless phone off of the charger and handed it to Lilly. "I'll wait for you outside."

Lilly made phone calls and Emma walked out to the barn. Emma fed the horses apples and waited for Lilly. "Do you want this door closed and locked, Emma?" Lilly called from the front porch.

Emma began to walk towards the house. "Just pull it shut. It will lock automatically." She bent over and picked up the bag of apples. "I am going to show you some of the countryside."

Emma opened the mustang door and slid into the driver's seat. Lilly pulled the front door shut, stepped over Sam and walked to the car. Emma drove down the drive and turned east onto the road. "I thought I would show you some of the lakes that the boys loved to fish and some of the other sights around here." She rolled the windows down and shifted gear.

The two women talked about Rylie and Jim and how they worked together and how they loved their family and life. Emma would tell Lilly about the lakes where Rylie took the kids and grandkids fishing and where he and Emma would go in the evenings after Kate moved out. They would camp and fish and enjoy each other's company.

"Rylie gave me so much happiness in the years we were together. We loved being together doing nothing at all." Lilly loved the beautiful countryside and listened intently to Emma's every word. "I have a stop I need to make in Topeka, Lilly. Do you mind?"

"No, not at all. I am at your mercy for the next week, Emma. You take me wherever you want and tell me whatever you want." Emma turned onto the new highway and headed north towards Topeka. As they traveled towards the city, Emma asked Lilly about her own life and family. She asked about siblings, parents and Lilly's fiancé.

"When is the wedding, Lilly?" Emma asked.

"We are planning on a fall wedding next year. We just haven't found a place to have it yet. We both want it outside and Kansas City really doesn't have what we are looking for. David suggested having it on an island but I want so many friends and family there that would not be able to attend if it were on an island."

"What kind of place are your looking for?" Emma asked with a smile.

"We both have agreed we want something simple and with a view and outdoors where everyone can enjoy the openness. My dress and the attendants' dresses are simple and the men are not wearing tuxedos, only casual suits. I want lots of earth tones and all of the colors of fall. Does that sound silly?"

"Heavens, no, it doesn't sound silly! Kate had her wedding at our place. She was so beautiful. Hey! What about the farm? We had hers under all of the trees by the barn. It was beautiful. She had a spring wedding but fall would be beautiful. You're welcome to it, if you want, Lilly."

"Oh, it would be a beautiful setting, Emma. Let me talk to David. Maybe bring him out in a couple of weeks to see the place. Would that work?"

Emma chuckled. "Like you have to ask. You should know by now that I love having folks some see my place."

Emma pulled into a large wholesale floral company. "Come on in with me, Lilly."

They walked into the shop. A large man of Hispanic decent greeted them. "Emma!" He gave Emma a huge bear hug. "Bobby, this is Lilly. Kate had her baby!" Bobby nodded to Lilly "Nice to meet you." He smiled and hugged Emma again. "What did she name him?" Emma smiled "Conner James. How many boys with James as their name do we have now, Bobby?"

"Let's see," Bobby said as he ran his hand through his thinning hair. "Michael named his and Keylock named his and Justin named his and now Kate. That son of yours lives on in all of those little guys. I have a picture of Michael's boy. Want to see?" He reached for his wallet before Emma even answered and pulled out a picture. It was a boy in his early teens, blond with an ear-to-ear smile.

"Good Lord, he looks like his daddy! Lilly, Michael is Bobby's stepson and he was one of Jim's dearest friends. Michael drove Jim's car to the cemetery the day we buried Jim. He drove right behind the hearse. Kate rode with him and so did Keylock, another dear friend."

Lilly smiled and looked at the picture again. Jim touched so many lives. Lilly was relieved that he was nothing like his father.

"I want huge bouquets with a single white rose in each to represent that grandson of mine. Can you get me set up?"

"You want one as big as the ones you do for birthdays and special occasions, same type of flowers but with the white rose?" Bobby asked.

"Yep, just like that. I knew you would do it. You always come through for me." Emma stepped toward a display and Bobby began gathering flowers in the cooler room. "Lilly, feel free to look around. Bobby is an awesome florist and he loved my Jim. He and his wife Brenda used to take Jim and Michael to the Ozarks each summer. Jim was like another son to them and Michael was just like one of my kids. Bobby makes all of the fresh arrangements for the graves."

Lilly walked around the shop and gathered in ideas of her own for that fall wedding she had told Emma about. She pondered over the idea of using the farm as the site for the wedding and wondered what David would think. He had seen the barn pictures and talked about what an awesome home it would have made for Emma and Rylie. He loved all of the pictures of the animals and Emma's flowers. It was definitely something to consider.

"Bobby, you do a great job as always!" Emma said as Bobby handed a bouquet to Emma and another one to Lilly.

"I want to see pictures of that new grandson when you come back in," Bobby smiled and waved.

"Tell Brenda hello!" Emma waved and walked back to the car.

Emma and Lilly talked about Kate's wedding and how she met Joshua. They talked about the other grandchildren and how much they meant to Emma. "Taylor is all grown up and she doesn't visit as often as she used to. Kelsi phones often. She makes sure Grandma is doing fine. The boys call once in a while or they come out and mow my lawn. Sometimes they will come out and ride the horses. With the age difference between the other grandkids and Conner, I imagine he will be spoiled rotten."

Emma drove into the cemetery. Emma and Lilly placed the bouquets on the graves. Again, Emma kissed her thumb and placed it onto each headstone. "We had better get this mustang back into the barn and think about what we are going to eat for dinner."

Chapter 12

After putting the mustang away, Emma and Lilly went into the house. Emma stood with the refrigerator door open and called out to Lilly in the dining room. "How hungry are you?"

"Emma, I had that big lunch. Let's just fix something easy." Lilly continued to go through photo albums.

"Sandwiches? Fresh vegetables? Fruit salad?" Emma asked.

"That sounds perfect."

They laughed and talked and looked at pictures as they enjoyed their meal. Emma told about how her parents met and Lilly talked about her own mother.

The conversation was kept lighthearted and Lilly knew Emma would bring Richard back into the conversation when she was ready. Lilly didn't want to spoil Emma's day with talk of such a dreadful memory.

Lilly again brought up the subject of having the wedding at Emma's and she could see the excitement on Emma's face.

"Wouldn't it be fun, Lilly? Think about the joy that would fill this place. Kate has all kinds of contacts when it comes to wedding design if you want to talk to her. I wonder how her first evening as a mom is going. Oh, how I loved having my babies! I loved every minute of the pregnancy and delivery. My children were my greatest gift but Rylie was a miracle too. He came along at a perfect time. Sometimes God puts those special things right in front of you when you least expect it. I know Kate will realize what a blessing her little boy is. There is something about a mother and son. I am not saying that because I lost my son. They say it is true. Mothers and sons and fathers and daughters. Boy, Kate got cheated on that one. She still had a relationship with her dad; it was just a strained relationship." Emma ate a grape. "I'm glad she had Rylie. They grew so close over the years. Rylie and Richard both gave Kate away in her wedding. Richard was an ass but Rylie remained a gentleman and he supported Kate. She never regretted her decision to include Rylie."

"How old was Kate when she married?" Lilly looked at the pictures of Kate's wedding. All of Rylie's children and grandchildren surrounded Kate as she stood in front of the barn. Standing on each side of Kate was Rylie and Emma. Richard was not in the picture.

"She was 26 years old. Did you notice that Richard is not in the pictures? He refused to be in anything that included Rylie or me. It broke Kate's heart that he was acting the way he did but I was not surprised at all."

"She made a beautiful bride, Emma. And look at you. You clean up pretty well." Lilly smiled at Emma. "What a handsome family, Emma. This is so nice to be able to see all of the pictures over the years and how your family has grown. And now you have a new addition with Conner James. You've been blessed, Emma."

Emma's smile faded. "Some days I feel that way and other days I feel I have been cursed. What I would give to have my boys here with me right now. Jim and Rylie would be so excited about a new baby. I know that, in spite of myself, I have had numerous blessings but along with those blessings comes a lot of heartache."

Emma began to clear the table. "Let me get this cleared and we will go sit on the porch and watch the sunset. I need to show you your room too."

Lilly started to help Emma and Emma motioned for her to sit down. "You keep looking at pictures. If you have any questions, I am more than willing to answer."

Lilly continued to look at Kate's wedding pictures. There was one with Emma helping Kate with the train on her dress. The pride glistened in Emma's eyes. Another one with Kate and Rylie and his sons. Picture after picture and none with Richard. How sad for Kate that he felt he could control the day that should have been special for the entire family.

"Lilly, are you ready to see your room? It's Kate's old room. I think that is where you will be most comfortable." Emma walked upstairs and opened the bedroom door. Lilly felt she was like stepping back in time. The room had an old iron bed with an antique quilt on it. Old black and white family pictures covered the walls and there was also an old quilt hanging on the east wall. On the antique washstand stood a picture of Kate and Jim when they were very young. Jim stood over her and held her gently from behind. Both children had large blue eyes and smiles that melted Lilly's heart. She wondered if those precious children had also been the victims of Richard's abuse.

"He was her protector from the day she was born." Emma picked up the picture and cradled it in her arms. "As he grew older, he became my protector too. He hated the way his dad treated me and I hated myself for the way I allowed him to treat the kids. It was out of fear that I didn't stand up to him but, over the years, I realized that I had to save my children from Richard and his controlling ways and his violent ways. I nearly waited too long."

Lilly didn't know what to say. She stood and looked at what had been Kate's room. Lilly could not imagine that Emma's children held it against Emma. Lilly felt Emma was being too hard on herself yet she could only imagine the guilt that Emma carried with her.

"Lilly? I will help you carry in your bags if you would like and then we can sit out on the porch." Emma smiled and set the picture back on the washstand.

The two walked downstairs and out to Lilly's vehicle. Lilly grabbed a large bag and handed Emma an overnight bag.

"Let's get you settled."

When they went onto the porch, Sam greeted them as if they had been gone a lifetime. As soon as Emma sat down, the fat gray cat jumped in her lap. Lilly sat in the chair beside her.

As they talked about Emma's garden and animals, the sun began to set. Lilly could see why Emma did not want to leave this place. It was so close to nature. The horses grazed in the pasture and Gracie chased two kittens into the barn. Life seemed simpler here and yet Lilly knew that Emma's life was far from simple. They sat on the porch until late evening.

"Lilly, I am ready to call it a night. How about you? This has been a full day. I promise we will jump right back into where we left off. Trust me, Lilly. I remember exactly where."

"I think turning in for the night sounds like an excellent idea, Emma." Emma closed up the barn and put the horses in their stalls. She finished the evening chores and locked up.

As Lilly prepared for bed, all the thoughts of her conversations with Emma ran through her head. It took quite a while before she fell asleep.

Lilly woke up several times during the night. She was not used to all of the different night sounds in the country and she was sure she heard Emma up roaming around a couple of times.

The moonlight cast a light on the washstand and Lilly could see the picture of Kate and Jim. Hanging on the wall above the washstand were pictures of Emma's grandchildren, Taylor, Brett, Marie, Kelsi and Dawson. Now Emma would have to add Conner James to the wall.

Lilly found it a reassurance that Emma had contentment in her stepchildren and grandchildren. With Kate in Denver it was good to know Emma had family close by.

Lilly lay there wondering if Richard had bothered Emma after Rylie died. She finally drifted off into a sound sleep.

Chapter 13

Lilly woke to the smell of bacon and other wonderful smells in Emma's kitchen. She slipped on her robe and went into the upstairs bathroom to freshen up. As Lilly walked downstairs she could see the front door open. She went into the kitchen but Emma wasn't there. As she walked towards the front door she could see Emma swinging on the porch swing. Lilly heard Emma singing "Amazing Grace".

"Emma?" Lilly pushed the screen door open.

"Morning, Lilly. I wondered when you would be waking up. I have breakfast ready. I decided to make a breakfast casserole and fry up some bacon. Hope you are hungry. I also made some homemade biscuits."

"Oh, Emma. I am used to a piece of toast so this will be a feast." Lilly sat in the chair and Sam sat down beside her.

"Beautiful morning, Lilly. How did you sleep?"

"I slept really well." Lilly didn't have the heart to tell Emma otherwise. Although Lilly did sleep well once she soundly fell to sleep.

"Kate has already called this morning. Mother and son had a restful night. She thinks they will either go home this afternoon or first thing in the morning." Emma began to swing again, her toes barely touching the porch floor.

Lilly ran her hand over Sam's head and scratched his ears. When she stopped, he would paw at her and then she would continue.

"We had better eat breakfast. I've already done the morning chores so I could eat a horse." Emma smiled and then whispered, "Don't let Sally and Pie hear that" and she winked.

The two women enjoyed a breakfast that could have served a family of four easily. Lilly enjoyed the biscuits and Emma had fresh honey from a neighbor's beehives. The casserole contained sausage, farm fresh brown eggs, hash browns, onions and cheese. Lilly doubted she would need another meal that day.

After clearing the table and washing the dishes, Lilly and Emma returned to Emma's porch.

"It's a new day, Lilly, my belly is full and I am ready to start where we ended yesterday. How about you? I am sure you didn't come here and take time away from your own life to just sit with me and swing on my porch."

"I want you to feel comfortable in talking to me, Emma and I want you to do it in your own time. Shall I get my notebook?" Lilly stood up from her chair.

"Yep. It's time. Go get it." The wind tussled Emma's hair and she brushed a strand from her forehead.

Lilly went into the house to get her notepad and returned to the porch to join Emma.

"Start whenever you are ready, Emma."

"Let me see. We ended with the neighbor approaching me with the fact that Richard had made sexual advances towards her daughter and some of the other neighbor girls. Is that right, Lilly?" Emma pulled one leg up under the other and stopped swinging.

Lilly read her notes. "That is it. You have a better memory than I do."

"Some things you don't forget, even when you want to." Emma looked out across the property. "I was embarrassed and ashamed. I told her I would take care of it. She told me that if I didn't, she would contact the authorities. I was so scared and I wasn't sure what to do. A part of me wanted him to go to jail and yet I had no idea where to turn. I thought about it all day. When he came home that night, I told him I wanted to start looking for another place to live. I said I wanted to move closer to the lake. I told him that he could have parties in a bigger house and we could think about getting a boat. That was the only thing I could come up with. I knew better than to tell him what was really going on. Richard sat silently for a few minutes. He stood and looked out the window. Then he turned to me and said 'Start looking for another house if that is what you want. Make it a place where we can entertain. You do all of the foot work and let me know what you decide.' He went downstairs and that was the end of the conversation."

"Did you look for another house, Emma?"

"I worked part time for a local doctor's office. After work that next day, I contacted a realtor and he came up with some houses to look at. It took me a week before I found something. I fell in love with the house and so did Richard. We made an offer and the people accepted it. Three weeks before we were to move, I found out I was pregnant with Jim. I was so excited but Richard wasn't. He accused me of cheating on him, said it wasn't his baby. That is when things really took a turn for the worst."

"Why didn't he want a child?" Lilly watched Emma's every expression.

"He never really said. I think it was because Richard was all about himself. I was to wait on him hand and foot and he did not want to share. I also think he didn't want someone else in the house that would know what went on behind closed doors."

Emma leaned over and took off her shoes. She smiled. "We moved into the new house. I was so excited about being pregnant. Richard and I had been married for seven years and I finally had something to look forward to. Now that I look back, I should not have been so selfish. I brought my babies into Hell."

"Was he abusive during your pregnancy?" Again, Lilly watched Emma's face.

Emma's brow wrinkled and she looked Lilly directly in the eye. "He was hot and cold. It was then that his sick sexual side started to come out. I was about five months pregnant when one day he came home from work and I could tell from his eyes that he was in a dark mood. His eyes would nearly turn red, I believe. I used to tell my friends that I had looked into the eyes of Satan himself. I hurried around thinking that he was angry because dinner was not on the table. He grabbed my hair and pulled me upstairs to the bedroom. I started to cry, thinking he was going to hurt the baby. I was begging him "Please don't hurt the baby. Please, please." Our bathroom was adjacent to the bedroom with the bathroom sink being outside the toilet and shower room. The sink was just divided by a partition in the bedroom. He grabbed his shave cream and razor. I stood motionless and scared, not knowing what he was going to do next. He turned from the sink and pushed me so hard that I fell to the floor. He sat on my chest and faced my legs and lower body. He tore at my skirt and underwear, tearing them from my body. I cried harder and harder, again begging him to not harm the child I carried in me. His weight kept me from taking deep breaths and I felt as if his weight would crush my chest. My cries became whispers due to very little air. I felt the cold shave cream on my pubic area. I tried to pull my legs together but he pulled them apart. Then I felt the razor. He was shaving my pubic area so hard that I could feel the warmth of my own blood as it ran down my buttocks. I begged and begged. When he had completely shaven my pubic area, he turned around to face me. He began to unzip his pants. I began to crawl across the floor, trying to somehow find safety. He grabbed me and turned me over on my back and put his knee on my belly. 'Do you want this baby to live?' he said. I nodded yes, not speaking. He took his knee off of my belly and lay down on top of me. "I want to know what it feels like to screw a little girl. Whenever I want to screw a little girl, you will cooperate or there will be consequences, bitch.' He thrust himself into me. It didn't take long before he was finished. Between his body fluids and my open cuts from the razor, I felt like I was on fire. Just as he climbed off of me, he kicked me in the leg and laughed. 'I like screwing little girls. See, bitch, moving away from the old neighborhood didn't stop me. You didn't think I knew, did you? Thought you were pulling one over on me, asking to move. Stupid bitch.' I stayed as quiet as possible, not wanting to agitate him in any way for fear he would follow through on hurting my baby." Emma stopped, tears in her blue eyes. "Jim" she whispered. "Lilly, I pray every night that he forgave me."

"Emma, I am sure Jim knew you loved him and that he did not hold it against you. You don't think Kate begrudges you, do you?"

"For years Kate would lash out at me over silly things and I think that was her bitterness coming out. Richard was not as hard on Kate as he was Jim in their early years but, as she grew into a young adult, he punished her for being a part of me. He never contributed financially towards her college education. Heck, he didn't even help pay for Jim's funeral and headstone. That man had so much money but he was so evil that he would not even share it with his own children. Kate has had a lot of bitterness and I can't blame her. But poor Jim was punished physically, mentally and emotionally. Kate's abuse was more the mental and the emotional turmoil he put her through. She always wanted to see the best in Richard because he was her dad. Over the years I think Kate began to realize that Rylie and I were the ones that she could rely on. She knew that Rylie and I had gone into debt for her college education and that Rylie bought her first car. We paid for so much over the years and Richard never contributed a cent. She realized more as she got older."

"Did Richard ever sexually abuse Kate?" Lilly asked.

"No. I believe Kate would have told me if he had. I had sole custody, a lifetime restraining order and only supervised visitation. It wasn't until much later that Kate would go to Richard's alone and by then I think she would have told me or called for help if he had tried something. She is a very strong willed young woman. I have never told Kate all of this because I think she would think I was such a fool for staying around. I let fear get in the way and, as the kids and I always said, a life lived in fear is a life half lived. Some things you don't want to tell your children about their father. After all, he was still their dad whether I wanted him to be or not. I am sure Kate would have said something about any sexual abuse. I worried every time she left for his house. What did I do to my babies, Lilly?" Emma's eyes filled with tears. "What did I do?"

"Emma, don't do this to yourself."

Emma scoffed and turned to Lilly "My Rylie used to tell me the same thing." Emma got out of the porch swing. "Ever been horseback riding?"

"No, I can't say that I have." Lilly hesitated.

"Come on, I'll take you on some of the back roads. You can ride Sally. She is as gentle as a lamb. I love just taking a ride around the farmland and enjoying the simpler things in life."

Emma and Lilly walked out to the barn. Emma saddled up the horses and explained to Lilly what she should do. "Don't be afraid, Lilly. Close your eyes and smell the hay. Run your hand across my sweet old Sally." Lilly ran her hand across Sally's mane and back. Emma helped her onto the horse. "I love the smell of a horse. Kate and I are both that way and Rylie finally admitted to us one day that he also liked the smell of the hay and the horses. He always joked that he didn't want to agree with the girls. Now take her reigns and follow me. Sally is so gentle."

Lilly did just as she was told and they rode out of the barn and turned north into a pasture. As they rode along, Emma told Lilly about each section of farmland and different trees and plants. She reminded Lilly that soon the trees would start to turn their fall colors. They noticed several squirrels scampering up the hedge trees.

"Sometimes at night you can hear the coyotes and an occasional bobcat. A bobcat sounds like a baby crying."

"I may have heard coyotes last night. At first I thought they were dogs. I heard an owl too. I don't know how you've kept from getting scared out here alone at night."

Emma ran her hand across Pie's mane and smiled. "Well now, remember that I had Jim and Kate when I first moved here and Jim was seventeen so I felt fairly secure. I was more scared of what Richard might do. He stalked me for years after the divorce. Heck, he bothered me up until nearly the end of his life. I don't know why he didn't just leave me alone. He did a little better after I married Rylie. The only way he hurt me then was financially. He took my portion of his retirement. And, as I have already told you, he never helped buy the kid's vehicles or helped with the funeral or Kate's education."

"Was he always that way, Emma?"

"Richard loved only one thing more than money and that was himself. When Jim was three years old I took up cleaning houses for extra income and Richard didn't know about it. I could buy Jim things with that money. Then as Kate came along, I began cleaning even more houses so that I could buy things for both of the kids. By then Richard knew I was cleaning houses but he thought I only cleaned two and he would ask for that money when he knew I had it so I kept the other income quiet. He would go so far as to label food like ice cream or popcorn with his name and threaten the kids if they ate any of it because it was his. Every Saturday he made me sit down with him and we would go over any checks that I had written for that week. I had to account for every thing with receipts. I was allowed $10 a month to go on personal items for myself like shampoo and feminine items. He was a self-centered man to the very end. He had always told Kate that he had willed her money and, when he passed on, she never saw a penny. It is still a legal battle and probably will be for years to come. Look at those clouds, Lilly." Emma pointed to some large fluffy clouds on the horizon. She stopped Pie and turned to look at Lilly. "People like Richard seem to get away with anything and others can't even catch a break in life. I always said he would never die because neither Heaven nor Hell wanted him. Guess he proved me wrong, huh?" She turned the horse around and Lilly followed.

"Come see the pond, Lilly." They crested a hill and the pond stood before them. There was a small boat dock with cattails growing on the northern edge. Two Adirondack chairs sat on the southern shore. Between the chairs were two cane fishing poles. "Sometimes I come here to forget and other times I come here to remember. Let's tie the horses up and sit for a while. We can start up again. You know, Lilly, there are times that these memories drain me. I am not proud of that part of my life but I also know that it is such a part of me. It is what has brought me here today." Emma slid off Pie's back, tied him to a post and reached for Sally's reigns. "Let me help you. How do you like horseback riding?" Lilly eased off of Sally's back and smiled. "It's relaxing, Emma. I am enjoying it."

Emma tied Sally to another post and motioned to the chairs. "This was Rylie's spot to get away. He would come here and fish. He loved to bring the grandkids here. There were evenings that we would just come and sit. We didn't need to talk. Just sit."

"It's really nice, Emma. I can see why you love this place so much. Yet it is surprising that you chose to live with such a distance between you and your neighbors. I know you say that you felt safe with the kids here with you but surely you had times that you were afraid."

Emma ran her hands up and down the arms of her chair. "There were plenty of times that I was scared. Richard made sure of that. He made sure I knew that he was still around."

"Emma, what happened that day that he abused you when you were pregnant with Jim? Did he leave after that? After he shaved you and sexually abused you, did he leave?"

Emma picked up a twig from the ground. "He locked me in the closet. He pulled me by my hair, bare from the waist down and bleeding, and pushed me into the closet. He put a chair on the outside and pushed it up under the doorknob. I have no idea how long I was in there but I was so relieved that he had left me alone, that I didn't care that I was in there. But, as the time went on, I started to get hot and feel like I didn't have enough air. I listened as hard as I could, trying to tell if he was still in the house. I sat on the floor and leaned against the wall and I started to sing old hymns as quietly as I could. I ran my hands over and over my belly and sang songs to my baby. I kept saying, "It will be all right. Mama will take care of you." And then I heard him in the room. I stopped singing. He began to laugh and say that I was going to run out of air. He said I would go without food and my baby would die. It was that day that I made myself the promise that I would never let him have the satisfaction of seeing me cry ever again. My bladder was full but I wouldn't let him know. He sat outside the closet for a long time and then he opened the door. He asked me if I was ready to come out. I didn't answer. I just stepped out. He told me to go clean up and he went downstairs. From that day on he would often lock me in the closet after a beating. To this day I can't stand to be in close quarters."

"What happened next, Emma?" Lilly watched Emma pick at the twig.

"Nothing else that day. I did everything in my power to keep from agitating him. I desperately wanted a healthy baby and I avoided any conflict with Richard. But . . . sometimes it doesn't matter how hard we try, the abuse will still happen."

"How long was it before it happened again?"

Emma continued to pick at the twig, not looking at Lilly. "It was February. Jim was nearly due and it was bitter cold. I had a doctor appointment and I didn't get home in time to have a hot meal ready for Richard. I had already taken time off from my job so that I could enjoy the last few weeks of my pregnancy and then be with the baby. Richard came home and I was just starting the meal. I asked if we could just have some soup and sandwiches. What a fool I was for letting him dictate what and when the meal would be. He began to shout and then he lit a cigarette. I was hurrying to get the soup ready and grill the cheese sandwiches. He took the cigarette and began to burn my arms. I kept jerking away. He would laugh and barely touch it to my skin. You know, Lilly, by this time in our lives I no longer told Richard I loved him to try to get him to stop. I had begun to tell him I hated him and that I wished he would die. I decided that, no matter what I said, he was going to abuse me anyway. He told me to shut up and leave him alone to eat. I grabbed a sandwich and went to leave the room when he said 'Better yet, you go outside.' I told him that it was freezing out and I wouldn't do that. He picked me up like a sack of potatoes, pressing my big belly against his shoulder and put me outside the back door. I had no coat and no shoes. He closed the door. I sat outside curled up against the house and waited until I could hear him go into another room. I started to walk to the neighbor's house. No one was home. As I was walking back to our house, Richard stepped outside. 'Get in here, you stupid bitch.' He pulled me inside. 'Go sit down and don't move or say a word or I will kill you and your bastard baby.' "And then?" Lilly leaned towards Emma and touched Emma's hand.

"And then nothing else. I just sat there and watched him stare at the television, not saying a word. My hatred was growing faster than that little boy I carried inside me. And let me tell you, Lilly, my Jim was a big boy. He was ten pounds, two ounces and twenty three inches long when he was born." Emma's face lit up. Lilly knew that Emma's children were the only good things that came out of her marriage to Richard. Lilly wondered why Emma stayed as long as she did yet she knew that fear had played such a big factor in all of Emma's choices.

"Tell me about the day Jim was born, Emma. I would love to hear about that special day."

Emma dropped the twig and turned to Lilly. "Let me tell you about that day! What a wonderful day, Lilly. What a wonderful day."

Chapter 14

Emma pulled her knees to her chest, crossing her arms around them as she sat in the Adirondack chair. She leaned towards Lilly. "March 15th. On a Saturday. That was when he was born. I went into labor about 1:00 in the morning. I woke Richard up at 5:00 and he got dressed to take me to the hospital. After they got me into a room, I phoned my family and Richard phoned his. Then we just had to wait. By 2:00 that afternoon, I was told I could start to push. Richard complained to a nurse that his shoulders and back hurt and asked if he could have a back rub. Would you believe that she actually gave it to him? Oh, he was such a charmer. He thought all women were put on this earth for him. Jim was born at 5:05 in the afternoon. My family had come over while I was in labor, which made Richard so angry, but I was so happy to have them there. What a blessed occasion, the birth of a child. Someday you will get to know what it is like, Lilly, and oh, how wonderful a child is to have in your life."

"How did Richard react to having a baby in the house?"

"I had to stay in the hospital for a week because I had some trouble since Jim was such a big baby. The night Jim was born, Richard went out with friends and I am sure he was out every night that week while I was in the hospital. I liked it because at least he wasn't with me at the hospital. We came home on March 22nd. That night we had a terrible snowstorm and the electricity went out. Richard gathered firewood and I sat in front of the fireplace and nursed Jim. When Richard came in to build a fire, he noticed that I had leaked onto my gown and the rocking chair. He backhanded me across the face, turned and began to stack wood in the fireplace. He never spoke or anything and then he turned around again and took a piece of wood and acted like he was going to hit me with it. I pulled Jim closer to me and looked Richard in the eye. 'What is it now, Richard? What have I done now?' I said. He told me I was so stupid to leak onto a nice piece of furniture. You know, Lilly, I didn't even know I had done that until he pointed it out. I think the warmth of my body, the warmth of the milk and the fact that I was trying to keep the baby warm, all contributed to me not knowing I had leaked. Little things would set him off. As for being happy that we had a baby, Richard was never happy about having children. He was happy with the attention the women gave him over his son but that was about it. Lilly, we had better head back to the house. We can finish there."

Emma took the reigns and handed them to Lilly and they both mounted the horses. They started back to the house. Lilly listened to Emma talk to Pie and both women chatted about the horses. As they came upon Emma's barn, a young girl with long brown hair approached them. "Taylor!" Emma shouted. "What are you doing at Grandma's?"

Taylor walked up to Pie and ran her hand across his mane. "Mom called and wanted me to check on you because you aren't answering your home phone or the cell phone. Where have you been?" Taylor's eyes were as dark as her Grandpa Rylie's appeared in all of the photos. She reached for her grandmother's hand. Emma slid out of the saddle and motioned for Lilly. "Lilly, this is Taylor Jewell. Taylor, this is my friend Lilly."

Lilly smiled and Taylor said "Nice to meet you." Taylor turned to Emma. "Grandma, you know how we worry about you out here all alone." Taylor wrapped her arms around Emma and squeezed her grandma's neck tight as she kissed her check. Lilly enjoyed seeing the closeness of the two, knowing that they were not blood relation but that a timeless love between Rylie and Emma had created a bond no other could break.

"You wouldn't believe what a tough old bird this old grandma is." Emma winked at both Lilly and Taylor.

"Yeah, well, Mom says you aren't as tough as you think you are." Taylor put her hands on her hips.

"Does she now? You need to put down those chicken wings, young lady." Emma took her hand and pulled one of Taylor's arms away from her hip. "The Good Lord isn't going to let anything get this old gal. There is still work left here on this earth for me to do. Like go see that new grandson!"

"How about that, Grandma? Did you ever think Aunt Kate would have a baby that big? Not as big as Uncle Jim though, huh Grandma?" The two walked with their arms around the others waist. "Lilly, come on up to the front porch. Taylor, you had better call your mom right now and tell her Grandma is just fine."

Emma stepped over Sam on the sidewalk and walked onto the porch. Taylor ran into the house. Emma and Lilly both sat down, Emma as usual sat on the swing. Within a few seconds, Taylor came out onto the porch with the phone in her hand. "Mom wants to talk to you, Grandma."

Emma rolled her eyes and stuck her tongue out at Taylor. "Tattletale" she whispered to her granddaughter.

"Hello?" Emma's feet began to swing back and forth as she sat listening to Melissa. "I know, I know," she said. "I will do better. I know it is only because you worry. But I am fine, I tell you. Just fine. Bye." Emma clicked off the phone. "Your mamma is too bossy and worries too much, young lady."

"You should be her daughter!" Taylor said as she stepped down the stairs of the porch and picked up a cat. She rubbed its belly. "I need to head back into town, Grandma. Now that I know you are fine, I can go home and get some work done. Brett will be out Sunday to mow your front lawn." She put the cat down, blew Emma a kiss and said "Carry your phone with you! Love you, Grandma."

"Love you too! Come back when you can stay longer, young lady." Emma waved and Taylor got into her car and drove down the drive.

"That girl worries way too much. Don't know what they would do if they knew all that I am telling you. They haven't a clue what all went on during those years. I have kept so much of this a secret. Sometimes that is what you have to do."

"You haven't told them about your past?"

"I've told Melissa and Denise some of it but not even close to all of it. Heavens, Lilly, my own children didn't know some of the things that went on. This is not something I am proud of. Most folks would think I was stupid for staying with Richard that long and letting those things go on. What they don't realize is I was so scared of losing my children and that he would find us if we left and he would make things even worse. Worse yet, he might follow through on his threats of killing me. Then my children would be left without a mother and their father would be in prison."

"I am sure people would not judge you, Emma."

"Then you don't know people, Lilly. I am sorry to sound so harsh but that is the truth. People can be so cruel. That is why I have kept this to myself."

Lilly watched Emma. "Are you ready to talk some more about your past?" Lilly was learning these memories seemed to drain Emma and Lilly believed that is why Emma would stop abruptly and shift to something else, something in the present and pleasant.

"Emma, whenever you are ready, I am."

"No better time than the present. This old bird isn't getting any younger. Where were we? Ah yes, we had brought my Jim home. Jim was two weeks old when Richard's mother and dad came to stay with us and see the baby. That made for a lot of work for me and I was a new mother. I waited on them hand and foot and tried to please both them and Richard. One day his mother called me into the kitchen. 'Look at how dirty your kitchen trash can is, Emma. Richard, come in here. Your wife needs to learn how to take care of a family.' I stood there just looking at her and the trashcan. Yes, it was dirty and yes, I needed to clean it but I had kept the house clean and taken care of Jim. I was cooking at least two meals a day for them and Richard had taken that week off to spend time with them so I wondered why he didn't help. For some crazy reason, I voiced those very opinions to Richard and his mother. He slapped me across the face and they both stood there and made me wash that trash can out with bleach water. The fumes were strong. Jim began to cry and I started to go upstairs. 'Hope you take better care of him than you are the rest of us!' Richard shouted as I went upstairs. I fed Jim and sat in his room rocking him and wishing I could find a way to get us out of there."

Lilly continued to write. "Lilly, do you think I was a fool? What is going on in your mind when I tell you these things?"

"Emma, I don't think you were a fool. I think you felt trapped and alone. You could not tell your family and Richard had isolated you from the outside world to the point that you had no one to turn to. No, Emma, you were not a fool."

"He continued to sexually abuse me, Lilly. I wasn't even healed from childbirth and he raped me. He raped me and then he stood over me and urinated on me. I threw up all over myself when he did that. He began to stay out all hours of the night when Jim was about four months old. I would sleep on the floor in Jim's room. It was such a relief when he wasn't home. I would start to get my hopes up that he wouldn't ever return but every time he came home. He usually smelled like alcohol and I knew he had been with other women. I looked forward to the nights that he would go out."

"Was it often? Did he stay out often?"

"Oh yes and I thought it was wonderful. I could be with my baby boy during the day and alone with him at night too. I didn't worry about Richard hurting us if he was away. But, as soon as that door would open, I knew I had to be on guard."

Sam chased Gracie onto the porch and knocked a plant over. Emma casually got up from the swing and went to the door. "I'll get a broom. Can I get you anything to drink, Lilly? Are you hungry?"

"Let me help you, Emma. I can clean it up while you sit. Just tell me where the broom is."

"It is in the closet in the kitchen. There is a dustpan there too. I am tired. I think I will let you do that. You're a good friend, Lilly."

Lilly came back out onto the porch. Emma sat with her eyes closed, toes barely touching the porch floor. Still Emma made that swing move slightly.

"Emma?"

Emma did not open her eyes but said "Uh huh".

"Are you all right?"

"Uh huh. Just tired for some reason. I usually can go all day and half the night. Don't know what my problem is."

Lilly swept up the mess. "What do you want to do with the plant that was in the pot?"

"Set it in that old box in the corner. That plant gave up the ghost a week ago and I'll just replace it with this one."

Lilly walked over to the other side of the porch and carefully set the plant inside the box. She turned to look at Emma. Emma still sat with her eyes closed.

"Emma, do you want to stop for a while? Am I tiring you?"

"Let's just go inside and sit in there. I really don't know what my problem is. I can go all day, I tell you."

Lilly opened the screen door and motioned for Emma to go on into the house.

Chapter 15

Emma walked into the living room and sat on the sofa. Gracie followed and sat at Emma's feet. "Sit down, Lilly."

"Do you need to rest? I can look at journals or pictures if you would like. I certainly don't want to tire you."

"Heavens, no. I'll be fine. Let's see. What else do you want to know about me? Shall I continue as we have been?"

"How about Jim's childhood? What was it like?"

"Jim was such a good baby and little boy. I only had to tell him no once and he would listen. Not my Kate. She would openly defy me and she was stubborn from the moment she was born. I will never understand why Richard was so hard on Jim. That boy tried everything to please his father. Nothing ever did."

"Why so many years between Jim and Kate?"

"Well, when Jim was three I became pregnant and Richard was furious. I was at the end of my first trimester. Richard was teaching me how to run our new riding lawnmower. As I was driving around the railroad ties that enclosed our garden, I cut it too close and hit a railroad tie. It didn't hurt the mower but it set Richard off. He told me to get into the house and he would make sure there was no damage to the mower. I went inside, with Jim following, and started to make him a cup of juice. Richard came into the kitchen. I felt the blow to the back of my head and I fell to the ground. Richard began to repeatedly kick me in the stomach. I could hear Jim crying 'Mamma' and, when I turned to make sure he was not in harms way, Richard kicked me in the head. I thought for sure he had broken my neck. I lay very still and then Jim crawled over to me. He kept rubbing my hair and saying 'mamma' over and over. When I was able, I got up, picked up my son and told Richard I was not going to allow him to do that anymore. I started for the car parked in the garage. I put Jim in and then I got into the driver's side. When I reached for the garage door opener, Richard reached inside the car window and took it off the visor. 'I'd like to see you leave now, bitch.' I put the car in reverse and he was crazy enough to stand between the car and the garage door, thinking he was some sort of superman, I guess. I watched him in the rearview mirror and eased the car back, pressing against his legs. Oh, how I wanted to just run him over. Richard continued to stand there. Jim began to cry and hug my neck. I knew I couldn't do that to my son; have him witness such a thing. I pulled back up a ways and Richard came to the side of the car. 'Get in the house and take your little bastard son with you.' I picked up that sweet little boy and started into the house. I slept in Jim's room that night on the floor. About 3:00 in the morning I woke up in terrible pain. I was bleeding and clotting. I went into the bathroom and gathered towels to place under me. I wanted to wake Richard but I was afraid of what he might do so I stayed next to Jim's bed, praying that the baby would be spared. Richard came in at 5:00 and told me to get up and make him breakfast. There was blood all over my clothes and legs. I begged him to take me to the hospital. I didn't want to lose that baby but he refused. I made him some breakfast and, when I was sure that he had left for work, I called our neighbor, Loretta. She took me to the hospital and she took care of Jim in the waiting room while I was in there. It was too late. I had already started to miscarry. They took care of everything and sent me home late that afternoon, telling me to call if I had any other problems. Loretta worked for the same company as Richard so he trusted her. She never asked how it happened and it was never discussed again. Richard was so relieved that I was no longer pregnant."

Emma turned to Lilly. "Lilly, would you bring me some albums and we will look at pictures together?"

Lilly went to the pie safe and retrieved several photo albums. She sat on the floor next to Emma as she lay on the sofa.

"Yes, open this one." Emma pointed to an album with a hand-quilted cover. Inside were pictures of Emma and Jim. There were some of Emma pregnant and others of both mother and son. "This is Jim's second birthday. That is my mother. He was the apple of her eye. My sister's kids were so much older than my own, fifteen and nine year's difference and my mother was thrilled to have another grandson. Since Richard no longer let me work outside the home, I could sneak up to my folk's house during the day and be back before it was time for him to get home. As time went by, he would even encourage me to go there. By that time he was openly having affairs and he would brag to others and rub it in my face. Like when he began to have an affair with a woman from his office in Topeka. Her car license plate read 'Green Eyes' and he would trade her vehicles and he would bring her car home for a couple of days every so often. When we would have guests over, he would proudly show off her car as if it were some sort of trophy. He would always say that it was 'their' car because they both had green eyes. I had grown callas to his ways with women and, if he was with them, he wasn't home beating or raping me. Look here, Jim with me when I was pregnant with Kate." Emma pointed to a picture of Jim and Emma, both with ear-to-ear grins. Mother and son anxiously awaiting their new arrival "Look at his smile! You know, he said he was going to have a little sister from the very start. He even practiced spelling her name so that he would be ready for her. I, on the other hand, was sure I was going to have another boy. I was so afraid to have a girl. I was afraid of what Richard would do to a daughter."

Emma turned the pages, sharing pictures of her life. "Here I am in the hospital after Kate was born. Look at Jim's face. That boy loved his little sister from the very beginning. Although he did complain some as she grew older but he would have fought to the death for her. There's Richard holding Kate. She was born in October and that following July Richard put in an in-ground pool. He said he wanted to be ready for when she would have her friends over to swim. He said he looked forward to seeing the girls in their bikinis. I thought to myself then that he was laying the groundwork for his sick sexual ways. I knew I would have to find a way out of there before he had a chance to harm Kate or one of her friends."

Emma ran a finger over a picture of the two children together, Jim holding Kate. "How they must have hated me. Richard could never tell them that they did anything right, he called them a bastard and a little cunt. What a stupid woman I have been." Tears rolled down Emma's tanned cheeks. "He wouldn't let Jim have friends over and, if I somehow allowed it, he would humiliate Jim in front of his friends. He encouraged Jim to have girls over and I discouraged it. Jim learned to have friends or parties outside our home where only I would be the parent representing the family. Richard NEVER went to a single birthday party. Heck, he didn't even know where their pediatrician's office was. He wanted no part of being a parent. I should have left when they were young. I waited entirely too long, Lilly. I wish I had just one more day to tell my son how sorry I am for staying with his dad and making Jim's life a living Hell. Just one more day." Emma's voice trailed off and she stood up. "I need to get a tissue. Are you hungry or thirsty?"

"You get the tissue and I am capable of fixing us a couple of iced teas." Lilly patted Emma's hand and headed for the kitchen and Emma went into the bathroom.

Chapter 16

Emma came out of the bathroom and Lilly handed her an iced tea. "Lilly, don't ever think my kids didn't love their dad. I believe they loved as only a child could love a parent but they also saw him for what he was. He was abusive, controlling, and selfish and they knew that. Kate gave him more credit than he probably deserved but that was her prerogative. It broke her heart when he refused to help her in any way. When Jim died, Richard called her boasting of his purchase of a new Harley Davidson motorcycle. That man nickeled and dimed his son's funeral expenses, refusing to pay, but he rode around on a motorcycle that he purchased with life insurance money from Jim's death. We had taken out a small policy when the kids were young and, even though it was purchased when we were married, Richard worked out a way to keep all of the money and not contribute to any thing regarding funeral and burial expenses. I hope he is burning right now as we speak." Emma covered her mouth and her blue eyes widened. "Guess that isn't a very Christian attitude, now is it?" She sat down on the sofa and pulled one leg up under the other. "Better yet, I'll take the floor. Let's spread these albums out on the coffee table and go over them." She knelt down on the floor.

"Emma, are you feeling better? You seemed so tired before." Lilly showed a genuine concern for her friend. "Maybe you need to eat something."

"Eat! Good Lord! What time is it? And I haven't even offered you a bite to eat!" Emma sprang from the floor and hurried toward the kitchen. "Forgive me, Lilly. What would you like to eat?"

"No, no. That isn't at all what I was getting at, Emma. You looked so tired and pale that I thought you might need something."

"Well, just to ward off any chance of hunger or anything ailing me, let's have a sandwich and some fruit. I'll get something set up and you go through those albums."

Lilly did as she was ordered and sat on the floor. She continued to look through albums, longing to know more about Emma and her life. As Lilly looked at a young Emma with her children, she wondered what it was like under the same roof with Richard. Did the neighbors know? How could Emma's family not know what was going on? Page after page of so many lives. Lilly made a promise to herself at that moment that she would tell Emma's story and hope that it somehow spared another victim of domestic abuse.

"Lilly, I got to thinking that, if you stay up later then this old bird, you could watch some videos." Emma handed Lilly a plate with a turkey sandwich, chips and fresh fruit.

"I would like that. Although I think this country air is making me so relaxed that I look forward to going to bed. Normally I am up half the night. Do you sleep well, Emma?"

Emma set her plate on the coffee table and smiled. "Well now, that is a tough one. There was a time when I was afraid to sleep but Rylie continued to assure me that it was all right to rest and that he was there for me. I had my nights and days mixed up for many years, let me tell you. That stemmed from when Richard and I were married and I was at home with the kids during the day. At night Richard was there so I could not sleep for fear of what he would do but during the day, after he left for work, I could rest when the kids napped. I felt safe then. I could rest for a few hours and then get my work done. We could slip off and clean a couple of houses on certain days, pocket that money for things that we needed or wanted and Richard could not harm us. Days were our safe haven. Nights were our Hell. Now I can sleep. Sometimes I wake up in a cold sweat, fully awakened by a haunting memory that has come to me in the night as a nightmare or a noise will remind me of sleepless nights straining to hear any sound that might be Richard coming to do us harm and it takes me a while to settle down but it is getting a little better. You know, I knew I wasn't safe until the day Richard was gone forever. That is when I knew it was safe."

"He actually bothered you after Rylie passed away?" Lilly could not imagine why he would continue to harass Emma after so many years.

"Yep. It wasn't long after Rylie passed that Richard made sure I knew he could still stir fears in me. I had come out to the barn to do chores one night. We had an old picnic table back there under those trees. I had just put up the horses and was headed for the chicken house when Richard came around the corner of the barn. He had a horse bridle and bit in his hand and was swinging it around. He grabbed me by my flannel shirt and threw me to the ground. Then he stood over me swinging that blasted thing around and around. 'Go ahead, bitch. Breathe, move, blink. Just do something so that I can bash your brains in.' I just lay there on the ground. I truly believed that, if I did move, he would finally finish me off, just like he had always promised. He continued to swing that thing closer and closer. I had an old dog named Rader and Sam, of course. They both came barreling out of the yard and Rader lunged at Richard. I began to scream that old dog's name because I knew he would die trying to protect me.

Richard swung at him and missed, giving me time to get up and run to the barn. I called for the dogs. Rader and Sam both came running. I waited with a shovel in my hand for Richard to come around that corner. The hair was up on both of the dogs' backs. We waited. Then I heard a car door slam. I looked through the crack in the barn door and saw Richard driving out of the drive. We waited until he got clear down the drive and then we came out. I ran to the house, hoping I would be able to call the sheriff before Richard got too far out of the county. As I came up on the porch, there lay one of my old female cats. When I picked her up, I knew she was dead. Under her body Richard had written the word 'consequences'. I called the sheriff and they came out and took pictures and filed a report. Of course, they said there wasn't any proof that he had done that to her and it could have been teenagers pulling some sort of prank. So, you see, Lilly, he wasn't ever going to completely leave me alone until one of us was in the grave. I guess the Good Lord decided to give me some peace in my later years from that evil man. Now I just want to be able to enjoy my life as best I can without my Rylie and Jim. I am so looking forward to going to see Kate and Conner. Gives me something to really look forward to." Emma turned a page and pointed to a picture of a shaggy standard schnauzer. "This is Rader, my best friend. Richard and I bought him when the kids were young. He was the most loyal friend I could have ever wanted in a dog. Of course, my Sam is loyal but he never really experienced Richard the way poor old Rader did. That dog protected both of my kids and me. I saw Richard beat and choke that dog too many times. He would have laid down his life for us. Rylie was the only man he ever trusted after living with Richard. That dog was always on guard. I still miss him to this day. I used to tell Rylie and the kids to bury me next to Rader, my best friend. He lived into his twenties. Mighty old for a dog. You know, Lilly, animals can sense so many things and I believe they have souls and that Rader and all of the other critters that have gone on before me are with my boys right now."

Emma patted Gracie's head and turned another page. "Here is Kate and Jim in the pool. She must have been all of seven years old and Jim was nearing his teens. Here I am with the kids and my friend Terri. Her boys were the same age as my kids and we met when Jim and her son were three years old. You know, this must have been right after I lost my kidney. Yep, that is when this picture was taken." Emma tapped her finger on the picture.

"Your kidney? How did you lose your kidney, Emma?" Lilly shifted her weight from one side to the other as she sat on the floor next to Emma. She took a bite of her sandwich.

"It was July. We had been to Table Rock Lake with our kids and other families from Richard's company. Richard was angry because Jim didn't want to learn to water ski and I would only ride on the tube behind the boat. The night we came back, he came into our bedroom where I was unpacking our bags. 'You need to do something about that sissy boy of yours. He let those girls show him up out there on the water. You've got yourself a real mamma's boy, Emma.' I started to walk out of the bedroom and not even acknowledge what he had just said. He grabbed me and closed the bedroom door. 'Did you hear what I said, cunt?' I looked him right in the eye and told him that boy was more of a man than he could ever be. He took his knee and thrust it into my stomach. I slid down the door onto the floor. He got down on top of me and continued to thrust his knee into my lower back. Over and over again, he would do that. I never let out a single cry because I was afraid the kids would hear. After he left the room, I went into each of the kid's rooms to tell them good night and gather their dirty clothes. I told Jim good night first. I told him I loved him and he asked me if I was all right. I told him yes. Then I went into Kate's room and did the same with her. About 4:00 in the morning I awoke with a terrible pain and vomiting. This went on until Richard's alarm went off. He told me to move out of the bathroom so that he could get ready for work. I was afraid to go into the kids' bathroom for fear they would see me so sick but I had nowhere else to go. After Richard left for work, I called my friend Terri and asked her to come get me and take me into the hospital. Of course, I first tried to get Richard to take me but he said no. After I called her, I called my friend Marsha who lived up the street. I asked if she would check in on the kids and make sure they were fine and that Terri was taking me to the hospital. A few minutes after I hung up the phone, Jim came into the bathroom where I was sitting on the floor with my head in the toilet. I was throwing up green bile. That boy would not leave my side. He sat in there with me. Soon Kate entered the room asking all kinds of questions. Jim took over completely. He fed her, had her get dressed. He was awesome. Terri lived in Lawrence so it took her some time before she arrived. Kate let her in the door. Kate kept asking me if I was going to die and Jim would hug her and tell her that everything would be fine. I remember he told her that it was probably something I ate."

Emma smiled and Lilly could tell that she was missing her son. "My children should have hated me. I will always wonder if Jim ever forgave me, Lilly. Nothing will ever change that. I can at least talk to Kate about it but not my Jim." She ran her fingers over the pictures again and again. "Terri took me to the hospital, with me throwing up all the way. She cussed Richard over and over. Oh, how she hated that man. When we got to the hospital, they immediately took me into a room. Terri said she would call Richard again and see if he would come to the hospital. By the time she got back into the room, they were sending me up to x-ray. They were sure my appendix had ruptured. When they gave me the results of the x-rays, they told me that my appendix had ruptured and they were calling in a surgeon. It wasn't until he got in there during the surgery that he found out that my kidney was so severely damaged, not only from that beating, but other beatings over the years. He made the decision to take both the appendix and what little was left of my kidney. When I came to in recovery, Richard and Terri were both at my bedside. Richard was playing the loving husband and Terri's eyes were shooting daggers at him. She stayed until I was completely conscious and then she said she would check in on me later. Richard, as usual, tried to charm her and flirt with her but she was not having any of that. The nurses thought he was quite a charmer but the surgeon came in that next morning and the first thing he said to me was 'You don't have to live like this, you know. There are places you can go to get help and protection.' I told him that, since I didn't work outside the home, Richard had always said that he would get custody of my children because he was the only one with an income to provide for them. I told him Richard had promised he would kill me if I tried to take the kids and leave. It took me four more years after that day before I proved him wrong. I finally overcame those fears of losing my babies."

Chapter 17

"What finally made you decide to leave Richard and why did it take another four years before you did anything?" Lilly finished her sandwich and began to eat her fruit. Emma took a sip of her iced tea and set her glass down. She ran her fingers through her hair and took a deep breath.

"Why did I finally leave? Well, the kids were fifteen and ten and I could not bear what was going on. Jim could not be a teenager and Richard was so sick sexually that I feared for my Kate. He had reached a point where he would answer ads in the newspaper asking for bi-sexual women. He would pretend to be me and answer these ads. Then he would try to set up a time for us to meet with them. He continued to have numerous affairs and it was even to the point that he would expose himself out from under his swim trunks when another female was over to swim or he would talk about Kate's little friends. I was so nervous about what he might do. Jim was so miserable and I worried that he might someday hurt his dad or, worse yet, kill him trying to defend me. Richard had decided we needed to move away from the only home our children had ever known and so we built a big, beautiful home in a new subdivision. I cried so hard the day we left our old house. That was the home where I had brought my babies home from the hospital. Both of the kids were so sad. I gave it a brief thought that maybe things would be better in the new house but, each time we had made some sort of change, I would think that and, each time, it made no difference. We were all settled into the house and I was planning on how I could eventually get out of there. Richard had agreed to let me have a part-time job as a bookkeeper for a local golf course and I kept my houses that I cleaned on the side. I kept those quiet so that I could put that money away. I did not know how long it would take to save up enough money to file. In the meantime, Richard had set up a motorcycle trip with some of his friends. We were going to go to Colorado. It was August and blistering hot. I had arranged for the kids to go to my parent's house while we were away. Oh, it was so hot that summer! The heat index was into the hundred's and he put us on that blasted motorcycle and off we went through western Kansas. By the time we reached Colorado, I had blood in my urine from the rough ten-hour trip and the heat and one kidney. You know, Lilly, on and on."

Emma pulled both of her legs up under her in a cross-legged style. She put her hands on her cheeks and pressed her cheeks downwards. Her eyes widened. "Oh, what a miserable trip. Richard very seldom took us as a family on a vacation, maybe twice in all those years. He took two and sometimes three trips a year with his male buddies. He wanted no part of including us in his trips. Why he decided to drag me along on this trip, I will never know. He did take Jim on a motorcycle trip when Jim was eleven. That man left my boy in a motel room in Las Vegas with a fever of 102. Then he went to the casinos and shows and left Jim in that room with no way of contacting him. Jim called me collect. I felt so helpless so far away and my child was so young and scared. Richard has always been about Richard." Emma put her head down and began to speak much quieter. "I was begging Richard on that trip to please let me rest and he could go out with his friends. I hated riding on that blasted bike. And there was one woman in that group that Richard thought was the greatest thing ever. Of course, he thought that about a lot of women. He became so angry that I would not jump at the chance to be with all of them. When I explained I had blood in my urine and I thought there was a problem with my kidney, he laughed and told me to get dressed and we were going to go to a casino and restaurant."

Emma put her head in her hands and spoke so softly that Lilly could barely make out her words. "I was so sick, Lilly. I was so sick."

"Did you tell the others how sick you were?"

"No, they were Richard's friends. I never really felt I could confide in them. I got dressed and did as he said. Later that evening he wanted to continue to gamble in the casinos so he let me go back to the room. By then I was running a fever and I wanted to go back home and see my babies and get well. When he came into the room at about 3:00 in the morning, I asked him if he would let me fly home. I knew I needed medical attention. I could no longer keep from crying and the tears began to flow. That, of course, made him happy. He loved to see me cry and beg for his mercy. It meant he was in control. He refused to either get me medical help or let me go home. For three days I went around with a high fever and blood in my urine. It was awful. I really thought I would never see my children again. Richard's friends began to ask me if I was sick and, when I told them yes, he became angry. One of the women wanted to help me but I believe she must have been told to mind her own business. We left for Kansas on the fourth morning. The ride home was miserable. By that time, I had such a fever and was in such pain that I truly thought I would not be able to stay on that bike. The whole time we were heading home, Richard would tell me how worthless I was and how wonderful this other wife on the trip was. He wouldn't stop for me to go to the bathroom or get something to drink. Our neighborhood was in a real hilly area and we were going up and down those hills when I decided to tell him that I wanted off. I didn't want to listen to him anymore and I wanted to walk the rest of the way home. He took his elbow and slammed it into my face so hard my nose bled. Then he began to go eighty miles an hour in those hills, weaving in and out. I was so scared! When we got home I went to our bedroom and called to check on the kids. My dad said he would bring them home that next morning. Just as I was about to hang up, Richard came into the room. After he beat me and put me in the closet, he left. I lay in that closet and knew that I had to complete my plan of leaving, whether I had enough money saved or not. For twenty-two years I had taken his abuse and I could no longer wait. In hindsight, I had waited much too long when it came to my kids. He came home several hours later, happy as a lark. For two more months I planned and planned, not ever letting on that I was going to file for divorce. I was afraid my family would not support me in my decision because divorce was against everything they believed but I also knew Richard would eventually kill me and destroy my children. I knew I had to save all of us from him."

Chapter 18

"When did you file for divorce, Emma?"

"It was November 20th. I woke the kids up for school after Richard had left for work. I took Jim into the kitchen and told him my plan. That boy was fifteen years old and so mature and supportive. I asked him to not say a word and he was not to come home after school that day. He promised to do as I had asked. We then agreed to not tell Kate until all of the arrangements were made. I put Kate on the school bus, called the mother of her best friend and asked if Kate could spend the night there that night. I made arrangements for the animals to be out of the house. At 9:00 that morning I met with an attorney. Within hours he had a protection from abuse order and had filed my divorce. I stayed with friends that night. Richard was served with the papers. That was one of the hardest things I have ever had to do. Both of the kids seemed to be fine with it but I know it had to be hard on them."

Sam began to bark and Emma got up off of the floor. "Sam! What are you barking at?"

Emma looked out the front window. "Good Lord! Melissa is here. Guess she didn't believe Miss Taylor when she told her Grandma was all right." Emma went to the door and Lilly got up from the floor and stood in the entry.

"That girl of yours didn't convince you, did she?" Emma opened the screen door and gave Melissa a big hug.

"I came to see for myself. Billy said to drive out here and see if you are being stubborn or not. Yes, Taylor said you were just fine and you had a guest."

Melissa offered her hand to Lilly. "My name is Melissa."

"Nice to meet you, Melissa. I have heard a lot about you and your family."

Melissa smiled and turned to Emma. "Are you telling stories on us?"

Lilly thought she had upset Melissa and said "No, no. Emma has done nothing but speak highly of all of you."

Melissa put her arm around Emma and squeezed her shoulders. "I know she did. She loves us as if we were her own."

Emma seemed to grimace as Melissa squeezed again and said, "I brought supper for you girls. Taylor said she didn't smell or see anything cooking in the kitchen when she came in to call me so I decided to make something for you two. You have to keep your strength up so you can fly out and see that new grandson. Do you want me to see if one of the kids will drive you there?"

"No, I think I will fly out and that way I can stay a while. Will Brett take care of my critters?"

"You can have Brett or Dawson come stay out here. I know one of them would welcome some time in the country."

Melissa took her arm off Emma's shoulder and reached for the door. "I'm gonna bring that food in. Hope you aren't picky, Lilly."

"Oh, no. Is there anything I can help you with?" Lilly stepped towards the door and both Lilly and Melissa went onto the porch. Melissa turned towards Lilly as she put one hand on her hip.

In an accusatory tone, Melissa said, "How's she doing? Are you tiring her? Is this story telling getting her spirits down? Does she want to see Kate?" Lilly was not sure if Melissa was very concerned or interrogating Lilly for information that Emma might not want Melissa to know.

"She lets me know if she needs a break and only once did she say anything about being tired. Why?"

"Her health isn't good. She will never let on, I'm sure. Lymphoma. She has been fighting it for a while. The doctor's did surgery and treatments but she just didn't bounce back like we had hoped. I think having this new grandbaby will bring her spirits up but I am worried about her health. We wish she would move into town but she won't hear of it. She's stubborn as a mule."

Lilly's heart sank. Emma had never let on anything was wrong. Why would something like this happen to Emma after all the other heartache she had suffered over her lifetime? Lilly walked down the porch steps and towards the gate. Melissa followed.

The two women gathered food from Melissa's trunk. "Meat loaf and cheesy potato casserole." She handed a bowl of green beans to Lilly. "Fresh from Jason and Denise's garden."

"Oh, Melissa. Maybe I should not have come. But I had no way of knowing! Will this take too much out of her?"

Just at that moment the screen door opened. "You girls had better not be trash talking on this old bird!"

Melissa flashed Emma a big, fake smile. "You don't worry about what we're talking. There isn't any trash to talk on you, now is there?" Her smile widened even more as did her big, brown eyes.

Emma pushed the screen door against Sam's hindquarters. "Just get the food and your behinds in here. You should know by now that I'm not going to let a guest go hungry." Emma began to close the screen door and Lilly could hear inaudible mumbles.

"Pay her no mind. She hates to think she can't take care of herself and right now she probably thinks I have overstepped my boundaries but, as soon as we walk in with the food, she'll be back to her old self. You just watch. I know her like a book."

Lilly wondered if Melissa truly knew all there was to know about Emma. She followed Melissa into the house, arms laden with food.

"Good Lord! Come set all that on the table. How many folks did you think you were feeding, Melissa?"

"I knew I was feeding just the two of you but this way you can have leftovers for lunch tomorrow. Just hush and enjoy the fact you don't have to cook tonight. I'm putting some of it in the refrigerator and you can warm it up. Did Brett call you about mowing your lawn Sunday after church?"

"Taylor said he was planning on it. Are you eating with us?"

Melissa turned to Lilly and whispered, "Told you she would get over those grumpies." She then called back to Emma from the kitchen. "Nope, I am heading home and eating the very same fixins with Billy. I doubled everything."

"Have you got time to sit a spell on the porch with us? I would like for you and Lilly to get to know one another." Emma reached down and picked up Gracie. She slid her arm into Melissa's. "Do you?"

"I'll sit with you girls for a little while." Melissa opened the screen door and Emma stepped onto the porch with Lilly and Melissa following. Emma sat on the porch swing and set Gracie down on the porch. Lilly and Melissa sat in the chairs.

"Melissa, when did you meet Emma?" Lilly asked.

"It was this same time of year. Rylie had met Emma less than a week before and he already wanted us to meet her." Melissa flashed a big smile at Emma. "He already knew she was the one for him, I think. Heck, what am I saying I think? I know! That man fell in love from the very first moment he laid eyes on her!"

"Stop it! You don't know that. There is no such thing as love at first sight." Emma blushed.

"Whatever. You know that is the God's truth. He would tell Lilly the same thing if he were here on this porch. Don't be denying it, Emma. God brought you two together when you both needed it the most. Tell her!" Melissa motioned to Lilly. Emma frowned and gave Melissa a short retort of "Tell her what?"

"Tell her that it was meant to be. Tell her how you met and then I will tell her how I met you. Tell her."

"Just stop it. She could care less about how we met. Right, Lilly?"

Lilly smiled, "Well, Emma. I am going to have to agree with Melissa on this one."

"Well, how in the Sam Hill are you two going to get to know one another if I am doing the talking?" Emma crossed her arms across her chest and took on a childish pout.

Melissa ruffled Emma's short hair and kissed her cheek. "Just tell her, Emma. If you don't, I will."

"Oh, fine. Kate was all of twelve years old and she begged me that Friday night to take her to the fair in town. She wanted nachos from one of the food vendors so I bought her nachos and I bought myself a pork tenderloin sandwich. It was a huge thing! All of the picnic tables were full except for a spot at a table with this man with five kids with him. I asked if we could sit there and he said yes. I watched how he interacted with those kids and I wondered where his wife was. He was so good with the kids and I remember wondering if he was a different man at home alone. I always did that because I knew things happened in homes behind closed doors. I had very little trust for men. Richard and I had been divorced three years and I had my doubts that any man was a decent man. I knew my dad was a good man but I trusted no one outside of family. I watched and watched. Then Kate wanted to go ride some of the rides. So, we left. She ran into some of her friends and asked if she could ride the rides with them. I said yes but then that left me alone to go to a concert that some band was putting on at the other end of the fairgrounds. I told her I would be back in an hour and where we should meet. In an hour I returned. There was Rylie standing by himself, waiting on his crew of kids. Why I spoke to that man, I will never know but I asked him if he was still doing his parental duty and he told me yes. I got so scared that I smiled and walked away. I could not believe I spoke to a total stranger!"

"Go on; tell her the rest, Emma." Melissa sat beside Emma on the swing and nudged Emma with her shoulder. "Go on!"

Emma rolled her eyes and lightly slapped Melissa on the leg. Lilly enjoyed watching their banter.

"He followed me. Asked if that was my daughter I had with me earlier. Then I asked if all of those kids he had with him were his and he said only one and the others were either her friends or cousins. We talked about silly stuff like the nice September evening and the companies we worked for. Silly stuff. Then Danielle came up. She was fourteen at the time, right Melissa?" Melissa nodded yes and Emma continued with her story. Shortly after Danielle showed up, so did Kate. She, of course, was jabbering about this friend and that and asking if she could spend the night with one of them. I said it was nice talking to him and he asked for my number. Crazy thing was, I gave it to him! That man could have been some sort of crazed ax murderer!"

Melissa leaned towards Lilly and said, "He called me as soon as he got home and told me all about this woman he had met. See, it was love at first sight, I tell you. I know because he went on and on about her. Right after their first date, he called and said he wanted us to meet her. Wanted our approval. Rylie's kids were very important to him and he wanted to include us in his decision to court Emma. Of course, we approved as soon as we met her and, since he was so smitten, we knew it was the right thing for him. He had been divorced for ten years when he met her. He had been looking for Emma for a long time."

"Stop it. You make me sound like I was a special catch. It wasn't that at all, Lilly. He was just lonely. It's not that he didn't date other women. His first marriage was far from happy and he was very cautious about women. Guess I was the only one that would put up with him on a regular basis." Emma pulled one leg up under the other. "Nothing special, I tell you. It was all about timing. Of course Kate and Danielle credit themselves since they had both wanted to go to the fair that night. How on earth did we get onto this subject? Melissa Joy, we were talking about when I divorced Richard before you showed up. I bet Lilly thinks I am so easily distracted, don't you Lilly?"

"Not at all, Emma. I enjoy hearing all of this and I know that we will eventually get back to what we were talking about. This is nice to spend time with you and Melissa. I really haven't had a chance to visit with family. The only time I saw Kate was the day her father passed away."

"Thank heaven for that." Melissa scoffed.

"Stop it right now." Emma patted Melissa on the knee. "Even you know that Kate loved her dad."

"Oh, Emma, what he did to you and the kids. And he even made life miserable for you and Rylie, you know that. That man was nothing but evil, I tell you. Just when we would think he was softening, Lilly, he would do an even more evil thing to one of them." Melissa twisted the end of her dark brown hair and her brown eyes widened.

"And the most sneaky feller you ever met. He could charm the teeth right out of a snake and then bite its head off, I tell you. I think he was related to the devil himself."

Emma pointed her index finger towards Melissa. "One thing about Melissa, she doesn't hold her thoughts back. Guess I should have warned you about that. After years of her and Kate being around one another, they both can set you on your ear. Lord, when they would gang up on my Rylie. He never did learn to not discuss politics and religion with these girls. And they would fight to the death for him and any other family member but they will also set you straight if they feel the need. Feisty, that's what they are."

Melissa looked at her watch. "Good night! I had better get back to the house. Billy Dean will be wondering if you two kidnapped me. I saw you are singing at church on Sunday, Emma. Are you coming, Lilly? What are you singing, Emma?" Melissa stepped down the steps and two cats intertwined between her legs.

Emma leaned back and sighed before she spoke. "I have something picked out but I haven't had the time to practice. You want to take my place?"

"No, I have to sing next week. I still think Lilly should come. How about it, Lilly?" Melissa turned and started down the sidewalk. She turned back again, raising her eyebrows and smiling.

Lilly stood up from her chair, "I was going to go back to Kansas City that morning but I might be able to stay around. I can't say when I was last in a church."

Melissa smiled. "It will be a treat." Melissa motioned towards Emma. "Wait till you hear that old gal sing. Emma, give your testimony and sing. Lilly would like that. Sounds like we will see you Sunday. See you then!" She turned back towards her vehicle and gave a backwards wave. "You girls clean that food up. And carry your phone with you!!"

Chapter 19

Emma walked back up the sidewalk and onto the porch. She took the toe of her canvas shoe and pressed it against a small chip in the porch floor paint. "She's bossy, huh? Thinks she can tell me what to sing, when to eat and when to carry my cell phone. Lord knows she and I have certainly had our differences. She wants to be in control. Kate can be the same way to a degree. Melissa is more of a manipulator and bossy. I know she sometimes means well. Those folks at church have heard my testimony. And the ones that haven't could care less, I am sure."

Emma looked at Lilly. "Don't feel you have to stay around and hear me sing. I don't know why they keep putting me on the schedule. Lord knows they need some new blood. I need to sit down for a spell." She immediately went to her porch swing and sat down. "Rylie said all he could see over that pork tenderloin the night of the fair was blue eyes smiling. He did love me. I had never known true love until Rylie. He was so good to my kids, Lilly. Rylie and Jim drove together to the same place of work every day for nearly three years. That formed a real bond. They were quite a pair, those two." Lilly sat down in the chair closest to the swing. "Richard never attempted to form a bond with his son, did he?"

Emma pressed her hands to her cheeks and looked Lilly right in the eye. "Richard built a wall between them that nothing would have ever torn down. Jim knew where he stood with his dad. Richard only cared about money and women. Not his son and not his daughter."

"I assume it was a nasty divorce."

Emma leaned back and put her hands behind her neck. "You could say it was nasty, all right. You know, Lilly, it becomes the most dangerous for a victim when they try to break that tie. When they try to end the relationship is when it gets scary."

"Did the kids feel threatened?"

"Heavens, yes. Jim watched his back constantly and he took it upon himself to see that Kate and I were safe. Kate was so upset because we never knew when or where Richard would show up and he called our house continuously. If he didn't call on my line, he would call on the kids' line. All night long he would call. I finally had to get a "no contact order" from a judge when it got to the point that the kids could not get any sleep. He knew how to get to all of us emotionally and he also knew our weaknesses."

"You say he knew your weaknesses. How is that?"

"Well, he would tell me that I would not be able to provide for the kids and then he would make me pay him whenever the kids went to visit. I paid for any food they ate, any movies, anything that he had to put out extra money for, I would have to reimburse him. He would send any receipts with Jim and then I would send him a payment. He would threaten to take the kids if I didn't. He knew that as long as he threatened to take my children, I would do whatever he said to keep them."

"When did you finally realize that he could not take them from you?"

"Jim was sixteen and he needed a different car because he had wrecked the original car I had bought him. I didn't have any money to buy him another car and I had only carried liability on his first car. Jim begged me to ask his dad for help so I asked Richard to please help us get a car for Jim. Richard asked Jim how much the car cost and Jim told him. Richard said he would meet me at the car dealership. We looked at cars and then he said to follow him to his place and he would give me the money. Said he had left his checkbook at home. How stupid I was! I did as he said and showed up at his house. That man grabbed me and dragged me into his house, raped me and tossed me out on his doorstep. He grabbed my face and spit in it and told me to keep quiet or he would take the kids from me because he could financially afford them. Why I didn't call the police, I truly cannot say. I tried screaming and no one came to help. It was during the day and I think all of the neighbors were gone. I went to my car with no money to pay for my son's car. Stupid! Stupid! Richard had never helped the kids and why did I think he would then? He could have paid cash several times over for a car for his son. I made a tenth of what he made. I drove to my doctor's office and they did an examination on me. Sad thing was, I had just had a hysterectomy three weeks before that. There was no way I should have had intercourse let alone something as rough as he had just done to my body. My doctor was furious and he documented it and asked if I would press charges. Again, I was afraid Richard would take my children and said no. That wouldn't happen in this day. Now the victim can't be scared into not filing because the physician and the police will do it for her. I went home and immediately Jim knew something was wrong. He saw the carpet burns on my face and he blamed himself for what had happened. I promised him at that moment that I would NEVER let Richard intimidate me into thinking that he could take those kids from me. Our divorce wasn't final yet because he kept filing for a continuance but my therapist asked for a psychological examination and Richard must have come up plum crazy because on the day of our divorce hearing, the judge ordered that I have sole custody with only supervised visitation. Why on earth did I let him scare me into thinking otherwise? I guess because he had brainwashed me so. But, because my son and I took the time to talk it over and he supported me, I knew I would NEVER do such a stupid thing again like I did on that day. And I would not believe that Richard could take my babies. That evening both of the kids and I went to a little car lot that offered financing and I bought Jim a little car. It was far from what that boy wanted but he was willing to settle and he NEVER complained. He drove that little car with pride. He drove it with pride because he did not need his dad to help us buy it. From that time on, Jim swore he would never ask his dad for another thing. And I swore that I would press charges if he EVER did another thing to me or to the kids. Sorry, Lilly, I guess I am jumping around a bit."

"Melissa talked about how evil Richard was. Does she know all that went on?"

"Heavens, no! Up until these conversations, much of what I am telling you has been kept a secret. Not even Rylie knew about all of this. I hate to think what he may have done if he had known. He kept calm when Richard was an ass at the funeral home making plans for Jim and he kept his calm when we were left with all of the debts. I know he was a fine man, but Richard could push any saint into losing it, I am sure."

"Emma, were there any good times with Richard? It is so hard to imagine that you stayed so long and that, even after you had divorced, you trusted him at times. Like meeting him in the car lot and following him home. I know many people would find it hard to fathom that you merely stayed out of fear."

"I have had two other people ask me that same question before. The first time I was asked, I thought and thought. Surely there were SOME good times, I thought. I couldn't think of any at that moment but the next time I was asked was from a dear friend whose husband had been Richard's best friend. I told her the good times were when we were with other people, either friends or family. I felt safe when others were around. The kids enjoyed those times too. We were safe until we went home or until our guests left our house. The best times were when I was with my kids while Richard was at work or on a trip. We had such good times. I missed the luxury of being able to be at home with them when I went to work full time but that was a small price to pay for our lives and our sanity. So, to answer your question, yes. Yes, there were some good times but the constant fear and the mental and physical abuse far out weighed the good. During the day, I always knew that he would be coming home and I would dread it so. When he was away on trips, I knew he would eventually come home. The kids lived in the same fear. Jim hibernated in his room most of the time and Kate learned to do the same as she grew older. There were nights when he would be late and, Lord forgive me, I would wish that he would be dead on the side of the road somewhere or that he had left me for another woman. I always hated to hear the door open because I knew my wishes had not come true. And he continued even after the divorce to haunt us."

The phone rang and Emma went into the house to answer it as Lilly stayed on the front porch.

"Kate! How's my grandson? Yep, I am leaving for Denver Monday the 20th and should be into Denver around 4:00 that afternoon. I will e-mail you my schedule."

There was a pause. "Yes, she is staying here with me. We were out on the porch just gabbing up a storm. No, Kate, I have just skimmed over our lives. Well, I've gone into some detail and some not. You are the one that suggested I do this, young lady. No, I am not overdoing it."

Another pause. "Yes, I am getting my rest. What is it with everyone thinking I can't take care of myself all of a sudden? You just worry about that boy and how to take care of him. Tell him Grandma is coming to give him lots of love."

Lilly stepped off the porch and headed towards the barn. It seemed so long ago that she had come to this farm to take photographs of this place. Emma's life ran through her mind. She passed through the trees where Richard had held Emma in fear. As she walked towards the horses, Sam walked alongside her. She knelt down on one knee and began to feel the tears well up inside her. She knew this was much more than just a story, this was someone she had come to know and someone that deserved more than what life had dealt her. Why did Emma stay so long and why did she succumb to Richard's threats even after the divorce? Did, in fact, her children harbor resentment, as she feared they had, for staying with him as long as she did? Sam licked Lilly's face and nuzzled his head against her hand. "Oh, Sam, poor Emma. How can a person live in such fear? Why did she stay?" Sam licked her face again.

"Lilly? Where are you?"

"Out here by the barn, Emma. I'm out here!"

Chapter 20

Emma walked up and ran her hand across Sam's back. "That was Kate. She is getting anxious to show that baby off. She sounds great." Emma knelt down and hugged Sam around the neck. "I wish she wouldn't worry about me. Lord, I've been alone here for quite some time and I do just fine. I tell you, between her and that granddaughter of mine. They treat me at times like I was one hundred years old or, worse yet, like a child. What have you and Sam been up to? Oh my word, Lilly, you look upset. Are you all right?"

Lilly stood up and wiped the back of her hand across her eyes. "Of course! Sam and I were just having a little chat, weren't we, Sam?" Lilly patted Sam's head and it was as if he smiled. His tail wagged and he stood up and started towards the barn, looking back once at the women.

Emma winked at Lilly and rubbed her stomach. "I think I am ready for some of Melissa's meal. You hungry, Lilly?"

"I could eat a little something, Emma."

"I tell you what. I'll head back and warm all of the food up and you can just spend time out here if you want. Well, unless you want to come in with me. Your choice." Emma walked toward the barn and looked inside. "Sam, you leave those chickens alone! They won't lay if you chase them around. I can't scramble you and Gracie your morning eggs if I don't have hens that lay, can I?" Sam followed Emma out of the barn and nuzzled his head against her hand. "No sweet talking, Sam. You just come to the house with me."

Emma turned in Lilly's direction. "What have you decided, Lilly? Are you staying out here for a while?"

"I think I will if you don't mind. I need to gather some thoughts and put some ideas together. Are you sure you don't need any help?" Lilly took a couple of steps towards Emma and Sam.

"Heavens, no, I don't need any help. All I am doing is warming up what Miss Melissa fixed for us. There's no trouble to that." Emma frowned. "What did she tell you that makes you worry over me and wonder if I need help? Did she sing like a lark on things that are personal?"

Lilly shook her head in an adamant negative motion. "No, no. She just said you had been under the weather and I am not to tire you out. And I certainly don't want to take advantage of your hospitality by not carrying my share of the load."

Emma giggled like a little girl. "Wait till I get my hands on her. I'll tell you what I will do. I will let you help me with some of the chores each day. That way you will get a feel for my daily life and I will get some help too. How about it?"

Lilly smiled and leaned up against the barn. "I think that sounds more than fair. So, for now, I will just spend some time out here and then this evening I will take a stab at learning how to do chores around here."

Emma began to walk toward the house. "Good enough! I will call you when the food is ready. Sam, are you with me or not?" Sam looked up at Lilly and then at Emma. Emma shrugged her shoulders. "Your choice, mister. And it's a tough choice. I'm offering scraps of food inside and Lilly is offering you good company out here." Emma continued to walk towards the house and Sam did not follow. Just as she reached the steps of the porch, he bolted from the barn entrance and ran towards the house. He abruptly stopped as he reached Emma and she ran her hand across his back and gave him a slap on his hindquarters. "Call if you need anything, Lilly!"

Lilly smiled and waved as she walked into the barn. In the corner of the barn were square bales of hay stacked neatly and nearly reaching the hayloft. Several bales were sitting alongside the towering mountain of bales. She sat on a bale of hay. Lilly thought of the lives affected by such a sad, terrible thing. How many others across the country bore the same heartache and abuse Emma and her children suffered? How many stay and never leave their abusers? Lilly wondered how she, as a journalist, could get the word out to others about the choices they had and the protection that was available. She thought about Emma's comment that the most dangerous time was when the victim tries to break the cycle of abuse. How many victims stay out of fear? Her thoughts weighed heavy on her.

Lilly pulled her knees up and wrapped her arms around them. From where she sat, she could see out the sliding barn doors. Beyond the grove of trees stood the pet cemetery where Emma buried her furry family members. Emma had briefly mentioned it to Lilly when they were on their horseback ride. Lilly walked to the animal cemetery. Each plot was marked with a small limestone marker and the name of that pet. Lilly's eyes followed each name until she came across Rader. She knew Emma had a special place in her heart for Rader because he had also been a victim of Richard's abuse. Each animal's plot had flowers planted around it. Lilly ran her hands through some marigolds and mums planted on Rader's grave. She began to count the small markers. She counted seventeen in all. Each one had been buried with love and each marker had been hand painted. Lilly could tell that a child painted some of the markers and possibly Emma painted others. The love and care given to this small area showed the kind of woman Emma was. She was a simple woman who cherished life and loved nature and the blessings bestowed upon her. She treated all equally and showed others by her actions the kind of woman she was. How hard it must have been to stay with Richard out of pride in those early years, not wanting to admit what she perceived as failure. Her fear of rejection by her family and eventually the fear that Richard instilled in her, kept her trapped in what potentially could have been fatal.

Sam and Gracie came rambling up to the pet cemetery where Lilly knelt. Gracie nearly leapt into Lilly's arms. She was besieged with animal licks and tail wags. Not far behind the dogs Lilly could see Emma walking towards her.

"Guess you couldn't hear me calling you clear back here. I knew Sam and Gracie would find you. I see you are checking out where we've buried our other loved ones. Do you have any questions about any of the markers?" Emma sat down on one of the railroad timbers that lined the cemetery. She picked a fading marigold bud from one of the plants. "Jim cried each time he had to help me bury one. That boy's heart was so big. I never turned down a critter my children brought home. I knew the animal needed love and I knew my kids needed the animal. We always had room for one more."

Emma stretched over to touch a marker. "Kate painted this one and those two over there. She was always bringing home cats. Oh, now wait. There was that time she brought a yellow lab pup from the school playground. She called me at work and asked me if she could. We ran an advertisement in the paper but no one claimed him so we kept him. But usually it was cats she brought home. Jim brought home all kinds of critters and I am not much better. I've been guilty of bringing a few home myself. And Rylie brought Sam home. I've already told you about Sam, haven't I?"

Lilly hugged Sam. "Oh, yes, I know about Sam. He is quite a character."

Emma stood up and brushed the seat of her jeans off. "The food's all ready to eat whenever you want."

Lilly gave Sam another hug and stood up, "I am ready. I'm going to need sustenance for those chores later on."

Both women, along with Sam and Gracie, walked back towards the house. Lilly opened the gate and Sam walked into the yard first. Emma laughed. "There are no ladies first with my old Sam. He believes in each one for himself. Sam, you've had some scraps of food so you need to stay outside. Besides, I think you smell like pond. Lilly and I may give you a good bath later this evening."

Lilly noticed the dining table was not set with food as she entered the house. Emma turned to Lilly, "I bet you're wondering where all of the food is, aren't you?"

Lilly placed a hand on the back of one of the oak dining chairs. "Well, yes, I am curious."

Emma smiled her huge smile, erasing her scar. "I've set us up on the sun porch. I spend very little time out there during the days in the summer but I love it in the evenings and on fall and winter days. Rylie put a little gas fireplace out there a few years ago and it puts off a gentle heat. It has the best view of any room in this place."

Emma walked through the kitchen and Lilly followed. French doors led from the south side of the kitchen onto the sun porch. Emma walked to a small iron table and two chairs that were painted white. Each chair had a bright yellow floral cushion on it. Emma motioned to the wall of floor to ceiling windows. "We had new windows put in when we realized we were not going to be able to turn the barn into a house. Rylie made sure we could alternate between screened windows or glass, whatever the weather called for. Sit down, Lilly."

Lilly sat at the table and Emma joined her. Emma bowed her head and said her usual prayer and Lilly bowed her head. Before Emma ended her prayer she spoke these words that touched Lilly's heart. "And, thank you, Lord, for my friend Lilly. I ask that she not stand in judgment over me and the choices I have made in my life. And, Lord, I ask that you bless Lilly and those that read her article about my family and me. May her article save some family from years of suffering and abuse. In Thy Name, Amen."

"Grab your plate and let's load up on this delicious food."

Lilly joined Emma in the kitchen and the women filled their plates. Emma carried the plate of sliced tomatoes, along with her own plate, to the sun porch. "I can never get enough of these things and it won't be long before they are out of season. My Jim would just bite into them like an apple. Wish he was here to see Conner James."

She cut into the tomato and said, "I bet you get tired of hearing this old bird say 'I wish', don't you, Lilly?"

Lilly patted Emma on her hand, "No, I can't imagine what it would be like to be in your shoes. You are a very strong woman."

Emma set her napkin on her lap. "Strength comes in many different forms, Lilly. Some folks would not think of me as strong. I have to ask for strength every day. And some days I feel so weak. There are days I wonder if I will make it through to the end of the day. I guess Richard gave me strength which would make him turn over in his grave if he heard me say that." She chuckled. "That gives me some gratification, that I achieved strength when it came to Richard."

They enjoyed their meal and talked about the evening chores. Lilly had no idea there was so much to do both morning and evening on Emma's farm. Emma talked about cooler weather coming soon and what it was like to do chores in cold weather. Lilly wondered if Emma would let others help her this winter since she had been ill. She also wondered how serious Emma's illness really was. Melissa had not gone into a lot of detail about Emma's illness but Lilly knew Emma's family was concerned about her.

"Lilly, go help yourself to more in the kitchen. More tomatoes?" Emma held the platter up and motioned to the large, juicy fruit.

"No thank you. I think I am going to get more cheesy potatoes."

Lilly returned to the table and took a sip of her iced tea, "Melissa told me cheesy potatoes were Jim's favorite. She said he liked them without onions and Denise or you would always make a special batch just for him. What other things did he enjoy besides tomatoes and cheesy potatoes? Did he have hobbies?"

"Well, you know some of his favorite foods. And he loved ice cream. Cars. He loved cars. Fast cars. And he loved animals. I guess I have told you a lot of these things. He loved his little sister and he was an awesome son. He would do anything for anyone. He worried so much about being like his father. Each time he would even come close to losing his temper, he would worry so I would have to remind that it was fine as long as he didn't hurt others. I could not get him to stop worrying about that, no matter how hard I tried. And he loved to laugh and tease others. But he didn't like anyone teasing the grandkids. I watched him get onto Danielle one time because he thought she was teasing Kelsi too much. He was always for the underdog."

Lilly took her plate to the kitchen sink and began to rinse it. "What are some of your favorite things, Emma? I guess I haven't asked you that and I really would like to know."

Emma brought her plate to the sink, rinsed it and loaded both of the plates into the dishwasher. She began to gather the leftover food from the counter and stove and put it in containers. She looked out the kitchen window, "My favorite things. Hmm. Well, I love the smell of autumn leaves burning. I love the touch of a kitten's fur. I love children and the sound of their laughter."

She smiled a distant smile as if she were back in time. "I love music. Not that loud stuff the kids listen to these days but old love songs, old ballads. I love jazz and blue grass. I love southern gospel and old hymns. I love sitting on my porch or taking a quiet ride on one of the horses. You already know that I love the smell of hay and horses. I love how loyal a dog can be to its owner. I love family and friends. And my favorite meal is breakfast and I enjoy having breakfast out. Rylie took me to the Corner Café every Saturday morning for breakfast. We always made sure it was in the budget. Oh, I could go on and on about what I like and love." She took a dishtowel and dried a pan.

"Emma, other than Rylie's children and grandchildren, do you have family here?"

"I have Rylie's family but not any of my own here in Kansas. My mother and father have gone on to Heaven. My sister and her family live in St. Joseph in the home my folks built when I was a teenager and we talk on occassion. But I have Rylie's kids and family and I have my friends."

Lilly sat at the kitchen table. "Any friends nearby? Lifelong friends?"

Emma sat in a chair across from Lilly, "Lifelong friends, you say?" She put her elbows on the table and rested her chin in the palms of her hands. "I guess you could say Richard got custody of what I thought was our friends except for my dear friend Marsha. To this day, she calls and checks on me. The friends I have now are friends I made after the divorce. And I guess that has been a lifetime ago when you think about it. And I have my friend Terri. I told you about her, Lilly. She is the friend that took me to the hospital when I lost my appendix and my kidney. She is quite ill but we keep in touch by phone or I sneak over to Lawrence once in a while and spend the afternoon with her. I think the one thing that hurt me when I divorced Richard was that people professing to be my friends believed him and turned against me. Marsha says that isn't the way it was but that those folks just didn't know what to do so they just didn't even call or check up on me. How can a person do that to another?" Emma frowned and looked Lilly directly in the eye. Lilly knew Emma expected a response.

Lilly thought for a brief moment and replied, "I don't know how they could do that, Emma. A true friendship should have a solid foundation." Lilly felt pleased with her response and hoped Emma felt the same.

Emma slapped her hand on the table, "I'll say an Amen to that!" She wiped her hands on the dishtowel and stood up. "Come with me." She motioned to Lilly.

Emma walked onto the sun porch and took a seat. "Sit where you can see out this window.

"Sit, sit." She motioned towards a large wicker chair with an overstuffed cushion in a deep red geranium pattern. Lilly did as she was told,

Emma closed her eyes and quietly spoke, "Now imagine that you are here alone and you have been the victim of mental, physical and verbal abuse for many, many years."

Lilly sat in her chair and tried to put herself in Emma's place. A lifetime of fear, even in what should have been the safety of her own home.

A twig snapped outside the sun porch and Emma smiled.

"Now imagine that you don't know if that sound was merely a twig snapping or the person that has held you victim all those years waits outside for you. Is that person watching your every move? Can they sense your fear?"

Lilly could feel her pulse beat more rapidly.

Leaves rustled in the trees. Lilly strained to see and hear. Was that a shadow of a man or was her mind and eyes playing tricks on her?

Emma had clearly made her point to Lilly. Fear had held this household and those that dwelt within it captive way too long.

Chapter 21

Emma opened her eyes and looked at Lilly, never taking her eyes from Lilly's, causing Lilly to feel somewhat uncomfortable as if Emma wanted Lilly to know the fear that had held Emma captive.

"I still feel him watching me. I know he can no longer harm me but for whatever reason, he still haunts me."

Lilly watched the trees. "Do you ever rest? Surely you know he is gone now. Now you can rest."

"He used to laugh at me when I referred to myself as a victim. He would tell me I chose to be a victim and I could leave any time but there would always be consequences."

Emma pulled her knees to her chest and hugged them, swaying slightly as she looked outside and then back at Lilly.

"Sometimes we, as victims, choose what might appear to be the easiest way and that would be to stay. Some folks might say I chose to stay in my situation because it was easy. In a way, I might have to agree. I chose to stay, in part, out of fear. Fear of the unknown is sometimes greater than staying in what you are accustomed to. The fear of Richard's threats and the fear of not being able to give my children what they were accustomed to played a part in my choice to stay in that environment. Some might think that, because I chose to stay in my situation, I deserved to be a victim. But when we choose to stay, we are forcing our children into being victims and that is out of their control. That is why a victim of domestic abuse needs to get out of the situation. For their own safety but, more importantly, for their child's safety."

Lilly looked at Emma, "What if there are no children? Shouldn't the victim get out?"

Emma's clear blue eyes widened, "Oh Heavens, yes! I am not saying that someone should stay in such a situation. I guess I feel that so many children are victimized because of the choices their parents make. But, of course, any victim should get out. Keep in mind that an abuser is going to become even more demented when the tie is being broken. Those were such scary times for all of us."

Lilly pulled her right leg up under the other and set her drink on the table beside her. "What do you think would have happened if you had chosen to stay, Emma?"

Emma stood and looked out the window. Her shoulders slouched and she spoke in a soft tone, "I believe I would not be here talking to you today. I believe he would have killed me or maimed me in such a way that I could not function. I believe that my children would have truly hated me if they had spent their entire teen years under the same roof with Richard. I believe that I had a small window of opportunity to get out and I took that moment and fled for our lives. If I had chosen to stay, so many things would be different. I am grateful that I had the strength to finally make that decision. I just wish I had done it sooner. But, there's no looking back. Take today and use it to the very fullest."

Lilly gave Emma a slight hug and said, "Emma, it is time to put it in the past. Who would have thought that you would finally be free from him after so many years? Who would have thought it would take so long for that freedom?"

Emma turned and smiled, her eyes brimming with tears. "Yep, who would have thought? Let's get those chores done so we can enjoy the rest of our evening. You'd better put on some different shoes. Have you got some old tennis shoes? If not, I bet I can get you all lined up."

After both women changed into different shoes, they went outside to the barn. Emma went towards the stacked hay and grabbed a hay hook that was in one of the bales. She used the hook to pierce the bale of hay. "Now I give the horses their hay in the evening and I open the gates to their stalls so they can get in out of the weather. A lot of times I just lock them in their stalls and give them grain but this evening I am leaving it up to them. Sometimes I worry about coyotes and such. That is why I have those two llamas out in the back pasture. We will open the gate so they can get in here with the horses. For some reason, coyotes don't come around if you have llamas. Most folks that have sheep keep a lama or two as protection from the coyotes. They make for a grumpy pet but a terrific watch dog."

Emma lifted the hay bale over the fence as if it was easy but Lilly knew that it had to weigh at least fifty pounds or more. She watched Emma go about her chores with such assurance and ease. Emma gave each horse a kiss on their foreheads and a hug around each one's neck. Emma told Lilly morning chores were different than those at night. She walked towards the chicken coop.

"The chickens tuck themselves in at night. All I have to do is check in on them and close the coop door. They don't stay out after dusk. And ole Romeo the Rooster will be calling me in the morning to let him and his ladies out." She turned towards the house. "I think Sam needs a bath. Are you ready to tackle that job?"

Lilly had grown to love Sam and she had no qualms about relieving him of his pond odor. "I'm ready."

Emma closed the door to the chicken coop and went into the barn. She reached for a leash that hung from a hook next to the horse tackle. "Samuel! Sam! Come here! She called his name two more times and he came around the barn, covered in cockle burrs. "Oh, Sam, where in the heck have you been? This is going to be more work than we thought, Lilly."

Lilly laughed. She felt so at home with Emma and her menagerie of animals. She truly admired Emma for her strength. She had decided she would call David later in the evening and let him know how much she loved him and appreciated him. Emma had made Lilly realize how precious love was and that some people never know how precious a gift it is. She watched Emma place the leash around Sam's neck; all the while trying to dodge his kisses and keep him in control. It wasn't going well and Lilly laughed so hard her side hurt. "Oh, Emma, what a sight the two of you are!"

Emma laughed, stood up and Sam jumped up on her, his tail wagging constantly. "Now see, Sam, you have given our guest quite a laugh with your antics. Let's see how entertaining you can be during your bath." She led Sam over to a small child's wading pool and handed the leash to Lilly. "Hold onto him when I turn on the hose cause he is going to go crazy, Lilly. Crazy."

Lilly grasped the leash as tightly as she could and braced herself. Emma turned on the garden hose and it took a few seconds of sputtering before the water came bursting out of the nozzle. Sam began to bark and dance around Lilly's feet. The leash became entwined around Lilly's ankles and she felt herself losing her balance. Before she knew it, she and Sam were both on the ground and he was licking her face and barking. Emma came running around the side of the house, dog shampoo in hand.

"Good Lord! What on earth happened here?"

Lilly was laughing so hard she could not answer Emma. Emma took Sam's leash. "Sit, Sam, sit!" Sam did as he was ordered, his tail still wagging. "Oh, Lilly, I am so sorry about his behavior. Are you hurt?"

Lilly sat up, still laughing. "No, no, I'm not hurt. You were right when you said he gets excited. How do you handle him by yourself at bath time? He's a wild one!"

Emma smiled and answered, "Just watch this. It's not that he doesn't want the bath but that he does." Emma turned, pointed to the little pool and spoke to Sam, "Sam, tub."

Sam bounced into the pool, his tail still wagging. He turned in circles and barked.

Lilly stood to her feet. "Well, would you look at that? No wonder he was so excited. He loves it, doesn't he?"

Emma took the hose and began to spray water on Sam. "Yep, he loves it. That is why I can't keep him out of the pond. The vet says he is part Labrador. Guess that explains his love of water."

The two women bathed the dog, both of them getting nearly as wet as him. After they had completed this final chore, Emma suggested they brush him and let him in the house for the night.

As they walked onto the porch, Gracie sat at the top of the stairs. She snipped at Sam as he walked by and gave Emma a loud bark. "As you can see, Miss Gracie is a bit jealous. She hates getting bathed but she doesn't want Sam to get more attention than her. Let's get him inside before he finds something to get into. Gracie, are you joining us or are you going to pout all night?"

Gracie followed the women into the house. Emma let Sam off the leash. He rolled around on the living room rug. Emma frowned. "Lilly, how about some ice cream after all that excitement?"

Lilly sat down on the sofa. "That sounds great."

They laughed and enjoyed talking about the ever so wild Sam and his bath time antics. After they finished their ice cream, Emma suggested they watch an old video. She went to the cabinet and began to take out videotapes. "Name your poison."

Holding up one video after another Emma listed each one as she held it proudly and announced, "When my kids were young, the kids as teenagers, after Rylie and I were married or just the kids and me."

Lilly walked over to join Emma and began to look over the tapes. "How about this one and maybe this one?"

Emma read the labels. "Jim was nine and Kate was four in this one. And this. You want to see when Rylie and I were married? All of our kids are in that one." She put one of the tapes into the player. "I have slowly been having these put on DVD and I hope to have them all done that way within a year. Then I will have to buy myself a DVD player. In the meantime, I watch the tapes. Sit down anywhere, Lilly."

Lilly sat on the sofa. Sam joined her. Emma sat in the recliner, her feet dangling. Gracie jumped up beside her. "Sam, you and Gracie need to get down. You're still wet." Sam gently eased off the sofa, turning to give Lilly a forlorn look. Emma set Gracie on the floor beside him.

Emma pressed the play button and the video showed a Halloween pumpkin and soon Jim appeared on the screen. He is laughing and seems to be dressed in a Ninja costume. Emma is completely focused on the image of her son. Lilly hears a man's voice. "Hey dumb ass. Get out of the way. I am trying to get a picture of the jack-o-lantern." Jim's eyes drop and his smile fades. Then a woman's voice. "Come here, Sugar. Stand with Kate and me." Lilly recognized the voice as Emma's. Lilly continues to watch the video. Emma is dressed as a witch and Kate is dressed as a cat. Emma keeps a close eye on both children as

Richard verbally abuses all three. As he pans the camera out his voice orders Emma to cast a "spell". The camera focuses on Emma. She waves her hand and says "Hocus, pocus, make us a happy family."

Lilly turns to see Emma's response. "Guess I wasn't a great spell caster, huh?" She pulled a pillow over her stomach. "Makes me sick to think I put those babies through that."

"Did he talk to them like that all of the time?"

Emma put the footrest of the recliner up. "Yep, most of the time. He did it to Jim more than he did to Kate. He would just fill her full of lies and promises. But poor Jim. He was terrible to my Jim."

"Emma, let's not watch these. We've had such a good day, let's not spoil it with such sorrow. How about the wedding video? Those were happier times. Let me change videos."

Lilly went and ejected the first tape, replacing it with the wedding video. She pushed the play button. Three young men in tuxedos are all smiling. Lilly recognizes them as Jim, Jason and Billy. Jim, being six feet, five inches tall, rests his arm on Jason's head. There is at least a foot's difference in height between the two teenage boys. A young Kate enters the room and all three boys begin to tease her. She stands beside her brother and looks up at him. He smiles an ear-to-ear smile and nudges her. The music starts and Jason and Billy leave the room. A woman Lilly guessed to be in her forties joins Kate. "Who is that, Emma?"

"That is my friend Terri. Kate was my maid of honor and Terri was an attendant. Rylie and I did not want a big wedding but both of our daughters insisted. Teenage girls. Always thinking in fairy tale terms. But now I am glad we did it."

The camera changes to inside the church. Rylie, Jason and Billy walk into the church, waiting for the attendants and bride. Terri and Kate enter. A small toddler, a little girl, enters carrying the flower petals in a tiny white basket. All those at the front of the church smile. As she reaches midway, she turns and changes her mind. Melissa appears in the frame.

"Who's the little flower girl, Emma?"

Emma wrinkled her nose and smiled. "That's Miss Taylor. She was fifteen months old. We wanted to include her so we decided to make her the flower girl. Watch, Lilly. Melissa coaxes her into going down the isle and then she runs to her Papa."

The music changed and Jim entered the room with Emma on his arm. She looked up at her son with her huge smile. When the minister asked who would be giving the bride, Jim proudly answered that he and his sister were giving their mother away.

"Proudest day of my life, I believe. Other than when I gave birth to my babies. I was so proud that Jim would do that. And he wore what he called a monkey suit. Trust me, that boy hated to dress up. And I put him in a tuxedo. His friends said it was only because he loved me so that he did that."

They continued to watch the video and when the wedding and reception were over, it changed to the farm. Lilly watched as the DJ played songs and people danced. The farm was beautiful. Flowers were everywhere. Tables were set with tablecloths and old Ball jars were filled with wildflowers. As Lilly watched, she knew that this was where she wanted to have her wedding. Emma was right. It was a perfect setting.

They watched the entire video and, when it was finished, Emma clapped her hands as if she had just seen an academy award performance. "Did you like the part where Jim and his friends sang to me? How about all that dancing? We had a good old time. Those were some good times when we were all together." Her voice softened. "Good times."

"That was such fun, watching all of you. What a special day that must have been for all of you. Your children got to finally see you happy."

Emma put down the footrest and stood up. "I miss the good times. We just didn't have enough years with all of us. Rylie and Jim's lives were too short. Way too short. Good Lord, look at the time! I've kept you up much later than I had planned. I am so sorry. You head on to bed and I will close up."

Lilly looked at the mantle clock. Eleven. "Emma, I usually stay up much later than this. You go on to bed and I think I will do some reading and maybe watch some more videos, if you don't mind. I have a couple of more hours before I will be ready to sleep."

Emma turned off the kitchen light. "Morning comes much sooner in the country. But, you do as you wish. Do you want Sam to stay down here with you?" She locked the deadbolt on the front door.

"I think Sam would be a perfect late night companion, especially now that he is clean." Sam wagged his tail and Lilly patted his head. Gracie barked.

Emma picked Gracie up. "Come on, Miss Jealous. You are sleeping in my room. Sam, behave. Lilly, if he starts to stand by the door, call me. I'll let him out. Sometimes he wants out just to chase a critter. I can usually tell which it is. Critter or bathroom. He should be fine. Call me if you need anything. Make sure you get a good night's sleep."

When Lilly was sure Emma had retired for the night, she called David from her cell phone. "Did I wake you?" There was a pause. "I just want to tell you how much you mean to me and how much I love you. David, I have found the place where we should have our wedding. I want you to come one day this week or on Saturday and see it. David, I want you to meet Emma."

Lilly stayed up and watched family videos after her conversation with David. Sam never left her side. She must have fallen asleep on the sofa. As the full moon cast a glow onto the living room wall, Lilly slept soundly.

Chapter 22

Sam's continuous barking awakened Lilly. He circled the sofa again and again, sometimes jumping on Lilly's legs as she tried to sit up. She heard a loud knock at the door and she turned to see a man smiling back at her through the leaded glass window.

Lilly stood and went to the bottom of the staircase leading to the upstairs bedrooms. "Emma! Emma, someone is at the door! Emma?"

Sam continued to bark and started to jump on the front door. The man took off his cowboy hat and pointed his finger at Sam through the window. He smiled as he spoke "Sam, you get down off Emma Jean's purty door. You get down." He looked in at Lilly, "Miss, is Emma Jean here?"

Lilly walked towards the front door and decided to open it since the gentleman knew both Sam and Emma. She reached for the blanket on the sofa and wrapped it around her and opened the door, "I thought she was but she doesn't seem to answer. Shall I go upstairs and look for her?"

Before the weathered cowboy could speak, Lilly saw Emma with a large watering can in her hand and Gracie beside her, walking down the drive towards the farmhouse. Emma waved and smiled, picking up her pace as she walked towards them.

Lilly felt awkward as she stood there with the stranger. He knelt down and began to rub Sam's ears, "Where's your collar, old fella? You'd better not run off with no tags." He looked up at Lilly, "Hell, he ain't about to run off from the good life. Looks like Emma Jean's been up to the cemetery to check on the boys, huh?" He stood and extended his rough, weathered hand, "Name's Zeke Lang."

Lilly shook Zeke's hand as Emma entered the gate. Emma set her watering can on the porch, "Ezekiel, I thought for sure I could get back before you showed up to shoe the horses." She wiped her hands on her sweatshirt, leaving dirty handprints on both pockets. "Have you met Lilly?"

Zeke extended his hand again and the two shook. Lilly smiled and nodded "Hello, Zeke, I'm Lilly. So nice to meet you."

Emma pulled her New York Yankees ball cap off and ran her fingers through her hair, "Let me run upstairs and clean up a bit. Zeke, you can go on out to the barn if you want and start on the horses and I'll catch up." She opened the screen door.

Zeke held the door for Emma, "Nope, I think I will sit out here a spell. I have something I want to show you on Pie's front hoof so I'll wait until you are out here."

Emma entered the doorway and turned back towards Lilly and Zeke, "Lilly, do you mind staying out here on the porch with Zeke and keeping him company while I wash up? I forgot my spade and had to dig in the flowers by hand. The iris had a few weeds growing in them. Can't have that. Everything needed watered. Looks like I've been making mud pies, doesn't it?" Emma held up her hands and Lilly wondered how she had earlier run her fingers through her hair with such a mess on her hands. Lilly chuckled.

Emma pointed a dirty finger at her and smiled, "You laughing at this old bird, Lilly Ballard?"

Lilly ran her hand across Sam's head, "No, Emma, I'm laughing with you. Zeke and I will wait out here on the porch for you." Lilly sat on the porch swing and Zeke sat on the porch steps. Emma closed the screen door and Gracie followed her upstairs.

Zeke's face was lined and tanned. It almost looked like leather and, when he took off his cowboy hat, his forehead was several shades lighter. He carried a can of chewing tobacco in his shirt pocket. As he leaned back on one elbow, he turned to Lilly and spoke, "Have you known Emma Jean long?"

Lilly began to swing slightly, "I've known her a few months. She's quite a character, isn't she?"

Zeke smiled. "I've known Emma a lot of years and I would say she is a character and also she has character. That woman has a heart of gold. Ain't no reason she should have suffered as she has all these years. Ain't no reason at all. She deserved better than to lose her boy and Rylie."

Lilly stopped swinging, "Zeke, did you know Jim?"

Zeke reached in his shirt pocket and pulled out his chewing tobacco can but did not open, merely tapping it against the palm of his hand, "Yes, miss, I sure did. He was a fine boy, that Jim. Didn't deserve the daddy he had."

Lilly leaned forward, "Did you know his father?"

"I knew of him and I seen him in action one evening. That man was pure Evil and Emma Jean and her kids should have got plum away from him a long time before they did. Evil, I tell you. That boy was a brave boy what he done that night."

"What did he do, Zeke?"

Zeke again tapped the tobacco can against his palm. "I was out at the barn with the horses. Don't think that man ever knew there was a witness to his evil ways. He raced his big, fancy truck up the drive and ran up on the porch where Emma Jean stood. She was trying to get back into the house but he grabbed her by the hair. Just as I was about to head for the house, Jim came out the front door. He spoke so calm to his dad. He said 'Dad, let go of mom and leave now before I call the sheriff.' That boy stood several inches over his dad and he stood so tall and proud that day. Protecting his mama, that's what he was doin, protecting his mama. That evil bastard let go of Emma Jean and turned and spat in his own boy's face. Jim never moved. He slowly reached for his mama and moved her behind him. By now Emma Jean was yelling at Richard and begging that boy to get in the house. Richard laughed and stepped down off the porch. He turned like he was going to come back up towards those two and must have thought better of it. I walked out of the barn cause I feared he was going to get into it with big Jim. He didn't. He just got in his truck and drove off. Emma Jean took her jacket off and wiped that boy's face, crying 'I'm sorry' to him the whole while. Big Jim just reached his arms around that woman and hugged her. He tussled her hair and I heard her say she was going in to get him a washcloth. I waited till she went inside and I went to the house. When I walked up on Jim, the biggest tears I ever saw were in that boy's eyes. I asked him if he was all right and he broke down. That moment broke my heart more than when I lost my folks to Heaven. It broke my heart to know how broken his young heart was. Emma Jean stepped out the door and handed him a wet cloth. She just kept saying 'I'm sorry, sugar, I'm sorry.' He told her it was fine and said he was going to go out to the barn. Asked me if I needed any help out there. Think he just wanted to get away. We started towards the barn and Emma Jean said 'I'll help too.' He turned to his mama and said 'Get back inside in case he comes back, Mom. Get back inside.' When we got out to the barn he turned to me and told me things that dad of his had done over the years. He cried and there were times I cried with him. Them folks never deserved what he put them through. To this day Emma Jean blames herself and will never forgive herself for what she done to them kids, having a dad like that."

The screen door opened and Emma stepped out, Gracie underfoot, "You want to stay for some breakfast, Zeke? I can whip something up real fast."

Zeke opened the tobacco can, looked inside and put the lid back on. "Ain't got time today. I'll take a raincheck. I got another appointment after your horses. Get movin, old woman." He slapped his thigh and Sam took that to mean that Zeke wanted to pet him and nuzzled his head against Zeke's hand. Zeke obliged with a pat on Sam's head.

Emma laughed and said, "Who you calling an old woman? How many years older than this old bird are you, Ezekiel?"

Zeke began to walk towards the garden gate, "More years than I care to recall, Emma Jean. Now that we have established that, let's get on out to that barn and get these horses taken care of."

Emma turned to Lilly as she followed Zeke, "Lilly, care to start some breakfast while Zeke show's me my Pie's hoof and we cuss and discuss whether they need shoed or not? I know they need their hoofs trimmed for sure. So, how about some eggs? There's ham in the refrigerator and hashbrowns in the freezer. Do you want toast?"

Lilly chuckled to herself and, once again, enjoyed Emma's bantering and her 'take the bull by the horns' attitude. "Emma, I will be more than happy to make breakfast. Zeke, are you sure you can't join us?"

Zeke ran his hand across the tobacco can in his pocket one more time, "No, maam, but I sure do appreciate the offer. I won't keep Emma Jean long. You go right ahead and start her some breakfast. She needs to keep up her strength."

Emma threw her hands in the air, "Here we go again! Folks thinking I can't fend for myself. Worrying about my eating habits, bossing me around. Ezekiel, why in the Sam Hill would you think I don't keep my strength up? Lord knows I can hay and chore with the best of them. Bet I could keep up with you, old man."

Zeke shook his head and motioned for Emma to walk through the open gate, "I reckon I can't argue with you on that. Even if I could, I wouldn't cause you would give me Hell, Emma Jean. Pure Hell."

Lilly gave a wave to the two as they walked towards the barn, bantering back and forth. Zeke turned back as they got a little further from the house, "Miss Lilly Ballard, it was right nice to meet you!"

"Same to you, Zeke. Don't let her work you too hard." She closed the screen door and walked towards Emma's kitchen.

Chapter 23

Lilly enjoyed preparing Emma's breakfast in the warm, inviting kitchen. She watched Sam and the beagle play what appeared to be a game of tag in the back yard. She wondered while she watched why she had never heard the beagle's name mentioned and made a mental note to ask Emma his name someday.

Lilly set the kitchen table and preheated the skillet for the fried eggs. As she opened the refrigerator door to retrieve the eggs, the front door opened and Emma entered.

Lilly set the egg crate on the table and walked into the living room, "Emma, how do you want your eggs? Over easy, medium?"

Before Lilly could finish, Emma responded curtly, "What I want is for Ezekiel Lang to let me pay him for trimming my horses' hoofs. I will not be some sort of charity case."

Lilly did not know how she should respond to Emma so she stood quietly beside the sofa.

Emma removed her shoes, "Sorry, Lilly. I just get so upset with folks thinking I need help, whether it is financially or otherwise. It will be a cold day when I ask anyone for help. The only one I ask for help from is the Good Lord Himself. If He can't help me, then there isn't a soul who can. I'm sorry I snapped at you. This isn't your fault." She began to walk towards Lilly, "If I could lay blame, I don't even know who I would blame. Now, to answer your question, I like my eggs fried medium. I can finish up breakfast, Lilly. There's no need in you having to since I am here. You're my guest."

Lilly knew better than to offer to finish breakfast since Emma was already feeling like others were doing too much for her. Lilly knew that Emma had been ill with lymphoma but she wondered if there was more to the story. Why were the local people concerned for Emma and also her family seemed concerned? She followed Emma into the kitchen, "Emma what is that little beagle's name? I don't think I have ever heard you mention his name."

Emma cracked two eggs into the cast iron skillet, "His name is Dog. Our grandson, Dawson, named him that when he first showed up here and it has stuck. Cute little fella, isn't he?"

Lilly was relieved that the conversation had become more light-hearted, "He plays so well with Sam. They have been having a good time out in the yard. I've enjoyed their entertainment."

Emma started to turn the eggs, "Guess I haven't asked you how you like your eggs. How about it?"

Lilly sat down at the table, "Medium. Over medium, please."

Emma turned the eggs and placed the bread in the toaster. "Then medium it is. What is on the schedule today? Is there anything you would like to do in particular?"

Lilly thought for a moment, "I am at your mercy, Emma. I should let you know that I phoned David last night and he is planning on heading this way one afternoon, if you don't mind. I believe we would like to have our wedding here at the farm. I watched those videos last night and realized how perfect this place is for such an event."

Emma smiled, "It is special, isn't it? I do believe that I made the right choice when I bought this place. You know, I thought I was doing such an injustice to my children, moving them here. They were raised with all new things, an in-ground pool, and a big house. But, you know, those were just things. We made this our home. This is where we belonged. They both knew that, I am sure. I know Kate will tell you that to this day. She loves this old place. She made so many friends here and has such fond memories. Did I tell you she was prom queen her senior year and she was voted best personality? That girl was so excited. You'd thought she had been crowned Miss America or something of the sort." Emma placed the eggs on a plate, buttered the toast and set Lilly's plate on the table. She returned to the stove and placed an egg in the skillet.

Lilly took a slice of ham off the platter and some hashbrowns. Within a few minutes Emma joined her at the table. Lilly bowed her head and Emma said the prayer, "Thank you, Lord, for the meal we are about to receive. Thank you for all your wondrous blessings. And Lord, take care of all our loved ones. Tell my kinfolk, especially my boys, to save a place for me at the table. I'll join them in your time, Lord, in your time. Amen."

The two women shared a casual conversation over breakfast and enjoyed one another's company as they ate and then cleared the table.

Lilly wiped her hands on a dishtowel, "Emma, I think I will take my shower if you don't mind. Is there anything else you want me to do before I do?"

Emma closed the dishwasher, "I can't think of anything. You go on and clean up and then; when you are finished I'll take my shower. Ezekiel got me out of my routine this morning, let me tell you. He showed up much earlier than I had planned. I know I have two bathrooms but I hate taking hot water from a guest. Besides, I need to go feed and water some of the animals. Now, you know where the fresh linens are, don't you?"

Lilly set her dishtowel beside the sink, "Yes, Emma. I'll join you as soon as I am finished and maybe I can help you finish with your chores."

Emma picked up the dishtowel and hung it over the stove handle, "Now, don't rush. If there are still chores to be done when you are finished, that would be great. No need to hurry, though."

Lilly went into the living room and folded the blanket she had used in the night. She went upstairs and Emma finished in the kitchen.

Emma went back outside to do the rest of her chores. She enjoyed the beautiful fall morning and filled each feed tub. She was just starting to fill the stock tanks with water when a bright yellow convertible pulled into the drive. Emma placed the hose into the stock tank and hurried towards the car. "Robyn! How in the heck are you? Oh, you brought the babies." Emma leaned into the car and began to unlock a car seat harness. "Come here, sugar. Look how you have grown"

As Emma took the little girl out of her seat, Lilly came outside. "Robyn, I want you to meet Lilly. Lilly, come out here! I have someone I want you to meet." Emma turned and gave Robyn a big hug.

Lilly walked towards the convertible. She noticed a slightly built brunette with big blue eyes. She was dressed in a business suit and she held Emma's hand as Emma held a toddler on her hip. As Lilly approached them, a little boy exited the car. He was probably seven years of age with sandy blond hair and he carried a soccer ball. Emma bent down and hugged him, "Lilly, this is my dear, sweet Robyn and her children, Lizzie and Skylar James. Robyn, this is my friend Lilly."

The two women shook hands and before they could speak Emma said, "You two have a lot in common. Robyn is a news anchor in Chicago and has a degree in journalism. Robyn, Lilly is the young lady that wrote the article about the barn."

Both women said "Nice to meet you" at the same time. Lilly spoke to Skylar, "I see you have a Yankees cap on. Do you like the Yankees?"

Skylar reached for his cap, "Emma and Momma do."

Emma tugged on his ball cap and adjusted Lizzie on her hip. "Come on in the house. I think I have some cookies for you two. What on earth brings you back to Kansas? I wasn't looking for you until Christmas."

Lilly watched Robyn as she spoke to Emma, trying to place why she seemed so familiar. As Robyn and Emma walked with the children to the house, Lilly realized who Robyn was. She had seen her in the photo albums with Jim, over and over again. She remembered Emma had told her Jim and Robyn had been engaged. Lilly followed them into the house. As Emma went to the kitchen to get cookies and the children followed, Lilly watched Robyn walk over to the bookcase and look over the pictures. Emma spoke from the kitchen, "Did you know Kate had her baby?"

Robyn walked to the kitchen doorway, "What did she end up naming him?"

Emma smiled, "Conner James."

Skylar took a cookie from Emma's hand and looked up at her, "That's my name", he said.

Emma knelt down in front of both children, "Why, you do share the same name, don't you? Do you want some milk with your cookies?"

Lizzie said yes and Skylar turned to his mother. Robyn said, "You can have some or you can have water."

He smiled and said, "Water, please."

Robyn helped Lizzie with her milk. "We can't stay long. I am here to see Dad. He had surgery yesterday and I drove in to help him for a couple of days. I know you probably get lonely so I brought the kids to see you and I want to go to the cemetery while I am here. Ryan had to stay in Chicago. He had some convention to go to."

Emma turned to Lilly. "Ryan is Robyn's husband and he is an architect in Chicago. Fine young man, fine young man."

Lilly thought she detected some sadness in Emma's voice. Moments like this had to be difficult for Emma. Her son's life was cut so short. These could have been her grandchildren. The life Robyn led could have been with Jim.

Emma picked Lizzie's cup up and asked if she wanted more milk. With an acknowledgment of 'no', Emma motioned for everyone to go into the living room. Skylar stopped in his tracks and looked up at Emma, "I want to see the horses."

Emma tugged on his cap, "Well, heck yes, you do. I'll take you out there. Did you know I just fed everyone and they're bellies are full? Do you ladies want to join us?"

Robyn sat down on the sofa. "I think I will stay in here, Emma. I've had a long drive and I know the kids are tired. We got very little sleep last night. You all can go if you want. Skylar, listen to Emma. Lizzie, hold Emma's hand."

Emma took both of the children's hands and walked towards the door. "Lilly, do you want to stay here and keep Robyn company?"

Lilly sat in a rocker. "I would love to."

Emma and the children went to the barn. Robyn was quiet for a moment and then spoke; "I think she gets lonely out here alone. I wish she had moved into town when Rylie passed but she insisted on staying out here. Does she seem lonely? How is her health?"

Lilly smiled. "From what I have seen, she certainly doesn't have time to get lonely. And I don't think she would live anywhere else. She is happy here and makes no bones about it."

Robyn rested one elbow on the overstuffed arm of the sofa. "But, does she spend too much time at the cemetery? Is she taking care of herself? She should be with Kate. She is out here all alone. Jim wouldn't want her to spend her last years all alone out here."

Lilly hesitated for a moment and then spoke, "Robyn, I've only known Emma a short time but one thing I am sure of is that this is where she belongs. She herself has expressed that to me. She wants to be here. She has had several visitors since I have been here and I think she keeps busy. You shouldn't worry about her."

Just then Lilly heard the children's voices and Emma laughing. She heard them step onto the porch. Emma called out for them to come outside. Lilly and Robyn stepped out onto the porch. Sam was covered in mud, head to toe. It was obvious he had shaken and Emma had received the brunt of the mud.

Lilly covered her mouth, her eyes widening. "What happened?"

Emma sat down on the swing, turning Lizzie around and going over her, looking for mud. "Well, I was so excited to see this bunch that I left the hose running in the stock tank. And, of course, Sam found the water and the mud. Guess you know what we will be doing again tonight, huh Lilly? Sky, did you get any mud on you?"

Skylar examined his clothing. "No, but Sam did, Emma."

Emma slapped her knee and lifted her leg slightly higher in the air, laughing, "I should say he did. I should say he did, little man."

Sam started to walk towards Lilly and Robyn, his tail wagging. Emma jumped up from the swing and reached for him. Sam slid out of Emma's arms and ran into the yard. Emma turned around, her clothes covered even more in mud, "Why, he is like a greased pig, I tell you."

Both of the children were giggling and the women laughed at Emma and Sam's antics. Robyn picked Lizzie up and kissed Emma on the cheek, "We need to go. I want to meet with Dad's doctor this morning and we still need to get to the cemetery."

Skylar tugged on Robyn's suit jacket, "Can I show Emma the flowers?"

Robyn wrapped her arm around his shoulder. "Of course you can show her. Run get them."

"Oh, wait! I'll just walk you out to the car and see them", Emma said.

Everyone walked to the car. Skylar opened the trunk door with his mother's remote, proudly smiling. "Look, Emma. We got the biggest ones we could find."

Inside the trunk was a large potted mum. It was a deep, autumn red. Skylar ran his fingers through the buds and blooms, looking at it with such pride. "It's the biggest, Emma. Cause Jim was big and tall, Momma says. And I've seen pictures and she is right. Right, Mom?"

Robyn's eyes filled with tears, "Right, Sky."

Emma hugged the little boy, "They are beautiful. The most beautiful mums I have ever seen."

Robyn hugged Emma and Emma gave her a kiss on the cheek. Emma held each child in her arms and told them how much she loved them and to be good for their parents. Emma buckled Lizzie into her car seat and Robyn and Skylar sat in the front. Taking one last look at the flowers, Emma closed the trunk door. She walked to the driver's side of the car. "Tell Ryan I said hello and tell your dad to take care."

Robyn patted Emma's hand as it rested on the door of the car. "I will. You take care of yourself. Send me pictures of Conner. Tell Kate to call or e-mail. Bye. Love you."

Emma stepped away from the car. "I love you too." She stood next to Lilly and watched as they drove down the drive and up the road to the cemetery, using her hand to protect her eyes from the morning sun. She turned to Lilly, "That was a nice surprise. They were pretty flowers, huh?"

Lilly put her hand on Emma's shoulder, "Yes, they were. Are you ok?"

"Heavens, yes. I knew she would be a great mother and wife. Jim knew that too. Ryan is a lucky man, he is."

Emma walked through the gate and up the sidewalk. "Guess I really need that shower now, huh?"

"Did you finish all of the chores or is there anything that I can do to help finish?"

Emma stopped and looked towards the barn, "Good Lord, I hope I did. What a mess that water made. I tell you what. Would you please go check on the water and I'll go in and shower? Better watch old Sam, though. He's a character, that dog."

Emma opened the screen door and Lilly walked towards the barn with Sam and Gracie following.

Chapter 24

Lilly checked and made sure the hose was turned off. She stood and looked back towards the house. Many of Emma's flowers were starting to fade and cottonwood leaves were beginning to fall off the trees. Lilly enjoyed hearing the sounds of the slight breeze rustle the remaining leaves on the trees. Pie came up behind her and nuzzled his head against her arm. Would Emma have to leave, Lilly thought? She thought of all of the drop-in guests that she had encountered these past few days and also on her trips before. Lilly was sure Robyn could rest assured that Emma was not lonely. And yet, she had a twinge of doubt. Emma was the kind of woman that would deny any sort of loneliness. She abhorred anyone thinking she needed any sort of help. Lilly wondered if that was part of the reason Emma had stayed in an abusive relationship; she did not want to ask for help or admit defeat. Emma was a proud woman and Lilly knew that.

Lilly rubbed Pie's ears and his eyes appeared as though he were drifting off to sleep. Sally grazed in the pasture, occasionally glancing Lilly's direction. Lilly ran her hand across Pie's nose, "Oh, Pie, the things you could tell. You were here when Richard would show up. You animals were the only witnesses at times. If only you could talk."

Lilly heard the screen door open and Emma stepped onto the porch. She shielded her eyes as she looked towards the barn. Lilly waved and Emma waved back. Emma walked towards the barn. "Did I turn off the water? Some days I think I am losing my mind, I tell you. I either can't remember a thing or I remember too much. What's the plan?"

Lilly stopped rubbing Pie's ear, "I really don't have one. I'm sure we have more to cover but you have already had a lot of excitement this morning if you want to wait."

Emma thought for a moment and said, "Shoot, that wasn't near the excitement this old bird has seen in her lifetime. Having company is just plain, old pleasure. It is such a pretty morning, how about we take a walk and just visit? Whatever subject comes up is what we will discuss."

Lilly frowned and responded before thinking, "You've already had a walk to the cemetery this morning. Don't you think that might wear you out a bit?"

Emma shot Lilly a glare and curtly responded, "I can walk as many times a day as I want and where I want. You know, I spent so many years being told what to wear, where to go and not go, when and what to eat, so on and so on. There's not a living soul that can tell me that I can or should or should not take as many walks as I like. I think you've been listening to too many folks, Lilly Ballard. If I get tired, I'll say so. But until I do, we are going to do as much as possible. I do want to give Sam his bath before nightfall since the evenings are getting cooler."

"I'm game for whatever the day brings if you are," Lilly said. She knew she had upset Emma in insinuating that Emma wasn't capable of 'keeping up'. She would definitely have to make a serious mental note to watch what she said when it came to Emma's health.

Emma put Gracie in the house but let Sam follow. Dog ran through the pasture, chasing two squirrels. Emma tied a zippered sweatshirt around her waist and said, "In case I get chilly." Instead of turning towards the east, Emma turned west and the two women, along with a very muddy Sam, began their walk.

Emma turned to Lilly, "Watch for bittersweet along the road. I want to cut some and make a wreath for my door. It is such a pretty added fall decoration. I picked some gourds last week and haven't done anything with them. My pumpkins didn't do well this summer with all the heat. Do you decorate for the holidays, Lilly?"

Lilly unzipped her jacket," I don't seem to have a lot of time and I travel so much. I decorate with just the bare essentials. I always put up a tree at Christmas but my Halloween and Thanksgiving decorating leaves a lot to be desired."

Emma walked to the side of the road and picked a small clump of bittersweet, "Why, Good Lord, I decorate for Easter, Fourth of July, Halloween, all of them. I don't think the kids and grandkids would ever forgive me if I didn't. I always enjoyed it when my kids were young and they would help me with the decorating. Now it is left up to me to do it all. Sometimes a grandkid will stop in and lend a hand but overall, it is this old bird on her own. And, you know, I like it because I do as I please. Sometimes I get a little weepy when I pull out an old ornament or come across a special memory."

Lilly stepped nearer the ditch where Emma stood, "Do you ever get lonely, Emma? Really, do you?"

Emma placed her bittersweet in the bag that she carried. "Good Heavens, Lilly. Don't you know that I don't have time enough to get lonely? There are nights when I lay my head on my pillow that I think of my boys and how I miss them or I think about what Kate might be doing at that moment, but you know, Lilly, I was much more lonely in my younger years than I am now and I had a husband and children. So many people can be the loneliest of lonely when they are sitting right next to another person. Richard made me feel so alone. I am so blessed that I had my children. And yet, I think they felt the loneliness too. We were so alone in that world. So alone."

Sam ran further down the road ahead of the women. Lilly enjoyed the fall air and looking for the bittersweet. A fencerow made of rock lined both sides of the road. In some areas the rock had either fallen down or someone had taken it. Lilly knew that those fencerows had been there for many years. She walked alongside Emma. "Emma, do you know who owns all of this land? Doesn't it make you sad that the rock fencerows are falling down or do you think someone has come along and taken the rock?"

Emma smiled, "Probably a little of both. That makes me think of a story. Not a happy one either. Care to hear it? Oh, and the Lang's own this side and the McCullough's own this side. I think both families own some five hundred plus acres. Poor old Rylie and Emma were lucky to have our little eighty acre plot."

Sam ran back towards the women and walked next to Lilly. She ran her hand over his back, picking at the dried mud. "I would love to hear your story."

Emma picked up a stick alongside the road and continued to walk, "Well, Richard and I had just built a new home and I decided I wanted to have a little flower garden surrounded with this native rock. So, I asked Richard if he would drive me in his truck down to the river road and we would gather some. Now, Lilly, the river road is a very primitive road with very few houses along it and it is right on the Kansas River. We, I am sorry to admit, found some fencerows and started to take some of the rocks. Richard told me I wasn't loading them fast enough into the bed of his truck. He said he was going to sit in the cab and I had ten minutes to gather more rocks. The slope was slightly muddy as I climbed up to the rock fence and I slipped. He laughed, called me a dirty name and drove off. I kept thinking he would come back but he didn't. I began to walk down that road, not knowing where it would end up. It began to get dark and I kept thinking he still would come back. He didn't. I walked and walked. I could hear the coyotes and the river running. It was so dark and I knew I had to try to stay on the road because the cliffs were on the north side with a hundred foot drop into the river. It began to get cold and I thought I could hear all kinds of critters. A couple of times I saw eyes glowing in the trees. Never thought of myself as a chicken but I was real scared that night. I walked for eleven miles to get home and when I got there, Richard was sitting on the front porch waiting. He said 'I'm hungry, cunt. Get inside and fix something to eat. And your kids have been wondering where you've been. I told them I didn't know so you had better let them know you are all right.' I walked in and checked on the kids, telling them that their dad had left me along that road. I told them I would have dinner in a little while. Oh, Lilly, the things I put those children through. I hope the Good Lord forgives me because I can't forgive myself."

Emma found more bittersweet and placed it in her bag. Lilly found another section where it grew abundantly. They gathered all the bittersweet they could and neither woman spoke for quite some time. Emma sat down on a rock along the side of the road and turned to Lilly, "Did I upset you Lilly? I thought you wanted stories from my past and maybe I have over shared. Sometimes I forget and I talk too much."

Lilly stopped and sat down on the side of the gravel road. "Emma, you haven't upset me. I think the more I get to know you, the more it saddens me to know of your life with Richard. I wish I could have known Rylie and Jim and I wish I could learn more about your whole family. But, by no means have you upset me."

Sam sat next to Lilly and licked her hands as she crossed them in her lap. She sat for a few minutes and then stood. Brushing off her jeans, she held her hand out to Emma to help her up. Emma took Lilly's hand and, as she stood, she said, "I was really scared that night on River Road. Richard had scared me plenty of times in my day but that was one of the worst, I do believe. My greatest fear was that I wouldn't make it home to my children and they would wonder why I had left them. I was scared."

An old, weathered Ford pickup came down the road. Emma motioned to Lilly to stay along the side and she held Sam. The truck drove past the two women, leaving a cloud of dust. Lilly could feel the grit from the gravel dust in her teeth. She tried to not take a breath until the air had cleared. Emma let go of Sam and he began to bark and run after the truck. He turned back around, appearing to be disgusted with the whole situation. Emma ran her hand over his tail. "Some new fella that moved in down the road. You can tell he isn't a local because he never waves and he doesn't slow down when he passes by. I took a plate of cookies down to his house to welcome him to the area. He just took them from me, never saying a word. Good thing I didn't really care for the plate cause he never brought it back. He has no respect for neighbors or the wildlife. I don't know if he has family or not. I never see anyone with him."

Emma and Lilly walked for quite some time, talking about the countryside and Emma's daily activities. Sam would occasionally scamper after something in the brush or chase a squirrel up a tree. Each time he would return to the women and either lick a hand or nudge them in request of a pat. After some time, Emma suggested they return to the house.

As they entered Emma's drive, Emma turned to Lilly and said, "Want to help me gather all of my fall decorations and we will put them out?"

Lilly enjoyed the thought of helping Emma decorate her home for the season. "I think that sounds like a perfect afternoon project."

Chapter 25

Emma and Lilly brought seven large plastic boxes up the basement stairs, each one full of decorations for fall and Halloween. Emma began to open the boxes and together Lilly and Emma decorated the house. As they opened the fourth box, Emma brought out a shiny ceramic skull head and ran her hand over it, "Jim's favorite Halloween decoration. It lights up. Good Lord, I can't tell you how old this thing is. I always put it on the sun porch and, when you are outside looking in, it does look mighty eerie. I put the pumpkins in the front window so as not to scare any little goblins that might visit. I remember the first year we moved out here and how disappointed the kids were that we didn't get any trick or treaters. But, we are so far out. Now folks from town bring their kids or grandkids out and some folks from church bring little ones so I have a few goblins that visit."

Emma filled a large basket with assorted gourds, bittersweet and silk leaves. She carried it to the entry and set it next to the antique washstand. Emma and Lilly spent nearly two hours decorating the house. After completing their work, they both stood back and admired each room. Emma turned to Lilly, "Now we decorate the porch."

Emma carried the last two boxes to the porch and opened them. Emma and Lilly strung lights in candy corn shapes and colors across the top of the porch. They continued to decorate until the final box was empty. Emma walked to the garden gate and stood facing the house. "She looks great, Lilly. Very nice." Lilly knew that Emma was referring to the house when she said 'she' just as she referred to her barn in the same manner. Lilly stood beside Emma and said, "I think we need to gather some of those corn stalks and put them on each side of the barn doors. How about it?"

Emma clapped her hands and laughed, "For a girl that does just the basic decorating at home, you sure are getting into this. Kinda fun, isn't it?"

Emma opened the gate and the two women, along with Sam, went into the field. They gathered stalks and carried them to the barn where they stood them against the barn door. Emma went inside the barn and came out with baling twine, "This should hold them together. Let's get this done and head into Lyndon to the EZ Rock Café for a bite. We'll stop while we are out and buy some pumpkins to add to all of this."

As if Sam understood the conversation, he ran towards the house, turning in circles occasionally and barking. Emma pointed her finger at him, "Sam, stop. You are staying here. And, when we get home, you are getting another bath."

With Emma's statement about a bath, Sam ran towards the baby pool, which still had some water in it from the night before. Emma ran to the side of the house shouting his name over and over. As Lilly watched their antics, she continued to be amazed at Emma's outlook on life after all she had been through. Lilly could hear Emma's contagious laugh and Sam's incessant barking. Lilly started to walk around to the side of the house to see if Emma needed help when Sam came running towards her. She could tell that he had been in the water and he was headed straight for Lilly with Emma in hot pursuit still shouting his name. Sam jumped up on Lilly, nearly knocking her down. He placed both muddy paws on her chest and licked her face.

Emma caught up with Sam and gave him a swat on his hind end. "Sam, what in Heaven's name is the matter with you? You have no manners anymore. I've got a good notion of setting you on the side of the road with a free sign around your neck. Good Lord."

Sam sat down next to Lilly, lowering his head in what appeared to be shame for his actions. Emma hugged his neck, "Sam, you're a hoot, I tell you. Never a dull moment. I never could stay mad at you with those big, brown eyes."

Lilly smiled and gave Sam a pat on the head, "Guess I will go in and change before we go to Lyndon."

Emma pulled off her cap, scratched her head and said, "I need to clean up a bit before we go. I do believe I've spent half my day dealing with dirt." She turned to Sam, "This isn't over, Mister. You are still getting a thorough cleaning when we get back."

Emma and Lilly changed their clothing and set off for Lyndon. Emma drove, all the while talking about her animals and her life in the country. She would occasionally refer to when the kids were young and to teenage parties at her home. She told Lilly that she usually kept it to parties outside with a bonfire and often the kids would set up tents and camp on the family land.

"I don't remember if I told you or not, Lilly, but Richard would not let the kids have many friends over. Maybe twice Jim was allowed and it wasn't until Kate approached her ninth birthday that he started wanting her friends to stay over. So, when we moved out here and they could have as many friends as they wanted, they had a good, old time. There are lots of memories at our little place. Lots of good memories. And I hope and pray the Lord lets me have many more.

Time to make more memories. Why, just think, Lilly, your wedding at my home will be an added memory. Gives me just one more thing to look forward to."

Lilly looked out the passenger window, "I look forward to that memory too. I will need your help and Kate's too. This is all new to me and with both of my parent's gone; it will be up to you and Kate to help me. David really doesn't care as long as we keep it simple. Neither one of us are into fancy, overdone weddings."

Emma turned into a gravel parking lot. The EZ Rock café was a small, pink building that resembled a diner in the 50's. When the two women stepped inside the door, they were greeted by a man dressed entirely in western wear, from his cowboy hat to his worn, scuffed cowboy boots. He tipped his hat and said, "Afternoon, ladies. You want the usual spot, Emma?"

Emma smiled and responded with "Yep, the usual."

The restaurant was decorated in 50's memorabilia and in the corner stood the grill of a 1956 Chevy that had been turned into a disc jockey station for karaoke nights. The cowboy led the women to a corner table. He placed menus on the table and smiled at Lilly. "Welcome to the EZ Rock, Miss. I don't believe I've seen you here before. Any friend of Emma's is a welcome guest here."

Lilly picked up a menu, smiled and said, "Thank you."

As the cowboy walked away from their table, Emma began to tell of the EZ Rock and its owners, Bill and Ellie. Lilly listened but, as she listened, she remembered Emma had told her that, in Emma's early years in Osage County, she chose to stay to herself but Lilly was learning that, even if Emma tried, she could not remain a stranger in this community. Small towns had very few secrets. Again, Lilly wondered how much these people knew of Emma's past. She knew Zeke Lang knew of Emma's past because he talked about his experience that night with Richard. But, who else knew and how much did they know? Lilly was sure Emma had tried to keep her past a secret and that she was ashamed of what she perceived as her weakness.

"Lilly?" Emma tapped Lilly's hand with her menu. "Are you still with me?"

"I'm here. Just thinking, Emma. I was just thinking."

Lilly picked up her menu and began to study it.

After a few minutes, a waitress with a very long, blonde ponytail came to the table, "Do you ladies know what you are having?"

Both women ordered and the waitress took their menus. Emma chatted with an occasional waitress or customer. Soon their food arrived and they enjoyed their meal.

After paying for the meals, Emma walked outside the door where she stopped for a moment. "Can you smell the leaves burning, Lilly? Now, you remember that is one of my favorites, don't you?"

"Yes, I remember. I can see why you enjoy it. Don't they have laws that require burn permits here?"

Emma smiled. "In Topeka they have burn permits and some of these smaller towns also have them. Another reason I am glad I live in the country is the fact that I don't need permission to burn my leaves. Have I told you about the time I set the old chicken house on fire when I moved into my place? That was a time when I should have asked permission, that's for sure."

Emma opened her car door and motioned for Lilly to get inside the car. They began to head back to Emma's farm and Emma told her story. "I hadn't been in the house long when I decided the chicken house was an eyesore and had to go. So, Jim and I set off to set that thing on fire. I had no idea that chicken poop would ignite like it did. Jim ran and grabbed the garden hose and I stood there in shock that I had set such a fire. It wasn't long and the Carbondale Fire Department arrived. Jim stood and talked to them after they had put out the fire. I think he was embarrassed that his momma had caused such a ruckus. I went in the house and brought out cookies and we all sat and had a real nice visit. I don't know how many folks he told that story to. We had trees that nearly died because the fire was so hot. Rylie and Jim had to cut the dead off those trees and that was nearly five years after we had set the fire. Jim said he was taking my matches away from me after that night. It became our little joke. Heck of a way to make an entrance when you move into a community, let me tell you."

Emma turned into a drive leading to a large, red barn. Several cattle stood at the gate watching as Emma's car drove past. Lilly wished she had brought her camera. The leaves on the oak trees were beautiful in their fall colors. At the end of the drive stood a small white cottage with bright evergreen shutters. Its porch was filled with every size pumpkin one could imagine. Emma stopped the car and turned to Lilly. "Let's get those pumpkins we talked about. It looks like Levi isn't home so we will leave our money in the box."

Emma and Lilly walked onto the porch. Two large gray cats greeted them. Emma knocked on the door. "Levi? Anybody home?" she said.

Lilly admired the pumpkins. Emma walked to the side of the house and came back with a child's red wagon. "Let's load up and get these pumpkins home."

They gathered four pumpkins into the wagon and took them to Emma's car. Lilly assumed they were finished but Emma returned to the porch and looked back at Lilly standing by the car. "You don't think we are going to settle for just those four, do you? We need some to carve later on for Halloween."

Lilly looked at Emma and seemed somewhat surprised at Emma's remark. "Do you still carve pumpkins, Emma?"

Emma laughed. "Well, don't look so surprised. Even an old bird can carve a pumpkin. There's no law that says you have to stop at a certain age when it comes to carving pumpkins and having fun, is there?"

Lilly walked onto the porch and picked up a large white pumpkin. "I want to carve this one. Well, that is, if I am around close to Halloween."

Emma waved her arms in the air. "Good Lord, you should know by now that you are welcome at my place any time. I want you to know that you are also welcome to take that pumpkin home and carve him for your own home."

Lilly set the large, white pumpkin in the wagon and said; "I'll leave it at your place, Emma. That gives me an excuse to come back the end of October. Maybe we can carve pumpkins together."

Emma began to pull the wagon towards the car. "That sounds like one heck of a deal. I usually have at least one grandkid that stops in to carve a pumpkin and waits for the seeds to come out of the oven. We may just make a party of it when the time comes."

The trunk of the car was full of pumpkins. Emma walked back to the porch and placed her money in a small box on the stair rail. As she closed the box, she gave it a pat on the lid, turned and ran her hand across one of the cat's tail and walked to the car.

She started the engine and turned to Lilly. "I'm ready to take these home and finish our decorating. Now don't forget Sam needs that bath too. Good Lord, this day seems like it has gone on forever. I think"

Before Emma could finish, Lilly's cell phone began to ring. "Hello." There was a pause and Lilly responded to the caller. "We have been decorating for fall and Halloween and we are just finishing a big purchase of pumpkins and taking them back to the house. What are you doing?" Another pause. "Oh, that sounds wonderful, David. Let me ask Emma."

Lilly turned to Emma and with an almost childlike face she asked, "David wants to know if this evening would be all right to come here and then he would spend part of tomorrow with us. May he?"

Emma's eyes widened. "Oh, Good Lord, I need to get home and clean the house. I'll need to give Sam that bath. What shall we have for dinner? Oh, Lilly, listen to me. Yes, yes, he is welcome. I had better get home and get busy."

Lilly told David that he was welcome at Emma's home, hung up and turned to Emma. "Emma, please don't fuss over things. David is no trouble and your home looks just fine."

Emma scoffed. "We've got all that mess out from decorations. All those plastic tubs and Sam shook mud all over the porch. And I'll need to put clean towels out and" Emma paused, "Listen to me. I think I sound like my mother when she knew company was coming. She wanted her house to look nice for folks when they came but I know a lot of this stems from years of living with Richard and he made sure I kept our house spotless at all times. I don't know how many times I would stay up all night because he thought the house wasn't to his specifications. Oh, Good Lord. That reminds me of when he wouldn't let me take both children to Sunday School because he was guaranteed that I wouldn't leave him if one child was left behind. He would insist that on Sunday mornings I had the house in order and a meal in the oven or crock-pot so that he could be fed at precisely noon. I would usually sneak out of church early in order to be home by noon. Then, as Kate grew older, I just quit going because I did not want to leave her alone with him on Sunday mornings."

Lilly rolled her window down slightly. "I will help you with everything you need to do. And, besides, I think your house looks great. We will clean up those storage tubs and give Sam a bath. Don't worry about your house. But, if it will make you feel better, I will help you clean or do whatever you need. David won't be in until around seven so we have plenty of time."

Emma seemed relieved with Lilly's suggestion. They drove home and unloaded their pumpkins and finished the chores. Lilly was brave enough to give Sam a bath while Emma prepared dinner.

When Lilly came into the house with Sam and Gracie at her side, the dining table was set for royalty. Emma had placed a beautiful set of dishes on the table and candles were lit. Fresh linen napkins and a tablecloth were also part of the setting. Emma had taken some of her bittersweet and made an arrangement for the center of the table along with some of her fall decorations.

Emma wiped her hands on a kitchen towel and stood next to the dining table. "Does it look all right? Haven't had dinner guests except for you for a long time. I want David to like it here."

Lilly ran her hand over the linen tablecloth and looked at the gleaming dishes. The candlelight reflected off the dishes and stemware. She could smell all of the mouth-watering fragrances coming from Emma's kitchen. "It is lovely, Emma. He will enjoy such special treatment."

Before Lilly could speak another word, Sam began to bark and she noticed headlights coming up Emma's drive. She was so anxious to have Emma and David meet. Sam ran to the front door and Lilly let him out.

Chapter 26

Sam continued to bark and run in circles as Lilly and Emma came onto the front porch. David's dark blue jeep came to a stop and the door opened. Emma held Sam as Lilly walked to the Jeep to greet David. Emma watched as they embraced and came towards the house. David was much taller than Lilly. He had a full salt and pepper beard. His black hair was also graying at the temples and, when he smiled at Emma, she noticed that his eyes were a deep gray. He was distinguished yet rugged and Emma felt at ease with him immediately.

Lilly introduced Emma and David and, when Emma extended her hand, David reached over and hugged her. "Emma, I've heard so much about you. This is such a pleasure. Lilly is quite impressed, let me tell you."

David's gesture seemed to embarrass Lilly. She wondered why he was not more respectful of Emma. She looked over at Emma to see Emma's response to his hug.

Emma seemed to blush. "Can't imagine being impressed with this old bird but I will take that as a mighty fine compliment. Have you eaten? I've got dinner on the stove. Come on in."

Lilly was relieved that Emma seemed fine with David's casual hug. David and Lilly followed Emma into the house. David held the door for Sam and Gracie. Emma turned around and in her most serious voice ordered both dogs to stay in the living room. Lilly was surprised when they both did as Emma told them to.

David admired Emma's table and how beautiful her home was and how warm and inviting she had made it. He asked about the homes history. Emma continued to answer his questions as she carried food to the table. Lilly offered to help but Emma insisted Lilly and David sit at the table. Emma finished bringing out the food and joined them at the table. She smiled and asked David if he would say the blessing. He smiled and bowed his head. "Dear Lord, thank you for the food we are about to receive. I ask that you bestow many blessings on Emma and her household. Amen."

Emma passed the green beans and said, "David, thank you for saying that prayer. My Rylie was so shy when it came to asking the Lord's blessing. He just stuttered and stammered and we finally agreed that I was in charge of the praying. I had no idea I would be on my knees in prayer so much later on in my life. I have begged the Lord for strength and I have begged Him for mercy. But, enough on that subject. You kids fill your plates and let's enjoy our meal."

As Emma and her guests ate their meal, Sam and Gracie began to ease across the living room floor on their bellies. Gracie stopped at the edge of the rug while Sam continued until he was next to Lilly. When Sam sat up next to Lilly, Emma realized what was happening and scolded Sam. "Sam, what are you doing over there? Are you being a bad dog? Gracie May, are you trying to ease into the dining room? What did I tell both of you?"

David chuckled. Emma frowned and then smiled. "Blasted animals. They certainly keep me on my toes. Rylie always looked forward to the day we didn't have animals in the house. Said I could have new furniture and new braided rugs in each room when they were all gone. I'm still waiting. I know full good and well that I will always have critters around. They keep me company. Heck, Rylie talked to them more than I did and he even grilled little cheeseburgers for Hootie. She would sit and wait until he was finished grilling and then he would let hers cool off a little and then serve it up for her. She lost a few pounds when Rylie went on to be with the Lord because I would not grill for her." Emma sat silent and seemed to go back in time for a moment and then said "That Rylie. You would have liked him, David. He was a fine man, my Rylie."

David set his fork down and wiped the corners of his mouth with Emma's linen napkin. "I also wish I could have met him. You will have to tell me stories and then, through your stories, I will know Rylie. Lilly tells me what a pleasure it is visiting with you here at your farm. She's fallen in love with this area. I look forward to having you show me around while I am here."

Emma lightly slapped the table. "I look forward to both. I can spin a yarn, that's for sure. Just ask my grandchildren. And I love showing folks where I planted my roots. You know, David, Lilly is talking about having your wedding here at the farm. What's your take on that idea?"

David reached over and took Lilly's hand. "I trust Lilly's judgment. She has truly fallen in love with this place so I am sure it will be a perfect setting. I look forward to seeing it in daylight."

Emma buttered another roll. "I can do you one better than waiting till daylight. I can show you our wedding pictures and that will give you a vague idea of what you two can do with this place. Of course, we didn't have the wedding here, just the reception. That's what we can do! I'll show you Kate's wedding pictures too. And I even have videos."

Emma took a bite of her roll and pinched off a piece, motioning for Gracie to come to her side. She gave Gracie the piece of roll. "Good Lord, listen to me go on. You might not even want to see pictures and videos. Don't let me bully you. You just tell me when you've had enough. Lilly, what do you think we should do this evening?"

Lilly took a sip of her tea and set her glass on the dining table. "I really don't have a plan. We will all just have to brainstorm and come up with something. I would like to take David out to the barn and show him around."

"Oh, Heavens, Lilly. Of course David needs to meet all of the critters and see the barn. I'll clean up after dinner and you two can take a walk out to the barn till I catch up. Sam will show you around. Right Sam?"

Emma bent down and looked under the dining table to catch a glimpse of Sam sitting next to Lilly. He lowered his head and looked back at Emma under the tablecloth.

Emma and her guests finished their meal. David and Lilly discussed the idea of their wedding at Emma's farm. David asked many questions about Emma and her family and Emma seemed at ease telling him about them.

After finishing their meal, David, Lilly and Sam went to the barn and Emma cleared the table and cleaned the kitchen. She put the leftovers in small plastic containers, labeled each and placed them in the refrigerator. After finishing, she invited Gracie to join her in the barn.

Lilly and David were standing near the horse stalls when Emma and Gracie entered the barn. Pie began to nay and Gracie chased a cat out of the barn. Emma walked up to Pie and kissed his forehead and he nuzzled against her neck. Emma giggled and kissed him again. She turned to Lilly. "What all have you shown our guest? Has he met Sally too? Did you tell him about the barn? Did you have enough light because I can turn on some more lights if need be."

David watched Emma. He wondered where the scar under her eye that ran to her temple came from. He guessed it was probably a horseback accident or farm accident. Emma's love for her animals intrigued David. She carried licorice in her jacket pocket and produced it to the horses. Pie was eager to take the entire stick of licorice where Sally took it gently and would bite off a portion at a time. Emma would occasionally run her hand across their manes and talk gently to them. She turned to David and handed him a piece of licorice. "Here, David. Feed some to the horses. Have you been around horses? Lilly and I will have to take you for an early morning horseback ride. Nothing like a ride on a nice, brisk fall morning. Rylie and I did that quite often. I hope you and Lilly enjoy as many good times as my Rylie and I had. Our lives are so short, David. You need to live for today."

Emma took Pie by his halter. "He won't hurt you. Just hand him his treat." Gracie barked just as David handed Pie the candy. David jumped and Lilly laughed.

Emma laughed and sat on a square bale of hay. Sam and Gracie sat next to her. She pointed her finger at David and said, "Don't let the horse know you are afraid. They can sense that. These two are so tame. I think Pie would sit in my lap like some old hound dog if I would let him. Never let them know, David. Lord knows I know how to hide my fears."

David sat on a hay bale across from Emma and Lilly stood beside him, placing her hand on his shoulder. David rested his elbows on his knees and leaned in towards Emma. "What do you mean by that, Emma?"

"I did my best to hide my fears from my children, Richard." Emma paused and leaned on a post behind the stack of bales. "Richard was my first husband. I don't know if Lilly has mentioned him but he caused a great deal of fear in this old bird. Anyway, I tried to hide my fears from him and my kids and even my own family and friends. There was one night I came out here to the barn. I had recently filed a Motion to Modify Child Support because my attorney advised me to. Jim was into his teens and times were hard. Richard had threatened me and said I would pay for going after his money. I came out here to the barn. I no more hit the door than I fell on my knees right over there in that empty stall. I was crying so hard and asking the Lord to please protect my babies and me. I prayed for financial relief. I laid my head on a bale of hay and sobbed. I heard someone come into the barn and I turned to see my dear sweet Jim standing next to me. He knelt down beside me and said, 'Mom, why do you pray to a God that hasn't helped you at all? After what we have been through, how can you believe?'

"I turned to him and patted him on the cheek. I said 'I would rather serve my God here on earth and die to find out He didn't exist than to not serve God here on earth and die to find out He did exist. I don't want to spend eternity in Hell, Jim and I certainly don't want you and your sister to.'

"Jim pulled his Yankees hat off and said, 'Mom, why did you marry dad? He is an Atheist and has made life so miserable for us. You did not share the same beliefs or interests. Did you ever love him?'

Emma sat on the edge of the bale and leaned in close to David. Lilly sat beside him, eager to hear Emma's response to Jim's question. Lilly was pleased that Emma had opened up to David, a total stranger. She had hoped Emma would be at ease with David and it was a bittersweet pleasure to see Emma share her life with David. Emma shook her head and said, "You never want to tell your child that there was no love between their father and you. I was as honest as I dared be with that boy. I said 'Jim, I did love your dad at one time. We were so young when we married and I truly thought I loved him. And, I did love him but, as the years went by and the abuse became worse, the love went away. I am so thankful you came along. And then your sister. But, in the same breath, I wish I had not made you a part of such a sad situation. I do believe that your dad wanted to love you as best he could. He wasn't taught love and therefore he himself didn't know how to love.'

"Jim stood up and seemed a little angry and said 'Don't make excuses for him, Mom. He has chosen to be the man he is. Don't ever make excuses for him. I know you are afraid of him and his threats. I will take care of you but someday I will be gone with a home of my own and who will take care of you then? Who, Mom?'

"I didn't know how to answer my son. It was not his responsibility to protect me and I hated that he felt he needed to. His friends say that he lived with Rylie, Kate and I until he was twenty two because he wanted to make sure Rylie was going to be able to take care of us. Rylie had some mighty big shoes to fill in that young man."

Emma picked at the twine around the hay bale. "Jim came home one day with a shirt he had bought and we lived by that motto each day. It said 'A Life Lived in Fear is a Life Half Lived'. Now, isn't that it in a nutshell, I tell you?"

Pie began to whinny and Emma stood up and walked towards his stall. David and Lilly sat silently, taking in all that Emma had said. It was David that broke the silence. "A Life Lived in Fear is a Life Half Lived. Give me some of that licorice, Emma."

Emma smiled and handed David two pieces of licorice. "You'll feel more comfortable with them after you ride them tomorrow. I promise. Let's get all these critters settled in for the night and go inside. Lilly, do you want to show David the routine or shall I?"

Lilly was still very solemn, still thinking about Emma and Jim. Still thinking about the fact that the petite, yet sturdy woman beside her had faced such sorrow and yet she remained strong and positive. "I think all three of us should do the honors."

Emma cut open a bale of hay with a utility knife and handed the knife to David. "Then all three shall share the chores. Show David where the llamas are and I will feed the horses and lock up the chicken house. Let's get the job done, kids. We're wasting time."

Chapter 27

A light drizzle began to come down as Emma, Lilly and David finished the chores. As they walked towards the house, the fall lights were glistening on Emma's porch. Two cats sat next to the pumpkins that lined the steps. Lilly pointed to the cats. "Look at their eyes. That black cat looks like a Halloween statue with her green eyes glowing. Oh, Emma, we really did do a good job, didn't we?"

Emma put the hood up on her jacket and then turned to Lilly, the hood covering her right side of her face and eye. "We did one heck of a job. It was nice to have someone help me too. Look at those tiny candy corn lights."

Emma turned to David and Lilly and said, "You young folks probably think this old bird is crazy. Here I am out in the country and I decorate my house. But, you know, if it brightens only one person's day, then it was worth the work of putting it up. And, look, it has already brightened our day."

They walked through the gate and onto the steps. Sam stood outside the gate and began to bark. David walked back to the gate and opened it for Sam. Emma tapped Sam on his nose with her index finger. "You need to keep up, Mister, or that's what happens. You almost got left out for the night, didn't you? Good thing David opened the gate. Now, wipe your paws before you come in."

Sam sat on the rug outside the front door and Emma took each paw and wiped it on the rug. Gracie stood patiently waiting her turn. David chuckled and Lilly nudged him with her elbow. He turned to her and raised his shoulders as if questioning why she had nudged him.

Emma opened the door and motioned for her guests to enter. She took off her jacket and hung it on the hall tree. Lilly and David wiped their feet and then Lilly decided to take her shoes off and set them next to the front door. She knew Emma took pride in how her home looked and she remembered that Emma had worried about David seeing the house in what Emma perceived as a mess.

Emma walked towards the kitchen. "Anyone want some cider, iced tea, coffee? Name your poison."

"Oh, cider sounds wonderful." Lilly said and David smiled in agreement.

Lilly and David heard Emma rattle some dishes and call to them from the kitchen, "Cider it is. Make yourselves at home. Lilly, show David around. This won't take me long."

Lilly took David upstairs and showed him around and they then came back downstairs. They began to look at the pictures of Emma's family when David noticed a large jar with marbles in it. The lid read "Count Your Blessings". David turned to Lilly and asked her what the jar meant. She responded, "I don't know. I just assumed it was decorative and never noticed the lid."

Emma walked into the room, carrying an antique serving tray with mugs of cider. Lilly pointed to the jar, "Emma, is there a story to this jar of marbles?"

Emma set the tray on the coffee table and motioned for them to have a seat. "Well, not many folks know about my marble jar and what it means to me. You see, when I was diagnosed with lymphoma, my doctors said three years was the most they could give me to live. That is one thousand ninety five days. So, I went and bought one thousand ninety five marbles and filled this old jar. Each day I take out a marble and throw it away. I throw it outside as far as I can. That is to remind me not to waste a single day. My boys weren't given a time frame on how long they had here on earth. No time to say good-bye or do all the things they wanted to do in life. I've been given a chance, a two-minute warning like they do in those football games. If I throw the last marble away and make it another day, then I beat those doctors' odds and, if I don't make it to another day and I still have marbles left, then I lived each of those days to the very fullest. That's all a person can ask, isn't it? That is why I have a marble jar." She took a sip of her cider.

Lilly fought to hold back her tears as she listened to Emma. David continued to look at the floor. Emma shook her index finger at her two friends. "Don't you two look so gloomy. Why, I've had more blessings than a lot of folks. I've been blessed with wonderful children and my Rylie was a gem. And now I have been blessed with a grandson that carries my son's name. I love my stepchildren and step-grandchildren. I have wonderful friends and such loyal critters. Don't the neither of you pity me. Why, I've seen doctors wrong plenty of times. Who's to say they know how long I really have? Now, drink your cider before it gets cold."

Gracie sat close to Emma, nuzzling against her leg. Sam stretched out on the living room rug. David thought about what a peaceful setting it was. His thoughts continued to go back to the previous conversation and Emma's outlook on life and death. He was so anxious to see her homestead and hear more about her. Lilly continued to sit silently and drink her cider. It was Emma that broke the silence. "Lilly Ballard, are you going to clam up all night? We're here to show our guest a good time. Shall we watch old home movies or look at albums? Lilly, what shall we do this evening?"

Lilly forced a smile and turned to David. "Anything in particular you wanted to do tonight?"

"I'm thinking the pictures and videos sound like a good idea. I would like to put faces with names." David took a final sip of his cider and leaned back on the sofa. "Tell me all about your family as we go, Emma."

Lilly knew that this would please Emma. Emma went to the bookcase and produced four photo albums and then took three videos from the video cabinet. She handed David the albums and started to sit on the floor next to him. David stood up, "No, no. You sit here on the sofa and I'll take the floor."

Emma didn't argue which somewhat surprised Lilly. She sat on the sofa and opened the first album. Just as she had done with Lilly, she began to point to each picture and tell David all about her children. David was focused on Emma's every word. Lilly sat and watched all the different emotions flood across Emma's face. It was as if she would go back in time as she looked at her children's baby pictures and told David all about their childhoods and their personalities.

The three friends looked at pictures and watched videos until late. Emma looked at the antique clock on the mantel. "Good Lord, look at the time. I'm going to head off to bed. You two are welcome to any thing in the kitchen and you can stay up and watch videos or look at albums and journals or all three things, if you like. I can't keep up with you young folks like I used to. I used to stay up with Kate all hours when she would come home on a break from college but those days are long gone. Sometimes Miss Taylor and I will have a slumber party and watch movies until late but not very often. I just can't keep up anymore. So, I guess what I am saying as I babble on, is you stay up as late as you would like. I will see you in the morning. I am thinking we should eat breakfast out. How's that sound to you?"

Lilly nodded her head in agreement and said "Corner Café?"

Emma turned off the kitchen light and picked Gracie up. "You bet." She carried Gracie with her and told Sam to behave.

"See you in the morning, Emma," David said.

Emma gave a backward wave and said, "Good Lord willing. Sweet dreams to both of you."

After Emma retired for the evening, Lilly went to the bookcase and brought back two more photo albums and some of Emma's journals. David took one of the journals and they sat next to one another and read:

December 23rd Richard left for a party this evening. I am sure Jim and I will be alone all night. The quiet is wonderful and the two of us are just sitting under the tree enjoying the lights and Christmas music. Jim loves the lights and ornaments. He has been so good about leaving the tree alone. Of course, he isn't even two yet. I can't imagine him going through the terrible two's. He's too good a baby to be "terrible". I wish Richard would never come home. I wonder which woman he will go home with tonight.

Richard says I can't go to my folks' house with Jim because it isn't safe to travel alone with a young child yet he won't go with me. I am going to go anyway and I will still be home later tomorrow to have Christmas alone with him. His parents will be here the day after Christmas.

December 24th: 9:00 AM—Richard has decided to go with us to Mom and Dad's. I think he cracked one of my ribs this morning because I am having trouble each time I take a breath or when I pick up Jim. It really hurts. I think he is afraid I will try to stay in St. Joseph if he lets me go alone. We will be back home tonight because he hates it at my parents' house. Calls them the crazy Holy Rollers. He keeps saying there is no God, there is no Christmas.

11:22PM—Richard has gone to bed and I am putting out the "Santa" presents. I just checked in on Jim. He looks so sweet and peaceful. I can't imagine life without him. My sweet baby boy. I hate that Richard is his father. What a fool I am. I'm coughing up blood but I think it will be fine. I've been through a lot worse and I need to stay well and strong for Jim. If Richard EVER hurts him, I think I would kill him. I guess these aren't very good Christmas thoughts, are they journal?

December 25th—Merry Christmas. I came downstairs with Jim to see what Santa brought. He is having such a good day. Richard is in having his coffee. I am sure he will want a large breakfast even though we are having a large Christmas dinner.

10:20 PM—Jim is sleeping. He had such a good day. He and I played all afternoon with his new toys while Richard watched football. I just finished getting the house clean for Richard's family tomorrow. I hope everyone gets along and has a nice visit. If I can keep all of them happy, maybe he won't make me suffer his "consequences" after they leave. Maybe.

December 30th—Sorry I haven't been able to write. I had to try to keep all of his family happy and him too. They did make over Jim and gave him some really nice gifts. Richard only hit me once while they were here. He will be going to a New Year's party tomorrow night so I will have some quiet time. But, I hate to think that he will come home after drinking and want to be with me. Maybe he will find someone there he would rather be with. Maybe he won't come home. Who am I kidding? Alcohol has nothing to do with whether he is nice or not. The only thing it does do is make him think all women want him even more than when he is sober. I wish I could leave.

David stopped reading. "Lilly, did you know all of this? How bad was it? Did you know?"

Lilly ran her fingers through her hair and held it in a makeshift ponytail. "Yes, I know most of what she went through. Or, at least a portion. It is much worse than this, David. Much worse."

David stood up, still holding the journal. "How could this happen? Why didn't you warn me about what she had been through? She's such a positive, sweet woman. Oh, God, how do these things happen?"

Lilly stood up and wrapped her arms around David's waist and looked him in the eye. "Emma is in hopes that, by telling her story, other women will realize they don't have to live like she did. They can get out of the abusive situation."

David leaned forward and rested his forehead against Lilly's. "She's so strong. What a crock this all is. She deserves better, Lilly. Anyone deserves better than that. What if she is right and all she has is the time left in the marble jar? She's missed so much in her life."

Lilly placed her hand gently over David's lips. "Don't ever think Emma has missed out in life. She would argue that with you. She was blessed with wonderful children as she told you earlier and Rylie thought the sun rose and set in that woman. What few years they had were good ones. She would not want pity from you, David."

Lilly took her hand away from David's mouth and took the journal from him and said, "As far as the marble jar, I don't want to think or talk about it. She will run out of marbles long before she runs out of time. She has to."

Lilly and David placed the albums and journals back into their places of storage and carried their cider mugs into the kitchen. Sam followed every step. Lilly turned to David, "I think Sam is spending the night with us. He's my best bud now that we have shared bath time together. Come on, Sam, let's call it a night."

David spent half the night awake thinking of Emma. He wondered what he and Lilly could do to help her around the farm on more than a temporary basis. He knew Lilly had grown fond of Emma and he could totally understand why. Maybe a good sleep would give him a fresh mind to tackle this. David always wanted to make things better. Seems like Emma mentioned Rylie was one to try to make things better. David thought some more. Yes, he surely could do something to make her life easier. He would talk to Lilly in the morning.

Chapter 28

David awoke to the sound of the front door closing. He sat up on the side of the bed and looked out the lace curtains. Emma and Gracie were walking towards the barn.

David slipped on his jeans and boots and grabbed his jacket, heading for the front door. As he put one arm into his jacket, he opened the gate with the other and called out to Emma. "Emma! Wait up."

Emma turned around and smiled, "Morning, David. You're up early. How did you sleep?"

"I slept very well, thank you. Where's Lilly?"

Emma opened the barn door. "The last I saw of her, she was heading for the shower. That girl makes no bones about wanting her breakfast. She wants to be ready when the bus leaves, let me tell you. Reminds me of my Kate. Are you up to helping me with the chores?"

David ran his hand across Pie's mane. "I'm looking forward to it. Where shall we start?"

Emma walked towards three large plastic drums. She took the lid off each and scooped out the grain with a large scoop. She handed David the scoop. "Put a full scoop in each feeder. Then we will put hay out for them."

Emma walked towards the back of the barn. She looked around, "Dog, dog! she called. A doghouse sat in the corner of the stall. David could see dog inside the doghouse, not moving.

Emma knelt on her knees and looked into the doghouse. "God bless his soul. He's passed on."

She turned to David with huge tears welling up in her eyes. "David, will you join me in burying my dear friend? We should let Lilly know. I'll get a shovel. In the laundry room is a shelf with old quilts and blankets. Please choose something for him."

Emma reached inside the doghouse and lifted Dog's body. She kissed his head and whispered in his ear. David turned to go to the house.

Lilly met David at the door, her hair in a towel. "Are we ready for breakfast?"

David kissed her on the cheek. "No, babe. Emma's suffered another loss today. Dog passed away in his sleep in the night. We need to bury him."

Lilly covered her mouth and felt the tears burning her eyes. "No, no. Not sweet little playful Dog. Oh, Sam and Gracie will miss him. How can we help? What do you need me to do?"

David walked towards the laundry room. "Emma said there are blankets and quilts on a shelf in the laundry area. We are to choose a special one for Dog. She is getting a shovel and I am guessing we need to get out there."

Lilly ran her hands across the blankets and quilts. She pulled out a tattered quilt. Some of the patches were done in colors of the earth and others had a fabric with cats and dogs on it. Lilly turned to David and held the quilt out. "How about his one?"

David looked at the quilt. "Is it too tattered?"

Lilly ran her hand over the quilt again. "It's been loved and used. Let's see what Emma says."

Lilly put on her sweater and they carried the quilt out to the pet cemetery. Emma sat on the railroad ties that lined the cemetery. She held Dog in her arms. She looked up as Lilly and David approached. "What did you pick out for this fella?"

Lilly held out the tattered quilt. Emma ran her hand across it. "Perfect. I made this some forty years ago with fabrics from some old clothes and an old fall tablecloth. Perfect."

David reached for the shovel. "Where do you want him buried, Emma?"

Emma pointed and said, "Right here next to Raider. So many kind souls rest here."

David began to dig. Emma wrapped Dog in the quilt. "I need to run in the house. I'll be right back."

David continued to dig and Lilly sat on the railroad tie, tears running down her cheeks. She couldn't remember a time she had grieved for an animal but things were different here at Emma's. Emma's animals were her family. Emma had taught Lilly so much about appreciating life.

Emma came towards Lilly, holding out a fork in her right hand. Emma slid the fork into the quilt around Dog's body, patting him and said, "The best is yet to come, Dog."

Emma lifted the beagle's small body and placed him in the grave. After suggesting that they each take a turn filling in the grave, Emma said a prayer.

When the three friends had completed the burial, with Gracie and Sam by their sides, Lilly turned to Emma. "Emma, what do you mean 'The best is yet to come' and why the fork?"

Emma slid her arm into Lilly's. "As a girl growing up and even now at church functions, the church ladies always say as they are taking your plate,

'Keep your fork, the best is yet to come'. I've always known that it meant a wonderful dessert was about to be set before me. So, I always bury my critters and my loved ones with a fork. My, isn't it nice to know that when we leave this old world that the best is yet to come?"

Lilly patted Emma's hand. "And, do you want the same for yourself? Do you want a fork, Emma?"

Emma laughed. "Heavens, yes. My family has saved a place for me at the Lord's table and I want to be ready. The best is yet to come."

Emma touched Lilly's damp hair. "You need to get inside and get that mane of hair dry if we are going to make it to the Corner Café. You and David go on inside. I need a few minutes out here to spend some time alone and finish the rest of the chores. Just some time alone. Now, get going, you two."

David squeezed Emma's shoulders as he walked past her and set the shovel against the barn. He turned and smiled at Emma. "Call if you need us."

"I'll be fine. I'll have to call the kids and grandkids when we get home from breakfast and let them know. He always went hunting with the grandsons. Now, go on." Emma walked back into the barn, and then turned to the pet cemetery. Gracie continued to sit by the freshly dug grave. "Gracie May, are you staying out here? Don't linger long."

As David and Lilly walked back to the house, Lilly began to sob uncontrollably. David stopped and held her in his arms. "She'll be fine, Lil. She has such an outlook on all of this. I've never seen anyone accept death like Emma."

Lilly buried her face in David's collar. "I can't imagine what this place would be like without Emma. She has to outlive the marbles, David. Emma needs to see this new grandson grow into a man. It's all so unfair. Why Emma?'

"I don't know why Emma. Some people have more than their share of grief. But you know she is fine with whatever comes. That grandson will know Emma. His mother will tell him all about her and you need to write all of Emma's stories down. He will have pictures, her journals, her videos."

Lilly pulled away from David in anger. "It's not the same. You know that. This family needs Emma. It's not fair, David."

"I know, Lil. I know it isn't fair. Let's get ready. You know she'll want to get to breakfast and back home to tell the kids. Go dry your hair."

David and Lilly went inside. Lilly went to dry her hair and David stood looking at all of Emma's family pictures. He picked up a picture of Emma and Rylie with all of their children and three of the grandchildren. He studied each face.

Emma opened the front door. David turned, still holding the picture in his hand. Emma pulled off her jacket. She smiled and used the toe of her right foot to grip the back of her left boot and pulled it off. She then did the same with the other boot. She pointed to the picture in David's hand. "Fine looking crew, huh David?"

"A very fine bunch, indeed. I look forward to meeting all of them someday soon."

Emma took the picture and held it in both hands as if to cradle a small infant. "I'm glad Kate has Conner now. Did Lilly tell you that I am going out to Denver to see all of them in just a few days?"

"I think one of you mentioned that. I'm sure you are looking forward to that."

Lilly came downstairs. "Are we ready?"

Emma laughed. "Sounds like we had better get this woman fed. Who's driving?"

David took his keys out of his pocket and rattled them in the air.

Emma set the picture down and put on her tennis shoes that were beside the door. She slipped one arm into her jacket and David helped her with the other arm. "I'll give you directions, David. Does that mean I can call shot-gun?"

Lilly placed her camera in her bag and looked puzzled. "Shotgun?"

David kissed Lilly's cheek. "It means Emma wants the front seat. You're in back."

Lilly shrugged her shoulders and mumbled "Shotgun. Never heard such a thing."

Chapter 29

Emma and Lilly convinced David over breakfast to stay through the weekend and attend church with Emma on Sunday. Emma promised horseback rides, visits with some of the locals and trips throughout the countryside and to the cemetery.

Lilly took several pictures of Emma with some of the local people at the café. David enjoyed watching Emma and her friends, listening to local stories and just the refreshing view of a small community.

As they were driving back to Emma's home, Lilly asked if David would stop the jeep and let her out to take a few pictures. Cattle grazed in a pasture nearby and Lilly took several pictures of them. She also enjoyed taking pictures of the barn in the background as it leaned towards the ground with its weathered barn boards.

Emma mentioned an old farmhouse that was vacant and asked if Lilly would like to take pictures of it. Lilly accepted the offer. Emma gave David directions to the old farm. As they came upon the abandoned house, Lilly felt sadness that such a beautiful home had been forsaken. The two-story home no longer had windows of glass. What once had been a front porch now leaned and only a few floorboards remained. Only an eyebrow window on the second floor still had glass in it. Vandals had painted 'bake sale' on the second story. Lilly took out her camera and began to take pictures.

Emma stood leaning against a porch post. "Poor old man Mills lived here up until the day he died. His kids all lived in the city, some in California and one in Minnesota. This old place had probably been paid for several times over. If they didn't want the place, they should have at least sold it to someone who did. But, no, they've let it sit here for the last ten to fifteen years and just rot away. That's my biggest fear. That our kids will let our place just sit there with not a soul caring to either live there or sell it. Kate has promised that won't happen but I still have that fear. I think I would have to come back and haunt them all if that happened."

David stepped onto the porch and reached for the door. Emma followed him. "Watch out for coons, skunks, you know, things that seek refuge inside old places like this. And, watch your step. This place is pretty shaky. I'll bet Rylie is turning over in his grave right now. He used to get on to me when I would do this sort of thing. 'Emma Jean, that's trespassing, don't you know?' he'd say. These Mills kids have given me permission to snoop about the place. Heck, I tried for three years to keep the flowers watered and free of weeds. One day I called those kids asking them what they wanted me to do with the flowers and the stuff left inside this place. They told me to dig up whatever flowers I wanted and take whatever I wanted. They didn't want to come back here. Breaks my heart to this day."

David held the screen door for Emma and Lilly. Sunlight came in through the bay window in the living room casting light on the old oak floors. Lilly could see the kitchen from the living room. Cabinet doors had been torn from their hinges, revealing dusty, empty cabinets with a floral patterned shelf paper. A large farmhouse sink stood proudly on one wall with a skirt still around the bottom.

Emma turned to Lilly and said, "I haven't been inside in a long time. Don't know if the stairs will hold us. I will leave it to your discretion. If you get up there, Lilly, you need to take pictures. It will break you heart. His clothes are still in the closet; the beds are still there. Most folks know to respect this place but those that aren't from these parts don't care. Vandals painted that sign on the outside of the place a year ago. I boxed up his Bible and paperwork and sent it to his kids in California. Never heard a word from them on that. I'm glad I sent it certified mail. At least that way I knew it made it to his family. Can't imagine not caring enough to even take care of your family's belongings. But, you never know what sort of father he was. We'll never know. Some folks say he was too hard on his kids and wife. She passed away when two of the kids were still at home. We'll never know now why. Those kids will probably take it to their graves someday. Take pictures, Lilly. Might make for some good magazine story or something. I'm waiting down here."

Emma sat on the bottom landing as Lilly and David began to walk up the flight of stairs. Emma could hear their footsteps and voices from where she sat. She began to sway slightly and hum as she waited. Lilly let out a shriek. Emma called up the stairs, "What is it? Are you hurt?"

David laughed. "Not hurt. Lilly found a mouse. She can't make fun of me for shying away from Pie can she, Emma?"

Emma chuckled. "A mouse. Lilly Ballard, you surprise me. I never had you for a squealer."

"It was merely a surprised squeal, Emma. That's all. Do you want to head home to call the kids?"

Emma stood up and looked up the staircase. "Whenever you are ready."

Emma heard footsteps and muffled voices. David appeared at the top of the stairs. "We're ready."

Emma brushed the seat of her pants. "Did you get any pictures?"

Lilly held up her camera and waved it back and forth in the air. "I've got plenty. You're right, Emma. It is sad to see all of this. I think the pictures will be a very memorable tribute to this place and what it once stood for."

Emma smiled slightly and walked towards the front door. "Then I am ready to go home. This has made me kind of sad. No, this day is sad. That's what it is. I've lost my dear friend Dog and then when I see such disregard for family and life, it makes me even more sad than I already was. I need to make phone calls to the kids. Kate will be so sad and oh, my grandchildren. Take me home, David. Please, take me home."

Emma was unusually quiet during the drive home. As they entered her driveway, Lilly noticed Zeke Lang's truck in the drive. Emma stepped out of David's jeep and walked towards Zeke. "What brings you here, Ezekiel?"

Zeke removed his hat and smiled at Emma. "I was passing by and saw your truck out so I thought I would stop. When there was no answer at the door and Sam and Gracie were outside, I got concerned. I didn't realize you still had guests."

Zeke gave a slight nod towards Lilly and David and said, "How you doing Miss Lilly?"

Lilly smiled and took David's hand. "I'm just fine, thank you. Zeke, this is my fiancé David."

Zeke extended his weathered hand to David. "Mighty fine to meet you, David."

"Nice meeting you too, Zeke."

Emma interrupted the conversation. "Why were you worried? Did you look to see if the mustang was in the barn? Maybe I took it on a ride."

Zeke reached for his tobacco can in his pocket, tapped it against the palm of his hand and put it back into his pocket. "Emma Jean, you know as well as I do that you keep that barn locked up tighter than all get out when you aren't home and yes, I did check the barn thinking you might be out there. What in the Hell has gotten into you, old woman? I ain't seen you this cantankerous in a long time."

Lilly stood next to Emma. "Emma lost Dog this morning, Zeke. She still has to phone her children and let them know."

Zeke put his hat on crooked. "What do you mean she lost him? Where in the Hell did he go? He don't run off. He ain't never been lost."

Emma raised her arms in the air. "No, no! Dog died this morning, Ezekiel. We found him in his house. Looked like he passed on in his sleep. We buried him in the pet cemetery with all the other critters. I want to let the kids know."

Zeke hugged Emma in an awkward hug. "Hell, I thought he done run off. Ain't like when we used to worry about Richard poisoning your critters. Remember when he poisoned old Tedward Bear? Jim was sure pissed about that one, wasn't he?"

Zeke looked at Lilly and David and seemed to blush. "Sorry, Miss."

He turned to Emma. "I'm so sorry, Emma Jean. And I ain't got no right bringing up that asshole on a day when your heart is so broken. But big Jim was sure pissed, huh?"

Emma patted Zeke on his broad shoulders. "Yes, Ezekiel, he sure was. But I don't want to think about that right now. I need to phone the kids. You are welcome to visit with Lilly and David if you would like. I'll be with all of you as soon as possible."

Emma walked through the gate and into the house. Lilly motioned for the men to sit on the porch. Zeke sat on the steps, leaving David a little confused as to where he should sit. He looked around and finally sat on one of Emma's wicker chairs.

Zeke again reached for the tobacco can. "Where you folks been? I'm guessing Emma took you to the Corner Café."

Lilly smiled. "You guessed right, Zeke. And then she took us to an abandoned farm. The Mills old place. I took my camera and took several pictures. Sad, seeing a place left like that."

Zeke shook his head in disgust. "Emma Jean ought not be doing that. Why, Rylie warned her all the time about going off and snooping in old barns and houses. She would say it was like going back in time when she would stand in them old places. She hates it when folks don't care for what they've been given. Even so, she could come across some old bum or a nutcase that would do her harm. She don't think sometimes. Crazy old woman."

Lilly felt as if she needed to come to Emma's defense. "She was very cautious and said she had not been in the place for many years. I'm sure she would not endanger herself or us for that matter."

Zeke smiled and set his hat on the porch floor. "Don't matter, Miss Lilly. One of these days she is going to piss someone off and get hurt."

Zeke's mention of pissing another off reminded Lilly of his earlier statement about Jim's feelings towards Richard and Tedward Bear. "Zeke, who was Tedward Bear? You mentioned that name earlier in a conversation."

"He was some cat Emma Jean drug home from a friend that could no longer keep him. Jim fell in love with that cat at first sight. They were quite a pair. That cat was wherever Jim was. The autopsy showed he had been poisoned. Emma Jean and Jim were both sure it was Richard because he had just given them his crazy consequences speech earlier that week. Whew, that boy was pissed. Jim and Emma buried Ted while little Miss Kate was at school. Don't know that she ever knew anything other than Ted was dead."

Emma opened the screen door. "Well, that's taken care of. I think Kate and Brett were most upset. I'm sure part of Kate's is hormonal right now. Poor Brett took it hard. They were buddies. What is going on out here?"

David stood and offered Emma his seat. Emma smiled and said, "Sit down, sit down. This is nice having friends here to visit. Have you had a nice visit?"

Zeke tapped his tobacco can against his knee and placed it back into his shirt pocket. "Been talking about crazy old women that wander into abandoned houses and barns. You know anyone like that?"

Emma glared at Zeke. "I am not a crazy old woman, Ezekiel. And, we were very cautious in that place. I haven't seen you trying to take care of it over the years. Who is going to take care of that place of yours when you are gone, old man? Why, you don't even have any children that will want it. I suppose I will be over at your place boxing up all your worldly possessions. If Nancy had not passed on, she would have taken care of all of it. But, then, that would have left her all alone. And, Lord knows it isn't any fun out here all alone at times."

Zeke ran his leathery hand across Gracie. "You're right on that one. My Nancy would have taken care of everything. She was such a strong woman. Not stubborn like some women but strong. Do you know that she's been gone goin on three years now?"

Zeke stood up. He turned to David and Lilly. "If you folks will excuse me, I think I had better move on."

Zeke hugged Emma in an awkward gesture. "Stay out of those old places, woman. I don't want to find you in the headlines some day."

Emma picked Zeke's hat up from where it sat on the porch. "Ezekiel, I didn't mean to upset you. I should not have brought up Nancy. I would never intentionally hurt you. I hope you know that."

Emma stood on her tiptoes to place Zeke's hat on his head. Zeke reached up to adjust it. Emma patted his back. "You know how I loved her. She was one of my dearest friends. We're going to the cemetery later; do you want to join us?"

Lilly could sense that Emma was trying exceptionally hard to make Zeke feel better. She sensed how badly Emma felt.

Zeke stepped down off the porch. "I'm fine. Don't fuss over me. And, yes, Emma Jean, I know how much you loved Nancy. It just makes me sad to think of how she suffered and how lonely I get at times. I don't know how you do it, being a woman and all. And that, old woman, is why I stop in to check on you. That is why I worry about you. Cause I care. Do you understand?"

Emma smiled. "I understand. And I appreciate it. I might not show it but I do."

Zeke walked to his truck and opened the door. "Hope to see you young folks again while you are here. When are you heading back to the city?"

Lilly stood by the porch rail. "We are leaving Sunday evening. We are going to church with Emma and leaving town that afternoon or early evening."

Zeke reached for the tobacco can but did not take it from his pocket. "Say an extra prayer for me. Lord knows I need it."

He turned to Emma. "Please stay out of the old abandoned places."

Emma used her hand to protect her eyes from the sun. "I promise. Feel better?"

Zeke started the ignition. "Much better. Bye."

Lilly and David stood next to Emma as they watched Zeke drive down the driveway. None of them spoke.

Emma opened the gate. "I hate it when I open my big mouth and put my foot in it. Poor man. They never had any children and now Nancy is gone. My heart aches for him and then I do such a stupid thing. Sometimes I don't have the sense God gave a silly goose, I tell you. None whatsoever."

Chapter 30

Emma and her guests spent the afternoon on horseback and fishing. David and Emma caught enough catfish for an early evening meal. As they rode back to the house, Emma suggested they take a trip after dinner to the cemetery and both Lilly and David were pleased with the suggestion.

Emma included David in cleaning the fish on the patio but Lilly chose to prepare the vegetables inside. Emma laughed as three barn cats hovered around her feet. David watched intently, asking questions now and then.

Emma pointed the tip of the filet knife at David and said, "Didn't your daddy take you fishing as a boy?"

David smiled. "No, he was on the road so much and we spent very little time together until I was sixteen and then we worked on cars together. I would have to say I missed out. Did your children go with their father fishing?"

Emma wiped her hands on a towel. "I can't say that they did. I do remember him offering but I don't think he ever followed through. Maybe Kate remembers a time but I sure don't. I tried to take them when I could. I remember there was one summer day I took them to the lake. Jim was in his early teens. He caught a small perch and the hook went into its mouth and through its eye. Oh, those kids were so upset. Kate was hollering for me to do something and Jim kept saying 'Can you save it, Mom?' Lord knows I did my best to save that little thing but after I got the hook out and set it in the water, I knew it wasn't going to make it and so did Jim but he told little Kate that it was going to be fine. Everything would be fine. He was always trying to assure her that things would be fine, no matter what the circumstance. How she misses him. How I miss him. Life has never been the same since he passed on. Parents should not have to lose their children, you know. Not ever."

Lilly came to the French door and opened it. "I have all of the vegetables ready. What shall I do now?"

Emma placed the fish on a platter. "Time for some fried catfish. Did you start frying those potatoes and onions yet?"

Lilly looked at the fish and then at Emma and David. "No, but the grease is getting hot just like you said. I don't think I have ever had a meal like this. Have you, David?"

David held the door for Emma. "I have had Cajun fried catfish but that is all. This will be a treat."

Lilly and David thoroughly enjoyed Emma's meal. After placing the dishes in the sink, Emma suggested they take the Mustang to the cemetery.

David helped Emma remove the tarp. Lilly tried to get into the cramped backseat and then decided to sit on David's lap in the passenger seat. As Emma drove to the cemetery, Lilly pointed towards Jim and Rylie's graves. "Right over there. That is where Rylie and Jim are buried."

Emma came to a stop and opened her door. Lilly and David followed Emma. As they approached the graves, Emma kissed her thumb and placed it on each headstone. She turned to David. "David, this is where my Rylie and Jim are laid to rest. See, there is a plot between the two of them. That is where I will be laid to rest someday. Rylie and I bought these other plots a year after Jim passed on."

Emma rearranged the flowers on both graves. She knelt in front of each headstone. David and Lilly stood quietly watching as Emma spoke to each as if they were standing there with her. "Boys, Dog passed on today. But, you both already know that, don't you? I am leaving for Denver on Monday but I will stop by on my way to the airport. I've brought Lilly and David here. I wanted David to see this place. I took him fishing and we had enough to fix up a mess of catfish."

Emma stood and ran her hand across Jim's black headstone. David asked about the bells on the cypress tree and Emma told him the story behind each bell. The three friends stood and talked about Jim's death and Rylie's. Emma had not shared much information about the day Rylie passed until this moment at the cemetery.

"He phoned me to say he was on his way home. He asked if I wanted him to pick up anything and I said no. He said he would be home soon. I decided to pack us a picnic basket and take him to the pond that evening. He drove in the driveway and I walked out to meet him. I loved the way his eyes nearly shut when he smiled at me. We embraced and I told him my plans. He wanted to change clothes so I waited on the porch. Seemed like forever and he didn't come out. I went inside and called his name but he did not answer. I knew something was wrong. I found him on the bedroom floor. He was having trouble breathing and having severe chest pains. I called 911 and waited with him. He kept saying, 'We haven't had long enough, Emma. I can't go now.' He passed before the ambulance arrived. They tried all they could but it was too late."

Lilly placed her arm on Emma's shoulder and tilted her head towards Emma's. "You've lost so much in life. I don't know how you do it. Why you had to lose both Jim and Rylie, I do not understand."

Emma's blue eyes glistened with tears as she patted Lilly's cheek. "We are not to question why, Lilly. Lord knows I have done my share of questioning Him on why He took my boys from me but I know I should not. I know that from the moment those boys were conceived, the Lord knew just how long each of them had on this earth and how their lives would end. It is His Will and I can't doubt that it was what should have been. That doesn't take away the pain. I can look forward to being with them again some day. The Bible says there will be no tears in Heaven but I think there will be tears of joy when we all get together again. Lots of joyful tears."

Lilly took Emma's hand and held it between her own. "I can't imagine having to make arrangements for two of the most important people in your life and remaining so positive and strong. You told me once that you spoke at Jim's funeral. I have never even thought about what I would want at my funeral."

Emma smiled. "I used to always tell Rylie and Jim about the things I wanted in my funeral and both of them would say there was no need in worrying about that. And then they were the ones that were taken from this earth and we had never discussed what they might want in their funerals. Of course, Jim was so young that we just didn't think about him passing on. Who would have thought? Now I have it all written down what I want including the songs. I might as well have the last say, don't you think?"

Lilly brushed her hair from her eyes and turned to David, Emma at her side. "Songs? I can't even think of any."

"Well, I have had my thoughts on this for years and I want 'Amazing Grace' and when folks are saying their last goodbyes; I want 'Happy Trails' by Roy Rogers and Dale Evans played. I want folks to remember the good times and celebrate my life, not grieve for my death. That's what I want. I want it to be happy because I will already be in a much better place than this old earth. I worry about Kate and hope she will be able to deal with the loss. She has suffered so many losses. She's strong. She'll be fine," Emma said as if to reassure herself and not her friends.

"I say we don't have a thing to worry about. You are going to outlive all of us, Emma," David said.

Emma slapped her thigh. "Wouldn't that be a hoot? That sure would show those doctors, huh? I think that will be my goal. Not to outlive my kinfolk but to outlive those that have told me there is no hope. Where would we be without hope? Think about how often we 'hope'. I hope you have a good day, I hope you feel better soon, I hope I win the lottery, on and on it goes. Thank goodness for hope."

Emma looked at her watch. "Good Lord, look at the time. We need to get back to the farm and do chores. I've kept you here way too long, rambling on. Rylie used to call me 'Ramblin Rose' when I would get on one of my tangents. Can't say the Lord didn't give me enough wind. He gave me plenty of that."

As they drove from the cemetery to the house, David and Lilly lightheartedly discussed things they would want in their funerals and Emma listened intently. She would chuckle at some of the silly songs Lilly would mention. "Lord, I shouldn't laugh. Look at me, choosing a song like 'Happy Trails'. I've got no room to talk. But, Lilly, would you really want the ABC song? Kid, you are a hoot."

The evening ended with the three friends watching more family videos and looking at pictures. Sam and Gracie performed with tricks that Emma had taught them and Emma told stories about her children and grandchildren. She even told stories of when her parents were young and how they met. As Lilly listened to Emma, she could see why Emma's children and grandchildren were always eager to hear her stories growing up.

After sharing a bowl of popcorn, Emma excused herself and retired for the evening. Lilly and David put on their jackets and took Gracie and Sam out before going to bed. Lilly sat on the porch steps and waited as David opened the gate for the dogs. Sam immediately ran towards the pet cemetery. David turned to Lilly and said, "I'll go get him. You watch Gracie."

Gracie waited at the gate for Lilly to let her into Emma's front yard. Lilly and Gracie sat beside one another, waiting for David. Gracie would occasionally nudge Lilly's hand in hopes of Lilly petting her. Lilly obliged.

After David and Sam returned, Lilly asked if they could stay on the porch for a while. They sat beside one another on the swing, both dogs at their feet.

"It's so peaceful here," David said quietly.

Lilly laid her head on his shoulder. "Won't it be beautiful for our wedding? I have decided I want Emma to give me away."

"Do you think she will do that?" David asked.

"Well, I never knew my dad and mom is gone and I can't think of a better person than Emma to give me away. I will talk to her about it when I feel the time is right. She is so excited about having the wedding here and she says Kate has offered to help with the arrangements and decorations. I think it would be perfect."

David kissed the top of Lilly's head, taking in the fragrance of her hair. "I think this place is the closest to Heaven a person can get here on earth. It's hard to imagine that Emma has had such hard times here. I'm glad that Richard is gone and he can no longer harm her or make her fearful. I just wish Rylie and Jim were still around here and it is a shame that Kate is so far from here. Although, Emma seems fine with it, doesn't she?"

Lilly brushed a strand of hair from her left eye. "I think Emma is happy if Kate is happy. She's been without Kate here since Kate left for college. Emma is happy when her children and grandchildren are happy."

David yawned and Sam stood up and nuzzled against David's hand. "I think Sam is ready for bed."

Lilly chuckled. "I think you are the one ready for bed."

Lilly, David and their canine friends went inside. David made sure all of the doors were locked and Lilly finished what little cleaning was left in the kitchen. As David turned out the lights, he turned to the marble jar. Another day had passed. Another marble now gone from the jar. He forced such thoughts out of his mind and picked up Gracie. "Come on, girl, let's go to bed."

Chapter 31

Lilly could not believe Sunday had already arrived. It had been so nice spending time with both Emma and David. Now it was the day they had to leave and go back to Kansas City and back to the office.

Lilly showered and dressed for church while David sat in the kitchen talking to Emma as she prepared breakfast.

Lilly entered the kitchen. David placed an arm around her waist. "You look pretty," he said as he kissed her cheek.

Emma turned from the stove. "You most certainly do. Let's eat and then I need to get cleaned up. Now, you kids keep in mind that I am by no means a professional singer. This is just a small church and we usually just have a church member sing a special on Sunday mornings. Nothing fancy. Understand?"

David passed the plate of breakfast sausages. "Yes, we understand. Still, I am looking forward to hearing you."

They finished breakfast and David cleared the table while Emma showered and dressed. Lilly sat at the kitchen table and read over her notes on Emma. She knew there was so much to learn and hoped Emma would someday tell more of her past. It was hard for Lilly to imagine that Emma had kept so much of her past from her children and her stepchildren. So many secrets that Emma was now sharing. Lilly was pleased that others might be helped through Emma's story.

David gave Sam a piece of sausage and Gracie the rest of the scrambled eggs. "You'll spoil them, David."

David winked at Lilly. "I'm sure Emma has never spoiled them, huh?"

Lilly stood up and adjusted each of the placemats on the kitchen table. "Good point."

David excused himself so that he could also get dressed for church. As he entered the living room, Emma came into the room. She wore a navy suit with a flare skirt just below the knee. She had a light pink camisole under her suit jacket with navy heels. It was the first time Lilly or David had seen Emma with makeup on. Her suit made her eyes a deeper blue than usual.

David motioned for Emma to turn in circles. She giggled but obliged his requested gesture. She placed her hand on her hip, then put both hands up and spun around several times. Gracie also went in circles and barked.

"Let me tell you, Emma Jean, you clean up beautifully. No wonder Rylie thought you were quite a catch. You look beautiful," Lilly said.

Emma scoffed as she blushed. "Whatever. Just a little makeup and my Sunday go to meeting clothes. Nothing special. David, don't you make me late."

David hurried towards the stairs. "I'll be down in fifteen minutes. I've already shaved and showered. Just a matter of putting on my Sunday best."

Emma took her Bible out of the bookcase and sat on the loveseat, thumbing through the pages. Lilly sat in the overstuffed chair. She felt slightly uncomfortable and wondered why she and David never attended church. As she sat there, she thought of her mother and how she never took Lilly to church or Sunday School. She raised Lilly alone, saying only that Lilly's father had died before she was born. Seeing Emma so devoted to her beliefs made Lilly wonder why her own mother had been against church. Even on her deathbed, she asked Lilly not to have a religious service. Lilly had never given it much thought until now.

David entered the room, turning around as he walked. Emma clapped her hands in a dignified applause. "I'd say we all look like Kansas royalty. Lilly, may we take your vehicle?"

Lilly stood up and straightened David's tie. "Of course, Emma. Now, exactly what is Kansas royalty?"

Emma laughed. "Just enough to look pretty but not enough to have folks bow before us."

Lilly opened the back door and seated herself behind David in the driver's seat. David smiled and went around to the passenger side to open the door for Emma. Emma curtsied and said "Thank you, sir." She winked at Lilly as she slid into the seat.

Emma gave David directions to the church. As they drove into the parking lot, Lilly noticed three white crosses in a flowerbed, each standing over six feet tall. The church was a small, white building with a green roof. Arched windows lined both sides and large double doors were at the entrance.

David parked the vehicle and the three friends walked towards the church. Emma reached into her purse and turned off her cell phone. David and Lilly followed suit.

Two older gentlemen greeted them at the door. The taller, white haired man smiled and extended his hand to Emma. "Emma Jean, I see you are singing this morning. It is always a treat. Who have we here?" he said as he extended his hand to David.

Emma introduced her friends and then showed them into the church. Lilly recognized several faces from the Corner Café and enjoyed seeing how many friends Emma had. Emma was greeted over and over, each time introducing Lilly and David.

The three friends sat together in a section of pews towards the back of the church. The congregation sang three hymns and an offering was taken. At the close of the offering, the minister stood and briefly spoke. He then introduced Emma as the special song for the morning.

Emma walked towards the platform, running her hands down both sides of her navy suit. She took a microphone and looked out over the congregation. Lilly listened intently as Emma spoke. "Many of you folks know me and some of you do not. I stand here before you today but for the grace of God. I would like to tell you a little about myself. Many of you have heard my story before but I have been asked to tell it again."

Emma walked slowly across the platform. "At the age of nineteen I married a young man that I knew the Lord did not have planned for my mate but sometimes we as human beings choose to go against the Lord's will. That is exactly what I did on that March day at the age of nineteen. After only three days of marriage, my husband began to beat me. There were times he would laugh and ask me where my God was as he was kicking and hitting me. Because I was raised that divorce was a sin, I chose to stay in that marriage. Two children were born, Jim and Kate. As they grew older, the abuse continued. Their father would beat me and then lock me in a room or a closet. While I sat alone, I would often sing old hymns and pray that the Lord would somehow save my children and me from this man. I had no idea that my children could hear me singing those songs until years later and then it became our code that I was safe as long as I was singing. One week the pastor had asked me to sing the following Sunday. I went and purchased an accompaniment tape to a song, practicing and practicing but not liking the way it sounded. My daughter came out of her room and said 'Mom, why are you singing this to music? It doesn't sound right at all.' I asked her how it should be sung and she said 'The way Jim and I always heard it, Mom, after Dad had left you alone in pain. Sing it the way we know it.' So I stand here today to sing that song. As you listen to it, remember that God watches over each and every one of us. Those times when we feel most alone, He is there. I am thankful for His amazing grace."

Emma began to sing the old hymn Amazing Grace. Her voice was clear and pure, each word coming from the depths of her heart. Lilly listened as Emma sang 'through many dangers, toils and snares, I have already come'. This was Emma's song. Lilly glanced around the congregation. Several people were in tears and others closed their eyes as they listened to Emma. Lilly looked at Melissa and Taylor with Billy sitting at their side. Taylor had her eyes fixed on her grandmother and she was silently singing the words along with Emma.

Jason and Denise sat next to them. Jason leaned forward with his elbows on his knees, looking at the ground. Denise gently patted his back.

Emma stopped singing. She smiled, her blue eyes smiled also. "I would like all of you to sing this last verse with me. Won't it be wonderful when we all get to Heaven and see our loved ones? Please, sing along with me."

The congregation stood and sang the last verse along with Emma. Lilly and David read from the hymnal and sang along. 'When we've been there ten thousand years, bright shining as the sun.' Lilly's voice trailed off as she watched Emma. Emma exuded strength like no other. Lilly had such admiration for this woman. So many people loved this small, determined woman in her community. Emma had no idea how admired and loved she was. Lilly wanted somehow to make things easier for Emma and she wanted to tell Emma's story.

The singing stopped. Everyone sat down and Emma returned to join Lilly and David. David patted Emma's hand and gave her a thumbs up sign as she sat next to him. Taylor turned around and winked at her grandmother.

The service ended and Emma motioned for the family to come to her. She introduced Lilly and David to everyone. Brett asked Emma if she had Sunday dinner prepared. Emma tugged on his right earlobe. "Now, what do you think, young man? When has your grandma let you go hungry on a Sunday afternoon? Besides, didn't you promise to do some of my choring for me?"

Brett's eyes were a clear blue and his smile was slightly crooked. He bore a scar across the bridge of his nose. "I think Mom and Taylor promised my services, didn't they? They promised my handyman services unbeknownst to me. Dawson swore he would help. What are we having for Sunday dinner, Grandma?"

Melissa slid her arm inside of Billy's. "We can't come today, Emma. The kids can do whatever they would like but Billy and I have made plans to go with some of the other couples in the church."

Emma picked up her purse and Bible. "Fair enough. The food will be on the table in an hour and anyone is welcome. Brett Dean, I assume you will be there. Miss Taylor, will you be joining us?"

Taylor kissed Emma's cheek. "I would like to but Stephen has invited me to lunch with him, Grandma."

Emma winked and patted Taylor's cheek. "Have you got a beau, Taylor Jewell? Good Lord, it was only yesterday you were in diapers. Where do the years go?"

Taylor blushed. "Oh, Grandma, it isn't serious. We are just going to lunch. That's all."

Jason and Denise hugged Emma and said they also had other plans but they would see her on their usual Tuesday evening dinner at Emma's house.

Jason smiled a crooked smile and said, "You know the only reason they got me here today was to hear you tell your story and sing."

Emma sighed and said, "Won't hurt you once in a while to set foot inside a church, Jason Ray. Lord knows its given all of us refuge when our hearts were heavy. You know your dad would tell you the same."

Jason kissed Emma's cheek and spoke teasingly "Be good".

Emma chuckled and responded with "I'm making no promises."

Brett put his arm on Emma's shoulder. "Grandma, I'm going to head on out to the farm. Anything you want me to do when I get there? Maybe eat?"

Emma pointed her finger at Brett. "We will be right behind you, young man."

Brett turned to David. "David, do you want to ride with me?"

David smiled. "I would be honored, Brett. You know, I've spent all this time with these two women and I could use another man's conversation."

The families went their separate ways and David and Brett led Emma and Lilly in the trip to Emma's home.

Brett started the conversation. "What did you think of Grandma's song?"

David was a bit surprised with Brett's openness yet knew he came by it honestly with Emma as his grandmother. "She has such a pure voice. It was not what I expected. She has a strong voice."

Brett tapped his hand on the steering wheel. "Strong voice for a strong woman. How much do you know about the story behind Grandma's song?"

"Only what she said in church. Can you tell me more?"

Brett turned off the radio. "My grandma would be locked in closets, bathrooms; anywhere that man could keep her locked in. My Aunt Kate and Uncle Jim would hear her through the heating ducts or late into the night, her voice would softly sing them to sleep so that they knew she was still with them. She's strong, let me tell you. I have seen her outwork most men. And she is the only woman that has ever stood up to my mom. There was a time my mom would try to boss and bully my grandma and grandma would have nothing to do with that. Now my Papa Beans hated confrontation. He was shocked at how bullheaded grandma was cause she always preached to all of us to turn the other cheek. But I think she decided in her midlife that she was no longer going to be pushed around by anyone and she stuck to it. I admire her for that."

"I must admit I have never met anyone like her. I know Lilly truly admires her. Did she tell you about her past and is that how you know about her singing after she was abused?"

Brett glanced at David. "My Aunt Kate told me a few years ago. We were sitting on Grandma's porch after an evening meal when Kate was home from Denver. Grandma's past was never discussed with me until that night. I said something about how I hated coming out here and doing her chores and Aunt Kate scolded me. She told me how Grandma had brought them to that farm and how hard she had worked to keep them there, sometimes holding down four jobs when Richard wouldn't pay what was owed. Grandma struggled with the fact that she could not keep Aunt Kate and Uncle Jim in the lifestyle they were accustomed to. She told me about how they would hear her being beat and how she would not cry out in pain or for help. Then they would hear her voice singing old gospel hymns but especially 'Amazing Grace'. Have you seen the sign that hangs in Grandma's living room? The one that says 'Amazing Grace'?"

"Yes, I believe I have."

Brett turned onto the gravel road. "It was a gift from my Papa Beans to Grandma not long before he died. She was so proud of that sign."

As the two men turned onto the gravel road, Lilly and Emma passed them, waving and leaving them in a cloud of dust.

David frowned. "Sometimes I wonder if that woman thinks about her own safety and now that of Emma's".

"I'm guessing she hasn't much experience on gravel, huh? I learned to drive out here in the country and Papa Beans would have strung me up if I had passed a person on these roads. I bet he is turning over in his grave right now as we speak."

Brett drove into Emma's drive. He pulled his truck near Lilly and Emma. "Are you women crazy or what? Grandma, you know better than that."

Emma waved her arms in the air in an exasperated gesture. "Brett Dean, my life is near over so why not enjoy?"

Brett hugged his grandmother from behind. "Grandma, please don't talk like that. You know you are going to outlive all of us."

Emma turned and looked Brett in the eyes, placing her hands on each of his tanned cheeks. "Don't ever say that again, young man. I want all my remaining babies to live on long after I am gone. I couldn't bear outliving another one of you."

"Oh, grandma, you know what I mean. You can't be giving up like that. We need you. Aunt Kate needs you. You are the only blood kin she's got. It isn't the same, you know."

Emma's eyes flashed. "It isn't the same, you say? Are you my blood? Heavens, no, but I have never thought of you as anything else. Remember in the old tree house that time when you wanted us to be blood kin? You took your little pocketknife and cut your thumb and then asked if you could cut mine. Good Lord, what kind of grandma agrees to such things? This one did. I let you cut my thumb and then we held our thumbs together. You said we were now and forever blood kin. Your Papa thought we had lost our minds when we came down from that tree house. But you were positive that was all it took. Child, you were my blood in my heart from the moment I laid eyes on you. Don't talk about Kate not having anyone again, you hear?"

Brett dug the tip of his boot into the dirt. "Yes, grandma."

Emma walked onto the porch. "Now, let's eat. Lilly, will you help me set the table? You boys can sit out here on the porch or I would appreciate it if you would water the horses."

Emma and Lilly entered the house. David turned to Brett. "Shall I change my clothes and we water the horses?"

"Heck, don't worry about changing. I'll get them set up. You can just supervise."

They walked towards the barn with Sam and Gracie at their sides. Brett looked at the ground the entire walk. David stopped walking and turned to Brett. "Are you o.k?"

"I hate it when she talks like that. I'm afraid she is giving up. And I hate that marble jar! Damn those doctors for not curing her. She's got me coming out here and videoing her doing chores, horseback riding, and all kinds of stuff so that we can give it to the next generation. She wants her great-grandkids to know about her."

David lightly touched Brett's sleeve. "I don't think she is giving up. I think she wants her family to face the possibility that she may be gone someday soon. As for the marbles, I think it is her way of showing those doctors they were wrong. I think she will toss the last marble and make it, well, make it maybe another day, maybe another year."

Emma came to the porch and rang the dinner bell. Brett called out to her "We'll be there in a few minutes, grandma. I haven't had a chance to turn on their water."

Emma wiped her hands on a dishtowel. "Don't take too long. It's on the table."

She opened the screen door, glancing back at David and Brett.

David and Lilly enjoyed the home cooked meal and lighthearted dinner conversation. Emma and Brett bantered back and forth. The smiles and the laughter felt so good to Lilly. She realized what she had missed as a child growing up. It was just Lilly and her mother and her mother did not like Sundays. Lilly wished she knew now why. Why didn't she ever question her mother? Emma was so open with all of her family. Lilly loved her mother but wished they had shared such openness.

Brett stayed until dusk. He and David trimmed Emma's lawn and took care of all the animals. Then they all sat on Emma's porch and, before Lilly realized the time, Brett announced he was leaving and David said they too should be getting on the highway. The thought made Lilly sad.

After Brett left, David went into the house to pack. Lilly and Emma stayed on the porch. Emma was the first to speak. "Now, you promise you will keep in touch, don't you?"

"Oh, Emma, of course. And you promise to call and give us a full report on that new grandbaby?"

Emma beamed. "You know it."

David stepped onto the porch. "You ready?"

Lilly could feel the tears burning her eyes. David looked into her eyes and gave her a look of 'don't cry'.

Emma hugged both of them and kissed Lilly on the cheek. "Lilly Ballard, you go write that story of Emma Jean. Don't let another woman think she has no other choice but to stay in such a relationship. Will you do that for me?"

Lilly struggled to fight back the tears. "I promise."

"And, as soon as I get home from Denver, I will call you. And we need to start planning that wedding. I will give Kate all the contact information and you two girls can get started. Now, we set it for September 23rd, right?"

"That's right", David said as he placed the last piece of luggage into his jeep.

Lilly turned to him. "Are you leading or following?"

He kissed her cheek. "I'm following."

They both got into their vehicles. Emma stood waving and smiling, with Sam at her side and Gracie chasing a calico cat. "Be careful. Drive safe. I promise to call when I return, Lilly. I promise."

Lilly watched Emma in her rearview mirror until she could no longer make her out. Emma waved the entire time they drove away. Lilly's cell phone began to ring. It was David.

"God that was hard", he said.

"I feel like we are leaving her all alone. I know we aren't and I know she is used to being alone but somehow I feel like I am letting her down."

"You write that article and do as Emma said. Then you won't let her down."

The drive home seemed to go on for forever. It would be three weeks before Lilly heard from Emma again.

Chapter 32

Lilly hurried from the shower and put on her robe as she answered the phone. It was Emma's familiar voice. "Let me tell you, Lilly Ballard, I have the most beautiful grandson on this earth. And he is so good."

Lilly smiled. "Oh, Emma, it is so good to hear from you. Are you just now getting back to Kansas?"

There was a pause and Lilly heard Emma sigh. "Well, no, Lilly. I had a little set back when I got home and I spent a few days in the hospital. But I am fine now. As a matter of fact, Kate and Conner are here with me. She seems to think she needs to be here but she needs to be home taking care of her own family and not me. She's leaving in three days and we wondered if you would like to come over and visit one day. Have you been working on wedding plans?"

Lilly's heart sank at the thought of Emma being ill. "Yes, I have worked on some things but I would like Kate's input. I would love to come see all of you. I can be there sometime late morning tomorrow if that would work for you."

"We will plan on seeing you tomorrow, Lilly. And tell David I said hello."

"I will. I am looking forward to it. See you tomorrow. Thank you for calling, Emma."

"Tomorrow it is, Lilly. See you then. And, Lilly?"

"Yes, Emma?"

"There's no need to thank me. It's a pleasure to hear your voice."

Both Emma and Lilly said goodbye. Lilly sat on the sofa, wrapping her robe around her. She had not noticed the room being chilly before but now it seemed to have taken on a slight chill. Her thoughts were on Emma. Why was she in the hospital? It must be serious for Kate to come home and take care of Emma. Lilly was anxious for tomorrow to arrive.

Emma hung up the phone and turned to Kate. "She'll be here late morning tomorrow. Now, I should probably get to the market and stock up. What shall we have to eat while she is here?"

"Momma, you are not going to overdue it. Lilly will be fine with either sandwiches or us going somewhere to eat. If I had thought you would make such a fuss, I would not have suggested you have her over. You need to keep up your strength and not try to conquer the world on a daily basis."

Emma scoffed and crossed her arms across her chest. "I don't want folks thinking I'm not a gracious hostess. There's never been a guest leave this house without a decent meal and sincere hospitality. And I won't start now."

Kate stood up from the loveseat and placed Conner in Emma's arms. "Take your grandson and enjoy him and I will go to the store. Or, if you insist on being a part of it, you can ride along. We can have a nice visit while we shop. How does that sound?"

Emma kissed Conner's hand and smiled. "That sounds much better. Shall we make a list before we go?"

Kate kissed the top of Emma's head. "Let's just fly by the seat of our pants and see what we come home with. I need to get you stocked up on groceries before I head home anyway. Of course, I have never seen your pantry without a year's supply of food in it. Who do you plan on feeding with all of that?"

Emma frowned. "I want to be prepared in case folks stop in or in case I can't get out for a while. Lord knows you kids are trying to coheres with the doctors right now as we speak and keep me locked inside this house. As soon as all of you turn your backs, I am outside with my critters, you know."

Kate smiled and reached for the diaper bag on the dining room table. "Just get your little fanny in the car and enjoy the company. Man, that Irish blood in those veins is stubborn. Sure glad I didn't inherit that," she said as she winked at her mother.

Emma carried Conner to the car and placed him in his car seat. She sat next to him. Kate started the engine and then turned to her mother. "Are you leaving Gracie out with Sam while we are away?"

"As long as he stays around, she will," Emma said. She rolled down her window. "Sam, you stay here and watch over things. No wandering off. You and Gracie stay on the porch. You hear me?"

Kate looked in the rearview mirror at her mother and smiled. She thought about all those years growing up and Emma never turning down a stray. Why, Emma had even taken in friends of Kate and Jim that needed a place to live. Sometimes friends stayed for a day and sometimes for a year. Emma would not turn someone or something out. Kate thought about her mother's illness and how cheated all of them would be if Emma did not win this battle. Kate felt the bitterness well up inside of her.

"Kate? Are you listening to me?"

Kate looked in the mirror. "Sorry, Mom. What were you saying?"

Emma ran a finger over Conner's forehead. "I said we should go on in to Topeka and consolidate our trips. We can go to Wal-Mart for diapers and toiletries and then on to the grocery store. Do you agree?"

"Sure. That sounds like a plan to me." Kate knew better than to argue or offer another option. Emma's mind was made up long before they left the house.

They finished their shopping at Wal-Mart. Kate thought Emma was getting tired and suggested Emma let Kate do the grocery shopping. As soon as she suggested it, she knew she had made the wrong choice.

Emma's arms went in the air. "Why in the Sam Hill do folks think I can't even handle shopping anymore? You are making this worse than it really is. By the way, did you throw out the marbles I told you to? You will mess up the numbers if we don't throw out for every day I have been gone. Did you do it, Kate?"

Kate sighed. She had forgotten to do as she was asked. "Oh, I forgot. We will do it as soon as we get back to the farm."

"I should have just done it myself. None of you like the marble task but it has to be done. I won't know if I beat the doctors if you don't do it the way I intended."

"Momma, you need to stop being so gruff. It's not like you. We will make sure it is done right. Now, sweeten up and enjoy this time with me and your grandson."

Emma looked out the window. "Lord knows you are right on this one, Kate. I'm sorry for being such a bossy grump. I'm sorry, Kate."

Emma kissed Conner. "And Grandma is so sorry she was naughty in front of her little man. I don't want you to remember me as an old crab. No, sir. No more crabbiness from this grandma."

The rest of the day was spent shopping and putting up the purchases. Kate noticed a few items that she did not remember placing in the cart. She laughed as she removed chocolate ice cream, cookies, four York Mint candy bars and bottled water from the grocery bag. She walked to the kitchen door with the cookies in her hand. She looked at Emma on the loveseat holding Conner. She smiled and then chuckled.

Emma looked up at Kate in the doorway. "What are you laughing at?"

"You and your chocolate. No wonder I fight cravings for chocolate. It's genetic. When did you sneak all of this into the cart?"

Emma winked. "Obviously when you weren't looking, huh?"

Kate shook her head and went into the kitchen. She continued to put the groceries away, listening to her mother's voice as she sang songs to Conner. It brought back so many memories. Emma was singing 'You Are My Sunshine'. Kate had heard that song so many times when she was growing up. She had always considered it 'their' song and now it was being passed on from grandmother to grandson. A rush of overwhelming sadness filled Kate. She missed her brother. She didn't have Rylie to phone for advice anymore and now her mother was fighting what she feared was a losing battle against cancer. She wondered why life had dealt this family such a rotten hand.

Kate thought of how her mother would scold her if she knew Kate was thinking these thoughts and wallowing in self-pity. She knew Emma would remind her she should be grateful for Conner and Joshua.

Kate placed the last item in the pantry. She walked into the living room where Emma and Conner were lying on the floor on one of Emma's quilts. Conner was asleep and Emma was lying there with her eyes closed but not sleeping.

"Mom, do you want to rest for a while in your room? I think I will put him in his bed and catch a little nap myself."

Emma sat up. "That sounds good. Now, you promise to also rest?"

"Yes, I promise. And, when we get up, we will eat and finish chores and get ready for Lilly's visit tomorrow. How does that sound?"

Emma smiled and kissed Conner's cheek. His cheek twitched and his mouth turned up on the left side in a slight smile. "That sounds like a heck of an idea", Emma said.

Chapter 33

Lilly arrived the following day in the late morning just as she had promised. She strained to see if anyone was on the porch waiting as she drove down Emma's drive. Sam came from the barn, barking and wagging his tail.

Lilly stopped her Jeep and stepped out. "Good morning, Sam. Where is everyone?"

Sam licked Lilly's hand just as the front door opened.

Emma wore blue jeans and a red sweatshirt. She had no shoes on and she waved a dishtowel in the air. "Good morning, Lilly. I am so glad you could do this. Come on in here."

Lilly opened the gate and Sam followed. She stepped onto the porch. Emma gave her a hug.

"Oh, Emma, it is so good to see you. I am so anxious to see Kate and Conner too. Are they inside?"

"Conner is taking his morning nap and Kate is putting on her face. Come on in."

Emma offered Lilly something to drink. "Do you have any iced tea made?"

Emma waved her dishtowel and said, "Is the Pope Catholic? Heavens, yes, I have iced tea. Have a seat and I'll be right back."

Lilly walked over to the family pictures. Obviously Emma had added one of her holding a beautiful baby. Lilly knew this must be Conner James. She picked up the photo to examine it more closely. Kate entered the room.

"Good morning, Lilly. I am so glad you made it." Kate touched Lilly's shoulder and smiled. Her deep green eyes seemed to smile just as Emma's blue eyes did when she smiled.

"Kate, you look wonderful. I certainly can't tell you just had a baby. How are you doing?"

"I'm great. Conner is such a joy. Now if I can get Momma on her feet, we'll be good to go."

Lilly frowned. "How bad is she?"

150

Emma walked into the room, carrying two iced teas. "I'll tell you. I can't turn my back for a minute without you girls talking about me. I'm fine, Lilly. It was just a little set back but I am fine now."

Kate rolled her eyes as Emma handed Lilly her tea. "You know you go to Hell for lying same as you do for stealing, Mom."

Emma turned to Kate. "Whatever. Do you want some iced tea too?"

"I can get it for myself, Mom. You sit down and visit with Lilly."

Lilly and Emma sat on the loveseat and discussed Emma's new grandson while Kate was in the kitchen. Kate came back with her tea and sat in one of the chairs. She took a sip of tea and said, "Did you bring your ideas for the wedding? What all have you done?"

"Well, I have my attendant's dresses ordered and I still don't have mine. I really need help with flowers and deciding on how to decorate things outdoors. Any ideas?"

Kate smiled and set her iced tea on the table. "I am full of ideas. We can make it as simple or as elegant as you want. You just say the word. I brought books and some drawings I have been working on. Where is your stuff?"

"I left it in the car."

Just as Kate was about to speak, Conner began to cry from the guest room. Emma stood up and said, "I'll take care of our boy and you girls gather up your ideas. Lilly, would you like to see our newest addition before you get your things from the car?"

"Oh, yes. I would love that."

Emma went into the bedroom and returned with Conner. He had a full head of dark blond curls and his face was round. Emma handed him to Lilly. Lilly looked at his tiny hands and his big round eyes. They were a deep blue. "Oh, he is beautiful. You are right, Emma."

Emma scoffed. "Did you think I would lie to you? Of course he is beautiful. Look at his parents!"

Kate nudged her mother. "Mom, show a little bit of humbleness, would you?"

"Why in the Sam Hill should I be humble when it comes to this? That baby is beautiful and we all know it. Here, hand him back to me and you girls start talking wedding while I change his britches."

Lilly handed Conner to Emma and picked up her keys from the table. She turned to Kate. "Should we sit at the dining table and go over all of this?"

Kate pulled her hair back in a makeshift ponytail. Lilly thought she looked tired. She wondered if it was the new baby or the stress of her mother's illness.

"I think the dining room table is an excellent idea. Mom isn't going to be putting on any feasts for us. We can eat at the kitchen table or in the sunroom if we plan on a meal. I'll get my stuff."

Lilly left for her car and returned with a box. Emma stayed in the guest room with Conner for quite some time before returning to the dining room. She carried Conner with such pride.

Lilly and Kate sat at the dining table going over wedding plans. Emma and Conner joined them. Emma smiled at Kate and said to Lilly, "Kate is the best when it comes to putting these things together. She isn't one of those fancy wedding planners but she has a talent like no other. You should see some of the Denver homes she has decorated and designed. She'll make this old farm look like a fairy tale setting. You hide and watch, Lilly."

Conner wiggled in Emma's arms and let out a small whimper. Kate turned abruptly to look at him.

Emma frowned and said, "It's just a whimper, Kate. He's fine."

Again, Kate rolled her eyes and said nothing. She turned the pages in one of Lilly's magazines.

Emma knew she may have hurt Kate's feelings and tried to make the conversation a little more lighthearted. "Kate, if I wrap a blanket around him and keep his ears covered from the cool, fall air; may I take him out on the porch?"

"Of course, Momma. Take him wherever you want. Maybe not the cemetery until you have a little more strength back. And I want to go with you when you do take him there to see Jim and Beans. O.K.?"

Emma wrapped a light blanket around Conner. "You're the boss. We'll stay around here, won't we Conner James? We'll be good this once, huh? Gracie, do you want to come hang out with the cool kids?"

Gracie began to bark and run in circles. Conner jumped at the loud barking noise.

"Then let's get on out of here. Let these girls do their wedding thing. Have fun, girls. We'll be around outside somewhere."

The screen door slammed and it was just a few minutes before Kate and Lilly heard the porch swing and Emma's voice singing.

Lilly waited a few minutes and then spoke. "Is her health failing? Is it getting worse?"

Kate set her pen down on the table and ran her fingers through her long blond hair. "It's worse. She had a terrible setback when she got back to Kansas. I think taking care of this place is too much for her. But I don't want her to sell it. This is our home. I doubt if Joshua can find work back in Kansas or Missouri that pays what his job in Denver pays and I hate to give up my business. But I don't know how long she is going to last out here on her own. None of the other kids or grandkids wants to move in here. As you can see, she is getting a little cantankerous. I think that will end when she is feeling better."

"When is that supposed to be?"

Kate leaned back in her chair and closed her eyes. "I have no idea. They are talking about some new treatment that might help. At first she argued that the treatments were worse than the disease but I think she is going to try it. I don't know how much time I will be able to take off work but I think I need to be here to help out. Some of the women from church have volunteered to come over and Zeke says he will take her to treatments. I am at a loss right now. My plate is so full."

Lilly's mind was racing as she tried to come up with solutions. "What about Rylie's kids? Can't they help out?"

Kate took a sip of her tea and shook her head no. "She says she doesn't want to have them taking care of her. She certainly won't allow Melissa to boss her around and she feels that it is not their responsibility. She says you draw the line somewhere when it comes to asking Rylie's kids for help. Taylor has already said she will come out three days a week and spend time with her and fix her a meal. I would feel better if someone was here on a full time basis."

Lilly blurted the word without thinking and wished she could take it back as soon as it left her mouth. "What about Hospice?"

Kate's green eyes grew dark and she glanced at Lilly and then looked down. "Lilly, if Hospice were here to help it would mean they thought there is no chance of getting well. That is not something we want to hear and I am thankful it is not an option right now."

"Oh, Kate. I wasn't even thinking. I am so sorry. Of course, you don't want Hospice here. We want Emma around for years to come. Sometimes I open my mouth before thinking."

Kate pulled out some sketches she had drawn of the farm and her ideas for the wedding and reception.

"Now we need to keep in mind that the weather could be cool and rainy. I thought we might rent a big tent. Here, look at these ideas."

Lilly and Kate looked over drawings and pictures and notes that they both had with them. They enjoyed one another's company and realized they had so much in common and similar tastes. It was over an hour before Emma entered the house with a sleeping Conner in her arms.

"I think I bored him with my songs and my stories."

Kate set her pen on the table. "I doubt that. I remember those stories and you can tell some pretty wild stories. Half the time my bedtime stories were so scary, I couldn't get to sleep. Now Jim loved his stories and his movies scary."

"He sure did but you weren't into the happily ever after stuff, Kate. I'm glad cause I had no Cinderella stories to offer you. I never did believe in fairy tales that made things easy on the princess. Never did."

Emma went to the guest bedroom and placed Conner in his crib. She returned with a receiving blanket in her hand. "You girls hungry? What are we doing the rest of the day? Are you spending the night, Lilly?"

Lilly had to chuckle at all of Emma's questions. "I can stay if you would like. I will eat whenever you and Kate are hungry."

"Mom, why don't we wait until Conner wakes up and we will drive over to Bill & Ellie's for a bite?"

"Sounds like a heck of a deal. I'm going to go rest a bit while that boy does and you girls wake me when it is time to leave. Do you need some rest too, Kate?"

"I'm fine. I think Lilly and I are going to try to get some of these plans set. You go rest and I will wake you when we are ready. I promise."

The afternoon was spent enjoying one another's company and a nice trip to Lyndon for a late lunch. Lilly enjoyed seeing familiar faces from her previous visits and it was such a pleasure to see Emma and Kate visit with the locals and show off their new family addition. Lilly looked forward to working with Kate over the next few months. She hoped they would form a friendship that would last forever.

After returning home, the three women spent some time on the porch talking about Kate's childhood and her own plans of a family. Emma held Conner in her arms with a blanket wrapped around him.

"I'm taking this boy inside. Do you mind if I give him his evening bath?"

"Of course not. Why don't you do that and Lilly and I will do the evening chores?"

Emma held the screen door with her hip. "That would be wonderful. Thanks, sis. Now, you'll make sure everyone is in the barn and you will make sure Sam and Gracie are in the house? Don't forget to feed the horses extra hay. And . . ."

Kate interrupted her mother. "Mom, I can handle it. I do remember how to do the chores on this farm. It will be fine. None of your critters will go hungry or without shelter. You go spend time with Conner. He loves his bath time."

Emma still stood at the door. Kate gave a motion as if to shoo something along. "Go, go."

Emma let the screen door close gently behind her. Lilly and Kate could hear her talking to Conner as she walked into the house. They both smiled.

"Let's get her chores done before she has a fit," Kate said.

The rest of the evening was spent tending to Emma's animals and then a quiet evening going over wedding plans. Emma sat and read a book but would add her ideas every once in a while. Lilly could not remember when she had spent such a pleasant evening. It was probably the last time she was here at the farm.

Before bedtime it was decided that they would all go to Emporia to a bridal shop and see if they could find a wedding dress for Lilly. As she lay in bed later that night, her thoughts would jump from one idea to another. Just as she drifted off, she thought of Emma. Tomorrow she would make sure Emma would give her away at the wedding. She desperately wanted Emma to do the honors.

Chapter 34

After several hours of shopping the following morning, Lilly found a dress that both Kate and Emma continued to rave over. They knew Conner was getting fussy and decided to head back towards home.

As they traveled toward Emma's, Kate brought up the subject of the upcoming holidays and how she thought Emma should just come to Denver. Emma said she would keep that idea on the back burner but she wanted to still decorate the house as she always did.

After much discussion, Lilly said she would come and help Emma decorate the house for Christmas. Kate turned to Lilly sitting next to her in the passenger seat. "Lilly Ballard, I do not think you understand what you are getting yourself into. My mother has a ton of boxes of decorations and she has been known to take over a week getting everything just like she wants it. When it comes to holiday decorating, she is a tyrant."

Emma leaned forwards from the back seat where she sat with Conner. "I am no such thing, Kate. I just want things to look special for the holidays. That's all."

They reached the house and Emma said she was going to take a nap. Lilly sat down on the sofa and Kate sat in the overstuffed chair with Conner on her lap.

Kate leaned her head on the back of the chair. "She starts this new treatment tomorrow. I am staying until I know how she does with it. I know she has all kinds of support around here but I will feel better knowing she is doing well with it. Do you think I am a terrible daughter by not moving back and taking care of her right now?"

"No, Kate. I don't think that at all. You and Joshua have your careers and now a new baby. Maybe you will be able to have her with you in Denver. I know that is not what she wants but it might be the only alternative."

"I don't know what to do. She can be so stubborn. I just don't think she is going to be able to stay here and I know that is going to break her heart."

"David and I are only an hour away and my job affords me the luxury of being able to come and go almost as much as I want. David can come over here too. We will help in any way possible. We have grown to love Emma. She's a fighter, Kate."

Kate sighed a deep sigh. "I think she is tired of fighting. It seems like she has had to fight one battle or another all her adult life. I think she is running out of fight. I never thought the day would come but I can see it in her eyes. She's tired. I just can't lose her, Lilly. Not now. I want my son to know her. She is the kind of grandma everyone wants for his or her children. And, neither Joshua nor I have any siblings to give our children aunts and uncles." Kate stopped. Her eyes filled with tears. "Jim would have been an awesome uncle. Conner can't miss out on not knowing Mom. He is already missing out on knowing his uncle. It's just not right, Lilly. Do you have siblings?"

Lilly pulled one leg up under the other. "No, I was an only child. It was just my mother and I. My dad died before I was born. Mom never really talked about him. When she was sick and I asked her if she wanted to be buried beside him, she became angry and told me she had no desire to do such a thing. You know, I never even asked her where he was buried and I guess she took that to her grave with her. I should have asked more questions growing up but I didn't. Make sure you tell your children all about their ancestors and their family history."

Kate ran her finger over the chintz fabric on the chair. "How sad that you never had siblings or a father. I am grateful that I had at least eighteen years with Jim. He did such cool things for me. He was the best."

Sam began to bark and run in circles. Before Kate and Lilly could get to the door, they heard Zeke Lang calling out Emma's name. "Emma Jean! Emma!" The truck horn began to honk.

Emma came out of the bedroom. "What in the Sam Hill is that old man up to now?"

Kate wrapped a quilt over Conner and Emma and Lilly stepped outside on the porch with Kate following. Conner whimpered as she covered his head with the quilt to protect him from the evening chill.

Zeke came running onto the porch. Lilly could see someone in the passenger seat and a child in the back seat of the extended cab.

"Emma, you need to call 911. I found these two on the road. She's messed up real bad. That bastard down the road has beat the shit out of her."

Emma looked towards the truck and asked, "Who? That fella that keeps to himself and is rude to everyone?"

"Yep. She's hurt, Emma. Hurt bad."

Emma turned to Kate and before she could speak Kate said, "I'm on it, Momma. I'll call for help."

Emma walked towards the truck. The young woman held a towel over her right eye. Emma's stomach turned as she fought back her own fears and memories. "My name is Emma and I am here to help you. We've called for help."

"No! He'll kill my boy and me if he knows I've gone for help. Please, no. No!"

Emma reached for the woman's arm and in a calm, soothing tone said, "Let me see how bad you are hurt. Maybe it isn't necessary but I think getting medical help would be a good idea."

Emma smiled at the boy in the back seat. "Are you hurt too?"

He looked down at the floorboard of Zeke's truck and quietly said, "No. But my mom is bad. Her eye is out on her cheek."

Emma quickly turned to Zeke and he shook his head yes in acknowledgment.

Emma opened the truck door. She turned to Lilly. "Lilly take this young man inside and get him something to drink and eat. See that he is taken care of, would you?"

Lilly's heart was racing. "Of course, Emma."

Lilly and Emma helped the boy out of the truck. Emma ran her hand through his dark hair. "Now, this is my friend Lilly and she is going to fix you something to eat. Would you feel better if Mr. Lang came inside also? My daughter Kate and her son are inside. I am going to stay with your momma and see if we can get her some help."

Zeke put his hand on the back of Emma's elbow and whispered in her ear, "There's a pickup turning into the drive, Emma Jean. We need to all get inside. I think it is this boy's pa."

Emma leaned into Zeke's pickup and spoke quietly to the young woman. "What is your name?"

"My name is Helen. Please don't let them take my boy away from me. He's all I have."

"Not a living soul will take that child from you, Helen. Let's get you inside until medical help gets here. Let me help you."

The towel dropped as Helen stepped from Zeke's truck. Emma's heart raced and she reached for the towel. Helen's face was already black and she tried to hold her eye back into the socket but it appeared all of the bones were fractured. Emma held Helen's arm and helped her hold the towel. "Just keep moving towards my house, Helen. Help is on its way."

Zeke held the door open for the two women. Kate met her mother at the door. "They are on their way. This is what I hate about being in the country. Lilly is taking care of the boy."

Emma helped Helen to a chair. "Just sit here and keep your head back. Would you like anything?"

Kate watched Zeke lock the front door. She walked over to him. "What are you doing?"

"He's at the end of the driveway. We don't want no more trouble. Did you call the sheriff too?"

"Yes, they are sending an ambulance and a sheriff. If he comes up here, I know Momma will rip him a new one and have him hauled off or, worse yet, shoot the son of a bitch.

"That is exactly why I ain't taking no chances. We're keeping this door locked until the sheriff gets here. I can't figure how he knows she is here. I picked her up on the side of the road. The boy flagged me down."

Kate pulled at her sweatshirt. "If he has any idea that you picked her up and he sees your truck here, he will try to come after her and talk her into coming home. Oh, how I remember those times of my own dad talking her into bringing us back. Telling her he would change. On and on he would make promises."

Kate looked out the front window towards the cemetery. "We all know that never happened. So much water under the bridge."

Emma was the first to hear the sirens. "Help is here, Helen."

The pickup at the end of the drive backed up and then turned and drove through a pasture towards his home. Zeke spoke quietly to Kate. "You think she will press charges?"

"It doesn't matter any more. The state will do it for her, if I remember right. She doesn't have to make the decision."

The ambulance pulled in front of Emma's house. Before the paramedics could get onto the porch, a sheriff's car pulled into the drive.

Emma met them at the door. She was trying to explain what happened when the young boy came from the kitchen. He walked to the paramedic and extended his hand. "My name is James Willis and my pop tried to kill my mom. Will you help us?"

The paramedic shook James hand. "We will help you and your mom. Are you hurt, son?"

"No sir, but my mom is in bad shape."

"Let's take a look at her. How old are you?"

"I'm ten, sir. Her eye keeps falling out of her head. He beat her bad this time. He used my baseball bat."

Emma turned to Kate. "Did you ask him his name when Lilly brought him in?"

Kate looked out the window, tears burning her eyes and said, "Yes. I wasn't going to tell you because I knew it would upset you. I knew it would bring back thoughts of Jim and what we went through."

The paramedics attended to Helen and Emma and James went onto the front porch to talk to the sheriff. They placed Helen on a gurney and Emma stepped aside so they could take Helen to the ambulance. As they came next to James, Helen asked them to stop.

"James, I'll be fine. These people are going to take care of things." She turned to the paramedic and said, "What will happen to my son while I am in the hospital?"

The sheriff spoke. "He will probably go into child protective custody until a family member arrives and can assure that he will be safe with them."

Emma stepped closer to the sheriff and looked him in the eye. "I don't think that will be necessary, Eli. He is welcome here until his family arrives. I am assuming it will be Helen's family and that you are getting ready to take care of the major problem here?"

The sheriff looked at Emma, then Zeke and at James. "I guess he can stay here. But I want assurance he is safe so I will go take care of the problem. And I will still have to notify Social Services about the boy."

Emma began to pace back and forth. "And you will let me know when it is safe?"

"Yes, Emma. I will let you know."

James kissed his mother's hands as he held them tightly in his. "Do you want me to ride with you, Mom?"

"I'll be fine. This way you don't have to sit at the hospital and wait. I am sure someone will bring you up as soon as you can visit. I love you."

"Mom, are you sure?"

Lilly and Kate stood on the porch, their arms touching. Lilly could feel Kate shaking.

Emma placed her hand gently on Helen's shoulder. "I will bring James anytime you want. Now, Helen, do you want someone to ride with you in the ambulance until your family arrives?"

A lump formed in Helen's throat and she made a deep moaning noise before she spoke. "My family has no idea what goes on behind closed doors. I have not seen them in over a year since Charles moved us out here in the country. This will come as a shock to them. But I want James to be with them. He'll be safe there. In my purse are all my contact numbers. Charles took all of my money and my keys but I still got away with my purse after he ransacked it."

The paramedic turned to Emma and said, "We need to get her to the hospital. She is going to need surgery and I hope they can save that eye. Animals like that bastard should be locked up and throw away the key."

Helen and James said goodbye. As they were placing Helen in the ambulance she asked for Emma. Emma walked to the end of the ambulance.

"Emma, will you come along? I'm scared. Will your girls take care of my son?"

Emma didn't feel it was necessary to correct Helen and explain that only Kate was her daughter. She smiled and said, "I will be happy to ride along."

The paramedic turned to Emma and suggested she take her own vehicle. That way she would have means of getting back home.

Kate walked up to her mother. "Are you up to this? You've been way too sick to be spending late hours. Why don't you let Zeke go?"

Emma walked back towards the house. "I need to get my keys. Kate, she doesn't have any one else. You make sure that boy is clean, warm and fed. I'll be back as soon as possible. She has no one here, Kate. No one."

Kate took a deep breath and decided she would not try to convince her mother otherwise. She hugged Emma and held onto her like a small child would when a parent leaves them in an unknown environment. "Be careful, Momma. They haven't arrested him yet."

"You keep the doors locked and don't hesitate to call the sheriff if need be."

Emma turned to Zeke. "Will you stay with these girls and little men until Eli lets you know he is in jail?"

"I sure as Hell will. I won't let no harm come to them, Emma. I swear on Nancy's grave."

Kate released Emma from the hug and kissed her check. The ambulance drove off. The sheriff followed them out of the drive but turned in the other direction towards the Willis home.

Emma walked to her car. Zeke walked with her. "Ezekiel, you take care of the chores so the girls aren't outside. I am hoping Eli catches him but I am afraid he has already left the county. Big, brave man that he is. I am so glad you brought her here. The girls will take care of the boy. He can help entertain Conner. I need to get going. I am praying they can save that eye of hers."

"Made this man nearly lose my supper when I came upon them. I hope they lock him away for life."

Emma started the engine. She patted Zeke's weathered hand as he rested it on the door of her car. "That won't happen and you know it. They need tougher laws against these kinds of people."

Zeke watched as Emma drove out of her drive. She was driving faster than Zeke cared to see but he made a mental note to not mention it to Emma. He knew she was on a mission.

Lilly stood on the porch and Kate carried Conner into the house with James following her. Zeke told Lilly he would finish the chores and be right in.

As Zeke walked towards the barn, he turned back towards Lilly. "Lilly Ballard, you lock them doors and don't open them until you are sure it is me. It shouldn't take me more than a few minutes. Now, go on and get inside that house."

Lilly did as she was told. She sat at the front window watching for Zeke to return. Kate and James sat on the floor and watched Conner. They were all quiet. There was nothing to say. All they could do was wait.

Chapter 35

Lilly saw Zeke walking back from the barn with Sam at his side. He came to the door and Lilly opened it.

Zeke pulled out his tobacco can and gently tapped it. "Didn't I tell you to wait until you were sure it was me?"

"I've been watching out the window. May I get you something to drink?"

Zeke chuckled. "What I need to drink is something Emma Jean don't allow in this household. I need something a lot more stiff than iced tea, Miss Lilly Ballard. Has she got any soda around here?"

"I'll look. Kate, do you know if she has any soda or not?"

Kate stood up and pulled at her jeans. Lilly could not get over all of the weight Kate had lost since the baby. She decided it was the stress of a newborn and her mother being ill.

Kate pulled at her jeans again and said, "I doubt if she has any. She only buys it if she thinks some of the grandkids are coming out. I'll look. Lilly, will you stay here with Conner? Zeke, do you want to show James the house and Jim's old bedroom? I think I will have him stay in there. Lilly, I will put you in Mom's room or on the sleeper sofa on the sun porch. Is that all right with you?"

"Of course. I had planned on heading home but I will stay another night. I think I will call David and let him know my plans."

Zeke took James upstairs and Kate went into the kitchen. Lilly phoned David and informed him of the day's happenings. Headlights shone into the front window.

Lilly excused herself on the phone and called out to Kate, "Someone is pulling in the drive. I can't make anything out just yet."

Just at that moment the car turned on its red lights and Lilly was relieved to know it was the sheriff. Kate called from the kitchen. "Don't open the door until you actually see the person. I'm on my way."

Zeke called from upstairs, "Don't open the door, ladies. We'll be right down."

Lilly turned to Kate. "I'm sure it is the sheriff. They have their lights on."

"You can never be sure, Lilly. Trust me. Don't ever open the door until you are sure."

Eli stepped out of the patrol car and opened the gate. Zeke came into the room alone. "Where's the boy?" Lilly asked.

"He's upstairs in Jim's room looking at some books Emma has in there. And he wanted to turn on the television."

Kate opened the door. "Did you find him?"

Eli took off his hat. "They caught him heading south on Highway 75. I imagine he was heading for the state line. He's on his way to jail. No ifs, ands or buts about it. I just hope we can hold him and get charges pressed while she's in the hospital. Where's the boy?"

Zeke reached for his shirt pocket and took his hand away, placing it in his jean pocket. "He's upstairs . . . . "

James walked down the stairs. "Did you get him? Can he get to my mom?"

Lilly thought of this young child more worried about his mother's safety than his own and she wondered if this is how it was for Jim and Emma. Emma always said Jim tried to protect both Emma and Kate. So many children lived this very same life and lived in fear daily.

Eli answered, "We found your dad and he is in custody. Your mom is safe in the hospital and we have a guard that will be outside her door. Emma will phone as soon as she knows anything about your mom. And your dad isn't able to get to either one of you. You're safe."

James looked at Conner lying on the quilt on Emma's living room rug. He looked up at Kate. "Don't think I don't love Pop. I do. But he can't keep hurting us like that. He just can't."

Kate sat down on the chair beside James. "I know you love your dad. No one is asking you to not love him. But he needs help and he needs to know he can't treat you and your mom that way. James, are there any animals at your farm that need fed and need attention?"

"Yes. We have two dogs and three barn cats. And my mom's chickens and ducks."

Kate stood and turned to Zeke and smiled. Zeke nudged her with his shoulder. "All right, Kate. I'll go tend to the animals. Eli, would it be all right if James came with me? Maybe you would like to go also?"

Eli radioed that he would be at the Willis farm helping tend the animals. He then turned to James. "Would you like to ride in the car with me?"

James eyes lit up. "Yeah!"

Zeke laughed and said, "I reckon that means I am in my old pickup alone. Poor old Zeke alone again."

Kate and Lilly both chuckled and Kate hugged Zeke. "Why, Ezekiel Lang, there isn't a woman in Osage County that doesn't think a ride in that old pickup would be a thrill. You know that."

Zeke blushed. "Ain't no woman compares to my Nancy. Reckon I'll just keep on being alone. And then there's them bastards like Willis out there beating their womenfolk. Don't make sense."

Kate whispered in Zeke's ear. "Remember he is still that boy's father. Don't talk like that in front of him. He can't help who his father is."

Zeke hugged Kate. "Right as always like your momma."

The two men and James left for the Willis farm and Kate and Lilly sat in the living room. Lilly was the first to speak. "How in the world did you live like this?"

Kate picked up Conner and said softly, "You learn to survive. You walk on eggshells. You live one day at a time."

The phone rang. Kate handed Conner to Lilly. "Hello?"

Lilly watched Kate and rocked Conner back and forth in a swaying motion. Kate said nothing but 'yes' and nodded her head. Lilly continued to watch. Finally Kate spoke.

"When are you coming home? Are you staying until the surgery is over? Mom, I think you need to come home. They can call us when she comes out of surgery and we can go then."

There was a pause. "He's been arrested."

Another pause. "How about you come home and we take shifts at the hospital? Zeke is still here and I am sure he wouldn't mind helping out. There's too many of us here that can take a shift. You need to get your rest."

Kate rolled her eyes. "Yes, momma. I expect to see you within the next two hours. Call from your cell phone and that way I will know when to expect you. I'm sending Zeke there to be with you. No arguments."

Kate sighed. "I love you too. Please don't get run down. You'll be in the hospital bed beside her if you don't take care of yourself."

Kate hung up the phone. "Every bone on that side of Helen's face is broken plus three ribs and they are going to call in a plastic surgeon to try to save her eye. Mom said it will be pretty extensive surgery and she has no idea how long. I think I talked her into coming home in a few hours and getting some rest. I am going to ask Zeke to go to the hospital and stay and have her come home."

Lilly pulled her sweater over her shoulders and handed a sleeping Conner to Lilly. "I could go sit with her. If Zeke will take me, I will sit with her. Or, if someone will give me directions to the hospital."

"We'll talk to Zeke when he gets here. They should be returning anytime now. I'm going to put Conner to bed. Will you listen for the phone?"

Kate took Conner into her room and Lilly sat on the sofa trying to gather the day's events.

Kate returned after a few minutes. Lilly took a deep breath and asked Kate, "Will you tell me more about your mom? She is so take charge and she reaches out to others in need. Why didn't she herself ask for help when your dad was so abusive?"

"Lilly, my mother is a very proud woman, as you know already. She was taught that divorce was a sin and that she should try to make it work. I know she finally divorced my dad because she was afraid for all of us. It was no longer about what her family would think but about the safety of her and her children."

Lilly leaned forward towards Kate as she sat down in the chair next to Lilly. "Go on, Kate, tell me more."

"After my mother found the strength to leave my dad, there was a time she tried to fight everyone's battle. I was eleven and we had gone to the local grocery store. A very large man and a woman about Mom's size were in the aisle where the eggs were. The woman picked up a carton of eggs and they slipped out of her hand, eggs breaking everywhere. He grabbed her by her hair and told her to get down there and clean them up. You could see the terror in her face. Momma wasn't afraid. She stormed up to that man and told him he was nothing but a piece of crap. Did he feel like a big man, treating his wife that way? I watched my little 5' 3" mother stand tall and proud against him. Then she knelt down on the floor with that woman. I heard her say 'You don't have to live like this, you know. There are shelters. Come with me right now.' The woman cried and told her she couldn't. So Momma said 'Then I will help you clean up this mess.' She used her bare hands to try to gather the broken eggs and that man stood over her, laughing and scoffing. She stood back up and looked him in the eye. She turned to me and told me to go get one of the men that worked there and tell them there had been an accident on the egg aisle. I was afraid to leave and I hesitated. 'Go on. This big man isn't going to do anything to me.' She held out her hand and helped that poor woman up to her feet. I hurried to get help. When we came back around the corner, Momma was wiping that woman's hands with her good jacket. I remember how proud she was of that new jacket and I couldn't believe what I was seeing. Momma had worked months to be able to save enough money for it and she took me with her when she bought it. Now she was cleaning that woman's hands. She held that woman's hands in hers and looked at the man again and said 'Someday you will pay for what you have done, mister. It may not be here on this earth but you will pay for it someday. I hope I am there to see it.' And then she turned and took me by the arm and walked away."

"What happened then?" Lilly asked.

"We got our groceries and when we got in the car she turned to me and said 'Never let anyone humiliate you like that and promise me that you will never let yourself be treated by a man that way.' I promised her I would never let it happen and I have kept that promise. I asked her sometime after that why she did what she did and why did she use her jacket to clean that woman's hands."

"What did she say?"

"She said she knew the humiliation that woman felt and she wanted her to know someone else was willing to be humiliated right along with her. That she wasn't alone in her embarrassment. And she said jackets wash but the human spirit takes a long time to cleanse. She was right."

Zeke's truck pulled into the drive. Kate looked out the window. "Zeke and James are back. Eli must have had to leave. They rode back together."

Lilly opened the door. Zeke smiled and said, "Did you look this time?"

"Yes, I did, but I assumed we were safe since an arrest had been made."

Kate stepped next to Zeke. "Nothing is for sure in a situation like this. Take every precaution." She turned to Zeke and gave him a big smile.

Zeke let out a moan and said, "What do you want?"

"Mom phoned. They are going to be doing surgery and I think we should take shifts at the hospital. Mom doesn't need to be up all night. She needs her rest. Would you take the first shift?"

"Kate Phillips, you are a charmer like your mother. I reckon I can go."

James looked up at Zeke. "I would like to go too. I want to be there for my mom. My grandparents won't be here until tomorrow according to Sheriff Eli. That gives me time to be with my mom. She needs me."

Kate looked at James and a rush of memories of a similar boy with the same name swept over her. She fought back the tears. "Are you sure you don't want to get a good night's sleep and then see her? She could be in surgery for hours, James."

"I want to be there for my mom. I can rest tomorrow. She needs me."

Zeke patted James on the back and said, "You're the boss, James. If you want to be there for your momma, then that is what will happen. Ain't no reason why you can't ride along. That way we can make sure Emma Jean comes home and gets her rest. I might warn you that she is a stubborn old woman. She can put up a fight when she thinks she is right."

James smiled. "She'll come home. I'll make sure of it." He turned to Kate and Lilly. "Thank you for your kindness but I need to be with my mom. Mr. Lang will bring me home in the morning. Sheriff Eli said it would be afternoon before my grandparents get here. And I will want to make sure my animals are fed. Do you mind?"

Kate looked at Zeke and back at James. "Make sure you listen to Zeke and, if you should decide you want to come back here tonight, you are welcome. One of us will probably be at the hospital in the early morning to take a shift with your mother. Maybe you will want to get some rest then."

James zipped his jacket. "We'll see. I need to see how mom is doing before I leave her."

"I understand." Kate said.

Lilly went into the kitchen and put some cookies into a zippered bag. She brought them out and said, "In case you need a snack while you are waiting."

Zeke and James both smiled and walked onto the porch. Zeke turned to Kate and, before he could speak, Kate said, "I'll lock all the doors. Sam and Gracie will be inside. I will keep a phone beside me. And I'm not afraid to call 911. You make sure Momma heads back here. And tell her to call so I will know when to look for her."

Zeke shook his head in what appeared to be disbelief. "Smarty pants. I will send that old woman home as soon as I get there. I will make her call."

Kate and Lilly went back inside the house. Kate locked the door. She turned to Lilly. "I'm exhausted. Want to call it a night?"

"I think I will wait up for your mother. I'll listen for the phone."

"Oh, Lilly, that would be great. Please have her wake me when she gets here. I know Conner will be awake for a feeding in a couple of hours so I am going to try to catch a little shuteye. Thank you so much. Now, you promise to have her wake me?"

"I promise."

Lilly fell asleep on the sofa shortly after Kate retired to bed. The phone rang. It was Emma saying Zeke was a stubborn old mule and she was on her way home. Lilly watched television until she heard Emma's car pull in the drive. She, of course, made sure it was Emma before she opened the door.

Emma looked tired. "Is Kate asleep?"

"She asked that you wake her when you arrive. She wanted to get a little sleep before Conner's next feeding."

"Are you sleeping in Jim's room tonight or shall I make up the sleeper sofa on the sun porch?"

"Oh, Emma, don't go to all that trouble. It is so late. I will either sleep here on the sofa or in Jim's room. Is she out of surgery?"

Emma took off her jacket. "No, not yet. It will be a few more hours. That boy isn't going to leave that hospital until he sees his mother."

Kate came into the living room. "I thought I heard your voice. Tell me what is going on."

The three women stayed up for another hour and Emma excused herself and went to bed. Conner awoke and Kate fed him while she and Lilly tried to discuss more wedding plans. It was difficult to do after such a day. Kate and Conner went into the other room to sleep and Lilly covered herself with one of Emma's quilts. It had been a long day. Sam lay on the floor beside her as she drifted off to sleep.

Chapter 36

Morning seemed to come much too soon for Lilly. She awoke to Kate and Emma talking in the kitchen.

Lilly entered the kitchen.

"Good morning, Lilly, How did you sleep?" Emma asked.

"Fine, thank you."

Emma filled Lilly in on the day's plans and asked if Lilly would stay long enough for Zeke and James to return to the house while Kate and Conner took Emma to her cancer treatment. Lilly tried to keep busy after Emma and Kate left, hoping it would take her mind off Emma's illness and the previous night's events.

The morning went quickly and Lilly was glad to see Zeke pull in the drive.

Zeke pulled off his cap and ran his fingers through his thinning hair. "They have Emma Jean in for her treatment and Miss Helen is out of surgery and doing well. James spent some time with her and now I think he is ready for a little shuteye and his grandma and grandpa to come pick him up. Have you done the chores?"

Lilly had a sheepish look on her face and said, "I let the horses out and fed the cats and dogs but I didn't take care of the other animals. I'm sorry, Zeke."

"Don't fret over it. I can have them all fed in no time. I think this fella is ready for some grub and a shower and nap. Aren't you?"

James smiled and nodded in agreement. He walked onto the porch.

"I think I can find something in Emma's kitchen that will fill you up. Thank you, Zeke, for feeding the animals. Let's see what we can find, James."

Lilly and Zeke enjoyed visiting while James ate his meal. By mid-afternoon James' grandparents had come to pick him up. Zeke and Lilly sat on the porch waiting for Kate and Emma to return. Zeke told of Nancy's courageous battle against cancer and all that Emma had done to help Nancy around the house.

Soon Emma and Kate returned. Emma waved as she came into the front yard. "I'm fine. That was a breeze. We stopped in to see Helen and her family was there with James. They are going to take her back home with them when she is well enough. She promised to keep in touch. This county needs a safe house for these victims, I tell you. She's lucky Ezekiel came upon her. Very lucky."

Emma sat on the porch. "That was so simple. Not a difficult doctor visit at all," she said as if she were trying to convince herself along with the others.

Kate looked over the top of her vehicle and made a face and shook her head. She lifted Conner from his car seat. "The physician said you wouldn't know how you are going to react until a few days from now. Probably within the next thirty-six hours. I'm calling Joshua and telling him I am staying a couple more days."

Emma stopped and turned to look at Kate. "Like heck you are. You are going home. I don't need help and, if I do, I will call."

Kate walked through the gate. "We'll see."

Zeke stood next to Lilly. "Emma Jean, if Miss Kate wants to stay and tend to your needs, let her. Drop that tough attitude, old woman."

Emma's blue eyes snapped. "I said I am fine and I am, Ezekiel Lang. If I need something, I can call you or a friend or one of the grown grandkids. Simple as that. Kate needs her own rest and time with Conner."

Emma sat on the sofa and motioned for Kate to sit beside her. "You know what I wish?" Emma said.

Kate put her arm around her mother. "What do you wish, Momma?"

"I wish I was rich and I could open a safe house for victims like Helen. A place where they could bring their children and feel safe. Someplace that had plenty of room to run. Only once did I go to the Battered Women's Shelter and it was an old house right in the heart of town. It had a tiny little yard. Jim was three. It was full that night and they had no place for us. They were going to set up cots for us if we had no other option so I called your uncle in St. Joe to pick us up."

"You should have never gone back to Dad then."

Emma turned to Kate and frowned, shaking her index finger at Kate. "Then I wouldn't have you. Guess the Good Lord thought it wasn't the right time."

Kate removed her arm from Emma. "Good Lord? Why did He let us go through what we did? Why is Jim gone now?"

Emma took her tissue she held in her left hand and waved it. "Truce! I should know better than to talk this with you. Someday you need to let your bitterness go, sis. And the sooner the better so you don't show it to your children."

Kate stood and walked to the window, pulling the curtain aside and looking towards the cemetery. "I'm not ready to let it go. Not yet. The day the doctors tell me you are cured and we have many years left, then I will let it go."

Emma sighed and laid her head back on the sofa. "Oh, Kate."

Lilly decided to try to ease the tension. "Emma, why couldn't you offer some of this land for the building of a safe house?"

Zeke stood behind the sofa shaking his head in a negative motion and frowning.

Emma lifted her head. "That might be an answer. What abuser would think to look for their victim out here in the country? Zeke, how much land would I need for something like that? I could donate the land if someone would offer the funds for the building."

Zeke reached for his pocket and then scratched his head. "Emma Jean, ain't no way you can handle a project like that right now. Put them ideas on the back burner for now and focus on yourself."

Emma leaned her head back and looked up at Zeke standing behind her. "I don't need your help anyway, old man. When I am up to it, I'll take care of it myself."

Zeke reached into his pocket and took out the chewing tobacco can, opened it and took a pinch of tobacco, bringing it to his mouth and then returning it to the can. He continued to hold the can in his hand. He ruffled Emma's hair. "Stubborn. That's all I will say."

Emma and Zeke bantered back and forth and Kate covered her ears and walked outside. Lilly stood and thought about following Kate. Zeke turned and spoke to Lilly. "We done pissed her off. She thinks we're fighting. Kate don't like nobody showing any kind of negative feelings, right Emma?"

"I'll go check on her," Emma said.

Emma opened the screen door. She placed her hand on Kate's back. "How bout you and I go in the Mustang to the cemetery? Zeke and Lilly are here to watch things. We can either leave Conner or take him. Your choice."

Kate leaned her head towards her mother's. "Just us, Momma. I will take Conner tomorrow when it is warmer."

"Fair enough," Emma said.

Emma walked to the front door. "We are taking a little drive to see the boys. Be back in a bit. Will you two tend to Conner for us?"

"I would be honored," Lilly said.

Emma and Kate were gone for nearly an hour and Zeke decided he should take care of Emma's chores and also his own place. "I think I will make sure the animals at the Willis place are cared for," he said.

After Zeke left, Lilly sat and rocked Conner while she waited for Emma and Kate. She soon heard them drive into the drive.

Lilly asked if Emma and Kate wanted her to stay and help with anything. It was decided mother and daughter would be fine and Lilly prepared to go back to Kansas City.

As Kate walked Lilly to her SUV, they discussed times they could go over finalizing wedding plans. It was decided Lilly and David would take a trip to Denver within the next two months. Both women looked forward to it.

Kate promised to keep Lilly informed of Emma's health and Lilly made Kate promise to have Emma call if she needed anything at all. Kate watched Lilly pull out of the drive. Lilly knew Emma's treatment had taken a toll on her because Emma chose to stay inside.

Kate returned to the house. Emma sat holding Conner. She looked tired. Kate wondered how long before the aftereffects of the treatments would take their toll on her mother. "Are you hungry?" she asked her mother.

Emma continued to rock Conner. "Not really. But you fix something for yourself. I think my little man and I will just sit here and enjoy one another. I doubt I stay up much longer. This has been a full day. Did Ezekiel get all my chores done?"

Kate smiled, thinking of her mother always wondering if things were taken care of.

"Yes, Momma. He took care of all of that before he headed home. He said he will check in tomorrow. I think he plans on helping as much as you will let him with all of your chores. And don't fight him either. He just wants to be a good friend."

Emma took a deep breath and let out a sigh. She kissed Conner's right hand. "I know he means well. And he is an awful good friend. Don't know what I would do without him at times. But don't go telling him that or he'll get the big head."

Kate chuckled and walked towards the kitchen. "I won't."

Chapter 37

It was hard for Kate to leave her mother and return to Denver. She continued to call daily and check on Emma. Each time she phoned, Emma would insist she was doing fine and that the treatments were going well.

Lilly and David made a trip to Denver and spent some time finalizing the wedding. Both couples enjoyed one another's company. It was decided that Lilly and David would try to stop in at Emma's over the Christmas holiday.

Kate and Joshua arrived at Emma's Christmas Eve. Emma did not greet them at the door. Kate handed Conner to Joshua as she entered the house. "Mom? Mom?" she called.

Emma came out of the kitchen. Kate was shocked to see her mother's appearance. Emma's hair was thinning and the circles under her eyes were extremely dark. Emma smiled, wiping her hands on a dishtowel.

"There's my gang. You are earlier than I thought you would be. I was just putting my pies in the oven."

Kate fought the burning tears welling in her eyes. She was overwhelmed with anger and fear. Why hadn't one of her stepsiblings phoned to tell her what Emma was like? Why didn't Zeke phone? Had Lilly checked in on Emma as promised?

Emma placed the towel over her shoulder. "Let me give this little man some sugar. Come here to your grandma."

Joshua handed Conner to Emma. Emma winked at Joshua and whispered, "It's fine. Things are just fine."

Kate felt she had to somehow address Emma's appearance without upsetting her mother. "Momma, has Zeke been here to help out? Is Taylor helping you around the house? Have you been making it to church on Sundays? Are you . . . .".

Before Kate could say any more Emma interrupted. "Folks are checking in. I sometimes make it to church when I am up to it and things are fine."

Emma looked at Kate and said, "What? Why are you looking at me that way?"

Kate crossed her arms. "Don't lie to me, Mother. You look exhausted. Why didn't you say you needed help and that these treatments are taking a toll?"

Emma held Conner close to her. "I am not lying and I didn't say they are taking their toll because they aren't. Don't start this with me. It's Christmas. Don't start it. Do you understand?"

Kate held her tongue. She glanced at Joshua. He looked frustrated and yet he gave her a slight smile. He turned to Emma. "Emma, your tree is beautiful as usual. Did you do it yourself this year?"

"Joshua, I know that is your way of trying to find out if folks are helping around here so I will just tell you the truth. Zeke went out and cut the tree for me, brought it here and set it up. I did all the decorating. Brett, Taylor and Dawson helped me with the outside lights and all the trimmings. There you have it. You know, when we first decided to have Christmas in Denver, I was all excited and then when I asked if we could have it here, I was afraid I might have trouble getting things done but everyone pitched in and look at how pretty it all turned out."

Kate could not believe she had let her mother talk her into changing plans. If she had known Emma was so frail, she would have had her flown to Denver. She decided at that moment it was time to take Emma home with them. She could not trust Emma to tell her the truth about her condition and she was sure Emma was pressuring the rest of the family and friends to keep her condition from Kate. Emma had a way of making sure Kate would not worry. She always said presentation was everything. If you present things in just the right way, folks will see things your way.

Emma held Conner and looked into his eyes and they both smiled. "He smiled! Oh, good Lord, he is growing so fast. Look at that little face. He smiled."

"Mom, if you would come out and stay for a while, we could get a doctor in Denver and you could be there to see Conner change each and every day. I want you to think about that. It would be perfect."

Emma smiled and turned her back to Kate. "We'll see."

Kate knew what Emma's "We'll see" meant. It meant no just like it meant no when Kate and Jim were growing up. Emma hated telling them 'no' so she would just say, "We'll see" instead. Kate could feel the frustration and anger building up inside but decided to let it go and try to have a decent Christmas. "How many of us will be here on Christmas Day, Mom?"

Emma swayed back and forth with Conner. "As always, I am not real sure. Ezekiel is coming and I have invited Rylie's entire bunch along with Lilly and David. I even phoned Helen and James but they are spending it with family."

Kate wished her mother had kept it a simple holiday gathering and wished it were a small gathering and Zeke. Emma was always including anyone and everyone for the holidays. Kate didn't mind when she was younger and Emma included friends but things were different now. Kate wasn't sure how long she would have her mother to share in holidays and she felt somewhat selfish.

Emma handed Conner to Joshua and turned to Kate. "I have some jobs for you while you are here. First of all, I want you to cut my hair. I don't want to go into town to the beauty shop and have the locals talking about 'Poor Emma'. Just shave it, Kate. And I want it done before folks get here tomorrow."

Kate remembered when Nancy had started losing her hair and Emma volunteered to shave her head. They did it on the front porch and Kate could hear both of them laughing and joking. She made a mental note to make things just as light hearted as that day years ago.

"I'll shave it after we put Conner to bed tonight. What other projects do you have for me?"

Emma went to the bookcase and took a note pad from the top shelf. "I've got my list all written down on this pad. It's my Bible right now. I will read it to you while you shear me tonight."

Joshua suggested he unload their luggage from the car and Kate sat down with Conner on her lap. "Sit down, Mom."

Emma obliged. Both women sat in silence until Conner let out a burp. Emma giggled like a little girl.

"He reminds me of your brother. Especially through the eyes."

Kate smiled. "Did that burp remind you of him also?"

"Heck, that burp could be genetic from either one of you. You were far from lady like as a little girl."

Joshua returned with the luggage and set it in the entry.

The family enjoyed one another and Emma relished in her grandson. After the evening meal, Kate put Conner to bed. The phone rang and Emma answered. "No, no. You're not calling too late. Kate and her family arrived here this afternoon and we have had such a nice visit. We are looking forward to seeing you. We will see you in time for Christmas dinner."

Emma hung up the phone as Kate entered the room. "That was Lilly. They will be here around noon tomorrow. That will give us time to have our Christmas in the morning as a family. Are you ready to give me that haircut?"

Kate frowned and Joshua gave her a hug. "I'll go take care of chores while you girls play beauty shop."

Kate kissed him and whispered, "Beauty shop my butt. Those treatments are causing her to lose her hair and this is what we have to deal with."

Emma cleared her throat in a loud cough. "I'm standing right here. I can hear you. There's not a blasted thing wrong with my hearing, you know. Just do what we have to do. It will grow back."

Joshua went outside and Kate went into the bathroom to get the hair clippers. When she returned to the living room, Emma had positioned herself on a barstool in the middle of the room, towel draped over her shoulders.

Kate took a very deep breath and slowly let it out. Emma turned to her and smiled from ear to ear. "Sugar, its only hair. Come on, let's make it fun. O.K.?"

"Ok, Momma. If I had known this, I would have bought you some scarves and hats for Christmas. Maybe we can have you fitted for a nice wig."

Emma pulled the towel over her head and laughed. "No wigs for me. I'm wearing Jim's old Yankee's ball cap and I will find some things to wear. They have such nice stuff now for cancer patients."

Kate felt that terrible feeling inside the pit of her stomach. Cancer. How she hated that word. She turned on the shears. Emma placed the towel back over her shoulders.

Emma settled herself on the barstool like an old hen would nesting. "Ready, set, go!"

Kate shook her head and began to shave her mother's head, tears burning her eyes. Her mind wandered to times long ago when Jim was alive and the three of them would go on outings together. Emma was always trying to make things an adventure. Then she would play a game she had invented that she called "If you could be". She would ask each of her children 'If you could be a tree, what kind of tree would you be?' and so on. It all seemed so long ago now as Kate struggled with the task of shearing her mother's hair and facing another holiday without her brother. She longed for Conner to know Jim and Rylie and she feared he might not have his grandmother around. Kate felt the anger replace the sadness.

"Kate Dog, what are you doing back there? Are you trying to dig right on through to my brain?"

Kate stopped the shears. Emma looked back at Kate. "I thought you would never stop shaving the back. Are you finished?"

Kate could not bear the sight of her mother with no hair. Emma's blue eyes smiled and she pulled Kate close to her. She held her against her small body. "Kate, it will be fine. Please don't let this ruin our holiday. This is Conner's first Christmas and I want it to be special. Try not to think about it."

Kate began to sob uncontrollably. "Why is this happening to you, momma? You, of all people, deserve a break in life. Why?"

"Now, sugar. I am no more special than any other person. Sickness does not choose someone because they are rich or poor. It does not choose someone because they have had a harder time in life than another. We may never know why it has chosen me but we will treat it with dignity and we will fight with all that we have. Don't be sad. Look at the blessings in my life."

Emma kissed Kate's cheek and said, "We need to get our rest. Christmas morning will be here and we need to rest up for Santa. He still needs to fill the stockings and eat his cookies and milk. You go on and I promise to get in bed soon."

"Let me help. I want to help you. I've never watched Santa in action and I think this would be an excellent time to observe him in action. Or should I say 'her'?"

Emma winked at Kate. "It doesn't matter what gender as long as you make the magic happen. Let's get busy."

The two women spent nearly an hour setting out the Santa cookie plate, filling stockings, leaving boot prints along the fireplace hearth where "Santa" had stepped in the ashes. Kate enjoyed watching her mother and listening to her sing the usual Christmas songs. She enjoyed helping create the same memories she had experienced as a child with her brother. Emma still signed packages from Santa. These were traditions Kate wanted to carry on to her own children.

Emma and Kate said their goodnights and, as Kate walked to her bedroom door, she watched Emma stand at the front window. Emma kissed her thumb and held it to the windowpane. Kate could hear her mother whisper "Sweet dreams" as she turned to retire for the night.

Chapter 38

Conner whimpered and Kate got up to get him out of his bed. She took a baby blanket off the bed rail and walked into the living room. The lights on the tree twinkled and she could smell cinnamon rolls baking. "Mom? Are you there?"

Kate walked into the kitchen to find Emma rolling out homemade cinnamon rolls with a bright red Santa hat on her head. Emma looked up and smiled. "Merry Christmas", she said.

"Merry Christmas, Mrs. Claus." Kate said.

She reached for the baking sheet with the freshly baked and iced rolls on it, taking a bite of the warm roll and closing her eyes. "Oh, how I miss your cooking. I need to learn how to cook like you and learn some of your recipes. Seems like I am so tired after working all day that I could care less about cooking. And now with Conner, I have even less time."

Emma removed another batch of rolls from the oven. "Enjoy each and every minute with your children. It goes so quickly. Enjoy both the good and bad. And take time to learn a recipe once in a while. I would love that."

Conner began to cry and squirm in Kate's arms. "He's wet and hungry. I'll change him and we can talk while I feed him."

Emma adjusted her Santa hat and called to Kate as she left the room. "Tell Joshua there's warm cinnamon rolls and presents to be opened. We're burning daylight."

Kate took Conner into the bedroom and Emma began to set the breakfast table. Soon Kate, Joshua and Conner arrived for breakfast.

Emma smiled and said "Merry Christmas Joshua. Santa came in the night and he left presents for all of us but especially your new son. Have a cinnamon roll and we will retire to the living room to open presents."

The family enjoyed the relaxed breakfast and then went into the living room. Kate began to open Conner's presents and set her packages next to her chair. After all the presents had been opened Emma knelt down and reached into the far corner behind the tall Christmas tree. "Why, here's one more package left back here with Kate's name on it. Here, Kate."

Emma handed a package to Kate with a deep red wrapping paper and gold ribbon. Kate looked puzzled but untied the ribbon. She gently unwrapped the package, sometimes looking up at her mother. Inside was a framed Halloween card. Kate turned to her mother and asked, "What's this?"

Emma smiled and said, "Read it, silly."

The card had been framed with both the front and the inside message showing. In a child's handwriting it read, 'To Katy. From Jim. Happy first Halloween.'

Emma leaned towards Kate. "He went to the hospital gift shop the night you were born and bought it with his own money. Of course that was on October 27th and we brought you home from the hospital on Halloween day. He had put up pictures he had drawn and balloons and sitting inside your baby bed was this card. He made me show it to you and read it out loud. I've kept it all these years along with so many other memories. I thought you should have it."

Kate hugged her mother and both of them shed tears. Kate looked over her mother's shoulder at Joshua and smiled. He held Conner in his lap. Joshua was an only child, never knowing the joy of having a sibling. He sometimes envied the bond Kate and Jim had. Kate kissed her mother's cheek and said, "I will hang it in a very special place where I will pass it often."

Emma's phone rang and she went to answer it. Emma said "Merry Christmas" as she greeted the person on the phone. The conversation was short and, as she hung up the phone, she pulled her Santa hat off, revealing her newly shaven head.

Emma sat on the arm of the loveseat. "Billy and Melissa are going to go to her family's Christmas gathering but Taylor and Brett will stop in this evening. Billy said he thinks Jason and his family will be here later but Danielle is not in town. She went away last night and is not returning until after New Year's. That girl is terrible about letting me know her whereabouts. I leave messages and she may or may not return my calls. Rylie always said Danielle dances to the beat of a different drum. Sounds like we may have a small gathering."

Kate was relieved in a way but also wanted to see the rest of the family. She knew she was being selfish in wanting Emma all to herself for the holiday.

"Kate? Are you listening to me?" Emma said.

Kate looked at her mother. "As a matter of fact, I wasn't. Off in my own world, I guess. What did you say?"

"I asked if you plan on helping me with Christmas dinner."

"Of course I do. Do you want to start things now?"

Emma chuckled and put her Santa hat on. "I was up at 4:00 this morning putting the turkey in the oven. I will need help with some of the other food. You have time to clean up and then help."

The morning was spent preparing the meal and at precisely noon Emma's doorbell rang. Emma opened the door and Zeke entered, arms laden with packages.

"Ezekiel Lang, what on earth are you doing bringing gifts?"

Zeke set the gifts under the tree. "Ain't none of them for you so just settle down. Them's all for the grandkids. I ain't missed a year yet, have I? Nancy would have my dog hide if I forgot the youngens."

"Ezekiel, some of my grandchildren are grown adults. They don't need gifts. If my family keeps having babies, you are going to go broke trying to shower them with gifts. Now, don't think I don't appreciate the kindness cause I do. It's that it can get so expensive. Unless you've come into some money and I don't know about it."

Emma nudged Zeke with her shoulder. Zeke looked at Emma and circled around her, looking up and down and then focusing on her head. "What the Hell did you do? You shaved it, didn't you?"

Emma ran her hand over her head and beamed. "Yes, Kate took the shears to me last night. I look pretty, huh?"

Zeke knew the toll cancer treatments could take on a person and he admired Emma's outlook. He remembered how Nancy and Emma would make light of the hair loss, the nausea and the fatigue. He knew he must also encourage Emma as she had encouraged Nancy.

"You look gorgeous. Why, I think I like having more hair than you do. That ain't saying much since I don't have much."

Zeke rubbed Emma's head and hugged her. "Gorgeous."

Emma smiled and put her Santa hat on. "And don't you forget it. Gorgeous sounds real nice to me. You can call me that any old time."

Zeke commented on the rich aroma coming from Emma's kitchen. Shortly after he arrived, Lilly and David came also. The afternoon was spent with gifts, delicious food and wonderful conversation. Emma kept glancing at the clock and then at the front door. Lilly and Kate offered to clear the table and do dishes. As they began to clear the table, Emma excused herself.

Within minutes Emma returned with her coat, gloves and hat on. Zeke was the first to speak. "Where do you think you're goin?"

Emma kissed Conner on the hand and smiled at her guests. "It's time for me to go see the boys. You don't think I would let Christmas go by without taking something to the cemetery, do you?"

Emma pulled a handful of bells from her coat pocket. "Every time a bell rings, an angel gets its wings."

Emma rang the bells, put them in her pocket and turned towards the door. "Anyone care to join me?"

Kate knew her mother was only being polite and that Emma really enjoyed this time alone at the cemetery.

"You go on. Joshua and I will go later and maybe Lilly and David will join us. You and Zeke can baby sit while we go."

Emma smiled and gave a backwards wave. She opened the door. Sam greeted her on the porch. She tugged on his tail and said, "Oh, come on. Get in the truck."

Kate went to the window and watched as her mother drove out of the drive. When she could tell Emma had nearly reached the cemetery, she turned to the others in the room. "Just where on earth are Rylie's kids? Do they realize Mom may not be here another Christmas? Now, don't get me wrong. A day without Melissa bossing all of us is just fine with me but I think it would have been nice if they had come. Surely the grandkids will show."

Joshua stood and hugged Kate. "I know they will. They love their grandma. Give them some time. And, Kate?"

"Yes?"

"You just admitted you are pleased with a portion of the outcome. Emma isn't complaining so you shouldn't either."

Kate shook her head. "She's hurting on the inside. You know how she is. She loves all of the family to be around. She's made all this food and bought gifts for all of them and not one has showed up. Do they know how sick she is?"

Zeke ran his weathered fingers over an ornament on the tree. "They know. Them grandkids have been out here. Jason or Denise stop in more than you might think, Kate. Jason's like his dad. Hates to see her in pain and is at a loss for words to comfort her. Brett says he can't stand to see her like this. Dawson stops in and Taylor brings a meal out once a week or so and helps with the laundry. Kelsi calls every Monday night. Her job at the modeling agency keeps her way too busy and away from family. Melissa says it bothers her to see Emma weak so she don't come out. They butt heads anyways so it might be best she don't come out. Hell, it bothers all of us to see her like this but we still come around. Don't rule them grandkids out yet, Kate. Not yet."

Kate walked over and hugged Zeke's neck. "We love you, Ezekiel Lang. You're like family. You keep better track of things than I do half the time. Why am I worried she doesn't have someone here? I'm so glad to know Mom has you nearby. Nonetheless, I plan on taking her back to Denver with me."

Zeke slapped his knee and laughed. "She is going to raise Holy Hell. Lands sakes, let me know when you plan on telling her so I can be far from the blast. She ain't goin to let you do that, Kate. Ain't no way. She loves her doctor here and this is her home. Personally I think it will make her worse to take her away from her comfort zone. That's just my thinking. You do what you want."

Emma's truck pulled into the drive with another car following her. Joshua stepped onto the front porch and Zeke followed. Lilly, David and Kate stood at the door.

Emma opened her door. Sam jumped out of the truck and ran in circles barking. She walked to the other vehicle. Brett and Dawson stepped out of the car.

Emma turned to the men on the porch. "Look who was at the cemetery. And Robyn and her family pulled in behind me. They can't come to the house because the little one is running a fever and sick so they are headed back to her dad's place."

Emma turned to Dawson and Brett. "Come on in. We've got plenty of food left over."

Zeke turned back to the front door where Kate stood. "Told you."

Kate stuck her tongue out at Zeke. Zeke smiled and said, "That's mature, Kate Phillips."

The young men joined Emma on the porch and hugged Joshua and Zeke. Zeke opened the door for them and all of the men motioned for Emma to enter first. She curtsied and entered the house.

Kate watched her mother and fought back the tears. So many times she had scolded her mother for dwelling on death when Jim died. Telling her mother to move on as Richard had. Emma once told her that it was not death that she dwelt on but the quality of life that was lost. She said she decorated the graves to celebrate Jim and Rylie's lives. Many times Emma would place flowers on a grave that was not decorated. She would worry that no one was celebrating the life that person lived and she took it upon herself to do so. Kate did not like going to the cemetery but tried to each time she came back to her mother's home. This place carried so many memories and many of them were not happy ones.

Emma took off her stocking hat and took the Santa hat from the coffee table. Brett was the first to speak. "Grandma, what did you do?"

Emma pulled the Santa hat onto her head. "I had Kate shave it last night. Why does everyone keep asking what I did when it is obvious my head is shaved?"

Dawson adjusted Emma's hat. "You are right, grandma. Brett is dumb. I, being very astute, knew exactly what you had done. You are making a fashion statement on behalf of all women in their sixties."

Zeke laughed and lightly punched Dawson on his arm and said, "You are so full of it, Dawson Orie. Good thing I wore my boots cause you are spreading it on mighty thick in here."

Lilly and David enjoyed being included as family and celebrating the holiday with Emma. As the evening drew to an end, Zeke, Brett and Dawson left for home. Emma stood on the porch and waved goodbye till she could no longer see their vehicles. She came back into the house, looking tired.

Joshua was the first to speak. "Emma, let us clean up things and you go on to bed. Conner is down for the night so we can spend time with Lilly and David and get this place in order."

"I am going to take you up on that one, sir. See you kids in the morning."

Emma hugged each one of her guests and said, "Don't stay up real late."

Kate rolled her eyes. "Yes, mother. We'll be good little girls and boys."

Emma frowned. "Don't patronize me, sis. I was just concerned that you all would be tired in the morning and Conner will be up early. Matter of fact, smarty pants, I will be the one up with him and you can stay up all night and sleep all day for all I care."

"Momma, settle down. I was just teasing you. Go get your sleep."

Emma's phone rang. "Who would be calling this late?" she asked.

"Hello?"

Emma put her hand over her mouth and smiled. "Taylor Jewell, I knew you didn't forget your grandma."

There was a pause and then Emma spoke. "I love you too. Merry Christmas, Tay."

Emma hung up the phone and turned to Kate. "She asked if Brett told me she would not be joining us and I told her he did indeed. She is mighty sweet on this fellow from church. She spent part of today with his family and part with her mother's family. She was worried I would be disappointed and I told her I am fine, just fine. Now, if you will excuse me, I am going to bed."

Emma retired for the night and the four friends set about clearing wrapping paper and cleaning the kitchen for the second time that day. Kate was worried about Emma being somewhat crabby. She attributed it to Emma being tired and removed it from her mind. She was disappointed Taylor did not visit but remembered when she was that age and the excitement of young love.

Lilly and Kate went over more wedding plans and the men looked through Emma's journals and letters.

David found a letter in one of Emma's journals and showed it to Joshua. They both sat reading it and Kate asked what they had found. Joshua replied "Nothing really. Just some letter. She probably should not have even kept it."

Kate frowned and reached for the letter. "Give it to me. Let me see it."

Kate read the letter as the others watched.

It read:

Dear Richard,

> *I have decided it is time you left Emma and the children. If we are going to be together then you must make this decision. I cannot wait any longer. Soon everyone will know and I have decided I will no longer keep this a secret.*
>
> *We belong together and no one should keep us apart. I forgive you for your actions the other night and know that it was simply because*

you are dealing with so much turmoil as to how to leave your family and start a life with me. I've used makeup to cover the marks and no one has noticed.

I am giving you another week to tell her it is over. If you don't tell her, I will. She must know what is going on and we are running out of time before everyone knows. Make this decision soon, my love.

Love forever,
Elaine

Kate looked up as everyone kept his or her focus on her. She continued to hold the letter in her right hand and said, "This does not surprise me. He was always having affairs. Obviously he decided to stay with us. It was mom that filed for divorce. Not him."

Lilly stood and said, "What does it say? It's from another woman?"

David turned to Lilly. "She may not want to tell you what it says. Just let it go, honey."

Kate handed the note to Lilly. "I don't care if you read it. Obviously you are the only one in the room that hasn't so you might as well. Nice way to end Christmas."

Kate looked up and then down. "Wherever you are, Dad, thanks for the Christmas present. Nice, Dad. Real nice. I'll never understand why she stayed as long as she did and why she put up with him being unfaithful all the time."

After reading the letter, Lilly folded it and placed it back into the journal. She turned to David and asked, "Is this where you found it? I think we should put it back exactly as we found it."

David nodded in agreement and Lilly put the letter back and closed the journal.

Joshua knew this had upset Kate and asked if she would like to go to bed.

Kate snapped at him, "Do I look like I could sleep right now? Anyone want to play a game of cards or something?"

The four friends played spades and hearts until after midnight and then retired for the night. Kate lay awake thinking about the letter. Little did she know Lilly was doing the very same thing in the next room.

Chapter 39

Lilly awoke to the sound of angry voices. She could tell it was both Emma and Kate. She stayed in bed, listening to the mother and daughter.

"I refuse to go to Denver with you! This is my home and if the Good Lord decides to take me to my heavenly home to be with Him, I do not want you to have to fly my body back to Kansas. Besides, my doctors are here, Kate."

"Momma, please consider it. It would be much better to have you where we could help take care of you and make you comfortable. There are excellent doctors in Denver. Probably much better than you have here."

"I'm comfortable right here at home. Besides, you have your own family to take care of and a career. I'm fine, Kate. I have folks from the church that check in on me and sometimes the grandkids come out and so many neighbors and friends. At least let me try to stay here longer. I promise to let you know if things reach the point I can't take care of myself or I am too tired to function on my own. Fair enough?"

There was a long silence. Lilly felt a twinge of guilt as she eavesdropped on this very private conversation. Still silence.

"Fair enough, Momma. But I am going to make phone calls to all sorts of people asking them to keep me posted on how you are doing."

"Then, so be it, Kate Phillips. You make your phone calls. Besides, you have work to do. We will be having Lilly and David's wedding here before you know it. It's been a long time since we had such a big gathering on this farm. And did you know I am the father of the bride and I will be walking Lilly down the aisle?"

"Yes, I knew that. You will make an excellent father of the bride. You've been a great mother and father all these years to us. Now is your chance to actually play the role of the father of the bride. Pretty special, huh?"

Lilly decided it would be a perfect time to walk in on the conversation and it appeared cooler heads were now prevailing. She opened the bedroom door and walked into the kitchen.

"Good morning, Lilly. How did you sleep?"

"I had a very restful night, Emma. And you?"

Emma sat in a kitchen chair. "Like a baby. I thought for sure you younger folks would sleep in since you stayed up late."

Kate excused herself when she heard Conner's whimpering from the bedroom. "I had better get him changed and fed before he wakes Joshua up. Joshua took the night shift. Conner was up three times. Too much Christmas excitement, I think."

Lilly looked at Emma. "What are you thinking, Emma?"

"Oh, I was thinking how quickly time comes and goes. All that build up and preparation for Christmas and now it is gone. You need to make sure you savor every moment, Lilly. Savor each and every moment."

Lilly touched Emma's hand. "You've taught me to never take a single moment for granted, Emma. Not one. Now, before we leave today, I want to take plenty of pictures of all of you." Lilly paused and then spoke "Emma, what were holidays like when Jim and Rylie were still alive?"

Emma smiled and took a sip of her tea. She ran her index finger around the rim of her cup, not looking at Lilly. "They were full of life. Lots of commotion and family. Rylie would grumble about all of the preparations and then he was always the first to get excited when it was time for all of us to gather together. Often my two kids and Rylie and I would stay up later after everyone had left and we would just visit about the day's events. We always enjoyed seeing the grandchildren open gifts. That was Jim's favorite. The children."

Emma looked at Lilly. "Funny you should ask about before the boys were gone. I sat here this morning thinking about how my life has been nothing but before and after. All our lives are before and after. Before I got married, before I had children, before I divorced, before Jim and Rylie passed on. Then I have after on those very same things. After I married, after the children, after this and after that. Now I face after I have been diagnosed. I pray it doesn't come down to before Emma passed on and after Emma passed on. Not yet, anyway."

"I believe you will be with us for a long time," Lilly said, not letting Emma know her true fears.

Emma stood and rinsed off a cup, placing it in the dishwasher. She turned to Lilly. "Everyone's life is a series of before and after, Lilly. Think of your very own life. What would you say?"

Lilly thought for a moment and responded. "My life is also a series of before and after. You are right, Emma. It is before and after grade school, before and after high school, before and after my mother died and soon it will be before and after my marriage to David. I also now can add before and after I met you, Emma."

Emma smiled and took a package of bacon from the refrigerator. "Indeed you can. Indeed you can."

Emma began to prepare breakfast and Lilly helped her. Emma decided to scramble eggs instead of taking orders. She told Lilly of her first breakfast with Joshua. "That boy wanted his eggs sunny side up and he placed them in with his hash browns and mixed it all up. I thought Rylie was going to lose his own breakfast watching that boy eat."

"How old were Kate and Joshua when they met?"

Emma sat down at the kitchen table. "Why, they were just freshmen in college. We had taken Kate out to Denver to attend college and, let me tell you, there were some mighty odd characters at that Art Institute. I happened to notice Joshua standing at the front desk of the dormitory and I told Kate he looked like a nice boy. What I really wanted to say was that I thought he looked normal compared to most of those young folks running around there. I later learned that I should not judge by appearance. Many of those young people were fine people and good friends to Kate."

Lilly chuckled. Just as she was about to continue asking more questions, Kate walked into the kitchen with Conner in her arms. "So you thought he looked normal did you?"

Emma laughed. "Heavens, yes. Of course, then I got to know that little Dickens. That boy has kept me on my toes ever since. I sometimes think Kate is raising two children. I often thought that with my Rylie. There were days I could have sworn I was living with a child. Now you both had better go tell those men of yours that breakfast is nearly ready. I'm fixing breakfast and then you are on your own for lunch. With all of these leftovers, we should be able to manage just fine."

Both Kate and Lilly did as they were told and Emma finished preparing breakfast. Joshua was the first to return to the kitchen. He hugged Emma and rubbed the top of her bare head. "Morning, Grandma."

Emma frowned. "Who told you I was your grandma? Do I look like your grandma? I don't think so."

Joshua laughed. "You just reminded me of Rylie when he would get that little rooster dance going on. He would get that head bobbing. Remember?"

"Oh, Lord. How on earth could I forget? That man and his banty rooster strut. Do I really look like that?"

Joshua nodded in agreement.

"Land sakes, I will have to work on that. I certainly don't want to go around here looking like I have some sort of attitude."

Joshua gave Emma a smirk. "Oh, no. You wouldn't want anyone to think you had an attitude."

Emma hit Joshua with her dishtowel. He hugged her and began to set the table.

Everyone had a nice visit and Emma's illness was not mentioned for the entire day. At day's end, Lilly put her coat on and walked to the barn. She sat down on a hay bale and thought about what a special holiday it had been. After some time, Kate joined her.

"Everything all right?"

Lilly pulled her coat around her and nodded. "Oh, yes. I just wanted some quiet time."

"I'm sorry. I'll leave you with your thoughts."

"No, Kate. Please stay. I would love to talk if you don't mind."

"Talk away. What shall we talk about?"

"Tell me more about your dad. That letter we found the other night. Do you think Emma remembers she has that?"

"Oh, trust me, Lilly. Mom remembers all of what she has kept and all that transpired over their marriage. Why do you ask?"

Lilly picked at the hay bale. "Oh, I don't know. I just can't understand why you would keep such a thing. A letter from some woman your husband had an affair with. Why would she do that?"

"I have no idea. Mom has held onto a lot of things that I could not understand. She has boxes of letters, pictures and all kinds of things that I thought should have been trashed. She always said she had kept them in case I ever needed them. I never understood why in the heck I would need those things."

"Do you think she will ever throw all of that away? Maybe that would help her deal with all the things he did to her."

"Your guess is as good as mine, Lilly. Don't ever try to understand my mother. They broke the mold when they made her."

Sam's ears perked up and Emma entered the barn. "Throw away what?"

Kate looked agitated. "How long have you been listening, Mom?"

"Long enough to know you girls think I should throw something away. Besides, I wasn't eavesdropping. I was coming out to see what was going on."

Kate pulled Emma's coat around her and buttoned the top button. "You need to take care and not be out in the cool air."

"Well now, Kate Phillips, who do you think comes out in this air and does the chores when none of you are here? Santa Claus? No, I do. Besides, it's a nice evening. This isn't cold."

Sam rubbed his right ear against Emma and then rolled on the floor of the barn. Emma rubbed his belly.

"What should I throw away?"

Kate took a deep sigh. "We didn't say you should throw anything away. We were wondering why you keep some of the things you keep. Old letters, cards and things of that sort."

"I keep those sorts of things in case someone might find them of interest someday. If I threw away things, then you would not have that Christmas gift of Jim's card, now would you?"

"You're right. But you do keep some silly things."

"Like what?"

Kate hesitated and decided to tell Emma about the four friends finding the note to Richard in one of Emma's albums.

"We found a letter to Dad from some woman wanting him to leave you and Jim and me. She was almost threatening him. Do you know what I am talking about?"

Emma nodded. "Yes, I do."

Kate rolled her eyes. "Well?"

"Well, what?"

Kate sighed a huge sigh. "Why did you keep it?"

"Because I thought it might be needed someday."

Lilly stood and walked to Pie's stall. She spoke softly, "I think that letter is in my mother's handwriting."

Kate's jaw dropped. "What?"

Lilly ran her hand over the rails of the stall. "I could swear that is my mother's handwriting and her signature."

Kate looked at Emma. "This is just too creepy. Mom?"

"This is not how I had planned this. I have a box of things we should go through. Shall I bring them out here or do you want to go inside?"

Kate frowned. "What do you mean?"

Emma looked annoyed with Kate's questions. "Let's go sit on the sun porch. I will have Joshua build a fire."

Lilly continued to look down at the barn floor. Emma stepped towards her. Lilly looked up, tears filling her eyes. "How did you know my mother? Is that what you are saying, Emma? You knew my mother?"

Emma touched Lilly's shoulder. "Let's go inside."

The walk from the barn to the house was uncomfortably quiet for the three women.

Emma entered the house and asked Joshua to start a fire in the stove on the sun porch. Joshua looked puzzled but did as he was asked.

Emma went into her bedroom. She later returned with a shoebox. She turned to Kate. "Shall we include the men or shall we go through this alone?"

Kate raised her arms in exasperation. "How in the heck should I know? I don't even know what you are about to show me."

Emma turned to the men. Joshua, would you mind taking care of bedtime for your son this evening? And, David, we women need some time alone. Do you mind?"

"No, not at all. I'll spend some time with Joshua and Conner."

Emma carried the shoebox as if it were a treasure. Lilly and Kate followed Emma onto the sun porch.

Emma sat on the wicker rocker. The silence was unbearable. She opened the box to reveal stacks of letters and cards. Then she lifted a baby picture from the box and handed it to Kate.

Lilly looked over Kate's shoulder. "That's me", Lilly said. "How did you get a baby picture of me?"

Emma motioned for both women to sit down. She was concerned that what they were about to hear would anger Kate and break Lilly's heart.

"I've kept these for many years. I didn't start to put it all together until just a few months ago and I was going to tell both of you but then I took ill. I guess the Lord thinks now is as good a time as any."

"Tell us what, Momma?"

Emma leaned back on the rocker. "As you know, your father loved women. He never really knew what being monogamous was. And, over the years, I learned to just keep my mouth shut and hope that someday I could get out of the marriage, which I did."

Lilly was confused as to how this was leading up to Emma having a baby picture of her.

Lilly held up the picture. "Emma, how did you get this?"

Emma closed her eyes and began to speak, resting her head on the back of the rocker. "Richard had many women but one in particular was a constant. He continued to see her for several years. She began to phone him. He would be away for days at a time, saying it was business but I was sure he was with another woman. Then the letters began to show up. He reached a point where he didn't even try to hide their affair. Then came the letter stating she was going to let everyone know. I assumed she meant let folks know about the affair. That wasn't it at all."

Emma opened her eyes and looked at Kate and Lilly. "She was pregnant and Richard was the father."

Kate covered her mouth and her eyes widened. Emma stood and placed her arms around Kate's waist, facing her. "I never knew what happened to that woman or the child she carried. The letters just stopped and I never knew what had happened. Then Lilly showed up. I began to put things together. I noticed some similarities in both of you and your father."

Kate pushed her mother away. "What in the Hell are you saying?"

Emma turned to Lilly and looked back at Kate. "I am saying I have reason to believe you girls are half sisters."

Lilly sat down and covered her face with both hands. "Oh, God. Oh, God. This just can't be happening."

"Now, Lilly. I'm not for sure. You and Kate can read the letters. There is even a birth certificate. But I think it is true. Your mother tried very hard to keep in contact and tried to get Richard to help financially and acknowledge you. I don't know if he ever even saw you. I am afraid your mother and Richard may have taken a lot of this to their graves with them. But, girls, I believe we should research as much as possible. Lord knows this is not how I wanted to tell you this."

Kate's eyes narrowed and Emma could see a familiar look that reminded her of Richard. "Why have you never told me this? Did Jim and Rylie know?"

Emma knew her answer would only infuriate Kate even more. "Jim had caught wind of it once from someone. He suspected he had at least one half sibling out there somewhere. When he confronted me with it, I told him that there had been a woman that had tried to tell Richard about a baby but that I had no idea if that child was still alive or where the woman and child had gone. I never confronted Richard with it. I found the picture in some papers after he moved out. He would throw away the letters and I would take them from the trash and keep them in this box. My heart went out to your mother, Lilly. What she must have gone through. And, yes, I told Rylie I suspected there might be a child somewhere but that I wasn't sure where or if the woman even wanted to be found."

"I need to take a walk." Kate said.

Emma touched Kate's arm as Kate passed her but Kate brushed off Emma's touch. "Katy Leigh, don't you do this. We are all hurting right now. Let's all sit and talk this out."

Kate turned back towards her mother, her deep green eyes filled with tears and anger. "I can't believe everyone in this family knew but me. That is a bunch of crap, Mom. Why didn't Jim tell me?"

Emma shook her head. "That, sis, we will never know. My guess is he wanted to protect you from more hurt from your father. But now we have the chance to make this right. You and Lilly are already friends and now you can also be family."

Kate walked from the room into the kitchen where Joshua met her. "Anything wrong?" he asked.

"Oh Hell, I just found out I have a half sister, that's all. Mom has been keeping secrets."

Joshua looked puzzled. "Your mom has another child?"

"No, Joshua. Dear old Dad couldn't keep it in his pants and apparently Lilly is his child. Or so Mom thinks."

Emma puffed up and stood in front of Kate as Lilly stood motionless. "Katy Leigh, you are being ridiculous. Think of how Lilly must feel right now."

Kate turned to Lilly. "Oh, Lilly. This has nothing to do with my like or dislike of you. I dearly love you and David. This has to do with yet another pile of crap that my dad has bestowed upon us. Not saying you are crap. I am just saying he never thought of anyone but himself and yet he always preached about his stupid 'consequences'. Did he ever think of the consequences of screwing around?"

Joshua was speechless. David entered the kitchen where everyone stood. "Want to let me in on the joke, guys?"

Lilly put her arm inside David's. "Let's step outside for a while. Kate and Emma need some time."

Emma raised her hand and said, "Whoa, whoa. Wait a minute. There is no reason you should have to excuse yourself, Lilly. This pertains to you as much as it does Kate. I say we all sit down, talk this over and read the letters. There is even a picture of you and your mother together."

Emma gave Kate a firm look. "Let's all be civil about this. No need in getting our blood pressure up. Life deals us a few curves and this is just a little one."

Kate hugged her mother. "Once again, you are right, Momma. This is just such a shock. I feel totally blindsided as I am sure Lilly does too."

Lilly nodded her head in agreement as she fought back tears. She felt betrayed by her own mother who had told her all those years that her father was dead and she also felt Emma had in some way betrayed her. Why did Emma keep her suspicions to herself for these months? Lilly was full of questions."

Everyone except Joshua went onto the sun porch where the fire cast a warm glow across the windows. The room was quiet except for the sound of an owl outside. Lilly was the first to speak.

"My mother seldom spoke of my father. We lived alone, just the two of us. This is such a shock."

Joshua came back into the room. Emma sat in the wicker rocker and turned to Joshua. "Is my grandson all tucked in for the night?"

Joshua smiled and said, "He most certainly is. Since Kate had already fed him, I had no trouble at all getting him to sleep. I think this country air is good for him. He's not used to so much quiet."

Kate reached for the box and handed it to Lilly. "Shall we begin our journey as half sisters?"

Lilly was relieved to see Kate's hostility had diminished and she was anxious to go over the box's contents.

Kate sat on the floor next to Emma and Lilly joined her. Both Joshua and David sat on the wicker loveseat.

Kate handed Lilly a letter and took one for herself. It was Lilly that spoke first. "Why don't we read them together?"

Kate seemed hesitant. "Oh, I don't know. Look at how many we have to go through. This is just overwhelming."

Emma began to slowly rock in her chair. "It isn't like you have to cover them all tonight."

Kate frowned. "We both go back to our homes tomorrow, Mother. We should have them read before then. Or are we going to each take a stack?"

"Don't you take that tone with me, young woman. Regardless of what the circumstances might be at this time, I am still your mother. And you will not talk to me in your condescending tone."

Emma's rocking became short, quick rocks and she pulled her sweater close to her shoulders.

Kate knew this had to also be hard on Emma. To know all these years that the man she married had fathered a child with another woman and to think that very child had become a part of Emma's life through some fluke. Kate knew how sacred marriage was to Emma and she knew the pain Richard's infidelities had brought Emma and her children. And to now have to tell Kate the truth and to have Lilly right there under her own roof.

Kate patted her mother's knee. "I'm sorry, Momma. I'm sorry I was so short with you."

"I accept your apology. Shall I read the letter aloud so that the men can also be a part of this or how shall we handle it?"

"Aloud would be fine with me," Lilly said.

Kate nodded in agreement. David squirmed in his seat, uncomfortable with the whole situation. Joshua leaned forward, resting his elbows on his knees. Emma had a captive audience. Kate handed the first letter to Emma.

Emma held the letter. "Wait. We should read them in sequence. The first one is on the bottom and the one on top is the most recent."

Lilly reached into the box and took the bottom letter. She handed it to Emma. Emma opened it and ran her index finger over it several times.

"Ok, here we go," Emma said.

"Dear Richard:

It has been a week since we last spoke. My heart longs to see you again. When you tell me you want us to be together always, I believe you but then you don't call or visit for sometimes days or even weeks. I don't know what to think.

Seeing you the last time with that other woman on the Plaza was more than I could bear. You say she is just a friend but I don't believe friends touch one another in the way you were. I saw you kiss. That is why I phoned you later that night and planned on confronting you with it. Your wife said you were not home. I told her it had to do with business. I think she believed me since we work for the same company.

I have not told my family I am seeing a married man because it would break their hearts. Do you really plan on leaving your family? I certainly don't want you to hurt your children. Are you sure you can get custody of them? I would be proud to help you care for them.

Please call soon. I long to hear your voice.

Love,
Elaine"

Emma looked up over her reading glasses. She raised her right eyebrow. "Well?"

Kate leaned her head against the rocker. "I think this is not fair for you to have to read these, Momma. You've already had the heartbreak of reading them who knows how many times and I think Lilly and I can handle reading them. We can read and pass them along. Don't do this to yourself. You have got to be exhausted. Are you sure you want to stay up or should you go to bed?"

Emma folded the letter. "I'm not tired but I will let you girls do your own reading. Just keep in mind that I believe she was being led on. As you read more, you can read between the lines that your dad was filling this poor woman full of lies. How hard it must have been when she realized she was never going to have him as a father figure to her child and that he would not support her or the child in anyway."

Kate stood up and put her hands on her hips. "Why would he be any different with her than he was with us? How many times did I hear him shout 'You wanted these kids!'? And tell you he never wanted us? Do you know how that made Jim and I feel knowing he never wanted us? Thank goodness you made up for him and told us over and over again how much you wanted us and how blessed you were to have us. He had better be thanking his lucky stars he isn't here for this one. Right now I would love to get my hands on him."

Emma slid her feet into her slippers. "Now stop. You don't mean that. There is no doubt in my mind that he has had to answer for the things he did. No need in getting upset with him now. He's gone and now we have to deal with this."

"Lilly, be glad he wasn't in the same household as you and your mother. He made a better father to Jim and me from a distance and that still wasn't any prize."

Emma walked to the doorway leading into the kitchen from the porch. "I'm having a piece of pumpkin pie and going to bed. Call me if you change your mind. And remember, you don't have to cover all of this in one night. We can run into town in the morning and make copies if you want."

"There is no way I am going to let the small town locals know about this and you know if you run into Thriftway, someone will start the gossip chain. Whatever teenager is working the customer service counter will run home and tell their mother or grandmother and then it will spread like wildfire. I don't know why you wouldn't let us get you that printer that also made copies. We could sure use it right now."

Emma waved her hand as she walked into the kitchen. "Goodnight."

Emma continued to mumble as she opened the refrigerator and fixed her pie.

"Momma, we can hear you!"

"Can you now? What was I saying?"

Kate rolled her eyes. "Something about you are going to eat that entire pie?"

Emma laughed. "And I think I said something about how much all of you mean to me and I love you!"

"Night, Emma," Joshua called.

"Goodnight father of my beautiful grandson."

The four young adults chuckled. Kate shook her head. "I have been blessed with a comedian for a mother."

The night was spent reading the letters and discussing what they had been dealt. Lilly and Kate noticed the birth certificate had 'unknown' listed where the father's name should have been.

Kate asked Lilly about her mother. Lilly hesitated and then responded. "My mother was a quiet woman that held so much bitterness. I think I now know where that bitterness came from. What she must have gone through. The denial and betrayal she must have felt. Each time I asked about my father she would tell me he died before I was born. She never married and she never dated. Surely she wasn't devoted to a man who would turn his back on her and his child?"

Kate knew the answer to Lilly's question. Emma was a devoted wife and mother and Richard turned his back on Emma and her children. Once Emma chose to leave Richard, he made sure Jim and Kate bore the consequences of Emma's decision. He would not help them in any way other than his court ordered child support. Kate thought back to those days. The times Emma struggled to buy Jim and Kate their first vehicles. She thought of the struggle Emma and Rylie went through trying to put Kate through college. Kate thought about the time Richard was passing through Denver and Kate's car had broken down in downtown Denver. Kate had phoned Emma and Emma had contacted a towing service. Emma asked if Richard might take the time to look at the car and see if he could find out what was wrong. He refused. He said he didn't have time. Those were the memories Kate tried to put at the back of her mind. She tried so often to remember a pleasant memory. Lilly was lucky, all right.

It was obvious from the letters that Elaine had loved Richard dearly. Richard was not capable of returning that love. Apparently he never made any attempt to see Lilly or to help Elaine support her. Once Richard found out Elaine was pregnant, he cut all ties with her. Her final letter summed up all her heartache and bitterness.

Richard,

You have made it quite obvious that you want nothing to do with our daughter or me. I will no longer send pictures or letters. Please understand that this means I never want to hear from you or see you again and, as far as I am concerned, you are dead. You have used me for the last time. Any woman that allows you to be a part of her life is a fool. You are evil hearted and I wish I had never seen your face. You took my love for you and you used it for your own gratification. The verbal and physical abuse, I am sure, would have only escalated if we had tried to make a life together. You need help, Richard.

You will never know the joy of watching this little girl grow up into a woman. For that, I am thankful. She will be told you are dead and I will teach her to hate the man that you are.

Elaine

Lilly stretched and leaned her head on David's knee. He looked at his watch. "It is nearly two in the morning!"

Kate yawned and said, "Conner will be getting up for a feeding in a while. I might as well stay up until he wakes up. What a night this has been. Oh, Lilly, who would have thought anything like this?"

David ran his fingers through Lilly's hair. She smiled and looked at Kate. Was Emma right? Is there such a resemblance that Emma put it all together? She studied Kate's face as she responded to Kate's question.

"I have always believed my father was dead and that, of course, I had no siblings. Now I find out I have two half-siblings. I now wish even more than before that I could have known Jim"

Kate smiled. "He was the best brother in the world. There will never be another one like him. You certainly missed out, Lilly. And I must say that Dad missed out on knowing you. I think your mom did a great job raising you alone. You really were better off, Lilly. Trust me on this. My dad just didn't quite know how to love."

Joshua sat silently looking at the floor. He spoke quietly. "Can you imagine what both of those women must have been going through? That man sure dealt out a lot of grief. You know, he and I never did get along but I tried to be cordial to him because it was always so important to Kate."

Lilly looked at the picture of her mother and herself. "I wish I had at least known him. Then I would have been given the option of liking or disliking him. I can see why Kate would have a love/hate relationship. After all, he was still her father regardless of how he treated her and her family."

Kate stood. "Beans was such a good step-father to me. Momma was so fortunate to have someone like him in our lives. I just wish they had had more years together. If you will excuse me, I am going to check on Conner."

Joshua stood next to Kate. "I think I am going to go outside for a while. It is such a beautiful night. David, care to join me? You are welcome too, Lilly, if you would like."

David was the first to speak. "I would love one more night of this country air. Are you joining us, Lilly?"

"No thanks. I think I will read some of these over again. You go on."

Chapter 40

Kate entered the bedroom and walked to Conner's crib. He wasn't there. She headed for Emma's room where the door was slightly ajar. She looked through the opening to see Emma on the bed with Conner by her side. He was sound asleep and Emma was crying and running her fingers over the bridge of his nose just as she used to do Kate and Jim.

Kate slowly opened the door. "Momma?"

Emma took a corner of the blanket and wiped her tears. "Yes, Sugar?"

"What are you doing? You should be sleeping."

"Well now, he whimpered and you young folks were busy so I just brought him in here with me. He went right back to sleep listening to his grandma sing. He's such a good boy, Kate."

"Why the tears?"

"Oh, they're tears of joy to a degree. I am happy to have been so blessed and sad to have lost so much. I have so many regrets. Think of poor Lilly. I am so sorry this all happened. I didn't want you to find out like this. I wanted to handle it differently. Not that I know how I would have done it but somehow differently."

Kate sat on the edge of Emma's bed. She studied Emma's face. There lay a woman who had suffered so many heartbreaks. She looked so frail with her shiny baldhead and the dark circles under her brilliantly blue eyes. Kate did not begrudge Emma for what had happened this night. She only wished Emma did not have to go through one more trial.

"Momma, why didn't you just throw all those letters and pictures away and no one would have ever known?"

Emma ran her index finger across Conner's forehead, down over his right temple, across his cheek and up the bridge of his nose. His lip twitched in what appeared to be a smile.

"I wonder what the future holds for this little guy. Kate, you must enjoy every single moment. Whether he has come inside covered in mud and tracks all over creation or he has been a perfect angel. Treasure each and every moment."

Kate kissed her mother's cheek. "I promise."

"And Kate?"

"Yes?"

"I'm sorry I somehow failed at keeping your dad content and faithful. I truly did the very best I could as a wife and mother. I am more ridden with guilt that I failed you kids. I'm just not sure your dad was cut out to be a husband and father and I believe he would have been unfaithful regardless. But maybe I am just trying to ease my own mind."

"Don't worry over it. He never had any intention of being faithful, Mom. Dad was Dad and let's just leave it at that."

Conner's eyes began to open. He squinted at his grandmother. Emma studied his face and began to quietly cry. Kate put her arms around her mother.

"Why are you crying, Momma?"

"If you ever say I said this, I will deny it, Kate, but I am scared. I always thought I could fight this battle and I was ready for whatever happened but now that this little man has arrived, I want to stick around and spend time with him. I want to be healthy so we can run and play, ride the horses and enjoy being a grandmother and grandson."

"Let's not worry about it. You are the strongest woman I know and you are going to beat this thing. You and Conner will have plenty of time together."

Emma wiped her cheek with the back of her hand. "I sure as heck hope so. But, on the other hand, if the Lord takes me, I will still have wonderful things to enjoy with my boys in Heaven."

Emma took a deep breath and slowly let it out. "You're right. Let's not worry about it."

Kate heard Joshua and David in the living room.

"I had better get Conner fed and back in his bed and you had better get some sleep."

"What time do you plan on leaving tomorrow?"

"I am guessing we will hit the road shortly after lunch. That way we will be home by ten."

Emma sat up and handed Conner to Kate. "Kate, I am so sorry all of this has happened. Good Lord, I had no idea how I was going to break my suspicions to you. Did you read all of the letters?"

"Yes. Lilly is still out on the sun porch going over them again. How did you put all of this together?"

"Well, Lilly would say something about her mother and she would mention things about where her mother worked and that she never knew her father. Then I studied both of your facial features and pulled out baby pictures. I would hold yours up next to hers. I played detective for months and months, not sure to this day if I have come to the right conclusion."

"Well, I am fairly sure you've come to the right conclusion. We've done some talking and comparing and we've read the letters. We have both agreed to the possibility of DNA testing or something along that line. I am going to research how we should go about this."

Without taking a single breath, Emma began, "I know it will never be the same but, if you are in fact half siblings, at least you will have someone. Do you remember that your grandmother on your dad's side had three children before she married your grandpa and they were adopted out and it wasn't until your dad was in his early forties that he found out he had three half siblings? What a mess that was. Your grandma had nothing to do with them but, as you know, I kept in touch with Della. I wanted her to know we accepted her. Your dad could have cared less but I felt she needed family and, after all, your dad and her were family."

"I totally forgot about Aunt Della. Wow, Dad followed in his mother's footsteps, huh?"

"Nah, not really. She had those babies before her marriage to your grandpa. Your dad did this during our marriage. Not the same."

Conner began to whimper. Kate kissed his forehead and then kissed Emma's cheek. "I'd better get him fed and get some sleep. You need to do the same. I love you, Momma."

"I love you too, Sugar. Sweet dreams."

Emma waited until she no longer heard voices in the living room and went to the kitchen to fix a cup of hot tea. As she entered the kitchen, she noticed Lilly still sitting on the sun porch reading the letters. Emma tried to be quiet so as not to bother Lilly.

As Emma warmed her water for her tea, Lilly stepped into the doorway leading from the sun porch to the kitchen.

"Emma, is everything all right?"

"Oh heavens, yes. I'm just a little restless and thought some warm tea would help. Are you holding up?'

Lilly nodded her head. "I'm as fine as anyone can be in a situation like this. I don't know how you did it. How could you stand knowing they had a relationship?"

"Oh, by the time your mother and Richard had become close, I had seen many women come and go and I knew Richard could not fathom what real love meant. The only part that always hurt me was that he would do this to his children. And, Lilly, I'm sure it wasn't his intention to hurt you. Richard was all about money. Had your mother not tried to get child support, he may have continued to see her and may have spent some time with you. But you have to remember this is the same man who itemized his own son's funeral expenses and wanted no part of helping the children he had from our marriage. Why should we think he would help you and your mother?"

"Kate and I plan on researching this until we get a definite answer. I will never understand why my mother did not tell me the truth."

"She may have been ashamed to tell you, Lilly. We will never know. I know I am ashamed of the fact that I stayed with him as long as I did and what I put my children through. I will question whether I was a good mother till the day the Good Lord takes me home."

Emma took a sip of her tea. Lilly took a long look at Emma, studying her face. This cancer and the treatments were taking a toll on Emma. Lilly made a mental note to discuss with David their role in making sure Emma was taking care of herself and making sure things were done around the farm. After all, they were only an hour away. An hour. All these years they had been only an hour from one another. Lilly could have known Kate and Jim. They could have been a part of the other's lives. So many years had been wasted.

"Lilly, I am sure both you and Kate will adjust to this. And I am sure your mother thought she was doing the right thing in not letting you know about your father. As a mother, I can only imagine how desperately she wanted to protect you from any heartache."

Lilly smiled at Emma. "Not all mothers are the same, Emma. Just like not all fathers are like Richard. I still wish I could have known him."

Emma frowned. "And I wish my children had not known him. But I can't look back. I would never trade the children I had and regardless of my opinion of Richard, he was their father. That will never change. And I will never forgive myself for letting him treat them the way he did. Even in death he treated his son with such disrespect. And for that, I am ashamed."

"Emma Jean needs to get in bed!" Kate called from the front room.

Emma walked from the kitchen to the living room doorway. "What in the Sam Hill are you still doing up?"

Kate raised an eyebrow. "Shouldn't I be asking you that very same question?"

Emma scoffed. "Sounds to me like you just did. How about we all go to bed?"

"Sounds good to me," Lilly said.

Kate hugged Emma and said her goodnights to both Lilly and Emma.

Morning would be here much too soon. Kate was upset that Emma had stayed up so late. Emma's rest was so important to her health. Kate would have to discuss it with her mother in the morning when they were both fresh.

Sam and Gracie both followed Emma to her room. "Good night" Emma called from her room.

"Night" Kate said.

Chapter 41

Emma slept late while Lilly and Kate made breakfast together. They enjoyed the privacy and time alone to discuss the previous night's event. Both studied the other's features and wondered if what they had discovered was true. Although neither one admitted it, both knew Emma's suspicions were true. Kate worried that Lilly would somehow treat Emma differently now that she had been told Richard was her father.

"Do you still want Mom to walk you down the aisle at the wedding?"

Lilly was somewhat taken aback by Kate's question.

"Of course. Nothing has changed. Your mom is so important to David and me. I absolutely adore her."

Kate took a deep sigh. "Oh, good. I think it would break her heart. She is so excited. You know, September will be here before we know it. I hope her health has improved by then and she will be able to enjoy all of the fun."

"We are just going to believe that she will be 100% better by then. Kate, do you think she will be o.k. here alone? David and I plan on making it a point to check in more frequently and spend more time here."

"Oh, Lilly, that would be wonderful. She is not going to come home with us to Denver. She's so stubborn sometimes. And now I have to admit to Zeke that he is right on this one."

"Anybody home?" a voice called from the living room.

Kate called from the kitchen. "In here."

Lilly gave Kate a puzzled look and said, "Who is it?"

Before Kate could answer Dawson and Brett entered the kitchen. Dawson took a piece of sausage and took a bite.

Kate gently slapped his hand. "What are you two doing here?"

Brett spoke first as Dawson chewed his sausage. "Grandma said be out here early. She wants some videos of everyone before you leave."

"Oh, great. She never said a word about it and none of us are even cleaned up," Kate said.

"Your grandma is still sleeping," Lilly said.

Dawson's deep blue eyes widened. "Grandma still asleep at this time of the morning? What did you do to her? Drug her?"

Kate began placing the biscuits on the cookie sheet. Dawson frowned at the can of biscuits.

"If grandma was awake, we wouldn't be having store bought biscuits. These city girls have no clue how to cook like grandma."

Kate hit Dawson across the arm with her dishtowel, reminding Lilly of something Emma would do.

Brett looked worried. "I'm going to go check on her. This is much too late for her. Something is wrong."

Kate touched his arm. "Brett, she was up until close to three this morning. Let her rest."

"Why did you let her stay up that late?" Brett replied curtly.

"Settle down. It was her choice and you know how she is when she sets her mind to something."

Dawson laughed and started to say something but Emma entered the kitchen. "Well, just how am I when my mind is set on something?"

Kate hugged Emma. "Stubborn. You are stubborn, Momma."

Dawson turned to his grandmother. "Grandma, they are making biscuits from a can. Do you believe that?"

Before Emma could answer, Brett began to scold her like a child. "What in the heck are you staying up so late for? Didn't the doctor say you needed all the rest you can get?"

Emma sat at the kitchen table and looked up at the four standing there. "The doctor says a lot of things but that doesn't mean I have to believe him. It's not his body that is full of some nasty disease, now is it?"

Dawson hugged his grandma. "She's right as usual."

Brett turned to his younger cousin. "Suck up," he said.

"Spoil Sport," Dawson replied.

"Jerk", Brett retorted.

"Stop this nonsense now. Be kind to one another," Emma said.

Dawson took a deep breath and looked at Brett. "Later," he said.

Kate excused herself to check on Conner but lightly slapped the back of both of her nephews' heads as she passed them.

Again Dawson's eyes widened. "Did you see that, Grandma?"

Emma shook her head, smiled and replied, "Yes, DW, I saw what your Aunt Kate did. Makes you pity poor little Conner, huh? She'll have that boy towing the line."

Brett took out his camcorder and began to video Lilly as she cooked the hashbrown casserole.

He narrated as he pointed the camcorder at Lilly. "This is Miss Lilly Ballard, friend of our family, as she prepares a lovely country breakfast for all of us with the exception of store bought biscuits. She is, after all, a city girl from the big neighboring city of Kansas City, Missouri. As my friend Ezekiel would say, 'She don't know no better'."

Brett continued to run the camcorder as Lilly shook her spatula at the camera.

Emma touched Brett's sleeve and said, "Brett Dean, I want you to take some of Conner today. I thought we might even try saddling up the horses and bundling him up and putting him on Pie."

Dawson slapped the top of the table. "Serious?"

"Yes, serious," Emma replied.

Brett turned the camera on Dawson and again began to narrate, "This is Dawson and he is concerned about our little cousin Conner taking over his role as the family roper and champion steer rider. He should be afraid. He should be very afraid."

Dawson's eyes narrowed as he glared into the camera. "You might want to consider the fact that we have to ride back into Topeka together."

Brett continued his narration. "Dawson Orie, I have reason to believe, is threatening me. If something should happen to me, please use this recording as evidence as to who may have had a hand in my demise."

"Would you two stop this? As you can see, Lilly, there is never a dull moment when these two are around. Poor Taylor never stood a chance around these two."

"Oh, Grandma. I might be a famous reporter someday," Brett said. "Like Robyn!"

Dawson chuckled. "Robyn's pretty. You're a dog, dude. Nobody wants to see your ugly mug on the television. Besides, aren't you going to college to be an oceanographer? Last I checked, there are no oceans in Kansas"

"I said that is enough!" Emma ordered.

Dawson gave Emma the look of an innocent child. "What? I was merely pointing out that Kansas has no oceans, Grandma."

Emma rolled her eyes. "Oh course your were, DW. Of course you were."

Kate entered the kitchen with Conner in her arms. "Joshua and David are up. They are taking their showers and then Lilly and I will have a turn after breakfast."

Dawson stood up, offering his chair to Kate. She smiled. He then held his arms out, motioning for Kate to hand Conner to him. She obliged.

"No roughhousing with him," Emma stated.

Dawson grinned and began to coo and talk to Conner. "Grandma thinks I am going to roughhouse with you. You're my bud. Nobody's going to hurt my little man. Brett and I are going to put you on Pie later and I think we should take turns having our pictures taken with you. Now Grandma probably thinks we are going to do some rodeo riding but old Pie will behave. We'll get you and Grandma on him. Why, we'll even throw these city girls on him and Sally."

Dawson continued to look into Conner's face. Kate touched Conner's hand and looked at Dawson. "I rode horses long before you were a glint in your dad's eye."

Dawson grinned. "No, no. I think Dad was glinting long before you were on a horse."

"Oh, Good Lord. Will you stop taunting your aunt? I thought I told you to behave," Emma said.

Lilly continued to stand at the stove, enjoying the family bantering back and forth. She had not experienced such love and closeness.

David entered the room. "Look's like a party in here. May I join in?"

Emma stood up. "I think we are going to have to move this party into the dining room. Do you girls want me to take over?"

Lilly opened the oven door and looked at the biscuits, waiting for some remark from at least one of the young men. "It won't be much longer. The casserole and biscuits should be ready soon. I think we can handle it, don't you Kate?"

Kate gave Brett a mischievous grin. "I think Brett can put down that camera long enough to help us set the table and finish up. Brett?"

Dawson spoke before Brett could reply to his aunt's question. "Ha ha. I've got my little man here in my arms and you are going to do sissy work."

Brett set the camera on the kitchen table and stood, glaring at Dawson. "Papa Beans was one of the best cooks I've ever known and he wasn't a sissy so you just shut your pie hole."

Emma leaned her head back and closed her eyes. "Oh, Good Lord, have mercy on us. Why did I ask these two to even join us? Lord, what did you fill these boys with this morning? Or should I ask the Devil what he filled you both with?"

Brett took a deep breath, reached for a potholder and kissed his grandmother's cheek. "We'll behave, Grandma. It's Dawson's fault, don't you know?"

Emma placed her hand over Brett's mouth and whispered, "Enough."

Emma, David, Dawson and Conner went into the dining room where Joshua joined them.

Soon the family gathered together for food and laughter. Kate was glad to see Emma enjoy this day. She knew it would be hard on Emma when everyone left and the quiet of nightfall set in.

Brett and Dawson took turns cam cording everyone. Kate enjoyed watching Emma with Conner on Pie. Brett and Dawson were very good at getting casual videos of everyone. David and Joshua took turns taking videos of Dawson and Brett. Everyone was dressed warm and Emma continued to check on Conner. It was an unusually nice December day with the afternoon temperature nearing 50 degrees. Most of the men shed their heavy winter coats and worked in flannel shirts.

Lilly and Kate felt Emma was getting tired and it was time for Conner's nap. Kate knew they had stayed well past their original departure time of early afternoon but everyone was having such a great time, she knew she should not mention it.

Emma and Conner took naps as the others put up the horses and set about doing some of the chores.

Lilly wondered if Kate would tell the two young men about their discovery the night before. Nothing was mentioned.

They all had time to sit on Emma's porch and discuss family. Kate and the boys told stories of Emma, Rylie and Jim. Joshua kept the camcorder recording as the stories were told. Each would recall a certain memory. Lilly listened closely as David held her hand.

Kate excused herself to check on Conner. After some time, Lilly also entered the house, leaving the men on the porch. It was Joshua who first spoke.

"I want both you boys to set a schedule of when you and Taylor can come out and check on your grandma. Zeke has also agreed to help. Kate and I will fly home two weekends out of each month. We need to know people are checking on her daily. She is getting weaker by the day with her treatments and she is not going to be able to keep up with this place. She has refused to go home with us. Will you promise to help out?"

"You know we will, Joshua. We already discussed this coming out here and we've already come up with a plan. Dawson is on Mondays, Wednesdays and Fridays. I am on Tuesday, Thursday and Saturdays and Taylor will bring her three evening meals a week. That leaves Zeke for Sundays. I figure he can bring her into town for church and we can take her and Zeke out for Sunday dinner and he can drive her home. How does that sound?" Brett asked.

"It sounds good to me but run it by Kate before you leave. Speaking of leaving, we are only going to make it as far as Hays tonight. It is getting too late in the afternoon to drive clear through."

Emma came to the front door and opened it. "You fellas staying out here all day? I've got some sandwiches and leftovers for lunch before you hit the road."

Dawson looked at his grandma and then at Joshua. "Grandma is psychic. She knew we were talking about you leaving."

"Quit talking that psychic stuff and get in here and eat," Emma said.

As soon as Emma left the doorway, Dawson told of how Emma had dreamt of Jim's death only a month before it happened. He said Emma had not told anyone except Rylie about it at the time and did not tell the rest of the family until some time later. Rylie said she told him it was the Lord's way of preparing her. Dawson then told that Danielle had lost a child at birth and that Kate had dreamt it months earlier. Only Emma and Kate and Rylie had known about that until Dawson was at the farm one day and his grandfather had told him about it.

Joshua said, "Grandma and Aunt Kate are psychic just like there is no such thing as ghosts. Only coincidences. Let's eat."

Dawson picked up his coat from the porch rail. "You believe what you want to and I am going to believe what I want. Grandma and Aunt Kate are physic, I tell you."

Joshua laughed. "The only thing your grandma and aunt are is psycho, Dawson. It goes with the gender."

Kate was standing in the doorway when Joshua turned to see her there as the men entered the house.

Dawson patted Joshua on the back. "You are so busted."

Joshua kissed Kate. "Just kidding, babe. Just kidding."

Kate merely said, "Um hum."

Everyone had a nice lunch followed by viewing the videos taken earlier in the day. It was a pleasant ending to what had been a pleasant day. Lilly did not look forward to the day ending.

Dawson and Brett were the first to leave, assuring Kate of the already planned schedule and asking that she send plenty of pictures of Conner. They hugged their grandma and she stood on the porch, waving goodbye until they were out of sight.

Kate and Joshua packed their things as Emma rocked Conner. Lilly listened from the kitchen as Emma sang to her small grandson. Soon Lilly heard Kate's voice.

"I want you to call me if you need anything. I am going to check in with you daily and everyone is aware that there will be no lying about how you are doing, that includes no lying from you. Understand? We will fly back at least one weekend a month if not two. Lilly and David are also going to be coming over and spending time with you. I think we have everything covered. Momma, please take care of yourself and don't be so bullheaded when it comes to accepting help from others."

Emma crossed her arms and said, "This is not a daycare and I do not need someone checking up on me every day. I am fine. Just fine."

Kate smiled, knowing how this must bruise her mother's ego to have to depend on others for help. She knew how independent Emma was and how she hated asking for help.

"I know you want your independence. Just patronize me on this. I will sleep better knowing you have folks checking in on you. And you know I need my sleep in order to take care of your grandson."

"Oh, Good Lord. Now you are playing the grandson card on me. That's just wrong. Plain old wrong."

Kate hugged her mother and said, "Just do this, ok?"

"Ok. But don't ever think I am doing it out of agreement with you. I'm doing it so you will hush up."

"I don't care why you do it just that you do it. I love you and I want you to get better. If that means asking others for their help, then that is what we will do."

"I've heard enough. I've made my promise so let's just drop it. Are you planning on driving straight through tonight?

"Joshua says we will probably stop in Hays or Colby and spend the night. I promise to let you know what our plans are and where we stay."

Emma pulled her sweater around her shoulders and said, "Good enough."

Lilly entered the room at the same time as Joshua. She smiled and hugged Kate. "Now you promise you will call and we will set a time to get together soon?"

Kate squeezed Lilly's shoulder. "Promise. We've got a lot of things to take care of. Not just wedding plans now. Momma and her secret letters, you know."

Emma began to tear up and walked to the living room window. Kate stood behind her mother and leaned her forehead on the back of Emma's head. "Please call me if you need anything. Who's going to shave your head? You know you can still change your mind and come home with us."

Emma turned around to face her daughter, tears running down her cheeks. "I'll be fine. I'm sure I can handle shaving my head. If I have problems, I will call Taylor to come out and help. I wish we weren't so far from one another. Kate, please forgive me for keeping the letters from you. I just didn't know how to handle it. It wasn't one of those take the bull by the horns things. I didn't want anyone to get hurt."

"Oh, don't worry about the letters. Lilly and I are now looking forward to getting to the bottom of it. It is still hard to imagine. I wish Jim was here to help us sort this out."

Kate hugged her mother, bending forward to kiss Emma's forehead.

Emma chuckled. "Me too," she said.

Kate wiped Emma's tears. "No more tears. Everything is going to be fine. Right?"

"Right," Emma said.

Joshua carried the luggage to the car as Kate bundled Conner into his car seat.

Emma knelt down next to Conner and began to talk to him as if the two were alone in the room. "Your grandma loves you more than anything. You take care of your momma and daddy and you call grandma if you need a story or a song. Grandma will be here for you. Let's pray your grandma is here always for you. And you remember your Uncle Jim and Papa Beans are your very own guardian angels.

Emma carried Conner to the vehicle and Kate fastened his car seat. Emma choked back tears as she kissed him and said "Grandma loves you."

Joshua patted Emma's hand and got in the driver's side as Kate hugged her mother, not wanting to let go. "Momma, please come with us. Or I will arrange a flight for you. I don't want you out here alone."

"Now, sis, I'm far from alone. I am going to be just fine. I have made my promises that I will do as the doctor says and you have arranged this Emma visitation thing so folks can keep you posted. The Good Lord will take care of things. Besides, I have Sam and Gracie here. And Zeke is not far away."

Kate held Emma close and whispered in her ear "I love you more than meat loves salt."

"And I love you more than meat loves salt. Now you go on and don't worry."

Emma stood at the gate and Lilly and David stood on the porch as Kate, Joshua and Conner drove away. Emma shielded her eyes from the afternoon sun as she watched them drive towards the cemetery. She turned to her friends on the porch.

"She's going to see the boys. I knew she would."

Lilly detected a sense of relief in Emma's voice. She knew how much it meant to Emma when Kate visited the cemetery. Lilly also knew how hard it was for Kate to make those visits.

Emma stayed outside for nearly thirty minutes, looking towards the cemetery. When the afternoon chill was more than she could bear in her sweater, she came inside. Lilly and David were gathering their things and also preparing to leave. Lilly remembered Kate had worried Emma would have a difficult time when the quiet of the night came and all her family had gone.

"You two taking off?" Emma asked.

"We need to get home. David has to be back in the office tomorrow and I am meeting with an editor. But we will give you a call this weekend. If you need anything, you feel free to call."

Emma smiled. "I will. You and Kate keep in touch with each other. Keep me posted on not only the wedding plans but on this half sister thing."

"I promise. You know Kate is already working on researching this further. And, Emma, don't blame yourself for what happened."

Emma rubbed her head. "Easier said than done, Miss Lilly Ballard. Easier said than done."

Emma walked David and Lilly out and watched as they also drove away. She rubbed Sam's ears. Gracie began to bark and jump up on Emma. "Little Miss Jealous. Come on in. Let's see what kind of trouble we can get into this evening."

The evening was quiet as Emma relaxed with her two dogs beside her. She searched the television for something to watch, occasionally talking to Sam and Gracie.

Soon she began to tire and decided to retire for the evening. She glanced at the grandfather clock in the living room, noticing that it was not even nine o'clock.

"Wonder when the kids will call," she said as she headed for her room. Sam and Gracie followed. Gracie nipped at Sam when he tried to enter the bedroom before her and Emma scolded her.

Emma drifted off to sleep. At eleven her phone rang. It was Kate letting her know they had made it to Colby and were staying there for the night.

When Emma hung up, she said a prayer aloud.

"Thank you, Lord, for my children and grandchildren. Please watch over them through the night. Watch over Papa's and Grandma's; Aunts, Uncles and cousins; all our friends and loved ones. Amen."

Chapter 42

The next two months were filled with doctor appointments and treatments for Emma. Everyone followed Kate's plan of keeping an eye on Emma and her health. In March Kate and Conner spent Jim's birthday with Emma. Emma was no longer losing weight and she seemed to have more energy.

As always, it was hard for Emma to see Kate and Conner leave. He was growing so fast and showed a few teeth when he smiled at his grandma. Emma took great pleasure in spending time with her daughter and grandson. Goodbyes were so hard yet Emma knew Kate's place was in Denver.

Lilly and David arrived Easter weekend to attend church with Emma and spend some time with her. Lilly thought Emma looked well and even had hopes of the treatments ending soon. Emma said the doctors had told her there might be a possibility of ending the treatments by summer. Lilly looked at this as good news.

Easter Sunday was filled with good company and good food. Zeke came to visit after the early morning church service. He took Lilly aside.

"So what do you think? Don't she look good? She even gained two pounds this last visit. Damn doctor won't talk to me when I take her in. He says I ain't family. He don't know Emma Jean is like a sister to me. Kate promised she would call and talk to him. Seems she is the only one he will share information with when it comes to her momma's health. I don't like being treated that way. He ought know I am her friend and I am the one that's been taking her each time."

"I'm sure Kate will take care of it, Zeke. If she said she would, then she will."

"Emma tells me you girls are officially half sisters. Now ain't that good? Now the neithers of ya have to be alone in your later years. Ain't nothing worse than bein alone."

Lilly was taken aback by Zeke's statement. She had no idea Emma had shared any information about this to anyone outside of those that were in the room the night they read Elaine's letters. Emma had stressed not to say a word to anyone as it would possibly spread like, quote, "wildfire". And she did not want any people from the church knowing. Lilly assumed that Zeke was such a dear friend, Emma trusted him with such a thing.

Zeke reached for his tobacco can, not taking it out of his shirt pocket. "Miss Lilly? Are you there? What in the Hell are you thinking?"

Lilly looked towards Zeke and he said, "Lord, I thought I'd lost you. You must have been a million miles from here."

"I definitely think she looks good, Zeke."

Emma entered the dining room. "What are you two talking about?"

Zeke again reached for his pocket. "Just stuff."

Emma patted his arm. "Just stuff, huh?"

Zeke's cheeks turned red. "Yep."

"Ezekiel Lang, you are the worst liar in all of Osage County. Were you talking about me?"

"Nope," Zeke said, this time taking the tobacco can from his pocket and taking a pinch. He looked at Emma and thought better of placing it in his mouth. Emma was very strict about tobacco and alcohol use in her home.

"Liar, liar, pants on fire," Emma taunted as she danced around the dining table.

"Oh, Hell. Now ain't that mature of ya. So what if we was talking about ya?"

"Well, that would be rude. Why don't you share what you were saying?"

Lilly decided it was time to intervene. "We were saying how well you look and it is so good to be together today."

Emma crossed her arms. "Um hum. Likely story."

Zeke frowned and said, "Emma Jean, that ain't nice insinuating Miss Lilly is lying to ya. That ain't nice at all."

"I will only say this once to you, Ezekiel Lang. You are right as rain. I should not do that. I just hope it was all good things you said. All good."

The friends spent the day on Emma's porch sharing stories and laughter. Lilly and David left at dusk and Zeke did Emma's chores for her.

Emma spent spring working in her flowers when she had the strength and by early June her treatments had stopped and the doctors said she was in a 'honeymoon' stage but not necessarily a remission. Emma told Zeke what the doctor had said as they returned to Emma's home from her final treatment.

Zeke took off his hat and scratched his head. "What kind of talk is that? What do they mean a 'honeymoon' stage? Why in the Hell can't they just come out and tell a person what is going on?"

"Now, Ezekiel, they did tell me. They said I don't need any more treatments at this time and I am satisfied with that. They said I don't need any more treatments at this time and I am satisfied with that. My hair will grow in and I won't be so nauseated and tired. It's good, Ezekiel. Let's just believe this is good."

Zeke pulled the truck over on the shoulder of the road. He turned to Emma and did not take his eyes from hers. "I can't bear to lose my best friend, Emma

Jean. You had better fight this thing. Your family and friends need you. Ain't none of us can bear any more heartache or grief in our lives."

Emma touched Zeke's arm and smiled. "Ezekiel, we are always going to have heartache and grief in our lives. That is the cycle of life itself. We are all facing death from the time we are born. And, yes, we've both had our share of heartache but we just can't dwell on it. We just can't or we'll just go crazy."

"Then call me crazy 'cause I can't seem to get it off my mind."

Emma laughed. "Then drive me home, Crazy."

Zeke chuckled. "Nut."

Zeke, Dawson and Brett spent evenings helping Emma with the evening chores. Brett continued to bring his camcorder and record Emma, sometimes without her even realizing it.

Emma's hair began to grow in and her face grew tan with the warmth of the summer sun. Kate and Conner continued to make at least one trip a month and everyone stayed with the original plan of helping Emma. With each passing day, Emma seemed to grow stronger.

As late summer arrived and fall approached, Emma, Kate and Lilly began to prepare the farm for the wedding. Emma kept Zeke and her grandsons busy with all sorts of projects. She wanted everything perfect for Lilly and David.

David tried to come as often as possible and Joshua's schedule seldom allowed him the opportunity to spend much time on the farm.

Emma decided one Saturday in late August to have Dawson and Brett paint the smaller barn that she called her chicken house. She sent them for red barn paint and brushes and rollers.

When they arrived, Emma was waiting with her paint overalls on. She stood with her hands on her hips, her hair growth reminding Dawson of tiny, white baby chick growth.

Emma clapped her hands together and said, "Chop, chop. Let's get this done."

Dawson carried two paint cans as he walked towards his grandmother. "Grandma, why are we doing this? We just painted this old thing two years ago."

"We are doing this, Dawson Orie, because we will be having a lot of guests here and I want things to be as perfect as possible."

Brett set his cans of paint on the ground and took a paintbrush from the shopping bag. "Yeah, perfect. Something you wouldn't know about."

Emma raised her arms in the air and exclaimed. "Oh, Good Lord. Boys, please don't play your games today. Grandma is just not up to it."

"Ah, Grandma, it makes our time go so much faster if you let us fool around," Brett said.

"Nope. There will be no fooling around on this day. I want this chicken house done by nightfall. I will stay right here with you and help."

Dawson grinned. "Are you helping or supervising?"

Emma swatted him with her paintbrush. "A little of both, young man."

Everyone worked each weekend to prepare for the wedding. Kate had decided to take some vacation time and spent the last three weeks before the wedding with her mother. She knew Emma would want her house spotless and everything outside in order. Kate soon realized how difficult it was to try to get things accomplished with a young child in tow.

It was late in the evening when Lilly phoned. Kate answered. Kate could hear the excitement and nervousness in Lilly's voice.

"I thought I would check in on how things are going. I will be there Friday and I am staying the week to help out and do my part. Did I wake Emma or Conner?"

Kate brushed her hair from her face. "Conner is down for the night and Mom is out on the porch swing. I am supposed to be bringing her two chocolate chips cookies and milk."

Lilly chuckled. "It's good to see her with her appetite back. How's she doing?"

"She seems to be doing really well. She has plenty of energy and she looks good. You should see the dress she has picked out for the wedding. We went ahead and bought it in hopes of you approving of it. It is so hard to find things that fit her with her weight loss. She looks great in it and I doubt she gains much weight between now and the wedding. She's gained seven pounds, Lilly. Isn't that great? Oh, she looks wonderful in that dress."

"Oh, I can't wait. I am so afraid she will tire herself out."

"You know how she is. Always wanting this done and that done. She's been to the cemetery twice today. She gets a little sad right before holidays and special occasions."

Emma entered the house. "Who are you talking to?" she asked.

Kate turned to her mother and whispered "Lilly".

Emma smiled and said, "Tell her I said hello. Guess this means I need to get my own cookies and milk. You girls will be on the phone all night."

Kate frowned and shook her head.

Emma went into the kitchen where she fixed her snack and then came back into the living room.

She sat on the overstuffed chair, pulling her right leg up under her and cupping her cookies in the palm of her hand. "Um hum. Just like I said. Jabber, jabber. You girls and your wedding plans."

"Lilly, Mom says hello and I probably should get off the phone and check on Conner. What time shall we expect you on Friday?"

There was a pause and then Kate said good-bye. She turned to her mother and shook her index finger at her. "Shame on you. You would have never let us kids interrupt you while on the phone. Shame on you."

Emma took a drink of her milk, her eyes smiling over the rim of the glass. She swallowed her milk and then spoke in a mocking child-like voice "Shame, shame on Emma."

Kate rolled her eyes. "Oh, mother."

Emma handed Kate one of her cookies and Kate declined the offer.

"So tell me what Lilly had to say," Emma said.

Kate filled Emma in on the conversation with Lilly and the plans for the week.

Kate and Emma spent the rest of the week preparing the house for the wedding. Emma decorated in her usual fall colors and decorations and Kate assured her it would be beautiful with Lilly's wedding colors. Lilly arrived on Friday. Emma and Kate were in the side yard raking a few leaves while Conner played nearby in his playpen. Sam stood on the patio nearby overlooking all of the activities. Gracie lay next to the playpen with her chin resting on her forepaws, a constant vigil on Conner.

Lilly hugged Emma and Kate and rubbed Conner's golden head of hair as she passed the playpen.

"Good Lord, Lilly, we've accomplished so much but I sure am thankful you are here. Kate has been working me like a dog," Emma said as she winked at Kate.

Emma looked happy and healthy. Her hair had grown and she wore its short haphazard length proudly. Her eyes sparkled as she motioned to Conner. "Isn't that boy growing like a weed?"

"He certainly is," Lilly responded as she turned toward Kate. "Are you ready for another one?"

Kate laughed. "No, no. I plan on enjoying him for quite a while before I even consider another one."

The morning was spent with plans of table placement and seating arrangements. They discussed more ideas and plans over lunch. Lilly and Kate talked constantly and Emma enjoyed being a part of their plans and preparations. Emma excused herself and put Conner's jacket on him and went outside. Lilly gave Kate a puzzled look.

"She just takes off, sometimes with Conner and other times she goes off alone. I found her one afternoon down by the pond, sitting in Rylie's fishing chair. I've found her all over the place. She says she is just thinking and needs some time."

"She looks great. Does she feel well?"

Kate cleared the table. "She seems to feel great. She has been tearing into housework and she sometimes goes without a nap during the day but retires early in the evening. The doctor says she is doing well. He still insists this is not a remission. I am going to believe it is and that she won't have to face another treatment."

Lilly and Kate finished clearing the table and went into the living room. Kate looked out the front window onto the porch where Emma sat on the swing with Conner. Emma caught a glimpse of Kate and called to her. "We're just porch sitting. You girls can come on out if you like."

Kate opened the screen door. "Just porch sitting, huh?"

Emma continued to swing as Conner pulled himself up on her. "Yep, just porch sitting."

Lilly and Kate sat in the chairs near the swing. Emma turned to them and asked, "Have you ever wondered why you've been put here on this earth?"

Kate immediately responded. "Now, you've always told me that you didn't want Jim to be alone when you were gone so you had me. Am I right?"

Emma smiled. "Yes, that is why I wanted another child. I worried that he would be alone with no family when we passed on. The Lord sure fooled me on that one, didn't he? I now believe I was blessed with you so that I would have some comfort when Jim died and so I would have the joy of Conner James. I think you were put on this earth for many reasons, Katy Leigh. I just hate that many of my choices in life brought you and your brother so much heartache. Rylie sat on this very swing one fall afternoon two years after we had lost Jim and he held me close to him and said 'I will never understand why so many bad things have happened to you, Emma.' Sometimes I ask myself that very question and then something will remind me that good things have also happened in my life. Why, just look at my blessings right here on this porch."

"I think I was put on this earth to use my talent to bring pictures of beautiful places to those who will only see them in print," Lilly said.

Zeke's truck drove into the drive. Emma sat Conner on her lap and he continued to squirm. "I wonder what that old codger is up to," she said.

When the truck drove closer to Emma's house, the women could see the bed of the truck was laden with all sizes and colors of pumpkins. Lilly hurried to the truck, hoping she could talk Zeke into selling her some for the wedding.

Zeke tipped his hat. "Morning, ladies. Morning, little man."

Lilly leaned over the bed of the truck. "Zeke, where on earth did you get all of these pumpkins?"

"Well, Miss Lilly, I grew them myself. I figured maybe they would add to all your girlie fall decorating for the wedding."

Lilly hugged Zeke. "Oh, Zeke, they are wonderful. Absolutely beautiful. I insist on paying you something for them. This had to take a lot of time and effort on your part."

Zeke seemed to blush. "It ain't no trouble at all. I did it for the fun."

Lilly lifted a perfectly round, white pumpkin and held it up for Emma and Kate to admire. "Kate, come look at all of these."

Kate stepped through the gate and she and Lilly began to ogle over each pumpkin as they lifted it for Emma to see.

"Ezekiel, you might want to get the red wagon from the barn for these girls to fill. I'll make you some coffee," Emma said.

"Mom, may we use the old antique wagon out south and fill it with hay and pumpkins like Jim and I used to do?"

Emma turned as she opened the screen door. Her eyes widened and she smiled a broad smile. "Oh, wouldn't that be pretty? Fine with me if Lilly wants it."

Zeke sat on the front bumper of the truck. "Reckon this means I need to hitch up the old wagon and pull it wherever these girls want."

Emma stepped inside the door and looked back at Zeke. "Right you are, Ezekiel Lang. I'll fix your coffee and you make these girls help. After all, it was Katy Leigh's idea. Put her to work."

Zeke winked at Kate. "You heard your momma. Ain't a soul on earth gonna argue with Emma Jean. Wait, that ain't true. I've heard you bicker with her."

Kate frowned. "In my younger days, Zeke. You couldn't pay me to argue with her now."

Zeke, Lilly and Kate worked on placing Emma's old wagon in just the right place for all the wedding guests to see as they entered the wedding. After some time, Emma came out with a thermos of coffee for Zeke and Conner in his stroller. She handed the thermos to Zeke.

Zeke tapped on his flannel shirt pocket, then reached for his chewing tobacco can. "Emma Jean, I need to talk to you in private for a minute."

Kate patted Zeke's arm. "This works out well. Lilly and I think we need some tiny, white lights woven in the hay and pumpkins. Mom, may I raid your storage boxes in the barn?'

"Of course. You know you don't need to ask. Whatever you girls need, you use."

Emma turned to Zeke with a worried look on her face. "Come sit on the porch with me."

Emma sat in a chair and Zeke sat on the porch steps, pushing Conner back and forth in his stroller on the sidewalk.

"Emma Jean, I've done something I'm afraid is gonna upset you. I should have talked to you first cause now I'm a getting cold feet."

Emma leaned forward in her chair. "What have you done, Ezekiel?"

"I asked Barb out to dinner on Sunday. Oh, I know I shouldn't have gone and done it. Why I just get lonely. You know how it is. Ain't no one ever gonna replace my Nancy but once in a while I would like to take someone to dinner. Am I wrong to feel this way?"

"Barb who?"

"You know, the waitress at the Corner Café. Sweetest gal. You know she's raised them grandkids of hers and she ain't had a chance to get out much. Not that she complains, mind you. Folks need other folks. Hell, if I didn't have you and your family, I'd done gone nuts a long time ago."

Emma stood from her chair and sat down next to Zeke on the porch steps. "Ezekiel, I think that is wonderful. Nancy would not begrudge you for wanting the company of others. Why, you've spent way too much time on me with my being ill. I should have thought of what this has done to you. You've been down this road before and here I am asking for your help. You go and have fun. Now take her someplace nice."

Zeke put his arm around Emma and hugged her. "I will go to my grave saying you are the closest thing to a sister I ever had. You're my kin, Emma Jean. Don't you ever think you have been a burden to me. I wouldn't have it any other way. I want to help you. I just want to go to dinner with someone once in a while. I can't keep on depending on you and yours to spend time with."

Emma pulled away from Zeke. "And why can't you? We love you, Ezekiel Lang. You are welcome day or night. Don't ever think different."

Kate and Lilly came from the barn, waving strings of lights at Emma and Zeke. Kate called out, "We found them!"

Zeke stood and ruffled Emma's short hair. "Looks like they are gonna need an extension cord. Reckon I'll head to the barn."

Emma stood. Zeke turned to her and kissed her cheek. "You're a fine woman, Emma Jean. I am proud to have you as my friend. Thanks for listening."

Emma winked at Zeke. "I want details of your Sunday dinner with Barb. Maybe the girls and I should go to breakfast in the morning and fill her in on what she is in for; dating an old codger like you."

Zeke walked through the gate. "Don't need no help from the likes of you and them girls, Emma Jean McMaster. You make them girls cook breakfast and stay away from the Corner Café. Now get your butt out here and see if them girls have done this to your satisfaction."

Emma clicked her heals together and saluted Zeke. "Yes, sir!"

Lilly ran up to Zeke as he walked toward the barn. "Zeke, may I ask you a question?"

Zeke looked at Lilly with a puzzled frown. "Go right ahead, Miss Lilly."

"Would you please dance the father/daughter dance at the reception with me? I know Emma is giving me away but I thought it might be nice to have the honor of dancing with you."

Zeke took both of Lilly's hands in his and faced her. "I would be the one that is honored. Never had a child of my own and I would be down right proud to dance with you."

Lilly smiled, tears welling up in her eyes as she spoke softly, "Thank you."

"I reckon this means I will need to get all gussied up. Last time I wore a suit was at Kate's wedding. That girl tortured me."

"I want you to wear whatever makes you comfortable."

"Now don't be telling Emma Jean. She'll be cinching my tie up and making all over me. That woman is nothing but a perfectionist. Always fussing over things."

Lilly looked at the ground. "She already knows."

Zeke reached for his tobacco can. "Oh, Hell. This calls for a pinch of chew. You get on back with the other women. And I will be honored to dance with you. Better wear your steel toed shoes."

Chapter 43

Lilly and David's wedding day finally arrived. The house was full of activity. Emma sat in front of the television, listening to the weather. She called out the forecast.

"High today near seventy-five. Clear with a low around fifty. Perfect day for a wedding!"

Emma walked outside and supervised the outdoor activities.

The florist arrived early and Emma's dear friend Marilyn arrived with the wedding cake. Emma announced Marilyn's arrival to David and Joshua. As she walked towards the reception tent to greet Marilyn, David asked Joshua how the two women knew one another.

"Emma and Marilyn worked for a non-profit law firm in Topeka. They worked together for over seventeen years. Marilyn was Emma's supervisor for years but they became such close friends and have continued to stay close after retirement."

Emma stood and admired the cake as Marilyn placed it on the table in the reception tent.

"I think this cake is even more beautiful than Kate's. Don't tell her I said that. It is gorgeous. Simply gorgeous."

Marilyn smiled at Emma. "Thank you. This is quite a set up. These kids have really gone all out."

"Lilly wanted it to be nice and not fancy but I think this is a little fancier than I pictured. Look at this tent! All those tiny lights on the ceiling and all the flowers. Lilly and Kate have done a beautiful job."

Emma insisted Marilyn sit down and the two women visited for over an hour when Kate called out to Emma that they needed her inside.

"I'll be there in a little while. Come out and say hello to Marilyn," Emma called.

Kate carried Conner outdoors. "Momma, we need you inside. You two can catch up on gossip later." Kate turned to Marilyn and asked, "You are staying for the wedding and reception, aren't you?"

"Of course," Marilyn responded.

"See, mother. You can talk later. We need your help now and you don't have enough time to sit on your tail and gab."

Emma tilted her head to one side and stuck her tongue out at Kate.

"Mature, Mom, real mature. Get your little tail in that house now."

Emma excused herself and hurried to the house. Kate followed with Conner in her arms. He was dressed in a tiny tuxedo and he was already beginning to fidget.

Emma laughed. "Get that monkey suit off that boy. He'll have it ruined before the wedding."

"Doesn't he look cute?" Kate asked.

"Yes, sugar. But I'm his grandma and I would think he looked cute in anything. Your brother would have a fit if he knew you had that child dressed up in a tuxedo."

Kate's smiled faded. "Conner will never know his Uncle Jim. I just hate that, Mom."

Emma hugged Kate. "I shouldn't have brought him up. It is just that he so hated getting all dressed up for these sort of things and that was the first thing I thought of."

Kate kissed Emma's cheek. "It's all right. He's with us in spirit."

"I need help with this dress!" Lilly called from upstairs.

Kate handed Conner to Emma and hurried upstairs. Emma kissed his nose. "Let's you and Grandma get you out of this suit until as close to the wedding as possible."

Emma undressed Conner and went into the kitchen where David sat drinking a cup of coffee.

"Are you nervous?" Emma asked.

"A little. Lilly has planned this for a long time and I want everything to go off without a hitch."

Emma smiled and said, "Oh, Lord. Seems like every wedding has a little hitch to it."

Emma giggled. "Get it? A hitch?"

David smiled. "I get it."

David held his arms out and Conner went to him. Emma sat at the table.

"Now see what spending time together does? Since you kids have become so close, my little man feels right at home with you."

Conner reached for David's glasses. "Tell Grandma how you and I are going to go hide somewhere and take off our tuxes. Your mom and Lilly can't torture us all day and night, can they?"

Emma watched quietly, thinking of how she longed for Jim and Rylie to be a part of all of this. She desperately wanted Conner to know his uncle and grandpa.

David could sense her sadness and spoke only, "They're here. Don't ever forget that."

Emma patted his hand and fought back her tears. "I know they are. I just wish they were here in body. I miss them more than you know."

"Mom? Mom! Where are you?" Kate called.

"In the kitchen," Emma said. "Good Lord, you would think we lived in a huge mansion, hollering like that."

Kate entered the kitchen. "Have you seen Joshua?"

"Last I saw him was outside helping set up the chairs," David answered.

Kate looked at Conner and then at Emma. "Where's his tux?"

"I took it off him and hung it up until closer to the wedding."

Kate walked out the back door of the sun porch, not acknowledging Emma's response to her tuxedo question. David shook his head.

"I'd better check on how things are going. Will you be able to handle Conner James for a while?" she asked.

David patted Conner's diaper padded bottom. "Of course. We still need time to plot our tuxedo get away."

Emma went to check on Lilly and then outdoors. Things were coming together. Kate had hung Rylie's antique railroad lanterns on shepherds' hooks, lining a pathway to the reception tent. All the colors of autumn filled the tent. Pumpkins were scattered throughout. On each table sat an antique ball jar tied with raffia and a votive candle in it, waiting for the dusk of evening to cast its glow on the room. A wooden dance floor had been set in the center of the tent with the linen covered tables surrounding it.

Emma walked towards Kate and Joshua. "This is absolutely gorgeous. You are so talented. I wish I had had the money to put something like this on for you two."

"Oh, momma. Our wedding was just as beautiful, don't you think, Joshua?"

"I know the bride was the most beautiful thing I had ever seen. And still is to this day."

Kate kissed Joshua. Emma cleared her throat. "We have no time for smooching. We need to get our work done so we can pretty ourselves up for the big day."

Afternoon arrived and it was time to get dressed. Emma went into her room. She put on her dress and stood before the full-length mirror, smoothing her dress with her hands. Her dress was a deep rich burgundy. She ran her fingers across her necklace, a gift from Jim. She put on her diamond earrings and looked at her reflection, nodding her approval. Lilly knocked on the door.

"Emma? May I come in?"

"Come in, Lilly. It's your turn to get dressed."

Lilly opened the door. "Oh, Emma. You look beautiful. Absolutely beautiful."

"Why, thank you, Lilly Ballard. Are you ready to put your dress on? What were you doing in it this morning?"

"The photographer came out and took a few pictures of me this morning. He wanted to take advantage of the morning light."

Emma chuckled. "Funny. A photographer taking pictures of a photographer."

Lilly smiled. "Will you stay and help me with my dress? Kate should be up here in a few minutes."

As Emma helped Lilly with her dress, Kate entered the room. Her hair was upswept and the forest green gown she wore made her eyes a deep green. Emma smiled with pride as she looked at her daughter.

"You look so pretty, sis. Absolutely gorgeous."

"And so do you, Mom."

Kate stepped back and looked at Lilly. "Oh, Lilly. You look radiant. Just wonderful."

After a few moments of mutual admiration, it was time for the guests to arrive. Emma stood at the bedroom window and announced each guest to Lilly and Kate. Soon the guests were seated and the time had come for Emma, Lilly and Kate to go downstairs to wait their turns.

The music played softly. Kate stepped out of the sun porch and began to walk down the aisle. Soon the music changed and it was Lilly's turn to have Emma walk her down the aisle. Everyone stood. Lilly's eyes were focused on David.

As Emma walked Lilly to the front of the aisle and stood before the pastor, David and the groomsmen, the pastor asked "Who gives this bride in Holy Matrimony?"

Emma stood beside Lilly and proudly said, "In memory of her mother, I do."

David took Lilly's hand and kissed Emma lightly on the cheek. She winked at him and turned to be seated in the front row.

The ceremony was a traditional ceremony. As the pastor announced, "Ladies and Gentleman, I would like to present David and Lilly Rollins, husband and wife," Zeke let out a big yee haw from the his seat next to Emma and everyone laughed except Emma who nudged him with her elbow.

"What?" he whispered.

"These folks are city folks and professional career people. Not country folk like some of us."

Zeke looked down at his new cowboy boots. "Well, sorry for being down right thrilled that they are hitched."

Lilly and David began to walk together down the aisle and Lilly smiled at Emma and Zeke. Zeke gave her a thumbs-up sign.

"See, she ain't mad, Emma."

The reception and dance filled the countryside with music and laughter. As planned, Lilly and Zeke danced the father daughter dance and David danced with his mother. The evening was filled with lots of food and fellowship. Kate kept a constant vigil on Emma, concerned that Emma would tire from the day and evening festivities.

Lilly watched as Emma was asked time and again to dance and not once did she turn a gentleman down. Brett videoed the evening activities, focusing on his grandmother the majority of the time. He often watched the professional videographer recording the bride and groom and tried to pick up a few pointers.

As guests began to leave, Emma sat in a chair. Kate had excused herself earlier to put Conner to bed and Taylor had agreed to stay in the house to listen for him. Zeke sat down next to Emma.

"Don't you think you should get some rest, old woman?"

Emma glanced towards Zeke and curtly responded. "You're older than me. Are you needing a nap?"

Zeke took a deep sigh and knew Emma was short with him merely because of the busy day and, whether she admitted it or not, her need for rest.

"You ain't danced with me yet. The band will be leaving shortly. Care to dance with me? I mean, if you ain't too tired and all."

Emma stood from her seat and held her hand out to Zeke.

David walked to the platform where the band stood and whispered something to the drummer. Within a few moments the band began to play the "Twist" and Emma and Zeke danced as if they were back in time, two young people enjoying life. The dance floor cleared and the remaining guests stood and watched the couple as they twisted and laughed. At the end of the song, the guests applauded and both Emma and Zeke took a bow.

Dawson walked up to Emma and asked, "Grandma, where did you learn to dance like that?"

"From your grandpa. Lord, I was raised that dancing was of the devil but your papa could really cut the rug and he would dance with me right here in the living room. He was so patient with me. I was born with two left feet but that Rylie had some talent. I even made him take ballroom lessons with me one winter not long before he passed on. We had fun, DW. We had lots of fun, your grandpa and I."

Emma stayed up until only a few guests were left and Kate insisted Emma get some rest. Kate assured her mother that the caterers would clean up their mess and the remainder would be clean before morning. Emma hugged Lilly and David, making them promise to phone her when they returned from their honeymoon.

After all the guests had left, Kate, Joshua, David and Lilly sat and watched as the area was cleared. Kate and Lilly kept insisting that they would help but everything was taken care of, leaving them time to talk before Lilly and David left for their late flight.

David was the first to broach the subject of the farm.

"We found Emma and Rylie's original plans for turning the barn into their home. It was purely by accident as we were helping Emma clean out some storage bins in the barn. Have you ever seen them? It is incredible."

Kate said she had never seen the plans and that the dream of turning the barn into a house had been cast aside for many years, when Kate was around fifteen.

"We would like to try to purchase the barn and turn it into our home. We would be near Emma and we could look after her and the farm. I would pay to build a new barn for Emma's animals and we would make sure she is taken care of and so are her animals. What do you think?"

Kate was shocked at the suggestion and wondered what Emma's response to such an idea would be.

"Wow, you totally broad sided me on this one. I am going to need some time. Yes, the idea of having you here if she needed you is wonderful but I don't know how I feel about the barn being turned into a house."

David leaned forward and placed his elbows on his knees, still wearing the tuxedo he had sworn he would shed earlier in the evening. "Would you consider going over the floor plans that both Emma and Rylie wanted when we return to the states?"

Kate nodded her head, agreeing to review the floor plans and said, "Mom may throw a huge fit that you even found them. Lately I never know what her reaction or mood is going to be."

David smiled. "We'll cross that bridge when we come to it."

The conversation led to Emma's health and chores and then to what a wonderful evening it had been. David looked at his watch and reminded Lilly that they should be leaving.

What had taken over a year to plan had come to an end and everyone was exhausted. Kate and Lilly hugged as they said their goodbyes and the men carried out the luggage for the honeymoon.

Kate and Joshua turned off the last of the lights and made sure everything was taken care of before retiring for the night.

As they lay in bed, Kate asked Joshua his opinion of the barn proposition. Joshua patted her leg and only said, "Get some rest, babe. We'll discuss it in the morning."

And Kate's response was, "Whatever." It reminded Joshua of something Emma would say and he chuckled.

Chapter 44

Kate and Joshua left the following afternoon, promising Emma they would return in late October for Kate's birthday.

They discussed the proposition of Lilly and David purchasing the barn and a portion of land around it. Kate was torn on how she felt about such an idea. Joshua said they should just wait until they had the opportunity of talking to David and Lilly and looking at Emma & Rylie's original plans.

Emma kept busy around the farm and continued to feel well, seeing her doctor every other week. Her grown grandchildren continued to help her as did Zeke and members of the church and community. She often had so many people at her home to help that she welcomed the quiet of the evening.

Kate, Lilly, Joshua and David met for a weekend in Chicago where David's parents lived. They discussed the offer on the barn. David was the first to speak.

"Kate, we are tired of living in the city and long for a place in the country. Your mother's place is only a little over an hour from our work and both of us often have the luxury of working from home. I promise you we would not veer from the original plans at all. Your parents did a wonderful job of planning it out and even had an architect draw up the plans. Look."

David opened the plans and Joshua and Kate looked over them.

"This is incredible," Joshua said. "Why didn't they do this?"

"I think the death of Jim and my college expenses took a toll. They never said that but I really believe that is what happened. Then they seemed content in the house and Mom filled the barn with animals and a place for the mustang."

"Emma only told me that life got in the way," Lilly said.

"Or death got in the way," Kate replied curtly.

Kate's cell phone rang and she looked at the caller identification. "Speaking of that little devil; it's her."

"Afternoon, momma."

"Afternoon, sis. I just got off the phone with Jason and Dawson. Dawson, Brett and Taylor want to bring friends out for a hayrack ride the weekend you will be here and I wanted to run it by you first. I thought I would call Lilly and David and ask them too but there is no answer at their place. I don't want this to cut into your birthday celebration."

"Good grief, mom. I'm way too old to worry about a party. Lilly and David are sitting right here with us. Shall I ask them?"

"What? No one told me that you all were going to be together this weekend."

"Well, mother, we have our cell phones and you can always reach us that way. This is a flying trip to Chicago. Dinner and theater tonight and back to Denver and Kansas City tomorrow."

"Hmmph. Where's my boy?"

"He's here with us. David's parents are going to baby-sit while we go out tonight."

"That's awfully nice of them. So, shall I plan on a hayrack ride that Saturday night? That will still leave us Friday night and most of Sunday to visit and celebrate your birthday. You talk it over with the others and let me know soon."

"That sounds fine with me as long as you don't go to a lot of trouble for it. Make those kids do the work. Are Jason and Denise coming? Billy and Melissa?"

No Billy and Melissa. They will be out of town that weekend but maybe Jason and Denise. Don't count on it. Probably just the kids and their dates. I never see Kelsi except holidays. I do get a card on occasion. Enough. I will let you go and you get back with me soon. Love you."

"Love you too, Mom. See you the end of the month."

Kate informed the others of the plans.

Lilly thumbed through a magazine and said, "We'll try to be there. Maybe that would be a good time to discuss this idea of the barn with Emma."

Joshua turned to Kate. "I thought I heard her say something about Kelsi."

"Just that she doesn't see her but gets a card once in a while."

"Now, she is Jason's step-daughter, right?" David asked.

"Yes. She married a boy she met in college. They moved to Minnesota and then New York after graduating. She comes back to Kansas once in a while but it is usually a flying trip and she doesn't have time to see Mom. They keep in touch by mail or by phone."

Lilly touched David's hand and said, "Shall we go for the hayrack ride and stay the night, hoping to approach Emma on the subject of the barn?"

David turned to Kate and said, "Kate, this barn is your inheritance. Emma has made it clear to all of us that she wants her home to stay in the family, if possible. We do not want to infringe on what is yours."

Kate ran her fingers through her hair. "I know the chance of us moving to the farm is slim. We love Denver and our careers and friends are there. But I want the farmhouse to stay just like it is. If Mom is willing to let you buy the barn, that is her choice, but I have reservations about ever turning loose of the house."

"Let's not worry about that. Emma is going to be around for a long time to take care of her house. This way we will be nearby to help her. We just don't want to step on your toes," David said.

Joshua put his arm around Kate, sensing she was still uncomfortable with the idea and said, "Let's see what Emma has to say."

The weekend of the Kate's birthday arrived and Emma was excited to see everyone. She baked a birthday cake and had worked all day Friday on treats for the hayrack ride on Saturday. Kate, Joshua and Conner arrived Friday afternoon with Lilly and David arriving that evening. Lilly brought up the subject of the barn purchase over dessert.

Emma sat quietly for quite some time, not looking at her guests. She ran her fork back and forth across her piece of cherry pie.

"Now, I never expected anything like this. Let me sleep on it. I'm not saying no and I'm not saying yes. I need to think. Have you thought about this, Kate?"

"Yes, I have and it is totally up to you. I will agree with whatever you decide."

"I'm porch sitting. You girls clean the kitchen and you men can do my chores. I need to think and I'm going to start it on the porch."

Emma walked to the coat closet and took her corduroy barn coat out, wrapping it around her shoulders. She walked onto the porch with Gracie following her.

The sound of the porch swing's slight creak was the only sound. No one spoke. Kate stood and began to clear the table. Conner sat in his highchair eating an Oreo cookie, smiling occasionally at his dad, teeth covered in chocolate.

David stood and said, "That went well."

"Whatever," Kate said. "If she needs the porch, then she's upset or thinking. Or both. I think we've hit both tonight. We've probably stirred a lot of memories and emotions."

Everyone did as Emma had instructed and went to bed much earlier than normal. Quietness filled the house. Kate could not sleep, wondering what was going through her mother's head and wondering what morning would bring.

Morning arrived to the sound of Emma in the kitchen rattling pots and pans. Kate and Lilly both came into the living room at the same time. They walked into the kitchen.

"Morning, mom," Kate said as she kissed her mother's cheek.

"Morning, girls."

Again quietness filled the room. Lilly hated herself for even bringing up the subject last night. She feared the entire weekend was ruined and Emma would turn them down, leaving this uncomfortable feeling between them forever.

"Are the boys sleeping in?" Emma asked.

"Conner woke up in the night so I put him between us and now he and his dad have taken over the whole bed."

"Lord, you used to steal covers, kick and carry on. Your brother was still as a mouse but not you. All over that bed."

"I know. You aren't going to let me live that one down."

David entered the kitchen and Emma turned to him, shaking a spatula at him.

"This is the way it is going to be. You can have the two acres that goes with the barn. I stay on the title until my dying day. No changing the plans and my new barn will look like it has been on this place for over a hundred years. You can't have the old barn until the new one is built for my critters and there will be a special place for the mustang. And nothing will be started until next spring. And no selling it to strangers if you decided you don't like the country life. Kate has first say on what is done with it if that time comes. No trying to bargain or change my mind. It is this way or no way. Understood?"

"You drive a hard bargain but I think we can agree to that. Lilly and Kate, what do you say?"

"She's the boss," Lilly said.

"I want you to make sure this is what you want to do, Momma. You're sure?"

"Sure as rain," Emma said.

"Then we will start making plans and I will draw up the plans for a new barn. Emma, thank you. I promise you won't regret it," David said.

Dawson and Brett arrived with their dates late afternoon and Taylor soon followed. Zeke arrived to hitch up the tractor to the hay wagon. He immediately announced he was in charge of driving and the young people were in charge of 'sparking'.

"Ezekiel, they don't call it sparking nor courting these days. What is it you call it now, DW?"

"We call it going out or dating, grandma. Get with the times."

Kate leaned over to Dawson and said, "Trust me; your grandma knows a lot more than she lets on. Don't let her fool you."

As the hayrack ride began, Taylor asked her grandmother to tell stories. Emma began to tell stories of her own mother's childhood in the south and then went on to her own childhood. Each time she would finish a story, one of the grandchildren would ask her to tell another story, often telling Emma the exact story they wanted her to tell. All the while Brett kept his camcorder focused on his grandmother as she told one story after the other. Once in a while he would pan across the guests, sometimes focusing on Conner as he sat on his grandmother's lap. Sam sat next to Emma as she told her stories.

The evening ended with a campfire and smores. Emma jumped up from her seat and said, "Oh, Good Lord, I forgot to bring out the birthday cake."

As she carried the cake outside, everyone sang "Happy Birthday" to Kate. It was an evening the guests would not soon forget.

Fall turned into colder weather. Thanksgiving passed and Emma celebrated another birthday. The marble jar was less than half full and Kate could no longer bear to look at it when she visited her mother.

Christmas arrived and Kate felt it was one of the best. Emma was in rare form, joking and preparing more food than ever before. David and Lilly arrived the day after Christmas and presented Emma with the new barn floor plans. She was pleased and gave them her approval. Emma knew spring would be arriving soon and she told David he could start in May.

Kate could not bear to think about the old barn being turned into David and Lilly's home but she wanted this to be her mother's decision so she kept quiet. Emma was no fool. She went into Kate's room that night and sat on the side of the bed. Joshua was still in the living room watching television and Conner lay sleeping in his bed nearby.

Emma ran her fingers through Kate's long hair.

"So, how long before you tell me what's bothering you?"

"Nothing is bothering me, Mom."

"Kate, I've been your momma way too many years to not know that you are holding something back from me. What is it?"

"I don't know if I can bear to see the old barn turned into a house. That will change everything."

Emma took a deep breath and let it out slowly.

"Kate, you and I know that life is all about change. Nothing lasts forever. I think seeing that barn built to the dream that Rylie and I always had will be a nice thing. Lord knows we could never afford to do such a thing. It would make Rylie proud to know it was finally being done. And a nice barn is being built for the mustang and critters. And I'll have folks nearby if I need them."

"It's just going to take some getting used to, I guess."

"It will for all of us. I think Lilly and David mean well and they are so excited about it. I'm not going to be around forever, you know."

Kate sat up in bed and said, "Is that what this is all about? Are you worried about this place after you are gone? And, by the way, you aren't going anywhere for a long, long time."

"No, no. I just think this will be a tiny step towards the day you have to deal with this place. I know deep in my heart that none of you kids or grandkids really want this place. Well, I know you want it but you can't move here so what happens to it, Kate?"

"I don't know and I don't want to think about it," Kate answered curtly.

Emma raised her eyebrows and said, "The day will come when you won't have any other choice than to face it. You had better be ready for that day."

Emma stood and, as she started to leave the room she said, "Love you more than meat loves salt."

"And I love you more than meat loves salt. That is why I can't bear to think of all of this. This is home. This is your home and that will never change."

"Never is a long time, Katy Leigh. Remember that. Good night."

Chapter 45

It was late February when Kate received the call from Emma's doctor.

"Kate, your mother's cancer is in her kidney and we need to discuss what needs to be done. Can you be in Topeka next week?"

"Yes, I will schedule a flight and I can be in your office on Monday. What time?"

Kate hung up the phone and Joshua knew from her face it wasn't good news.

Kate sat at the kitchen table and covered her eyes. "We've been going there monthly, Lilly and David look out for her, Zeke is there more often than not. How did we miss this?"

"Babe, none of us can look inside Emma. It just happened to hit her kidney. She'll be fine."

"Joshua, she only has the one kidney. Oh, God, this just can't be happening. Dr. Sands is waiting until I arrive and I will be there when he tells her. That alone is going to piss her off. She is going to think we've been keeping it from her. You know how she hates that."

"Do you want me to come too?"

"No, a sudden visit will tip her off and if we both show up, she'll know for sure something is up. I'll go with Conner and your mom can take care of him on Sunday night and Monday."

Kate slept very little the next three days, anxious to get to Emma's and face this head on. She had learned that from her mother. Face things head on. Take the bull by the horns. That was Emma and now Kate carried that very same trait.

Emma and Dawson met Kate and Conner at the airport.

"This is such a nice surprise, Sis."

Emma immediately took Conner and began to make over him, not noticing Kate's constant stare.

Kate noticed Emma had again started to lose weight and her dark circles had begun to return under her eyes.

Dawson tried to engage Kate in the usual teasing and banter but soon realized she was not in the mood.

The drive to the farm consisted of Emma constantly talking about the local gossip and how much Conner had grown in three weeks.

After the evening meal, Emma asked how long Kate planned on staying and was surprised when Kate said at least a week. Kate made light of the idea that she wanted Conner to spend a couple of days with Joshua's parents and that she wanted to spend some time with Emma without the usual hustle and bustle of extra guests.

Emma studied Kate's face as she made excuses for the extended visit.

"You never could lie. So, why are you really here?" Emma asked.

"I told you. I want some time alone with you."

"Liar."

"Stop it, Mom. I can't believe you think I am lying."

"I don't think it, I know it. Why in the Sam Hill are you here?"

Kate knew there was no getting around the truth so she told Emma the recent findings. She went into as little detail as possible, hoping that would suffice until they could meet with the doctor on Monday.

"So, who else knows this that hasn't told me? What other secrets are you keeping from me?"

Kate knew Emma was upset.

"Only Joshua knows. No one else knows. No grandkids, no friends, no one else."

Emma raised her right eyebrow. "Well, good. We can get this taken care of without the whole world knowing. I want no more talk of it until we get to the doctor's office on Monday. You understand?"

"Yes."

Kate spent the weekend helping Emma take down Valentine decorations and putting up St. Patrick's Day decorations. They decorated Jim's grave both knowing March brought yet another birthday that Jim and Rylie would not celebrate.

Kate took Conner to Joshua's parents on Sunday afternoon and Emma rode along.

Monday morning arrived and still neither Emma nor Kate spoke about the cancer. The ride to the doctor's office was unbearably quiet for Kate. Emma sat in the waiting room, thumbing through magazines, occasionally pointing out a recipe to Kate.

The nurse called Emma's name and both Emma and Kate went into the doctor's office.

"There's no reason to act like I don't know what is going on here. I pulled it out of Kate so let's just get on with what our next step will be," Emma said.

The doctor knew Emma well and knew the best approach would be to be straight-forward with her.

"Emma, we found a large cancerous mass on your kidney. Of course, we will want to do a biopsy and then discuss treatment. I also have reason to believe it may have returned to other parts of your body."

Kate let out a moan. Emma knew that moan. It was the same gut-wrenching moan she had heard from her daughter the night Jim died. She did not want to be the one to bring that heartache to her daughter once again.

Emma gripped Kate's hand and looked at the doctor. "Find out what and where it is and have a plan by the end of the week. Kate needs to get home to her work and family and I don't have time for lolly-gagging around, wondering what the plan is."

Dr. Sands smiled and looked over the rim of his glasses at Emma and Kate. "Shall we plan on a biopsy tomorrow morning and I want to order an MRI and other tests too."

Kate leaned forward in her chair. "Dr. Sands, what about an organ donation?"

"Let's see if it is only in the kidney and then we will discuss the options, Kate."

Kate phoned Joshua from her cell phone on the way home from the doctor's office. Emma sat quietly looking out the car window. Emma listened as Kate told Joshua of the conversation with the doctor. Kate then phoned her mother-in-law to let her know Conner would need to spend another night in Kansas City.

Kate hung up the phone and looked at Emma. Emma turned and looked at her daughter. "Ice cream. That's the ticket. Run by G's and get me some brown bread ice cream."

Kate smiled, remembering her childhood when ice cream was the cure for everything. Emma always used ice cream for any hurts her children had.

They sat at G's and ate their ice cream, telling one another stories of memories of ice cream trips long ago. They laughed and they cried, never discussing Emma's illness.

Emma woke early, making blueberry muffins, Kate's favorite, for breakfast. The ride to the hospital was quiet until Emma reached into her purse and pulled out a disc. Kate looked at it and smiled.

"Remember this?" Emma asked.

"Of course. You recorded that for Papa the year after Jim passed away. It was for Father's Day and then everyone wanted a copy of it. You used to say you were going to be a famous rock star. And I would remind you that it was all gospel music and how would you be a rock star?"

"Yep. I think I gave out over three hundred copies that year. Your grandpa had so many people wanting it and then I began to speak at seminars for work and those people wanted them too. That was fun recording it."

Emma put it in and they listened to her voice sing old gospel hymns. Kate thought back to when she was young and Emma gave her a copy. Kate seldom listened to it then, filled with bitterness over her brother's death. So much had changed since then. She listened now wondering how her mother sang those songs only months after losing her son. How did Emma go to memorials and tell her story and sing?

They drove into the hospital parking lot. Kate turned off the ignition. "Ready?" she asked.

Emma smiled. "Ready."

Kate sat in the waiting room as Emma went through test after test. The nurse wheeled Emma out in a wheel chair and Kate could hear her mother saying, "I don't need this thing. I'm not an invalid, you know. I can walk perfectly fine. Just stop this thing right here. I don't want my daughter seeing me wheeled like I'm sick."

The nurse obliged Emma. Kate waited until Emma stood beside her chair, acting as if she had never known about the wheelchair incident.

"Are they finished already?" Kate asked.

"Yep. Said the doctor will call this afternoon and set a time to meet with us."

They stopped and ate a burger at the Corner Café before going home. Barb and Zeke had been seeing one another at least once a week and Emma enjoyed teasing her about it.

Barb laughed and hit Emma with her cloth that she was cleaning a table with.

"Now, you know what it's like being all alone. Adult conversation once a week is mighty nice. Them grandkids of mine are all in their teens now and they ain't got time for grandma like they used to. So many of us have lost our spouses and it's hard. Why, look at you, Emma. You've lost your son and your husband and now you're fighting your own battle. It ain't fair, I tell ya. It just ain't fair."

Barb hugged Emma and Kate could see the tears in her eyes. Both women had suffered so many losses in their lives and that was a bond many could not understand.

"You just keep your eye on that Ezekiel Lang. He's a feisty old coot," Emma said.

Barb smiled. "I've known Zeke going on forty years and there ain't nothing he could do that would surprise me. He's full of the devil."

Emma sipped her tea. "Nah, I've looked the devil in the eye and Ezekiel is just a kitten compared to the devil. He just wants us to think he's full of the devil."

Barb laughed, her arms laden with dirty dishes she had cleared from a large corner table. "Ain't that the truth?"

Kate and Emma finished lunch and stopped by the cemetery on their way home. Kate did not like the cemetery visits but knew they meant a lot to Emma so she obliged.

As they entered Emma's front door, the telephone was ringing. Emma hurried to the phone. "Hello?"

Emma would occasionally nod her head and say, "Yes, I see. Of course, I understand."

There was a pause and Emma said, "She is right here. Would you like to speak to her or will it wait until we see you in the morning?"

Another pause and then Emma handed the phone to Kate. "He wants to talk to you for a moment."

Kate took the phone and Emma sat on the arm of the chair. Kate also did more listening than talking and ended the conversation with "We'll see you tomorrow. Thank you."

Emma continued to sit on the arm of the chair, not looking at Kate and not speaking. Kate put her arms around Emma and began to cry.

"Now, sis. Don't get upset. You've got to be strong. We'll figure something out. No need in shedding tears over this."

Kate took her hands and held Emma's cheeks in them and looked into Emma's clear blue eyes.

"Momma, he said it is in your kidney and more lymph nodes. This is not good."

"Ah, heck, this is just another bump in my life's road. Stop fussing over it. We'll know more tomorrow. Let's have a nice evening. Let's ride out to the pond. Go saddle the horses."

"Don't you think it will be too cold?"

"We'll bundle up. It will be fun."

Kate shrugged her shoulders and put on her coat and gloves, knowing Emma needed this time on horseback.

"I'll have them saddled in fifteen minutes. You come out then. And dress really warm."

Emma saluted Kate as she left for the barn. Emma watched until Kate was out the gate and on her way to the barn. She knelt beside the chair and began to pray and weep like a child.

"Oh, dear Lord, please don't bring Kate any more heartache. If you plan on taking me, please don't put her through watching me suffer. Lord, take me quickly. Lord, if it is your will that I go home to be with you and the boys, please take me quickly. I can take the suffering but it's Kate that doesn't deserve to go through another heartache. I'm ready for whatever you bring as long as you don't hurt my baby girl in the process. Please, Lord, please."

Emma wiped her eyes and stood up. She went into the kitchen and washed her face with cold water. She went into the bedroom and she dressed warmly as Kate had instructed. She went downstairs and put on her boots, walked out the front door and told Gracie to stay inside as she closed it behind her. When she arrived at the barn, Kate had Pie and Sally saddled and Sam waited beside Kate.

Kate looked at Emma. "Ready?"

"Ready as rain," Emma said.

The ride was peaceful and there was a thin layer of ice on the pond. As they rode, Kate could see the horses' breath in the air. Emma stopped Pie near Rylie's fishing chairs and dismounted Pie. She tied him to a tree and Kate did the same with Sally.

Emma sat in Rylie's Adirondack chair, resting her head on the back. Kate stood near the pond, tossing a rock to see if she could break the ice.

"This is one of my favorite places. It is so peaceful. You know, Rylie and I came here often after you left home. It seemed to help us with the deafening quiet of our empty nest. Sometimes I would fish with him and other times I would read while he fished. I feel close to him here. I feel closest to Jim when I am working with the horses or in the mustang and closest to Rylie out here. Today I have the best of both worlds."

Pie whinnied as if to remind Emma that he too felt Jim and Rylie's presence here. Emma smiled.

"I feel closest to Jim when we take our rides in the mustang or when I am in the mountains. He and I never spent time together in the mountains but I know he would have loved their beauty. I can't imagine how much it hurts to have lost him. Now that I have Conner, I know a mother's love and I just can't imagine what the pain must be like. Oh, Momma, this just can't be happening. It just can't"

Emma patted the chair beside her, motioning for Kate to join her.

"Kate, if it is my time to go, then we should be glad we had time to say our good-byes and to spend time together, knowing that our time left is short. Jim and Rylie were both taken from us without any chance to say goodbye or I love you. We never had the chance to tell them all things we so desperately want to tell them now. You and I are being given that chance. A chance to tell one another all our inner most secrets and all our feelings. A time to laugh and cry. We, in some sick, strange way, are being blessed with an opportunity we never had. You didn't get to say goodbye to your dad. Never have you had this chance. Take it and use it to its full advantage. Heaven knows I certainly don't want to die. I want to spend years watching Conner grow and I want to teach him all kinds of things. But, if I don't have that opportunity, then you will have to tell him all about me and teach him all the things you know I would have taught him."

"It's not fair. I've lost everyone."

Emma patted Kate's hand. "No you haven't. Why, you've got your own family to love and cherish. Granted, you should not have suffered the loss of your brother, but parents pass on. Someday your children will be faced with losing you. It's nature's way."

It's crap. That's what it is. I should at least have the joy of having someone left in my life."

"You do, Kate. You have Conner and Joshua. And, as hard a pill as it was to swallow, you have Lilly. Now, no more talk about death. Lord, we're killing me off and we haven't even talked to the doctor yet about the full prognosis and treatment. Come on, let's ride a little further south and then turn back towards home. It will be too dark to ride soon."

Chapter 46

Dr. Sands greeted Emma and Kate as they entered his office. Emma was full of questions.

"How bad is it?" she asked.

"Emma, this is very serious. It is a large mass on your kidney and several lymph nodes will need to be removed. I'm going to try radiation and chemotherapy and try to at least save your kidney. Going on a donor list is my last choice."

"What if I am a match?" Kate asked.

"We can check on that and, if you are and you and your mother choose donation, we can do it. My concern is that the cancer is spreading quickly."

Kate pounded her fist on the arm of the chair. "What happened to this crap about a honeymoon period?"

Dr. Sands took a deep breath and, before he could speak Emma said, "I guess the honeymoon is over, huh?"

He smiled at Emma and said, "Yes, Emma, the honeymoon is over."

"I never was one for long honeymoons," she quipped.

Surgery and treatments were scheduled and Kate made phone calls to Lilly and Emma's friends and family.

Joshua flew into Kansas City and stayed with Kate during Emma's surgery. Lilly, David, Dawson and Zeke were also there.

Emma was moved to an assisted living facility during the first two weeks of her treatment, constantly complaining and worrying about the farm.

It was March 12th when Emma was allowed to return home. She was in good spirits and began to regain her strength. Kate and Joshua brought Conner to the farm to spend some time, which seemed to help Emma. Kate knew this would be a hard week. Jim's birthday was March 15th and Rylie's was March 22nd. Family and friends dropped in throughout the week. As suspected, Emma insisted on decorating the graves. Lilly and Kate went to see Bobby at the florist shop and he filled the back of the SUV with flowers, insisting they keep both him and Brenda informed of Emma's health and assuring them Mike and his family would be out to see her on the 15th.

As promised Mike and his family arrived at Emma's the afternoon of March 15th. Emma was thrilled to see Mike and Becky and they brought James with them. Mike told stories of the times he and Jim spent together and Emma was a captive audience, listening attentively to stories Kate knew Emma had already heard.

As it was time for Emma's guests to leave, Kate walked them onto the porch. Mike lit a cigarette and said, "How bad is she?'

Kate was surprised at his question.

"They haven't said much other than they are going to be doing these treatments. She has already said she will not continue the treatments if there is little hope."

"You know your brother would want her to fight this. She's a scrapper. She'll fight with all she has."

Mike hugged Kate and told her he would be out every other weekend. He made promises on behalf of Jim's other friends that they would also stop in.

Kate waved as they drove out of the drive and then turned to Lilly as she came out the front door.

"That was a boost for her," Lilly said.

"Mike can always cheer her up. He is so much like Jim and has phoned her every single Mother's Day since Jim passed away. He always tells her he loves her. Jim's friends are the closest she has to having him. I know I am here but they remind her of him and sometimes that is what she needs."

By week's end, Emma had grown weaker and Kate insisted she again see the doctor. Kate told herself it was because Emma had tried to entertain any guest that came by. Kate phoned Lilly and told her Emma was again going in to see the doctor. Lilly asked that Kate keep her informed and said she was willing to help whenever Kate needed.

Dr. Sands examined Emma. He insisted she get more rest and prescribed an anti-nausea drug and asked if he could speak to Kate alone. Emma pointed her finger at the doctor and said, "Anything you have to say to Kate, you can say to me. I am not a child, you know."

Dr. Sands smiled at Emma, longing to be able to find a cure for this kind, spirited woman.

"I want you to have some privacy to get dressed, Emma and I want to go over some things with Kate."

"Things? What sort of things? Like I said, I am not a child, doc."

Dr. Sands motioned for Emma to leave the room and dress. Emma mumbled and frowned as she left the room. She turned back toward the doctor and said, "Tell Kate in front of me what you have to say. I'm not leaving this room. Just pretend I'm not even here if you have to."

The doctor took a deep breath, turned to Kate and spoke slowly. "I think she should know about my time frame on treatments while she is in Denver. You and I can discuss those things when she is at home. You and I have plenty of time to discuss treatments and the consequences of those treatments."

Emma scoffed as she said, "Hmm. Consequences. Not a word I like, doc. Not at all."

Kate knew her mother was referring to a lifetime of consequences from Richard. Kate wondered if Emma had both kidneys, would she stand a better chance of fighting this cancer? Richard always threatened consequences and even from the grave, his abuse left Emma with consequences. Kate filled with bitterness inside and wished things had been different for all of them.

Emma excused herself from the room to dress and Kate sat down in Dr. Sands' office. He looked over Emma's chart and spoke to Kate.

"The most she has is a year. I believe we are fighting a losing battle. It is time to start extensive treatment in hopes of a miracle but I believe you and the family should prepare for what in most probability is the inevitable with such invasive cancer. I have my doubts about even continuing with treatments."

Kate's eyes burned with tears and she could feel her ears turn red, something her mother had always teased her about. Emma always knew when Kate was angry because her ears turned bright red.

"Thank you for letting me know. Does she know? Kate asked.

"Your mother is a very bright woman. There is no doubt in my mind that she knows how ill she is but does not want to let on in hopes of keeping up appearances for you and your family."

"She's always looking out for us. Now it is my turn to look out for her."

The doctor opened the door and Kate left his office, her stomach in knots. She tried to fight the tears and knew she had to regain her composure before she saw her mother.

Emma was standing in the waiting room reading a magazine. She looked up as Kate entered the room.

Emma put her arm around Kate's waist and smiled up at her.

"Now don't stew over this. Doctors don't know everything, you know. I don't even want to know what he said cause I think he is Dr. Gloom and Doom right now. I'll be fine, sis. Either way, I'll be fine."

Kate turned to Emma. "I don't want either way, Mom. I want you healthy and here with us. I'm going to take a leave from work and stay at the farm with you for a while."

"Like heck you are. I am not so bad off that I need a full time nurse. You are needed in Denver."

Kate walked outside to the car and opened the passenger door for her mother.

"We'll see," she said.

Kate and Emma returned home to find Lilly and Zeke preparing the meal. Emma excused herself and said she wanted to rest for a short while.

When Kate was sure her mother was out of earshot, she informed Lilly and Zeke of Emma's prognosis.

Zeke sat down at the kitchen table and covered his face with his large, weathered hands.

"Not Emma Jean too. Damn cancer. Not Emma Jean too."

Lilly's mind was a blur. She was trying to think of a solution and trying to fight the reality of it all.

"David should put a rush on the barn remodeling plans and building the new barn. We can't wait until May as he had promised Emma. We need to be here now. That makes the most sense, Kate. We can be here until you can make arrangements to stay with her full-time. I'm calling David."

Kate was too emotionally exhausted to argue with Lilly and knew what she was suggesting made sense. Lilly phoned David from her cell phone and Kate and Zeke continued to sit at the table, neither speaking.

Lilly entered the kitchen.

"He is lighting a fire under the project. Emma will be fine with it if David approaches it from the right angle and not from the urgency of her illness."

Kate continued to look down at the table and merely said, "You're right."

Zeke abruptly stood up from the table and left the room. Both women heard the front screen door slam. Lilly walked to the window and watched Zeke. He sat on a step and reached for his tobacco can, taking a pinch. Before he could put it in his mouth, he tossed it into the yard. Sam sat down beside him on the front steps of the porch and licked his face. Zeke broke down and began to cry.

Kate stood beside Lilly and said, "He can't bear to go through another loss to cancer."

Lilly turned to Kate and said, "You can't bear another loss, Kate. You've suffered so many. This is so unfair."

"Yeah, well, as we all know . . . . life's not fair. I will not let her suffer. I don't care what it takes; she isn't going to suffer. She's suffered so much in her lifetime and I refuse to watch her suffer in the end."

Emma called from upstairs. "I can't sleep so I'm coming downstairs. If you girls are talking about me, it is time to stop. I am walking down the stairs."

Both women began to giggle as Emma called out each time she took a step. As she stood on the landing, she smiled at Kate and Lilly and said, "I am getting close so no talking, understand?"

"We understand, mother," Kate said with a grin.

"Now let's all put on our happy faces and not fret over this. Where is Ezekiel?"

Lilly pointed to the front door and said, "He stepped out for a few minutes."

Emma shot Kate a brief glare. "Did you tell him whatever gloom the doctor told you?"

Kate nodded her head as if she were a small child just being caught and scolded.

"Oh, Good Lord, Kate. Sometimes we have to lie in order to keep folks from getting hurt. You know better than that."

Emma looked out the window and said, "Oh, crap. That old man is crying his heart out to Sam."

She turned to Kate. "Get your butt out there and say something to take his mind off this. Ask him to chore or something. If you can't get the job done, then I guess I will."

Kate kissed Emma's cheek as she passed her on her way out the door. Emma watched as Kate sat down next to Zeke, placing her arm around his broad shoulders. Kate leaned her head towards Zeke and Emma could tell they were both crying.

"Oh, land sakes, now they're both bawling. Guess I'll go out there and make them cheer up."

Lilly reached for Emma's arm and said, "Emma, maybe you should let them have this time alone."

Emma turned to Lilly. "And exactly what did she say the doctor told her?"

Lilly cringed, knowing that she had brought this on herself by stopping Emma.

"She merely said the doctor isn't hopeful about the treatment."

Emma raised her hands in the air and said, "Duh? I'm no doctor but I know that. He should not have upset her like this. I ought to go back to his office and give him a piece of my mind."

Lilly could not think of a response so she stood before Emma in silence.

Emma brushed Lilly's bangs from her face and leaned her forehead on Lilly's.

"We are not going to dwell on this. We are going to get the new barn done, move the mustang and the critters and you and David can start on the old barn. We'll make it fun."

Lilly saw this as a perfect opportunity to inform Emma that David was moving the project to April.

Emma tilted her head and asked, "And when did David decide to do this? Last I talked to him; he was still planning on May 1st."

Lilly thought of Emma's earlier comment that sometimes you have to lie to protect another person from the truth.

"I spoke to him earlier while you and Kate were gone and he informed me then of his plans. He's in hopes that you won't be too upset."

"I see," was Emma's only response.

Conner cried from the bedroom and Emma said, "You're saved by the bell, young lady."

She went into the other room and Lilly hurried into the kitchen to finish preparing the meal.

Kate and Zeke sat on the porch for quite a while until they could no longer bear the cold March wind.

The next few days were spent with quiet conversation and reflection. Emma agreed to David's plan and plans were made to deliver the supplies the following Monday.

Kate caught Zeke with his hand in the marble jar one afternoon.

"What are you doing?" she asked.

"For every marble Emma Jean throws away, I am throwing away two. I ain't gonna let her think this beat her. She is going to outlast that damn marble jar," he said.

"Good thinking. Of course, you know she keeps close track of it."

"Not no more. She just walks in here and takes out the marble and throws it out. I think it ain't the same no more."

"Then go for it," Kate said as she hugged Zeke.

Kate and Conner returned to Denver on Saturday and Emma agreed to phone if she needed them. She and Kate agreed Kate would take some time off within the next month and she would spend time with Emma at the farm.

Lilly stayed with Emma throughout the weekend.

Early Monday morning Zeke arrived at Emma's place, excited to wait along with Emma for the barn supplies. He had only been there an hour when David drove into the driveway.

David went over the new barn plans with Emma and she was pleased to see he had planned an actual garage addition to the barn for the mustang.

"Oh, David. I just can't wait now that I've seen it on paper. When do they start?"

"Well, since we're supposed to have some really nice days this week, I am going to try to have the concrete poured and ready soon."

The supplies arrived after lunch and David spoke to several contractors. It was decided that concrete would be poured by the end of the week.

On Friday Zeke again arrived at Emma's, this time carrying a beautiful teak lounge chair in the bed of his truck. Emma walked onto the porch.

"What's that for, Ezekiel?"

"That, Emma Jean, is for you to sit on and watch the men build your barn. I've been working on it. I phoned Marilyn and she is making you some real nice cushions to go on it. After all, we don't want you suffering from tired butt while you supervise them men. Those fellas have no clue what sort of supervising they are gonna get. Why, you can work a man harder than any man I've ever worked for."

Emma looked sad and said, "Why, I never meant to do such a thing, Ezekiel. I certainly hope you don't hold that against me."

Zeke lifted the chair out of the truck.

"Hell, Emma Jean, don't be taking things so serious. I'm just joshing ya."

He asked Emma to direct him to the perfect spot for watching the barn building. She motioned to a spot not far from the worksite where she would be in the morning sun.

After placing the chair in its designated spot, Zeke offered to do Emma's chores.

"I've already done them. You can't take all my pleasure from me, Ezekiel Lang. Choring is one of my greatest pleasures. I love the smell of the hay and the animals. You can't do them all the time for me just yet."

Zeke rubbed the back of his hand against Emma's cheek.

"You let me know when the time comes that you want me to do them full time, old woman. Just say the word."

Emma's eyes welled with tears and she whispered, "It won't be much longer, Ezekiel. Not much longer. But I plan on outliving the marbles. I'll show those doctors. Not much longer, old man."

Zeke quickly turned his eyes from Emma's, hoping she would not see the fear in them. Zeke knew what pain and heartache this disease could bring. He didn't want that for his dear friend.

Only time would tell if Zeke would see his hopes of Emma not suffering come true. Very little time, he was afraid.

Chapter 47

By Mother's Day weekend, the barn was framed and Kate and Conner were staying at Emma's full time. Each morning Emma would make her way slowly to her lounge chair with the magnolia blossom print cushions on it and she would watch the men work. While they were building the new barn, plans were being made of starting the old barn renovation as soon as the new one was completed. David drove from Kansas City to Emma's at least four times a week, sometimes bringing Lilly along with him.

Emma had several guests stop in on Mother's Day. By late afternoon things had grown quiet on the farm and Kate asked if Emma was ready to go to the cemetery as she always did on special occasions. Conner chased Gracie around the dining room table as Emma answered Kate.

"I forgot to get flowers. Oh, Kate, I forgot to get flowers. I think I'm losing my mind, sis."

Kate held up a bouquet from behind her back and smiled.

"I've got you covered, momma. And you are not losing your mind."

"Have you got the book?"

Kate smiled and held up the children's book *Where the Wild Things Are*. This book had been Jim's favorite as a child. Each Mother's Day, Jim's birthday and the anniversary of his passing, Emma would go to the cemetery and read aloud quietly as she sat at the gravesite. Kate had given Emma a new copy of the book one Christmas and Emma began the tradition of reading it to her grandchildren. Kate feared Conner would not know the joy of hearing his grandmother read it much longer before he went to bed each night at her home.

They arrived at the cemetery and Emma placed the flowers on the grave. Kate watched in silence. Then Emma sat down beside the grave, looking at the picture of her son and opened the book. Conner sat on his mother's knee and listened attentively while his grandmother read the book, holding up each page for him to see as she read it. Kate knew her mother had the book memorized but she continued to read it as if she was reading it to her children at bedtime.

The days Emma, Kate and Conner spent were treasured. Emma began to no longer walk to the barn and she grew weaker with each day's passing. By Memorial Day weekend the new barn was complete. David had hoped it would be sooner but weather that spring had put the construction behind. All of Emma's family arrived to help move everything from the old barn to the new one. Everything except the mustang. Emma insisted she be the one to drive the mustang into its new home.

"Momma, how are you going to get out to the barn? I think I should drive it. I think you are too weak."

Zeke picked Emma up from her lounge chair, scooping her into his arms as if she were a child.

"She's got a ride to the barn. Let's go, old woman," he said as he carried her.

Emma's family stood, many in tears, as they watched this mountain of a man carry what was now his frail, dying friend, to the barn. Emma waved to her family as she was carried away to drive her son's car one last time.

Kate walked towards the barn. The sound of the engine reverberated as Emma drove towards the new garage addition. Emma waved as if she were a pageant queen. She carefully pulled the mustang into its new home, smiling the entire time. Waiting to carry her back to the house was Zeke. He stood silently, knowing what a reverent time this was for Emma. He knew she would tell him when she was ready to go back to the house. Kate walked towards Zeke and stood beside him, putting her arm inside his.

David turned to Lilly as Emma opened the car door and he kissed her forehead. There was no need for words. Everyone present knew how important this moment was.

All of Emma's family waited until she motioned to Zeke before they approached the garage. Dawson was the first to speak.

"Good job, Grandma. Wouldn't Uncle Jim be proud?"

Zeke leaned down into the driver's side of the mustang, careful of the frailty of Emma.

Emma smiled at Dawson. "He is proud, Dawson Orie. I know he is."

The afternoon was filled with family and a picnic. By dusk most family members had left. Kate and Lilly began to clean up.

Kate did not look up but merely said, "It won't be long now. We've had hospice out here for over a month and last week the nurse said it won't be much longer."

Lilly was surprised by Kate's frankness.

"Are you sure?" she asked.

"Look at her, Lilly. She can't walk across the room anymore. I bathe her each morning. I know they are right. She isn't happy like this. You know how she hates to depend on others. She's ready to go."

"Do you want us to stay?"

"No, Joshua is taking some time off work and we should be fine. I promise to phone if she gets worse."

That night Emma called out to Kate asking if she would come into her bedroom.

Kate stuck her head inside the door.

"What's up?" she asked.

"It is time we had a talk. Come sit beside me."

Kate sat next to Emma on the side of the bed.

"I want to go over some things with you. Now, you know where my Will is and you know about all of my insurance policies. But there are some things you don't know and I should tell you."

Kate did not want this conversation but knew Emma felt it necessary.

"What?" she asked.

"In the closet are all of the videos Brett has been taking. I have labeled them. Most are for you and Conner but some are for the grown grandkids and some are to do whatever you please with. Brett even recorded me reading "Where the Wild Things Are" so you can play it for my grandchildren. Please continue to read it at your brother's grave. All of my life's journals are stored in the closet. Almost fifty years of journals. You've got a lot of reading to do. And there is a small safe with important papers and jewelry. The combination is written down and taped inside a shoebox on the top shelf. I have a small policy that I have left for Ezekiel. He's like family and he struggles financially. It might help him a little. Lord knows it isn't much. Any questions?"

"No, Momma. No questions."

Emma ran her index finger across Kate's forehead and over the bridge of her nose.

"I want you to be happy. Don't grieve for me. I'll be fine. It's you I am worried about. I would agree that this isn't fair. It isn't fair for you. But you need to get on with life. Enjoy all the things I never got to enjoy. Teach my grandbabies that life is a gift and to never take it for granted. Never let the sun set in anger. Love and cherish Joshua and your family because you are not promised more than the very moment you breathe. You already know all this but I am going over it one last time. And remember, I'll be waiting at the crossroads for you. The boys and I and all those that have gone on before you will be there when your journey is complete. Live a full, happy life. Live it for me and Jim and Beans."

Kate could not hold the tears back any longer. Emma held her in her arms and ran her hand through Kate's hair.

"Let it all out, sis. You've held it back way too long. Let it out while I'm here to hold you."

Kate cried herself to sleep in her mother's arms.

The next morning, Emma ate very little breakfast before asking if Kate would help her out to her lounge chair. Joshua and Kate both carried Emma to her chair.

Each morning they did this very same thing. Emma watched as work on the new barn began. Kate sometimes brought one of the horses up to see Emma. Sam and Gracie never left Emma's side. Gracie positioned herself under Emma's chair each morning and Sam sat beside Emma, placing his head on her lap.

June 5th arrived with Kate reminding Emma that it was Emma and Rylie's wedding anniversary.

"Do you want me to take you to the cemetery?" Kate asked.

"No, not today. We might spend our anniversary together."

Kate attributed Emma's comment to the pain medication. She did take time to phone Lilly and let her know Emma's condition was worse and Lilly said she had already promised herself to be there later that afternoon. David had been keeping her posted on Emma's condition since Lilly last saw Emma on Sunday.

Kate spent most of her time with her mother and Joshua helped with the household chores and Conner. Zeke arrived around noon. He brought a light blanket that one of the local women had made for Emma. He placed it across Emma's legs and immediately Gracie jumped on it. Zeke started to take her off and Emma insisted she be allowed to sit there on the soft blanket.

Zeke ran his hand across Emma's forehead as if testing her for a fever. As he walked towards the barn, he called back, "Don't fuss at me if your new blanket smells like dog, Emma Jean."

Kate sat beside Emma as Emma began to sing softly.

"Sing with me, Kate. Better yet, you sing to me."

"What shall I sing, Momma?"

"Sing *You are My Sunshine*," Emma requested.

Kate began to sing the song. It had been Emma and Kate's song since Kate was a baby. Kate sang it through one time and looked at Emma.

"Again," Emma whispered.

"You are my sunshine, my only sunshine. You make me happy when skies are gray. You'll never know dear how much I love you. Please don't take my sunshine away."

Kate choked back the tears. She looked at her mother. Emma was motionless.

Kate's cries became sobs.

"Momma? Momma?" she cried but Emma did not answer.

"Zeke! Joshua! Come quick!" she cried out.

Chapter 48

Kate could not believe it had been nearly a year since Emma had passed away. Conner talked constantly as they drove from Denver to Carbondale. Mother's Day was Sunday and Kate was determined to make the trip in good time.

She drove into the driveway where Lilly stood outside the barn, waving.

"There's Lilly," Conner announced.

Kate looked at Emma's house, freshly painted. Lilly opened the passenger door and looked in at Kate.

"They just came out to see the place and it passed with flying colors," she said.

Kate took Conner out of the seat and said, "Let's see it."

Nearly two hundred yards from Emma's house stood a large farmhouse, newly constructed. The women and Conner walked towards the house.

"Wow, it has really come together in the last month," Kate said.

They walked onto the wraparound porch and through the front door. Inside was a main gathering room. Also on the main floor was a kitchenette, three bedrooms and two baths. The second floor held another three bedrooms and two baths. In each bedroom stood a double bed, twin bunk beds and a crib. The house looked as if it had always been on that site and the rooms took you back in time.

"We have cots available if needed," Lilly said.

"It is beautiful. She would be so proud," Kate said.

Zeke walked into the room, taking off his hat and kissing Kate's cheek.

"She is proud," he said.

"What time do our guests arrive?" Zeke asked Kate.

"The bus arrives at six tonight," Kate answered.

"That only gives us an hour and a half. Lord Almighty," Zeke said.

Lilly patted his arm and said, "Its fine. It's just fine."

David helped Kate carry her luggage into the barn. Kate's breath was always taken away when she entered it. Seeing Rylie and Emma's dream come true meant more than Kate had ever imagined it would. She often wondered if Emma regretted not being able to live in the barn as she and Rylie had hoped. She reassured herself that Emma had no regrets when it came to the farm.

"Mind if I run to the cemetery before company arrives?"

"Go right ahead. Conner, how about Zeke takes you for a ride on Pie?"

"Yeah! Can I Mom?" he asked.

"Sure. You go right ahead," Kate said as she took her set of keys from her purse.

Zeke looked at Kate and asked, "You taking it home next weekend?"

"Yep. I drove that rental here and I'm turning it in and I'm taking the mustang home. We bought a home on ten acres in the mountains. Joshua built a two car garage just for it and Jim's tools."

"That's a good thing, kiddo," Zeke said as Conner jumped on his back for a ride to the barn.

Kate drove the mustang into the cemetery. She walked to the graves, kissing her thumb and placing it on each headstone. She stood before Emma and Rylie's headstone.

"This is a good day, Momma. I hope this is what you always wanted and we make you proud."

Kate stayed at the cemetery for quite a while, telling stories and just enjoying the quiet. She could remember a time when she hated coming here but now it gave her some peace. She looked at her watch and walked to the mustang. She drove slowly down the gravel road, hoping to keep as much dust off the black car as possible.

By 5:45 pm Kate was pacing back and forth on Emma's porch. Lilly stood at the gate with Sam beside her. Zeke, David and Conner waited near the barn.

"Here comes the bus," Lilly said.

A large, blue bus pulled into the drive and stopped. Besides the driver, it held four women and seven children. They began to step off the bus.

Kate was the first to speak.

"Welcome to Emma's farm. I am Emma's daughter, Kate and this is Lilly." Lilly smiled and nodded.

Kate continued. "I would also like to introduce you to Lilly's husband, David. That is Zeke and this is my son Conner. These folks are here to help make your stay as comfortable as possible."

"Follow me and I will show you where you will be staying," Lilly said as David and Zeke began to carry the small amount of luggage.

Inside the new house Lilly began to tell each woman about the accommodations.

"Each room has plenty of room for you and your children. There is a small kitchenette where you can prepare snacks and lunch. Breakfast and dinner are held in the main house where the meals are prepared for you. Every Wednesday night we will hold a mandatory group meeting. Your safety is of the utmost importance to us here at Emma's farm. The sheriff's department patrols these premises hourly and both this house and the main house have an alarm system."

Lilly turned to Kate and said, "Kate, would you like to tell them more?"

Kate began to speak. "We ask that you keep your room and the bathroom you use clean. There is a large laundry room next to the kitchen. Please take care of your own laundry. Let me show you to your rooms and then we will go to the main house."

Zeke and David carried the luggage into the entry and set it down. Zeke tipped his hat to each woman as she passed. Memories of Richard stalking Emma on this very spot crossed his mind and he smiled that Emma had finally won. She had her safe haven for battered women. He looked at the large oak mantle which read *A Life Lived in Fear is a Life Half Lived*. Emma didn't have many years of not living in fear. Zeke hoped these women had longer.

After touring the safe house and seeing their rooms, Kate took the women and children outside. They began to walk from the safe house to the main house. Kate looked down and saw one of Emma's marbles shining in the newly excavated dirt. Grass seed surrounded it but the sun captured its brilliance. Kate bent over to pick it up. She ran it in and out of her fingers, never taking her eyes off the shiny, purple and yellow symbol of Emma's triumph.

Kate turned to the guests and said, "Over this farmstead you will find marbles. When you find one, please take it inside the main house and wash it. In the dining room is a large jar with the words 'count your blessings' inscribed on it. Please dry your marble and place it in the jar as you count one of your blessings."

She turned to Zeke and Lilly, tears welling up in her eyes. Emma's dream of making a safe place for battered women and their children had finally come true. Little did Emma know that Ezekiel Lang was not as impoverished as she had believed. Zeke took the life insurance money and, along with a portion of his savings, he built Emma's dream.

Lilly spoke to the guests as they entered the main house. "Our dear friend Helen is here each day to prepare your morning and evening meals."

Helen stood at the kitchen doorway and James looked around from behind her, smiling at the other children. Helen still bore scars from her beating under her eye and across the bridge of her nose. She had been so excited when Kate phoned her about the safe house. The opportunity to help others made her so thankful she had returned to the community near Emma's farm. James had grown into a fine teenage boy who adored his mother and enjoyed being with Emma's family.

Pictures of Emma and her family hung on the staircase wall and adorned the living room.

"Are there any questions?" Lilly asked.

"How long will we be able to stay here?" a fair-skinned woman with dark hair and eyes asked.

"You may stay here until you find permanent housing, employment or whatever it is you need," Lilly answered.

When the question/answer session was over, Zeke escorted the women to the other house. Several of the children watched for marbles on the ground and so did their mothers. Kate stayed on Emma's porch. Helen came to the front door and looked through the screen.

"You o.k. Kate?" she asked.

"She should be here for this, Helen. She's missing the best part."

Helen came out and sat in the chair next to Kate.

"She's not missing it. She is the best part. Think of all she did to help others. We are just carrying on what she started. Emma is the best part, Kate. Your mother's dream has come true."

Kate leaned her head back and closed her eyes, clasping her hands across her stomach.

Helen touched her hand. "When are you due?"

"In November. I hope it is on Momma's birthday. And I want it to be a girl."

Helen smiled and merely said, "It is" as she walked back into the house.

After the evening meal, the new residents of Emma's farm went back to the large house and Kate stayed in Emma's house. She called Lilly on the house phone.

"Hello?" Lilly said.

"Want to watch some videos with me?" Kate asked.

"I'll be over in five minutes. Is Conner asleep?"

"Zeke took him into town for ice cream. I thought we could just sit and watch old videos. David is welcome too."

"See you in a few minutes," Lilly said as she hung up the phone.

Kate gathered a few videos. She was glad she had made copies for herself, Lilly and the rest of the family. Zeke had also requested copies of some. She read each label on the case and smiled as she opened one and put it into the disc player.

Lilly entered the house and wiped her feet on the entry rug. "David is working on a project and said start without him."

"I already put one in. Do you mind?" Kate asked.

"Of course not," Lilly answered as she sat on the sofa.

They both sat focusing on the television. Taylor appeared on the screen, smiling and pretending to be a television announcer. The camera turned to Emma as she sat on the front porch. Lilly and Kate both noticed it had been in Emma's healthier days as her face was tanned and round.

Taylor held a microphone up to Emma as she asked, "Mrs. McMaster, would you tell us what your greatest dreams and adventures have been?"

Emma tilted her head and smiled into the camera. "My greatest dreams have been to be a mother, then to be a true friend and to help others in need. Oh, and to someday see my boys again. But that day is a long ways off. My greatest adventure? That would be life. My life has been my greatest adventure."

The camera turned back to Taylor and Kate's mind wandered to simpler days. She remembered the first time Emma brought Kate and Jim to see this place. She sat looking at the television but thinking of her mother and brother. She thought about her first meeting with Rylie and how she grew to love him over the years. She thought of his quiet tolerance of being called 'Beans'.

Lilly interrupted Kate's thoughts. "Zeke and Conner are back. Do you want to continue with the video or shall we stop it until you get Conner in bed?"

Zeke carried Conner into the house. Conner was barely awake and Kate motioned for Zeke to put him in Kate's room.

"I think we will stay here tonight, if you don't mind. I want to sleep in my old bedroom."

Lilly did not argue. After all, this was still Kate's home and she owned everything but the barn and the small plot of land around it. Maybe they should not have made it where two meals a day and weekly meetings were held in Emma's house. But Lilly reminded herself that Kate had specified those very things. Lilly was tired and did not want to worry about it on such a happy day.

Zeke offered to walk Lilly back to the barn and hugged Kate as they left. He turned back and said, "Lock up."

"I always do, Ezekiel Lang."

Zeke smiled as he thought about Kate's response and how it reminded him of Emma.

Kate tucked Conner into bed and stepped out onto the front porch. She looked towards the safe house where only two rooms remained lit. She hoped this would provide the safety and security these families so desperately needed. She sat in the darkness, slightly swaying on the porch swing and listening to its gentle creak.

After escorting Lilly to the barn, Zeke walked towards his truck. The moonlight cast shadows from the picket fence, standing like tall, thin soldiers guarding the farmhouse.

"I see you on that swing, Kate Phillips. I thought I told you to lock up."

"Not just yet, Zeke. Come sit with me for a minute."

Zeke opened the gate and Sam followed him. He reached for his pocket that no longer held a tobacco can. He smiled. Emma would be proud that he finally quit chewing. He sighed as he eased down onto the porch steps.

Kate sat on the steps beside him. She looked out into the starlit sky.

"This has been a good day, Zeke. Momma would be proud."

"She is proud, Kate. She is proud. Ain't no stopping us now. Her dreams live on. And Kate?"

"Yes Zeke?"

"Your momma is proud of you."

Kate winked at Zeke and said, "I know. You are right, Ezekiel Lang. Right as rain you are. Right as rain."

Zeke chuckled as he said, "Acorn don't fall far from the tree, Kate. You are your momma's daughter."

He smiled as he hugged Kate. They sat in silence as they watched the starlit Kansas sky over Emma's porch. A slight breeze gave the porch swing enough motion to lend a gentle creaking sound as it swayed back and forth, as if Emma herself still sat there enjoying the evening with Kate and Zeke. Zeke felt it was Emma's angelic way of her approval and her affirmation of pride in Kate and the work her family and friends had done to accomplish her dream of a safe haven for so many in need. And he knew that old porch would hold more secrets as the years went by. After all, it would always be Emma's porch where many a friend and many a stranger found refuge from life's bitter storms.